Mine Would Be You

Mine Would Be You

K. JAMILA

Mine Would Be You © 2020
Copyright © 2021 by K. Jamila

All rights reserved. No part of this publication may be reproduced, distributed, or transmitted in any form or by any means, including photocopying, recording, or other electronic or mechanical methods, without the prior written permission of the publisher, except in the case of brief quotations embodied in critical reviews and certain other noncommercial uses permitted by copyright law.

This book is a work of fiction. All names, characters, locations, and incidents are products of the authors imaginations. Any resemblance to actual persons, things, living or dead, locales or events is entirely coincidental.

Editing: April Alvis
Cover: Murphy Rae, www.murphyrae.com
Formatting: Elaine York, Allusion Publishing,
www.allusionpublishing.com

Dedications

I.
For anyone scared of love—keep dreaming, keep believing.
Love will come to you.

II.
To Jules—I love you to Saturn and beyond.
I hope the love you deserve finds you when you're ready
and I hope it's the brightest light in the sky.

Playlist

"Traitor" – Olivia Rodrigo
"Older" – Sasha Sloan
"Mine Would Be You" – Blake Shelton
"Enchanted" – Taylor Swift
"Notice Me" – Role Model
"I Guess I'm In Love" – Clinton Kane
"Take My Time" – Harry Hudson
"Wanted" – Hunter Hayes
"Homesick" – Kane Brown
"Pessimist" – Julia Michaels
"Kiss Me" – Sixpence None the Richer
"Hey Stupid, I Love You – JP Saxe
"Get Away with It" – Lacy Cavalier
"King of My Heart" – Taylor Swift
"Put Me Back Together" – Caitlyn Smith
"My Somebody" – Trent Harmon
"Missing Piece" – Vance Joy
"Stone" – Alessia Cara
"All I Need" – Christina Aguilera
"Lucky Ones" – Lana Del Rey
"Butterflies" – Kacey Musgraves
"Daylight" – Taylor Swift

One | Nina

" **D**o you miss him or the idea of him?"

Her eyes gaze into mine from her seat across from me in the gray and blue office space as I contemplate the question. I cross and uncross my legs, leaning into the black leather couch. Its warm, supple material feels comforting on my back. The theme of the room folds around me like a blanket: gray and yellow accents, the gray armchair she sits in, light yellow walls. A desk is pressed against the wall to my left, and two full bookshelves add color on either side. My feet tap lightly on the shag carpet.

"I miss parts of him, the familiar parts, the good parts. I'm over him," I sigh, rolling my lips into my mouth. "But this wave of . . . missing him hit me last week, and it hasn't gone away."

The sight of my therapist's round face morphing into a smile provides a sense of comfort. As if my sentiment is normal. Expected even.

"It's normal to miss someone who was a part of your life for so long. It doesn't mean you're not over him."

I let out the breath I was holding deep in my diaphragm.

"Myles was a big, important part of your life. He was around for a lot of big events. High school, graduation, the beginning of college, and unfortunately, the beginning of your postgrad life.

It's okay to miss him." She pauses. "Do you have any desire to get back together with him? If he came back, would you give him another chance?"

The answer is immediate. I know without a doubt, even in the depths of my brain currently flooded with all the things he did *right*, I don't ever want to date him again. Ever since I started therapy almost two years ago, I knew I didn't want to be with him after everything. I just needed a little guidance to help me see that.

"No."

"Good, I'm glad to hear that. It shows that the things we've worked on are in fact working. In times like this, when those feelings are reemerging, this is when you must remind yourself of why you don't want to be with him. You have to remember the negatives."

I look away from her prying eyes because for a long time, for most of my teen years and early young adult life, all I wanted was Myles. And I've been without these aching thoughts for so long that the sudden appearance of them is jarring. But Marissa is right. I have to remind myself of the list I made when I first started with her. Of all the negatives. Of every single reason I wrote down to remind myself I *don't* want him.

Because I don't.

"It just feels like a warning. I know that sounds crazy, but it's like something is coming. Like he's going to show up. I know that I'm probably insane, but it's just a feeling."

Since we ended things, I've had no insight into his life, aside from the last time I saw him, eight months ago outside my parents' house in Brooklyn. When we first broke up years ago, we vowed to stay friends. Truthfully though, I couldn't do that and watch his life on social media. He's been muted on all accounts ever since. Allowing me to keep the façade of friendship open without torturing myself by watching his life play out. Without me in it.

"That's not crazy, but I don't want you to dwell on that. Instead, I want you to go home and find that list. Read them one by one, okay? Remind yourself of your own worth outside of his faults," she says softly, as if she has a viewfinder into my thoughts.

My teeth grab onto the inside of my lip as I nod, and our session comes to a close. We schedule my next appointment like usual, every three weeks on Tuesday at 5:30 p.m. I exit the building, and my boots click on the dirty gray pavement of the New York city street as I make my way to the nearest subway station, consciously avoiding the drops of gum and the murky puddles.

The usual car horns and construction beeps of the traffic fade into the background as my thoughts run back to Myles. While I recognize these thoughts of missing him, it's different than it used to be, back when I first started therapy. There used to be a twinge of pain or pricking at my eyes whenever I would think about him. A heaviness on my chest.

Now, it feels like the memory of him sits on my skin, like the rays of a heat lamp.

It's all over and all-consuming, but it's painless. Which is nice.

I guess.

Though I'd much rather not feel him at all.

The feeling still makes me want to skip this unbearably crowded subway ride and crawl into my bed. Preferably with a sleeve of Fudge Stripe cookies and a large bottle of wine while Jenko lays his calico body on top of my stomach.

My phone vibrates in my back pocket as I enter the subway train, and a message from Harper appears, telling me she's currently picking up takeout from one of our favorite restaurants, Soybean. Sloan always joins us, and it's been our Tuesday night tradition for years now.

Since Harper and I work in Tribeca together, we often take the same train to and from. But some days our schedules are completely different. Sometimes I go to the gym in the morning and Harper sleeps past her alarm. I have therapy on Tuesday nights, and she does yoga after work. Hence our separation.

Tonight, I know that no matter how much I may want to, Harper will by no means let me wallow in self-pity over the feelings that the memories of Myles are causing. Instead, she will drag all she can out of me and attempt to make me feel better.

Because that's who Harper is. My fiery, red-headed, *we do not let our shitty exes get us down* best friend. She also practically hates Myles, and since I can't hate him no matter how hard I've tried, it's nice to have her to break me out of my rose-colored memories when I need her to.

The subway ride home to our two-bedroom apartment on the East Side passes in a flash. Glancing around at everyone bundled up in coats and gloves in the warmer-than-usual, but still cold February in the city, I pull my old, black and gray checkered coat closer around my body until I'm in the warmth of my building.

I kick my shoes off on the rug near the shoe rack Harper insisted we have so we don't drag unnecessary New York dirt into the clean space. The apartment is empty except for Jenko sitting on the windowsill of the fire escape. The exposed brick of the living room lights up as I flick on the lights and lean down to scratch him between the ears.

After shrugging off my coat and setting my work bag down, I grab three wineglasses, and while I wait for Harper and Sloan to arrive, I pour myself a large glass of the white Moscato that we all love. I shuffle into my bedroom and shrug on some large gray sweats and a sweater before placing myself at the counter with the TV playing another rerun of *Sex and the City* until they both arrive.

The smell of food wafting down the hallway alerts me to Harper's presence before she appears in the kitchen. "So, I see therapy went well," she chides as she drops her keys on the counter and takes in my very full wine glass.

I raise it in a fake "cheers" before taking a very long pull of the liquid.

"Swimmingly, actually."

She just shakes her head before taking her long red hair out of the bun she had it wrapped in for yoga class. After setting three plates on the counter, she pours her own glass of wine, her eyes flickering up to the TV when she's done, focused on the episode we've both seen countless times.

"I'm just going to wait for Sloan to get here before I bug you about therapy."

I roll my eyes. "You know I'm not required to tell you about my therapy sessions."

Harper gives me a deadpan look.

"Fine, maybe I'll be drunk enough it won't bother me."

She clinks her glass to mine, grinning despite my blank stare. "That's the spirit."

Soon enough, before we've both downed our first glasses, there's a quick knock at the door before I hear it open with the extra key we gave Sloan. Harper starts setting out the food, chicken pad Thai for me, spicy something or other for her, and curry for Sloan.

I take the liberty of pouring Sloan a glass and refilling the other two.

Sloan's holding her mail in her hand, and she's not dressed in her usual salon attire, which means she stopped by her own apartment before coming here. She drops the envelopes on the counter and drapes her coat over her chair as she takes a long sip of her wine. Her deep brown curls just touch the tops of her shoulders in the pink camisole and cardigan combo, complimentary against her dark brown skin.

"Hello, ladies." She smiles as Harper slides each of our plates in our direction. "How was therapy?"

"*¿Cómo crees?*" I mumble in frustration with my lips on the edge of the glass.

They glance between each other before their eyes fall back to me. Both know that over the last week or so Myles has been at the forefront of my mind, that I have been missing him, so they shouldn't be completely surprised by the words that I speak next.

"We talked about Myles."

Harper frowns around her food while Sloan keeps her warm brown eyes focused on me and nods encouragingly. I take a bite of the pad Thai, taking my time because I really don't want to spend any more time on him than I already have.

"I told her that it feels like he's going to show up. Somehow, someway."

Harper turns her gray eyes on me with the focus of a hawk. "You don't want him to, right?"

"No. It's just I haven't been reminiscent, haven't missed him, in so long. And it's not like I miss him in a way that I want him to come back and apologize. I don't ever want to touch him or be with him again."

"Thank god," Harper mumbles as she takes a sip of wine.

"Harps. Be nice," Sloan scolds.

If Sloan was an object, she'd be your favorite blanket from childhood.

Harper would be a samurai sword.

I take a sip of my own wine. "It's just weird. I'm sure it'll go away."

"Well, you know what my advice is. You need to get laid," Harper mumbles over her food, eyes flickering between me and the TV. "Or go on a date. Or something."

Jenko meows from his spot on the gray armchair as if to say, *she's right you know,* and Sloan bites her lip as she nods as well. I'm not saying they're wrong.

It's been over two years. *Dios ayúdame.*

"You know it's not that easy."

It's not that I physically can't—instead, I mentally can't—if I'm not comfortable with someone, I don't want them to touch me. I clam up and get nervous, and hook-ups make me intensely uncomfortable. Myles was my first everything. He knew me like the back of his hand. After that ended, all the dating I've done and attempted one-night stands, courtesy of my friends' encouragement, have failed. Hence, the never-ending dry spell.

"Yeah, well, I'm still undyingly determined to find you someone." Sloan tugs a curl, and I watch as it bounces back up. I've always been jealous of her curls. Mine are wavier, looser, never quite enough. "I don't think you're crazy, by the way. Maybe it is a sign of something, who knows."

I nod as I take another bite. We fall into a comfortable silence, one where there are no conversations of Myles or getting me laid, just the comforting problems of Carrie Bradshaw from the TV. Only after two more episodes, one bottle of wine down, and a clean counter do I break out the makings of homemade brownies and the second bottle of Moscato.

Sloan is bent over her pile of mail and her open laptop. Probably pouring through appointment requests for the salon and replying to customers on her waiting list. She's a wildly successful hair stylist down at Fringe on the Lower East Side, an extremely popular salon.

Harper twirls on the stool where I previously sat, clutching her wine glass, with her eyes glued to the TV. I pull my hair back into a ponytail and break two eggs into the bowl over the sugar, vanilla, and oil. I mix the ingredients together as I get to the good part. The cocoa powder, the flour, and the chocolate chips.

The oven beeps, letting me know it's fully preheated, and I stop twirling the now chocolaty batter long enough to spray the pan with PAM. I spread the batter into it but leave a healthy amount for me to spoon out. Because eating raw brownie batter will solve everything, I just know it.

Just as I place them into the oven and grab the spatula topped with chocolate, Sloan's hand shoots up to cover her mouth, a loud gasp escaping as she stares at the paper in her hand.

"What?" Harper looks at me, eyes wide.

"Holy shit. Holy freaking shit."

There is a blush pink envelope ripped open on the counter with cursive lettering on the front, but the square she holds in her hand is what has her undivided attention. I'm still more concerned with the brownie batter resting on my spatula.

"Go get your mail," Sloan says.

Her voice is muffled because her hand is still covering her mouth. I cock my head, my eyebrows furrowing together as I taste the first glob of brownie batter.

"Sloan, what the hell!" Harper says as she leans in to read it while simultaneously trying to finish the rest of her wine.

"Oh my god." Her eyes shoot up to me as shock spreads over her face.

"Will one of you idiots tell me what is going on?"

Harper doesn't say anything as she finishes off her wine before she stands up. Her red hair falls forward as she searches in her bag and pulls out our mail and two identical pink envelopes, both with the same cursive lettering that's on Sloan's envelope.

I'm three more globs of brownie batter in before she slides me a pink envelope. I pick it up with my other hand, and I feel both of their eyes burning a hole into my forehead. It's addressed to me, obviously, so I tear open the seam and pull out the contents.

The pretty pink envelope is discarded, but my heart stops when I realize what I'm holding. Light purple and pink flower accents line the edges of the textured paper.

Your presence has been requested
To celebrate the union of

My eyes glide easily over the introduction and focus on the two names.

They are perfectly centered in jet black calligraphy.

My heart beats painfully slow in my chest.

Emma Tate & Myles Henderson

I blink. And blink again. Hoping the words will rearrange themselves in a way that makes sense. But my heart feels completely dead in my chest as my eyes travel further down the paper. Before I finish reading, I gulp the rest of my third glass of wine.

Harper and Sloan do me the honors of sliding over their own refilled glasses.

Saturday, the 21ˢᵗ of May, Twenty-Twenty Two
Six in the evening at the Midtown Loft & Terrace

I stare blankly at the perfect piece of paper in my hand. With the perfect cursive. With the address of one of the best views in the city. In May.

Myles is getting married.

Two | Nina

"**N**ina, give me the bottle and the phone, please."

The bottle of whiskey is clutched closely to my chest. White Moscato just wasn't cutting it anymore. And I can't seem to pull myself away from Myles's Facebook page, which I searched up just for this moment. It's filled to the brim with engagement pictures of him and *Emma Tate*.

It's perfect. She's perfect. Everything looks fucking perfect.

To go along with their perfect invites and soon-to-be perfect wedding.

Light brown hair flows past her shoulders and around her impeccable, oval face. Her entire face is symmetrical; her eyes aren't too far apart or too close. Her nose is just slightly upturned above her lips, which are painted red in all of their engagement photos.

I raise the bottle to my lips, ignoring Sloan's quiet request for me to give it up. "I can't believe this."

The liquid burns going down my throat, and it warms me from the inside out. Two years is a long time retrospectively. But when you break it apart it isn't. For him to be engaged and getting married in a few months, a few months past our two-year breakup point—it still feels like it happened quickly.

Maybe it's because my two years were spent differently.

Mine were spent in therapy, addressing my faults, my attachment style, my issues and how they and Myles's behavior may affect me going forward. Going over and over our relationship and where it went wrong. I had to repeatedly remind myself that nothing I did was the sole reason for the end of us.

Not to say I'm blame free, but I was more often the one in pain than the one causing it.

I can't help but spiral back into us for a moment.

He won't look at me.

That's all I can think about as we sit on the stoop outside my parents' house. The sun is beating down onto my sweatshirt-covered shoulders in early spring. It should be warm, but I'm just cold. Goosebumps are spread all over my arms and down my spine.

He looks beautiful, but he almost looks foreign back in Brooklyn. It's his Easter break, his last one before he graduates, and he's already got this fresh graduate glow. I'm jealous that I still have a year to go. I'm jealous he's so far ahead of me. But I'm not jealous of how distant he looks on the stoop we've sat on for years.

He looks unfamiliar, unknown, next to me. Because he's never not looked at me.

From when we were running around as kids in the playground or streets of Brooklyn, he's always looked at me.

But I guess that's unfair of me, to want him to look at me one last time, since I'm officially ending things. Ever since he left for school, things haven't been right. We've been on and off and on again, repeatedly. But I didn't know how to be in a world without him all that time.

Little did I know, I was living in one, I just wasn't aware.

And I'd rather be alone than be strung along and led on

only to realize it'll never be the same. We'll never be best friends again. We'll never spend the fourth of July together, never celebrate our birthdays or holidays again. I'll never cheer him on in the stands again. He'll never watch me with hazy eyes as I try on my favorite latest fashion trend in the dimness of my room.

"I know I'm ending it," I start quietly, "but it's been over for a while, hasn't it?"

I'm scared of the answer, even though I know it. We used to never run out of words to say, never have awkward silences, never fight. But all we've done, all we do, is walk on eggshells around each other.

As if we're both scared of stepping on a crack in our foundation and watching it all crumble.

He crosses his arm, and his eyes flicker to me. I look down at the concrete.

"You're the one ending it, so you tell me."

The words are harsh, but I hear the hurt underneath them. We both know the truth, but that doesn't make it hurt any less.

"You don't get to be mad at me, Myles. Things haven't been the same since you left for college years ago. You don't treat me like I'm someone you care about. And I'm not going to sit here and wait for you with my breath held until you make up your mind anymore."

He sighs and finally really looks at me. My eyes start to prick, and I can feel my throat tighten as I dig my nails into my palm.

"I love you, Myles. I've loved you since we were kids running down this street. But we'll never be those kids again." I laugh, but it's shallow and dry. "You're not in love with me. You haven't been for years. I won't chase someone who's made it clear I'm not what they wanted for years. It just took me until now to see it."

Now it's me who can't look at him.

"I never meant to do this to us, to you. I'm sorry, I mean that. I just didn't know how to let you go. You were a part of my life for so long, and I didn't think we'd end up here. I never meant to do this," Myles says, but the words feel empty to me.

It's hard to believe it, after seeing the videos and images of his social life when he was away. The same girl appearing in all the pictures or videos during his senior year. He went from never hiding anything from me to always turning his phone away or ending our nightly facetimes early or canceling plans. I was never an anxious person.

Until I became one.

I don't want to be mad, even though anger pricks at my skin. I just want to let him go.

"I'll always have love for you, Nin, forever," he says, his deep brown eyes pouring into mine.

We look at each other, communicating a million things both of us could say out loud but choose not to. I could ask him to try again. But I won't. He could beg me for another chance. But he doesn't. And the small part of me that wants him to is scratching at my skin, waiting on the back of my tongue.

His lips are pushed together in a sad, closed-mouth half-smile, and my eyes are brimming with tears, but I hold them in. I don't want to cry in front of him anymore. I don't want him to see me vulnerable ever again.

And I say the one word I shouldn't, but I do it anyway.

I extend a shaky hand. "Friends?"

He gives me a soft smile. "Friends."

My heart constricts because I know it's a lie. I'll never call him with good news, he'll never tell me about his day, and we'll never walk through the familiar streets again.

We'll never really be friends again.

The bottle is ripped out of my grasp. Harper is standing over me with the alcohol in her hands. Sloan is looking at me with sad eyes, *you're over your ex, but he's getting married, and it sucks* eyes. Jenko is watching the whole thing from the windowsill. His tail flicks lazily up and down as he watches us with lethargic eyes and perked ears.

"You cannot drink this whole thing tonight."

I lean my head against the wall from where I'm seated on the floor. Harper's face softens as she bends down.

"I know it sucks, Nina. But you will feel even worse when you have to wake up and go to work tomorrow. We can drink this wedding invitation into oblivion on Friday, I pinky promise."

I grip her pinky with mine as she pulls me up, and the three of us take seats on the couch. They both make space for me in between them, and I crawl into it as they cover me with the black fuzzy blanket from our couch. My skin is still warm from the alcohol flowing through me, and I can't stop picking my lip as I keep rereading that invitation and replaying our relationship.

Harper hands me the pan of brownies. "I said we couldn't get trashed, but we can eat our feelings."

Even Jenko, who really only likes me and doesn't like being crowded by anyone, including my best friends, pads over and curls onto my lap. His tiny body warms me as he purrs in my lap, and I rest my head on Sloan's shoulder.

Harper's manicured nail is tracing shapes on my arm, and I can't help it as the tears finally come out. It's quiet, no noise except the occasional beep of a horn and the TV, but it feels like a part of me is chipping off for good. Myles has been locked away in a box for so long.

A happy, closed, muted box. And that invitation was the hidden key that opened it. Most of me is happy for him. I'm happy he found someone.

But a very small, miniscule part of me is painfully aware that someone isn't me.

Another part is upset at how easily he moved on, and that I'm still here. Alone.

Those parts escape me through tears that crawl down my cheeks and land in quiet spatters on my thighs.

I blink away as much as I can and lean my head back onto the couch. To my left I'm surprised, though I shouldn't be, to see wetness in Harper's eyes. "Harps."

She glares at me through the two tears dripping down her cheeks.

"You know whenever you cry, I cry. And I don't know, I hate him. For everything he did. And I never wanted you two back together, but it's still the same Myles we all grew up with. And he's getting fucking married."

My lips quirk into a smile, and I pull her into my arms, where she cuddles her orange-red hair into me. Jenko adjusts to make room for the new addition, but he doesn't run away, and Sloan holds us all together.

Harper is all hard edges and sharpened knives, but when she loves you, this side materializes. Ever since we were kids, whenever I cried, you were bound to see Harper in tears with me. Although, her tears were always accompanied with a glare. She hates crying, but she's also a sympathy crier.

She is fully aware of the irony.

"He's getting married," I echo, biting the inside of my lip as I usually do.

"Are we going to go?" Sloan asks quietly as if I might combust, which is possible, or as if Harper might completely lose it. Also possible.

"Yeah. Yeah, we are. It may be depressing, but I need to see it. That final nail in the coffin." I pause. "I'm also going to look hot. We may be over, and I may be in therapy, but it's a need."

That brings a chuckle out of them both.

"You know it's okay to put yourself out there, Nina. I know you're okay—happy—on your own, but you don't have to be alone. It's okay to open yourself up." Sloan's voice is quiet as she says it, but it doesn't change the pang of fear I feel at the words.

Even the idea, the possibility, of doing that, of doing *love* again, is terrifying. To get hurt like that again. When I'm alone, the only person that can hurt me is me.

Love means letting someone else have the ability to hurt you.

And I've had quite enough of that.

"I'd much rather sit inside my well-guarded, fortified castle, thank you very much."

Harper lifts her head. Her gray eyes are still slightly watery, but they pierce into mine. "You can't sit here with Jenko forever."

I gently cover his ears and scowl at her. "Watch me."

He purrs on my lap, and the conversation drops, thankfully. I'm in no position to talk about the idea of me opening up to someone or dating. I just want to wallow.

We sit there for a little while more, letting the episode play out before Sloan stands up. "I have to be at the salon super early tomorrow. Are you gonna be all right tonight?"

Her brown eyes watch me, hesitation appearing in them as she does. "Yeah, I'm gonna be fine. I'm just going to bed, and I'll be fine until Friday."

She pulls me into a hug and holds me tight. I squeeze my eyes shut to stop more tears from flowing out the sides and down my cheeks. My head is pounding just slightly, like it always does when I try to hold in the tears, but I ignore it.

After placing a quick kiss on my cheek and hugging Harper, Sloan slings her bags over her shoulders and bundles into her coat as she walks out the door, bidding us goodbye. I can feel Harper's eyes on the back of my head.

I turn. "I'm gonna head to bed. I'm starting to get a headache from drinking."

A lie because I never get headaches or hungover. Harper knows that too.

"Nina."

I gather Jenko into my arms, the vibrations of his purring sending a flood of calming waves over me. "I'm fine. I'm just gonna go sleep it off. I'll see you in the morning."

She watches me closely as I head down the hallway to my room. I press my back against the door after I shut it. The warm yellow glow of my lights welcome me in with the green of the plants on my windowsill.

Photos and collages I've made of my favorite old *Poze* covers and photoshoots are framed together above my bed, certain quotes and photos front and center. Piles of old magazines like *Harper's Bazaar, Cosmo, Vogue,* and others sit under the window and at the foot of my bed.

Pictures of the three of us from childhood are framed around my speaker on the mahogany dresser from my family that matches my bed frame. Pictures of my family also line the dresser. Various perfumes and a collection of makeup sit to the side, and candles are haphazardly thrown around the surfaces of my room: the dresser, the window, and my nightstand.

I walk over the pink fuzzy rug that matches the blanket over my gray comforter and bury myself into it. Jenko curls tightly into my stomach as I lay on my side after shutting the lights off.

Darkness floods in from the space between the windowsill and where my curtains stop, letting only a faint glow from the city streetlights in. It surrounds me as I lay there, unable to stop reminiscing on the relationship that used to be mine. Every wrong and every right. I couldn't stop the tears even if I wanted to.

I bury my face into the pillows so that when Harper walks by, like I know she will, to listen for my quiet sobs, she won't hear them.

Tomorrow I'll wake up and pick myself up. Walk myself through my routine—gym, breakfast, work—and I'll be okay. I'll remember that I'm happy here with my friends and on my own.

I'll be okay.

But for right now, I've accepted it's okay to be sad about Myles getting married. About officially losing someone who was a part of me for so long, even after letting him go.

The last piece of him that had a hold on me is being chiseled off my shoulder with a pickaxe.

And despite me wishing it wouldn't, it still hurts.

Three | Nina

I thought this week would never end.

Between having to write four articles for work on different upcoming trends, making final edits for the March magazine, the wedding invitation, and my undying desire to drown my sorrows in alcohol as an unhealthy coping mechanism, it feels like years have passed.

To make matters worse, my parents also got invitations to the wedding which resulted in a two-hour phone call with them on Wednesday. My mom kept flying in and out of Spanish as she asked how I was, when this happened, and other questions I had no answers to, all between cursing Myles out in Spanish, even though she used to love him.

My dad was much less animated as he took the phone. He quietly reminded me that he never liked Myles, which he didn't, and when he quietly whispered he loved me more than anything, I broke down in tears. He let me cry to him in silence and told me that my favorite meal would be waiting on the table on Sunday afternoon if I wanted to venture into Brooklyn. Which I would. I could use the company of my parents and their cooking.

But finally, after a long, exhausting week, it's Friday.

As the night sky deepens and the city lights up, leaving rays of building lights on our apartment floors, I am no longer concerned with my pity-inducing feelings.

Because before that invitation and before the flashing warning signs of me missing him, I was doing fucking great.

Correction, I *am* doing fucking great.

I am done shedding tears over someone I know I'm better off without—at least for now. With our speaker playing my favorite songs throughout the apartment, I am becoming myself again.

Jenko is sitting on my vanity as I apply the finishing touches on my deep red lipstick.

He watches me with perked ears before I pick him up in my arms, letting the black robe fan out around my legs as I dance to the song. His body vibrates as he purrs, and I lose myself in the lyrics, lose myself in the excitement flooding through my body as I embrace this feeling.

Harper appears in my doorway, hands on her hips as she watches me with a bright smile.

I spin around, gracing her with my own smile, a full one for the first time since Tuesday, and she dances with Jenko and I as she holds our signature pre-game cups in her hands, fully decorated in shades of glitter and phrases we used to say all the time.

As we spin around, I take in her outfit. She's dressed in a black, corset-detailed bodysuit, held up with dainty silver chains, tan joggers, and black sock booties. Her orange-red hair is mussed into the perfect messy ponytail, and a dark smoky eye and lip tie the look together. She pulls away from my hand. Her cheeks are flushed, but her gray eyes twinkle with excitement.

"All right, lay it on me. What are you wearing tonight?"

She crosses her legs as she sits in my vanity chair, taking a sip out of her cup and handing me mine. We got them on our senior year spring break trip to Key West. Best investment we ever made. I grasp the cup with a smile as I take a slow sip, letting the drink enter my bloodstream.

Jenko hops out of my arms and onto my bed, curling himself into the mountain of pillows, and I hold my robe closed as I show her what I have picked out. A black leather skirt with a slit on one side and a black, sheer, long-sleeve bodysuit with detailing that will wrap around my chest, all to be paired with thigh-high black boots.

Simple but effective.

"Fuck yes. You'll look amazing," she squeals as she sips again, kicking her legs in excitement as I disappear into the bathroom to get dressed.

I look in the mirror. My brown eyes stare back at me, and for the first time this week, they're bright and filled with anticipation. No pain, no yearning, nothing but the electric energy running through me. My wavy hair falls in loose curls, framing my face, and the make-up is painted on like my mother taught me. When I was younger, I was obsessed with how she and her best friends would spend hours gossiping and painting on lipstick or the perfect cat eye, listening to Selena and old East Coast rap.

As I take in the sheer bodysuit and the black leather skirt that makes my short legs look miles longer, I feel like myself. Someone who has fun, who goes out with her best friends and isn't concerned with exes or love or anything but being happy within herself.

I grab my cup and my boots before heading into the kitchen, where the speaker is blasting loud music and where Harper sits. I tip the cup back, enjoying the familiar burn.

Harper's nails click against her phone until she looks up. "I know I said it already, but you look fantastic. Sloan said she's getting changed now and will be here in ten."

Before Sloan gets here, I pour three shots of tequila that we can toss back paired with salt and lime. And in the meantime, I scroll on Instagram and other social medias, pinning new fashion trends to my Pinterest board and adding things to my online shopping cart I most definitely do not need but won't stop myself from buying if a good sale comes along.

Harper looks up from her phone again, on which I'm willing to bet the Tinder app is pulled up, and looks at me deeply. She takes a sip from her silicone straw before she speaks.

"I think you should download Tinder. It's time."

I shake my head. "Nope. Give it up."

She rolls her eyes as she swipes left again. "For me?"

"No."

I tap my French tip nails against my cup as I finish the last sips and start to feel the telltale effects of alcohol. My cheeks are hot, and my body warms from the inside. I ignore Harper's deep sigh as she attempts to guilt me into the app.

I hear Sloan's signature knock on the door and the sound of her key as she enters.

Her tight curls bounce as she enters the kitchen, dancing on beat to the song playing, and grins as she takes in our outfits. She's got on her signature nude lipstick, which compliments her dark skin perfectly, and her winged liner is sharp, as usual.

A long sleeve white crop top cuts off perfectly above her midi-length leopard print skirt with a slit up the left leg. She's got a simple black belt with gold detailing wrapped around the skirt and simple black booties to tie the outfit together. She looks flawless.

"We look hot." Sloan grins.

Her eyes focus on the shots of tequila, wiggling her eyebrows at us, and we all grip our shot glasses after sprinkling salt on our hands,

"You guys ready?" I say breathlessly with a smile, and my two best friends grin.

We tap our glasses to one another, raise them to the sky, touch the table, and toss the liquid back, relishing the burn.

Bar Ten is radiating infectious energy.

The entire place is vibrating as the bass of the early 2000's pop and hip-hop songs blast through the large speakers on both floors.

Downstairs is more conversational. The walls are lined with TVs playing various sports on different screens, there's a pool table and shuffleboard along with high top seating lining the walls, and then of course the large bar. And the loudest noise you'll most likely hear is the roar of everyone talking to one another over the music.

Upstairs is the dance floor. Three smaller bars are placed in corners of the room that surrounds the DJ of the night, and the rest is all strobe lights and people grinding on each other. This spot is known for having the best DJs in this part of New York. Luckily, we come here often enough the bouncers usually give us a smile and send us on our way past the line after a quick flash of our IDs.

At this point, I don't even know how many shots we've taken.

My cheeks are on fire, and I probably have the appearance of someone who applied way too much blush or is extremely embarrassed. Sloan is singing along loudly to every song that plays overhead, and I've had to pull down Harper from standing on a high top at least twice. Because in her eyes, dancing on the floor is nowhere near as fun as dancing on a table.

I've also fought off at least four creepy men on the upstairs dance floor, and I need another drink to cool me down immediately. Or one to pour on the next man that approaches me. Whichever is more pressing at the moment.

"I'll be right back. I need a drink," I say to my friends, whose hands are intertwined as they dance around to the song, and I toss them a smile as I make my way downstairs.

The lights are slightly blurred in a multitude of colors as I finally reach the bar, an effect of the amount of alcohol I've consumed tonight. But I like it. I'm enjoying the buzz. The sheer feeling of aliveness flowing through my body, from my toes to my fingertips.

I stand on my tiptoes to eye my surroundings, trying to make my short frame appear taller among the crowd around the bar. My view is interrupted by someone much taller than me on my tiptoes. I lean back, stumbling slightly before I catch myself on the counter. He's at least 6'2 with tanned skin and loose blond curls that falls over his forehead in a way that makes me want to run my hands through them.

He's turned away from me, talking to someone on his left, but energy burns off him.

It's lively and warm and all-encompassing.

His head starts to turn, and I force my eyes forward to await a bartender, tapping my nails on the countertop. The hairs on the back of my neck rise as the heat of his gaze sticks to my skin.

I've been cold all week. Between constant goosebumps and tears, I couldn't shake the chills no matter how deep I burrowed into my blankets with my boiling hot coffee.

But right now, my skin is prickling with warmth.

I turn, and my eyes connect with his.

Not only are his eyes blue, like a deep cerulean blue that I could sink in—drown in—his smile is bright and enticing. All surrounded by a sharp jawline and double dimples.

To put it simply, he's gorgeous.

His face lights up further if that's possible, like he's walking on sunshine as he looks at me. I don't deny that the slow trail of his eyes down my body causes an intense butterfly sensation in my stomach.

But I raise an eyebrow as he looks at me, keeping my face neutral, as if the way he's looking at me and the sunshiny smile are having absolutely no effect on me.

And the dimples?

My god.

I break away from the intense gaze as the bartender comes over with a small smile and asks me if I want the usual, to which I nod. She asks him for his order and disappears to go make them.

He leans down, resting both forearms on the bar to make us eye level with each other. His shirt sleeves are rolled up to his elbows and the collar is unbuttoned at the top where his tan skin peaks out. His arm just barely grazes mine.

And I'm not sure if it's the buzz or him that causes the spot to burn along with a flash of heat in the pit of my stomach. My mind goes blank briefly, distracted by everything about him.

Either way, I like it.

"Hi."

His voice is deep and unwavering and at the same time, light and airy. It draws me in and washes over me. All in one simple word.

I struggle to keep my face straight.

"Hi," I say, making a move to hand the bartender my cash, but before I can he's sliding her a credit card. "Thank you, but you didn't—that wasn't necessary."

His smile never falters as he takes a sip of what looks like an old fashioned, and I wrap my lips around the straw in my own drink. Turning, he leans his back against the bar, looking down at me.

Those blue eyes are the brightest thing in the darkened bar.

"No need to thank me. I wanted to."

I cock my head as I watch him carefully. Not caring that it seems as if I'm studying him like a piece of artwork hanging in the Metropolitan. Because the way he smiles, the sharp cut of his jaw and his eyes.

He belongs in a museum.

And I want to take it all in.

"Are you here alone?" he asks, eyes roaming for a second before landing on me.

With his eyes trained on mine, I can't help but notice the crackling electricity between us in this small space. Somehow separating us from everyone else, even though we're surrounded.

I roll my eyes, biting my lip to hide my smile. "My friends are upstairs."

"Friends. Okay, good."

"Good?" I twirl my finger in the condensation on my glass.

"I prefer that response to boyfriend."

My cheeks flush despite myself, and I know it's not from the alcohol this time as the heat spreads up my neck and over my face.

"Just because I didn't respond boyfriend doesn't mean I don't have one."

He nods slowly. "Do you?"

"No."

The smile on his face expands, both dimples deepening. "Good."

I step away from the bar so I'm directly in front of him just as someone bumps into me from behind, causing me to stumble. I manage to keep my drink upright, but his hand wraps around my arm and grips my elbow to steady me.

Goosebumps spread over my skin. And not the bad kind that I got familiar with this week. The good kind. The kind that makes you forget about every other thought and focus on the skin-to-skin contact going on.

Our eyes connect as I look up, feeling confidence surge through me as he slowly unwraps his hand from around mine.

"Girlfriend?"

His tongue darts out, licking his lip. "Nope."

"Well, come on." I reach out to the hand that was just on mine.

His dimples pop. "Already can't let go of me, huh?"

"Oh, *Cállete*,"

He raises an eyebrow, and if it's possible his smile widens. "I don't know what that means, but I'll do whatever you say."

The urge to smile is fighting to come out.

"Do you want to come dance with me or not?"

He's watching me with those deep blue eyes, and the essence of his presence is so different from anyone else in the bar. Everything about it is alluring, enchanting. He reminds me of a summer day at the beach. When the waves are calm for a moment so you can wade in and let the water envelop you instead of blindly diving headfirst into the crash.

"Never wanted to do anything more."

Four | Nina

know with unyielding certainty I am not in my own bed.

I'm not even in my apartment.

Qué demonios.

The brightness flooding in from the large windows onto the light gray walls of the large bedroom is completely foreign to me, and there are three things I can gather through my barely open eyes at this very second.

One, I'm buttoned backwards into a men's dress shirt.

Two, there is a wall of pillows next to me.

Three, I am certain there is someone on the other side of those pillows.

A groan crawls at the back of my throat as my head pounds like a jackhammer, but I am terrified at waking up whoever is lying next to me, so I stay quiet. I move slowly to take in my surroundings, sitting up a tiny bit from under the down comforter.

My phone is on the nightstand, my shoes are haphazardly on the floor, and my skirt is still on, though uncomfortably so. I lean up, peeking my head over the pillow wall to see blond, curly hair and a well-toned and tanned back.

His arms are curled under his pillow and the band of his boxers peeks out before the comforter covers the rest. Even sleeping, his muscles stretch taut as he breathes, shifting when he does.

I lay back and pull the collar of the shirt up and over my face, slightly concerned with why it's on backwards, and sit in my thoughts for a minute. The amber and suede scent surrounds me, and I breath in deep, getting the tiniest hint of vanilla and letting it comfort my spinning head.

There is no way I slept with him, that's for certain. But if not, why didn't I get a ride home? Did I tell Harper and Sloan I was leaving with him? Why am I in a buttoned in backwards? Why the hell is it so bright?

"Morning, sunshine."

My heart almost bursts out of my chest at his morning voice and the intrusion it has on my running thoughts. How did I get from the dance floor to his bedroom?

I remember his hands on my hips, the touch lighting me up under the strobe lights last night. The way he held me close to him as the music played, the way I enjoyed it. Leaned into him, relished the feel of him on me. The way he moved his hips in sync with me.

I remember kissing him.

The memory is hazy at best. Just the phantom feeling of his lips on mine. That's it, but it's there.

I pull the shirt away from my face. Those eyes are focused on me like they were all last night, and his full lips are pulled into the smallest of smirks.

My teeth grip my lip, nerves spreading under my skin.

"Hi," is about all I can muster in this moment. As my eyes flicker between us, between the pillow wall and the button up and him, my brain feels like mush. "Did you, uh, do all this for a reason?"

He smiles fully as he watches me put together a small puzzle piece of last night. He sits up, leaning against the headboard.

Those stupid, beautiful blue eyes are even brighter in the sunlight, and I've never liked the color blue so much in my life.

Not that I would ever admit that to him. But it's true.

"I did."

My face turns hot; my cheeks are on fire. "What was the goal?"

"Protection measures for myself of course. As much as I genuinely wouldn't have complained, you were also extremely drunk, and if we hook up, I'd want you to remember it. And more importantly, enjoy it."

He says it so casually, so nonchalantly, like it's nothing. His voice is low and soft since he just woke up, and I swear I catch the smallest hint of an accent, but I can't place it. I also can't escape his words: *I want you to remember it. Enjoy it.*

While we didn't hook up, his words hold some truth because he's the first person I've felt sincerely attracted to since Myles and my failed one-night stand attempts. The fact that we didn't hook up because of my drunkenness says more for his character than anything, and the thought alone sends heat straight between my legs.

"So, you thought a pillow fort and makeshift straight jacket would save you?"

He runs a hand through the soft blond curls on top of his head before extending into a stretch, causing his muscles to tighten up, and my eyes are hyper focused on him.

"It did the trick." He laughs softly, and the sound washes over me.

Those eyes flicker to mine, and they soften, moving slowly over my face, taking in every blush-covered inch.

"But to be honest, I wouldn't have minded if it didn't."

Oh my. Heat pools instantly in the bottom of my stomach.

I want nothing more than to bury my head into this shirt and back under the covers—that are much softer and more expensive than mine—and go back to sleep. My eyes have adjusted to the room. Three huge windows line the bedroom walls, and I can see the New York City skyline clearly. The entire skyline. Every single building is crystal clear.

There's a flat screen on the wall across from us, two armchairs by the windows, and a tall bookshelf with a record player and books lining it from top to bottom. The walls are gray, and the furniture is simplistic, but the room doesn't feel cold. It's homey. There are pictures on the dresser in frames and a few art pieces on the wall.

The bed rustles, and my eyes flicker back to him. He's turned on his side, leaning on top the pillow wall. I bury myself deeper into the covers and watch as a lazy smirk falls onto his lips as he watches me.

"*¿Qué?*" I say quietly.

His eyes flicker with humor. "I know what that means, smart ass."

I purse my lips to keep from grinning.

"Now is as good a time as ever, but I never got your name?"

"Nina."

He extends his arm, breaking the pillow barrier, and the backwardness of this does not escape me. Learning a man's name already in their bed, it's a whole new world for me.

"Nina," he says it slowly, like he's testing it out, and my entire body erupts into tingles as he says it. Like no one else has ever said my name before. It's a wildly confusing and alluring feeling. I want him to say it again, over and over. "I'm Jackson."

I reach my arm out from under the covers and connect my hand with his. As I study him, the features of his face, I couldn't see a name fitting him any better. I sit up, and his eyes don't leave me as I adjust. I can't decide whether to focus on Jackson or the striking view that sits a few feet away.

"It's beautiful," I say to him, softly because part of me is scared if I speak too loudly, this calm little bubble with this *stranger* is going to pop. And I'm not sure I want it to.

"It sure is."

The same feeling I got at the bar last night spreads over my skin. His infectiously warm energy causes my own skin to prickle with warmth, and that's how I know he's not talking about the view. My eyes flicker away from the New York skyline and back to his cheeky grin, and as much as I wanted to keep my straight face, my lip falls from between my teeth at the sight of those damn dimples.

My phone vibrating angrily on the nightstand breaks the silence and our eye contact, and I reach for it. It's ten a.m., and Harper's name flashes across with five new text messages.

Harper: *I hope you had fun. Are you coming home soon? Are you* still *having fun? Be safe. We're brunching when you're back.*

Por el amor de Dios. I am in for a questioning.

I pull up the ride app and call one immediately. I draw my legs out from the bed to see a glass of water on the nightstand, and he gives me a nod when I look at it questioningly. I gulp it down as I pull on my shoes and realize this is going to be a painful morning-after outfit ride, especially when I take this shirt off.

"Well, I have to go." I motion to the app. "But thank you. For last night and for the pillow wall."

After putting my shoes on and regretting this outfit to the fullest, I realize I'm still buttoned in backwards. I run a hand through my hair and glance at him.

"Can you help me out?"

"Out of my shirt? Anytime."

I bite the inside of my cheek at his cheesy line, but my stomach is going wild. I haven't been this affected by a man since

Myles—or maybe ever. The others I tried with never caused the butterflies to erupt or my cheeks to burn.

"All right, *galán*, just help me."

I shake my head as I see his eyes flicker with curiosity. Hopefully, he'll forget what I said by the time he can pull up Google Translate.

But still a smile forms on his lips again as he stands up and walks around to me. His fingertips brush over my spine like a whisper as he slowly unbuttons the shirt. My breathing hitches as he moves my hair over my shoulder to get the last few buttons. He lets his fingers brush my neck longer than he needs too, and my entire body pulses.

I need to get a grip. Immediately.

"Thank you," I mutter, shrugging the shirt off and practically throw it at him.

"Anytime," he whispers back, still extremely close to me, and his breath hits my neck. I spin, needing to get away from his dangerously wispy fingers and charming eyes.

I straighten my shoulders, still buzzing with nervous energy but not wanting him to see that as he walks me out through the ridiculously nice apartment. I can't help but drag my eyes over him.

He's got a few freckles spattered over his smooth skin, and when he turns around at the front door my eyes go straight to the low-riding band of his pants. The thoughts that fill my head cause whatever coolness I was feeling to disappear as I glance up to see him watching me with one eyebrow raised and a buoyant expression.

Part of me wants to drop dead at being caught looking.

Before he can say another cheeky word, I'm uttering him a rushed goodbye, and I'm out the door pressing the elevator button. I climb in, with his eyes on me the whole time.

"Nina, wait!" he shouts.

I shrug my shoulders as the chill spreads over me at the sound of my name.

But the elevator doors are already closing, too late for me to stop them, and his figure disappears as I lean my head back on the cool silver doors. I brush my fingers over my lips as I descend, trying to chase the ghost of the memory I have of his lips on mine.

We were here, not at the bar.

From what I gather it was in the hallway next to his room. I was pushed softly against the wall, and my hands were curled into the nape of his hair. And I just barely remember the softness of the curls and smoothness of his skin.

The quick flash of his dimples.

His hands cupped my cheeks, and I vividly remember his thumb brushing over my skin, those intense eyes focused on me before he leaned forward slowly and pressed his lips to mine.

But that's where it ends. After that, it's all a dusty blur.

As the elevator door opens with a ding, I realize I forgot something. It was probably the same reason he shouted after me.

I don't have his phone number.

• • •

"You didn't get his number?" Sloan asks incredulously as she sips her mimosa. Harper is leaned in next to me, eyes focused like she's waiting for me to spill something else.

I down the rest of my mimosa.

"I could barely think straight. I was so confused; my brain wasn't functioning. You don't think I'd like to have his number? Or his last name? I can't even internet stalk him now."

I could go back to his apartment but that's taking it too far, even for me.

"Oh, babe, it's okay." Harper says, taking a sip of her disgusting Bloody Mary.

I grab the pitcher of the endless mimosas I ordered before letting my head fall into my hands. The sun streams in the large window we're crowded against at our favorite brunch spot. It's unusually sunny for a mid-February day, and I'm basking in all the sun I can get. After I called a ride home in my outfit, I walked in to my two best friends awaiting my return. Sloan was spread out on the couch with a coffee mug and her tight curls in a bun while Harper was curled into the armchair with her eyes closed.

As soon as I entered, their heads whipped around to me and the biggest, cheekiest grins I'd ever seen spread over their faces. I tried to ignore them and made a beeline for the shower, but they just followed me, taking their seats on the steamy bathroom floor as they bombarded me with questions.

The hot water was the only thing that could wash away the blurry night and the embarrassment sitting on my skin. The only thing I didn't want washed away were the images of a blurry kiss against an apartment wall. Even now, the ghost feeling of his lips are enough to send a blast of heat over my body and to flood my cheeks pink.

I break off a piece of the chocolate chip muffin. "He built a pillow fort between us because I was so drunk. Said if we hooked up, he'd want me to remember."

Harper lifts her head from where it rested on my shoulder moments ago, and her mouth falls open.

"He didn't."

"He did," I say, frowning. "I'm an idiot. How is it that the one person I was attracted to is too nice and sweet and builds a pillow wall? Because I was too drunk? And I don't get his number? What are the odds?"

Even after showering and getting somewhat ready, we all have a disheveled energy surrounding us. That's loud and clear by the pitcher of mimosas, Harper's third Bloody Mary, and an overwhelming number of appetizers.

My hair is in a loose bun on the top of my head, curls framing my bare face. Sloan's curly hair is pulled tight into a cute puff with a simple headband, and Harper's hair falls in waves down her back. We're all dressed appropriately because Harper wanted to get some photos today, and her camera sits on the edge of the table.

"I'm going to assume stalking him is out of the question?" Harper's eyes light up. I stare blankly at her. A smile plays at her lips. "You should honestly get a comedy show or something."

"We'd be such a good supporting cast," Sloan sighs and finishes her own drink.

"Honestly, even though nothing frisky happened, I'm proud of you. He was hot. Like really hot. Even his name is hot."

I roll my eyes as Harper wiggles her eyebrows and leans forward on her elbow, and Sloan nods in agreement. They had seen me dancing with him upstairs, and I had avoided them just so their eyes wouldn't pop out of their heads.

"Jackson. Yeah, he is hot. Like disgustingly attractive."

"Well, I'm sure you'll see him again," Sloan says, always the picture of optimism. She can turn any situation around if she tries hard enough.

I latch onto her brown eyes with my own. "What are the odds of that, Sloan, seriously?"

"Like negative ten," Harper chimes in.

"All I'm saying is you never really know."

Our food arrives after our resident optimist has finished speaking. I turn and watch people pass by the window, clad in jackets on their bikes. Groups of friends walk by in hordes, clutching their shopping bags, and cars turn down the street one after another.

I try not to feel discouraged at the stupid, silly encounter, at the fact that I'll most likely never see Jackson again. It's funnier than anything else, and I know I'm just being dramatic, but still, it's another tally on my bad luck in love journey. While I've accepted that maybe it's just not for me, at least not right now or anytime soon, those brief moments had felt like a new chapter. But it was just another paragraph on an already turned page.

Five | Nina

Sundays are my favorite day of the week; they always have been. Especially after the week I've had, I need it.

It's even better today as I clutch my mug, which is filled with my mom's homemade chocolate en Leche de Coco, as the steam floats upwards. The smell of my mom's empanadas frying, along with rice and my dad's sweet potatoes, fills the house. It's a strange mixture, but I think they're trying to give me all my favorites in one night.

I also know my mom made torta negra cake for dessert, and I saw a quart of the homestyle vanilla chip ice cream my dad always used to buy in the freezer. All to make me feel better.

I take a small sip, letting the chocolate and coconut milk take over my taste buds.

My bedroom is the same—it always is every time I visit. Maybe a stray box with random knick-knacks, but for the most part it's unchanged. I lean against the doorway as I look around. It feels different today, maybe because everywhere I look there is a memory of Myles and me waiting to jump out.

My bed, where we used to lay for hours while I made him watch *21 Jump Street* for the thousandth time. Or when he couldn't keep his hands off me after my junior year homecoming and we had our first mini hook up. I remember it so vividly because he was the only person I wanted to touch me. The only hands I wanted on my hips or my legs or anywhere else.

Or my window seat, my favorite place in the whole world, where I'd read my magazines or cut them up to make collages. He'd always help me, hand me the glue or the poster board, and I would put on ESPN so we could watch sports together while we did it.

It's also the place he first told me he loved me.

The sun has started to stream in through my open curtains, just barely touching the carpeted floor and the foot of my bed. I don't know why I'm awake before my alarm, but I know Myles is too.

Because even though his head is on my chest and his arm is curled around mine, his fingers are tracing circles on my ribs softly. Like butter.

He has to go soon, since I snuck him in last night and he is most definitely not allowed to spend the night. My hand is on the back of his neck, just to touch him. I see his eyes flutter open, and he adjusts so he's practically covering me and I'm under the full weight of him. But I don't mind. I smile down at him as he rests his chin on his hand. The moment is peaceful. The only sound around us is the early birds chirping outside my window as he looks at me.

"Hey, can I tell you something?" he asks.

He says it quietly, and I nod as his deep brown eyes soften. I run my finger over his jaw and his lips before he speaks. Enjoying how the rising sun gives his dark skin the slightest glow. He leans further up, so his face is directly above me, our lips so close they almost touch but don't.

"I love you."

I stare at him, almost positive I didn't hear him right. That it's just early and my brain isn't working right.

"What?"

He smiles, it's soft and easy, but he smiles as he presses our lips together and punctuates each word with a kiss. "I. Love. You."

A stupidly goofy grin spreads over my face as I pull him down to really, fully kiss me. Relaxing into the feel of his hands on my cheeks and the softness of his lips.

And in the early morning sunlight filling my room with soft rays that promise a great day, I can't imagine this moment any differently.

"I love you too."

I blink as I come out of the memory. There's an immense pressure on my chest, but it's not painful or overwhelming. It's just there, filled with reminiscence. The cold, hard fact that that moment is forever a memory now. That Myles and I are like a tiny box tucked into the corner of my brain where those memories, those moments in time, will always be.

But like my therapist always told me in the beginning, a few deep breaths, take it one step at time, and the feeling will fade. Over time I won't always get the feeling of nostalgia—of wishing for a relationship that was never going to last—or the heavy chest. The memories will always be there, but they'll get smaller over time and will be just that, memories.

The sound of dishes and silverware clinking draws my attention away from my room. I give it one last look before shutting the door and walking down the stairs.

"¿Estás bien, mija?" My mom asks as she checks on the empanadas when I enter the kitchen.

"Sí, Mamá. I'm good."

Dad is playing the CD I made him for Father's Day when I was sixteen years old. It's filled with our favorites from that year and from when I was young. I know he's doing everything in his fatherly power to make me feel better. Just like my mom is. The music floats throughout the house and trickles into the kitchen.

"*Matrimonio? Seriamente? Quién se cree que es?*" *Marriage? Seriously? Who does he think he is?*

"*No lo sé, Mamá.*" I exhale. "But if he's happy that's all that matters."

"*Está bien no estar bien, mi amor.*" *It's okay not to be okay, my love.*

I don't answer as Dad appears, leaning in the doorway as the late afternoon Sunday sun shines through the windows. I pull on the strings of an old hoodie of his that was tucked away in the back closet, biting softly on the end.

Sun rays illuminate the space. The walls are yellow, my mom's favorite color, which my dad insisted they paint the kitchen. Bright plates and dishware and colorful artwork hang on the walls, and pictures of the three of us and some with Harper and Sloan cover the fridge.

I love living on my own. But this Brooklyn house will always be home, and I've never been more thankful for it or my parents.

Dad goes to stand next to Mom as she flips the empanadas for the last time, his brown skin just a bit lighter than hers and mine. My dad is black and white, and my mom is Colombian, hence the mix of skin tones between all of us. He wraps an arm around her waist and presses a soft kiss to her temple. Just standing there in her presence, in her space. The love between them is clear as day as he starts to dance around her to the beat of the song and she shoos him away, though there is a goofy grin on her lips.

They're the epitome of the lucky ones. I know I want that one day, what they have.

But I don't think I want it anytime soon.

Looking away, I watch the swirls of the coconut milk in my drink instead.

My parents always treated me like a princess for sure, but today, the treatment is above and beyond. My plate is served with at least three scoops of sweet potatoes, two scoops of rice, and six empanadas. I don't complain as we dig in, their eyes on me the whole time in that gentle *make sure she's okay* parent look they have.

And I barely have any time to digest my dinner before my mom is serving us slices of torta negra cake. When she places mine down, she presses a slow kiss to my forehead. I'm cried out from this week. Shed all the tears I felt I needed to. But being here with them, I can't help but feel the emotions start to bubble again, just a different kind.

I savor the mix of the cake and the vanilla ice cream, letting the flavors melt on my tongue and fix all the little cracks in my heart. Because my parents and their cooking can most definitely do that. After we finish, my mom shoos my dad out of the kitchen, and I can hear the music turn up just a little. I grab plates and silverware to help her, but she stops me.

My mother's black hair is cut short to her shoulders, but it's as glossy as ever, and her brown eyes twinkle with that motherly instinct as she looks at me. Her brown skin is smooth and soft as she reaches forward and tucks my hair behind my ear.

"*Te amo, mija*," she says, pulling me into a tight hug, and I close my eyes and just stay there in the embrace. She pats my back. "Okay, go see your dad. He wants to talk to you."

I nod as she kisses me on the cheek. My phone and keys are tucked into the hoodie as I enter the living room. It's cozy. A couch lines the back wall with two recliners on either side to face the TV, leaving the window clear for light to come through. He's seated on the couch. I fall down next to him, where he lifts his arm for me, and I curl into the embrace.

He presses a soft kiss to my forehead. "You okay?"

One of my favorite songs on the CD is playing, "God Only Knows," and I let the song wash over me. "Yeah, I'm okay."

"If you're not, that's okay too. But I know I raised a strong girl, and I know you know that you deserve better and that you'll be okay."

I smile, fully aware we couldn't have this conversation without a dig at Myles. "I am, I swear. I was sad this week. It was just surprising is all. But I'm better."

He squeezes my arm. "I love this song. Remember I'd play it every Sunday morning while we made waffles before your mom was up?"

My lips quirk into a smile at the memory. We used to jam out to random songs every Sunday, always changing up the playlist as we surprised my mom with waffles, though it became less of a surprise and more of a tradition. Without fail, we would play this song every week.

"Regardless of how you feel, I know it sucks right now, no matter how much you tell yourself it doesn't. I never liked him. I know, I'm your dad, so it's expected that I say that. But something just wasn't right,"

My dad doesn't get sappy often, but I hear the little crack in his voice as he coughs to hide it. I feel like I'm seventeen again, when Myles first broke up with me before he left for college, right before my senior year, and I stayed cuddled on the couch between my parents. They watched all my favorite movies on repeat with me, cooked me all my favorite food, and barely left me alone until they were sure I was okay.

I'm twenty-three. I'm grown up. I should be able to handle this on my own. But being here with my parents today has been the best thing I didn't know I needed.

"One day there will be someone that comes along and makes you realize Myles was never even an option for you."

My eyes flutter closed as I lean into his side further. Thankful more than ever for my dad.

"And I don't know if it's possible, but one day you'll find that someone who loves you more than me or tries to. But that someone is not him, and until that day and every day after, I'll be here. I love you, Nina."

As his words wash over me, I feel warmth. Whether it's the heat coming through the vents, the fullness from the meal, my dad's embrace, or a sign of healing, I savor it. It's the first time I've felt genuinely okay all week. Even though I feel unlucky in love, in life sometimes, I know that's just a phase. Just a part of becoming an adult, of growing up.

I know that this time will be filled with ups and downs, like life always is. That you can't have any flowers without a little rain. That the beauty of life is seeing the clear blue sky after a storm.

I know the wedding will be the finale of Myles and me. Our last goodbye. A book being glued shut for good. And that will probably hurt a bit. Or a lot.

Regardless, I find comfort in knowing he's happy, and I find comfort in the fact that therapy allowed me to be happy with myself. To be happy without him. Going out, brunching with my friends, and being here with my parents reminded me of that girl.

That I was so good without him. That I still am.

This week drew me back down, pushed me under the waves and covered me in clouds, but right now, as the darkness disappears and the sun starts to peek through the clouds, I feel like my head is finally breaking the surface.

"**Y**ou cannot wear black to a wedding, Valentina Scott." I groan, pulling my robe closer and avoiding Harper's hawk-like eyes. My closet is staring back at me, but nothing is calling to me. All I want to do is pull on my signature black dress, but I can't as that is apparently against wedding etiquette. So I've been told.

Sounds like bullshit to me.

I take a sip of water, trying to hydrate before this monstrous event.

The last twenty-four hours have been a ride.

And honestly, I really should have a reality TV show. Named *Valentina's Missteps, Mishaps, and Misfortunes. Featuring Harper and Sloan.* Because not only did we all wake up hungover after Sloan's birthday celebrations yesterday, but apparently when we were drunk, I also begged Sloan to cut my hair.

And in her just as drunken daze, she agreed to it.

So, in a completely rational decision, I have lost about six inches of hair.

Loose curls that used to hit midback now brush my shoulders. When we woke up in a haze, I'd be lying if I said I didn't shed a tear.

"Then what are my options?" I ask, exasperated.

"What about the light blue one?"

"That gray one?"

I set my water down and run my hands over my face. All eyes are on me. Jenko's ears are perked from where he rests on my vanity, Sloan is leaning comfortably against my pillows, and Harper is spinning in my vanity chair.

They both look great. Sloan is stunning in her yellow maxi dress. It's backless and strappy and compliments her dark skin perfectly as her hair bounces around her in perfectly tight curls. The nude heels she stole from my closet compliment the outfit perfectly along with her signature jewelry.

Harper looks gorgeous. Our matching tattoo is visible on her ribs, the three flowers to represent each of our birth months. She's dressed in a long sleeve emerald romper that has cutouts right over her rib bones. Her hair is done in her signature purposely loose ponytail. Nude block heels and silver jewelry tie it all together.

So, all that's left is me.

"Wait, the red one. Wear the red one," Harper practically squeals as her gray eyes light up.

"Can I wear red to a wedding?" I turn, searching for this dress until my eyes finally find it, tucked away in the corner of my closet. And I don't care about etiquette anymore. "Oh. It's perfect."

Sloan holds up her cup. "I'll drink to that."

While I am almost positive that red is against some wedding dress code, I don't care. I bought this dress from a cute little boutique in Brooklyn on a whim. The editor at *Poze* had complimented one of my first articles, and I bought this as a celebration.

It's absolutely perfect.

It's satin, with a V-shaped neckline and thin straps, and hits right about mid-thigh. It cinches at the waist and makes my small chest look ten times better.

I slip inside my tiny closet and put it on, and when I come out, by the big grins on my friends' faces, I know it's the one. My hair brushes the tops of my shoulders, and even though it made me sad earlier, I feel pretty badass right now.

"Let's get this pregame properly started, ladies."

• • •

I am bouncing with nerves as the taxi pulls up outside of the venue, fighting memories that pound at my head.

Not even the warm May breeze or the buzz of the alcohol in my blood can stop the nervous energy radiating off me. The Midtown Loft and Terrace is towering above us as our heels click on the pavement, and I'm clutching my purse so hard my hand is turning white.

I won't even have my parents to help me through this since they had a previous engagement on the same day, a big work party for my dad and his architecture company getting a huge deal. Not that I think they really would've come anyway.

Harper and Sloan surround me, linking their arms through mine as we reach the door. The doorman smiles at us, and we're greeted with a sign with instructions for the *Henderson Wedding*.

The ceremony is on the rooftop, and the reception to follow is a few floors below.

A rooftop wedding in May with a view of the city to die for. I don't know if it gets any better.

"We got this. Worst comes to worst, I make a scene and Sloan hauls your ass out of here." Harper whispers in my ear as we climb into the elevator, and the problem is, I know she's dead serious. She would absolutely do that for me, and Sloan would absolutely drive the getaway car.

"If it helps, I've got a stash of SweeTarts in my purse if you need them," Sloan offers, and I laugh for the first time all day.

I'd be lost, dead in a ditch, if it wasn't for these two.

The elevator dings, and we step out onto the rooftop. It's breathtaking.

The sun is at a perfect height in the sky, painting a warm glow over the city and the ceremony setup. There is an arch set up for the altar, with smooth white chairs lined up and arranged to create an aisle that's decorated with light purple and pink flowers and gold accents. It's not the tallest building, we can't see the tops of every skyscraper, but it makes you feel immersed into the city. There are two groomsmen waiting to greet people coming off the elevator, to lead us to our seats, and I recognize both from high school. Soft smiles come over their faces when they land on us.

"Hey, superstar, how have you been? Harps, Sloan, what's good?"

I keep the forced smile on my face as we embrace Lewis, Myles's high school best friend, and I let myself gain a little bit of comfort from it. A small piece of happy history.

"I've been good. Figured I'd see you guys here," I say as I embrace the other old friend, Drew. When I make eye contact with them, there is a thinly-veiled twinkle of sympathy, but I ignore it and the annoyance that follows.

"Come on," Lewis says to me with a smile, and I loop my arm with his as Sloan and Harper share Drew. They walk us down to the middle of the groom's side, and we take the first three seats, with me in between my two friends.

He leans down and places a kiss on my cheek. "It's good to see you, seriously. We'll catch up at the reception."

I smile, but it's forced. The reality of seeing all his old friends, who were just as much my own friends, hits me hard. It's a tortured feeling, seeing how far removed I am from everything I used to be a part of. As if Sloan can sense my growing unease, she reaches over and grips my hand, giving me a gentle squeeze.

My hair floats lightly as a breeze passes through. Even high up, it's warm as the sun beats down on us and people start to trickle in. The rest of the bridal party stays hidden, just Lewis and Drew leading people to seats on either the bride's or groom's side. I recognize a good amount of people on the groom's side, getting a few waves and soft hello's before they take their own seats.

I try to keep my thoughts focused on Sloan's hand holding mine and the beautiful view. Briefly it reminds me of waking up in that high-rise apartment, although the view from the apartment was much higher, clearer. It was captivating.

"Oh, here we go." Harper places her hand on my shoulder.

Myles is walking his parents down the aisle.

He hasn't seen me yet. He's deep in conversation with his mom and dad, whom I absolutely adored when we were together. I still do, but I haven't seen them in years. With the warm, big smiles on their faces and twinkling eyes, it's easy to see how happy they are for him. The sight makes relief bloom in my chest. My heart squeezes as his mom sees me first, and her smile widens as she blows me a kiss, like she used to.

I give her a smile back as his dad finally sees me, throwing me a wink like always, until my eyes finally land on Myles. There's a soft, blissful expression on his face, and the joy is clear in his brown eyes. A million things float through our wordless conversation that seems to stop time just for a second.

It's bittersweet, knowing we loved each other but still ended up apart.

I never thought I'd be *watching* Myles get married, that's for sure.

"I'll be home before you know it." Myles says, forcing me to look at him on my window seat. He leaves for college tomorrow.

"I'm just nervous." I bite my lip, not explaining further. About the long distance. About how I'm terrified he'll forget about me and find someone better.

He cups my face. "Don't be, Nina." Before I can protest, he kisses me softly and takes all my fears with it. "I'm not looking for anyone else. I don't want anyone else."

Exhaling, I fight to force that memory out, force his voice out of my head.

Because that's exactly what happened. He may not have been looking, but he did find someone else.

I turn my head forward as they start to move past, breaking our eye contact. My eyes prick a bit, but I blink until the feeling disappears. He takes his place near the justice of the peace, who gives him a small handshake and a smile. Myles turns, his eyes scanning the full seats of the ceremony space.

Just as they land on me, as our eyes connect, the music starts, allowing me to turn away, ignoring the overwhelming emotions growing in my chest.

I recognize most of the groomsmen as expected, maybe one or two from college, then Lewis and Drew, and when they walk by, you can see a peek of the fun-colored socks they all have on. Their respective bridesmaids, who all look stunning, are dressed in long lilac gowns to stick with the theme.

But as the best man steps out with the maid of honor, I swear to god my heart steps out of my chest and jumps off the edge of the building.

This has to be a joke.

"Is that . . ?"

"No fucking way."

I'm almost shocked by the curse word that leaves Sloan's mouth and not Harper's, but my brain is short-circuiting as my mouth practically falls open.

"Am I being punked?"

It's Jackson. My weird, attempted, not-quite one-night stand.

My hand goes limp in Sloan's as he starts walking down the aisle with the maid of honor, and my eyes are glued to him.

His blond curls are the same short length, and his smile is as bright as the sun shining over us. The only difference is he's in a suit. A crisp, clean black suit that fits him like a glove. Even with the fun red socks peeking out of his dress pants, he looks immaculate.

The maid of honor and he are in a quiet conversation as they walk, and he hasn't seen me yet. Thank god. I'm not sure I want him to because between him and Myles, I might actually step over the side of the building.

I duck my head, letting my short hair cover my face as he passes our aisle, and even so, that pure, bright energy radiating off him reaches me. Sloan gives my hand a squeeze and Harper latches onto my other one. Myles gives him a big grin and a handshake as he steps up to take his place next to him.

My mind is running a million miles an hour as an instrumental song starts playing.

I let my eyes flutter close and take three deep breaths.

When I open them again, my skin is tingling with warmth. My eyes connect with those deep blue eyes, and my heart stops all over again.

Jackson has a lazy smile gracing his lips, and a look of ironic disbelief passes over his features. Like he can't believe I'm here but isn't mad that I am.

Sloan, all those months ago at brunch with her stupid blind optimism, was right. *All I'm saying is you never know.*

The odds of me seeing him again were, as Harper said, negative ten.

More realistically, negative twenty.

For him to be standing here, as Myles's best man is absolutely mind-numbing to me. Part of me wants to scream. Part of me wants to laugh. Most of me wants to leave.

I don't know what to do.

As I turn to wait for the arrival of Emma, I feel two sets of eyes on my back.

One sends yet another wave of nostalgia and sadness over my skin. The other is setting my skin on fire, like the tequila shots Harper gave me, coursing through my blood.

I'm not prepared for this at all.

The appearance of Emma and her dad getting closer draws me out of my spiraling thoughts. She looks prettier than the Facebook pictures I stalked. The dress is unreal. It's off-the-shoulder lace bodice cinches at the waist and disappears into smooth white fabric in a mermaid style. Her shiny brown hair is half up, half down and flows down her back. As she looks up at Myles, her smile is soft and genuine. Light pink lipstick and soft make-up adorn her face.

Myles's eyes have been completely focused on her, but when she turns away to hand over her flowers, they flicker to mine. It's quick and fleeting, and if I wasn't looking, I would've missed it.

They drop back to Emma as she takes her place, and I let out the breath I didn't know I was holding. My eyes flicker to Jackson as he stands tall and proud watching the ceremony.

The only explanation is that they met at University of Georgia, which makes sense. I heard almost nothing about Myles's life when he was away. Between our off and on drama, I never asked. Rarely looked on social media because I became obsessed with what he wasn't saying to me and the posts on every platform. I was anxious, and it wasn't healthy. So how would I have known who his new best friend was?

How the hell is this my life?

My friends squeeze my hands tightly as the vows begin with Emma.

"When I went away to college, I expected to come out with a degree and a few friends. When we met freshman year, we were instant friends. And I thought if a friendship with you was all I got, then it would be enough. But when you asked me to be your girlfriend the summer after we graduated, I can't explain the pure joy I felt that I would finally get to be with you."

My heart stops in my chest as I register her words.

"You are the best part of my life. The gift that college gave me. And I'll forever be thankful for deciding on that school and deciding on you. You help me when I need it and push me to be the best I can be. I can't imagine doing life with anyone but you."

I can't hear anything else as the blood rushes past my ears, and Harper's nails are digging into my palm painfully because she knows exactly what's affecting me. All the back and forth, all the anxieties and insecurities I had, every time I asked what was different for four years straight. Why he didn't kiss me as often. Why we didn't talk about the future anymore, why the *I love yous* only came when he was drunk. Why we were constantly on and off again.

And when we officially broke up—for the fifth time—over spring break during his senior year, I knew what he wasn't saying. Knew that the girl that was constantly off to the side or in pictures, the ones I did see, is the one standing at the altar. Maybe he didn't truly cheat, I'll never know, but I know that while he was creating something with her, he was destroying what he had with me.

While I was back home, wondering if we'd be the same or ever get back together fully. While I was still in love with him. He met Emma.

He was falling in love with Emma.

"He's so full of—"

"Harper. Stop. Please. We're happy for him."

Happy is not the right word, but I'm hoping if I repeat it enough, I'll mean it.

I see Harper pout out of the corner of my eye. Even though her words are harsh, and she mostly came for me, I know this sucks for all of us. Myles was all our friend for a good chunk of our lives. Even he and Harper were kind of close when they were younger. So even though she'll never admit it, and part of her hates him now, I know Harper is sad at the loss of her old friend. That he wasn't the person we thought he was.

Unexpectedly, while I am angry, more hurt than anything, a sense of closure also comes. I wasn't crazy all those years. I wasn't making things up.

My eyes flicker to Jackson, whose eyes are already on me, and recognition flashes in them even from here. Like he's putting the pieces together, like Myles always mentioned an ex, and here she is in the flesh. The same girl he met months ago in a bar.

Myles's voice draws me back. "You're the love of my life, Emma. You're it for me, forever and a day and more. I'll always be there for you, when you need me to be and when you don't. Life has been a whirlwind since I met you, and I hope it continues that way, with us holding hands through everything. I don't care what happens, as long as you're by my side."

There is a sense of finality that washes over me, even though my chest cracks in half, as the two look at each other with sickly but somehow charming love in their eyes.

I shut the last open door that is Myles and I, and I feel nothing.

It's done. It's over.

The wedding party descends the aisle after the kiss, and my heart is pounding. Myles gives me a fleeting, soft smile, and I return it, despite everything I'm feeling.

But it's the flash of the dimples and a wink of a deep blue eye Jackson gives me that sends my emotions into a different type of overdrive.

I am in no way prepared for the rest of this day.

Welcome back to another episode of Valentina's Missteps, Mishaps and Misfortunes. *Featuring Harper, Sloan, and guest appearances from her ex Myles and his best man and her weird one-night stand Jackson.*

Seven | Jackson

All the missing pieces came together easily when I saw her sitting in the crowd.

She looked different than the two times I'd seen her before. Once in a crowded bar—and in my bedroom—and once in an old, grainy photograph that Myles used to carry around.

My head turns as I follow the newlyweds into the reception area to take pictures. Myles and Emma look ridiculously happy as they hold hands, listening to the instructions of the photographer as the wedding party watches from the sidelines. The windows behind them showcase the buildings of New York lighting up as darkness falls. I smile, my hands tucked in my pockets, standing next to Emma's best friend, but my head is somewhere else.

Nina.

All I can seem to focus on is Nina.

The girl from the bar in February. The same girl sitting in the crowd at Myles's wedding. Every time I turned my head over and over trying to figure out why she seemed so familiar the past few months comes to a head. She's Myles's ex-girlfriend, who he dated all through high school, off and on through the beginning of college, and had known practically his entire life.

All talk of her stopped his junior year when he started to seriously be interested in Emma. I wasn't around, I had graduated by then since I was three years ahead of him, but something doesn't sit right.

The look on her face during the ceremony replays again and again. It was during their vows, and I could tell she thought she hid it well. But I saw it. How her shoulders tensed and her eyes had widened briefly, a sharp pain flashing in them. Her cheeks had turned pinked as she listened, but I had no idea what could've set her off.

Turning my eyes back to Myles and Emma, I see the girls are walking up to take their pictures with the bride. Myles lands by my side with a huge grin.

"How you feeling, man?" I pat him on the back with a big smile.

He shrugs, glancing at the ground with a headshake before looking back up. "Married." His eyes move to Emma, who smiles warmly back at him. "Thankful as well."

"You guys are great. I'm happy for you. We all are."

"Thanks for standing up there by my side."

I pat him again on the back. Despite me being older and graduating before he did, we just hit it off. We worked well together on the field and ended up in the same circle. Before I knew it, we were extremely close, two peas in a pod despite the years between us. Another person I added to my ever-growing family. I was happy to stand by him up there.

But I can't deny the questions I have about the timeline of his relationships. I want to ask him about Nina being here, but I doubt his wedding is the appropriate time.

Luckily for me, one of his old buddies from high school enters the conversation. "Did you see Nina out there?"

Myles raises a brow. "We invited her."

"No, I know that, dumbass." Drew rolls his eyes, and we chuckle. "You never told us she was coming."

"Yeah." Myles nods. "We're good. I wanted to."

The conversation falls off after that as we're pulled in to take pictures. The camera flashes a million times with the city in the background. We follow the careful instructions of the photographer, lifting our pant legs to show off the brightly colored socks underneath, and standing around Myles, and eventually posing for a full wedding party photo surrounding and celebrating the couple. Time passes, and we're getting ready to enter the reception area. As the other groomsman enter ahead of me, cheers from the guests ensue over the music, and it repeats.

When I enter, my eyes search the room for Nina without a second thought. It takes a moment before I find her, but I do. There's a barely-there smile on her lips, her now shorter hair is tucked behind her ear on one side, and her eyes widen slightly when she meets my gaze.

I grin because I genuinely never thought I would see her again. The guarded exterior, pink cheeks, and pretty brown eyes. That's all she was for the past few months. Just a girl in a bar that I couldn't stop thinking about.

Her smile doesn't widen when she sees me, not that I expect it to, but for some reason it just makes my own smile grow. I know I probably shouldn't be as enamored by her as I am. Considering she used to date my best friend for years and we've only met one time. But I'm not sure if I give a shit enough to *not* pursue her.

He's married now, moved on. It shouldn't matter what I do or who I date.

And knowing I shouldn't, the whole reception, my eyes keep finding her in the room. How her hands move when she talks while dinner is served. The way she watches with a tight smile and studies the table during the first dance. How she actually smiles when Myles dances with his mom. The way she casually sways to the songs overhead when the dancing has fully begun.

Or how animated, happy she is when she's talking to her friends, showing me glimpses of the girl I met months ago.

Nina's just as gorgeous as she was that night. The red dress she has on compliments her warm brown skin, full lips that are always slightly pouty, from what I remember, and big brown eyes that are somehow soft and cautious all at once. I may not know her well at all, but from what I've seen, no matter the situation, she carries herself with a quiet but formidable confidence.

I take a long pull of the old fashioned in my hand as I lean against the wall taking a break. Roman, my longest and closest friend aside from Myles, walks my way. "Who are you looking at?"

Roman is Emma's older friend from childhood, but we met freshman year of college when he came to play football. He's basically been my other brother ever since. Knows me better than I know myself some days.

With a quick nod in Nina's direction, he pockets his hands. "Brown hair?"

"Nina, Myles's ex-girlfriend."

He whistles lowly, taking a sip of his own drink. "Oh. Shit." He grins.

I shrug. "It's not a big deal. I met her a few months ago in a bar and didn't realize who she was until today."

I especially notice how she squares her shoulders and glances at her friends when Myles asks her to dance. Despite myself, I take a long drink, my eyes glued on both of them as he walks beside her to the dance floor. Her shoulders are held back, tightly so, and she tucks a piece of hair behind her ear before letting him guide her into a dance.

Roman shoulders me, the grin faded into an amused look on his face. "You're staring."

I exhale. "I don't think I care."

He chuckles and pats me on the back. "Well, go talk to her after then. She looks—" He hesitates, and I finally tear my eyes away to give him a questioning look. "Miserable. She looks miserable out there with him."

This time I chuckle, finishing the drink and spinning the glass in my hands. Roman's right. She does look miserable. They're standing so far apart it's a miracle they touch at all, and in the background, her friends are staring without a single blink. The music plays overhead, and they spin slowly, among the crowd on the floor. Nina looks almost anywhere but directly at Myles.

"All right, well, I'm going to leave you to pine and go." Roman pats my back with a grin as he strides away before I can respond. Directly towards Nina's friends, specifically the red head.

Seems like I'm not the only one infatuated with someone at this wedding.

Obviously, I'm not going to interrupt whatever is happening in that conversation between the two of them., but I know without a doubt, I'm not leaving without talking to her again. Without chasing whatever high I felt when I met her in February. No matter how brief it had been then.

Easily, I keep my eyes on her, study her. It's weird to be seeing her here after that night in February. Trailing my eyes over her slow-moving figure, I appreciate the red against her warm brown skin, the way it hugs her curves and flares, and the scattered black ink on her skin. Everything about her has captivated me since we met.

Luckily for me, Emma strides towards them with a smile, and I bide my time, watching and waiting until Nina walks away. So I can swoop in and make her forget about Myles entirely.

Or at least, I'm going to try.

Eight | Nina

"I'm really glad you came."

The inside of my cheek is raw from biting it so hard. Every so often the familiar metallic taste fills my mouth.

I look up, forcing my lips into a soft smile. "I'm happy for you. You look really happy."

We sway in silence to the beat of the song, and I feel my friends' eyes on me. They're both seated at our table, bent forward on their elbows watching me like a parent watches their child on the playground for the first time as they sip their drinks. Although, between death glares at Myles, Harper is also talking to a handsome man sitting to her right. By the knowing look on Sloan's face, I know she's interested.

Myles's hands are placed very lightly on my waist, and I hold my own awkwardly on his shoulders. It's weird. Tiptoeing around each other. There's a strange amount of a space between us—the kind that would totally be appropriate at a middle school dance. I don't particularly want to be dancing with him, but when he came over after food and speeches while Emma was dancing with some of her friends, I was already two drinks in, and I felt like I couldn't say no.

I wish I had, because it's as if we're dancing on a glass ceiling, looking down at the sheer height beneath us, and if we make one wrong step it'll shatter into a million pieces, and we'll go with it.

"I am, really," he says, but he trails off. His shoulders tense under my fingertips as he takes a deep breath. "Nin."

Instead of the old feeling I used to get, heart flutters and sweaty palms, I flush with annoyance. Because he doesn't have the right to call me that anymore.

"I just wanna say, I want to tell you—"

My heart thunders in my chest, not sure what kind of sentence his jumbled words are going to form. Thankfully, Emma appears next to us, effectively cutting him off, a warm smile on her face as she taps his shoulder and glances at me.

"I'm sorry, can I steal him away?" she asks, kindness dripping off her tongue, and I return the smile, dropping my hands and stepping back from Myles without a second thought.

I can breathe again.

"Of course. You look stunning, by the way. That dress is to die for."

Emma lets out a soft laugh. "Thank you, I got very lucky."

She pulls me in for an unexpected hug, and I freeze. It takes me a second before I return the gesture with a simple pat on the back. I see Harper's eyes practically fall out of her head.

"You look stunning yourself. I'm happy Myles's old friends could make it. It's like a reunion, and I know he's happy to see you all. Thank you for coming."

Old friends.

I kind of want to laugh. I also kind of want to cry.

"Of course, I'm glad I could make it. You both look very happy." I fake a smile as her eyes flicker to Myles. The joy is radiating off her like a space heater, and it eliminates some of the awkwardness. At least between us.

With a parting nod I make a beeline for the open bar, the smile falling off my face. Myles's gaze burns a hole into my back. I'm thankful for the cool surface of the bar top, and the bartender greets me quickly with a smile.

"Three tequila shots, please."

Luckily, I stress ate enough bread at the buffet that these shouldn't have an immediate effect on me—just enough to make me feel better than I do. I close my eyes to take a deep breath before the bartender comes back. In and out.

Estoy bien, estoy bien.

"Fancy seeing you here."

I open my eyes to see three tequila shots lined up and Jackson's tall frame leaning against the bar next to me. His lips are pulled into a cheeky smile as he raises an eyebrow at me. The warm energy he's always emitting surrounds me. A contrast to the dark city in the windows behind him.

"Yeah, what are the odds?" I mumble, knocking back two of the three shots as he watches me. I signal for one more and slide the fourth shot to Jackson. He picks it up, and the ring on his middle finger makes a tapping sound against the tiny glass.

"I should've recognized you." He studies me, and I him. I like him like this. His suit jacket is off, with the sleeves rolled up, and the bow tie is much looser. He looks more comfortable. His eyes flicker to me after ordering his old fashioned.

"Why would you have?"

"Myles showed me a picture once or twice. After practice his freshman year, we all got drunk and he was talking about you. He talked about you a lot. You're not someone I'd forget."

Any other time it would be weird talking about an ex, but either it's the liquid confidence flowing through me or that I feel comfortable around him. For a second, I almost forget that I'm at Myles's wedding.

I lean my elbow on the bar top, trying to fight the flush crawling up my neck, and look up at him, because even in heels I don't close the height difference much. "It doesn't matter."

"No, it doesn't," he says with a smile, and my heart flutters, but I keep my face straight as his eyes leisurely glide over me. "I probably shouldn't say this, but he's kind of an idiot. For letting you go."

He pauses and picks up his glass, taking a slow sip as the words wash over me.

"Actually, I take that back. I'm happy he did."

My mouth parts briefly before I recover, but internally my heart has dropped into my stomach. His eyes twinkle as if that was the exact response he wanted. Instead of responding, I use the moment to catch my breath and hold up the third shot, clinking my glass with his, and toss it back.

Finally, my words return. "You're just saying that."

He raises a brow as his eyes darken. "I don't say anything I don't mean."

I open my mouth to respond, but I'm genuinely speechless, and my mouth closes only to gnaw on the inside of my bottom lip. Jackson smirks, giving me a fleeting glimpse at the dimples, and he holds out his hand after finishing off the old fashioned.

"Come on, let's dance."

My eye flickers between his hand, his face, and my friends watching this whole thing. "Why?" Harper has stopped talking to her wedding man briefly as her and Sloan both give me thumbs up with painfully obvious grins on their faces.

"Wasn't it you who asked me to dance months ago?" He raises a brow, eyes twinkling.

I flush. "I was drunk."

He doesn't budge. "Well, I'm asking you now."

I roll my eyes, but I place my hand in Jackson's despite it. A slow song is playing in the background, but I barely hear it over my own heartbeat. A flash of heat goes throughout my entire body as he cups my hand in his. Palm to palm, we walk to the dance floor.

His hands immediately encircle my waist with all the confidence in the world as he pulls me close with no hesitation, and my breath hitches. My hands intertwine behind his neck, feeling just a brush of a blond curl on the surface of my skin. If I was an inch closer, our chests would be touching.

"So, I take it by the look on your face during the vows something was wrong?"

His voice is soft, and I take a deep breath. But I don't miss the unsaid words that he was looking at *me* during the ceremony. The thought warms my entire body.

"You noticed?"

He nods.

"College was weird for us. We weren't together, but we were obviously living different breakups. I guess. But it doesn't matter. He met Emma, and he's happy now."

I thought he was happy with me, but I was wrong.

I pause, looking away from Jackson's watching blue eyes, and focus on the slightly crooked bowtie around his neck. On his hands on my waist, my hips. And I wish my dress was thinner so I could feel their heat.

His eyes burn a spot on the side of my face as we sway for a second in silence.

"I don't know all—or really any—of the details like you do, but whatever it was that happened, it does matter. His friend or not, he's wrong for not being clear," he says, shrugging as if it's that easy, that black and white. He looks down at me. "But I guess I wouldn't be dancing with you if it worked out differently. So, I won't complain."

I shake my head softly, my eyes flickering back up to his. Unsure of who exactly this honest, open man really is. And why he's spending time with me.

Jackson has a way with words, and everything he says sticks to my skin like mist. A small part of me knows I'm dancing, flirting even, with Myles's best man. But that is the sober, more rational part of me, and the tequila is doing a good job of pushing that away.

"You cut your hair." He dips me to the song before pulling me back up. "And we match."

He pauses our dance and lifts his pant leg dramatically, as if on a runway, to show me the red socks he has on. They match my dress perfectly.

This time, a tiny smile breaks through at the sight of him giving me a fashion show on the middle of the dance floor.

His smile is wide, both dimples flashing at me, like he doesn't care who sees.

I feel the gaze of many eyes on us, but I don't look away from Jackson and his addicting energy as he pulls me back into the beat of a second song, slower this time, and we fall into step. This time his hand holds mine up by his chest as the other finds its place on my hip.

"Took you long enough to give me a smile."

"*Eres un tonto,*" I mutter as my free hand lands on his shoulder. The muscles under my fingertips move as he laughs, and I can't help but thumb over them gently.

"You're killing me." He leans down to whisper in my ear, "I'm going to have to learn Spanish to keep up with you."

"Maybe I don't want you to keep up with me."

Jackson raises a brow. "I don't think that's the case," he says. So self-assured.

My skin flushes as his cheek brushes past mine. And I hear the accent again. It's soft, hardly there, but I hear it. It's not overbearing at all—instead it's light. Barely a hint half the time. "Charming southern boy, are we?"

He grins. He's always grinning. I kind of like it. "So, you figured it out?" I nod, and he continues. "Born and raised in

Georgia. Was only right to stay there for school. And somehow I ended up here."

"I bet that southern appeal works like a charm for the girls," I say, because I'm not blind to the number of eyes that have been on him all day. From the ceremony to now, it's like he's impossible to miss. He's bright and warm, and when he walks into the room, people's eyes go to him like a moth to a flame.

"Jealous?" He raises his eyebrows, those blue eyes sparkling.

"Never," I say as he dips me again, but slower this time.

His hand slides lower on my back to keep me stable, and his fingertips brush the open skin above the back of the dress. The brief contact sends little sparks up and down my spine, like lightning bugs, and my pulse speeds up as my skin sings under the softness of his touch.

He shakes his head softly, his short curls unfurling near his forehead as we fall back into step, and he gives me a gentle smile.

"You've got this energy around you. It's strong but quiet, like a brewing storm, but it's there. I like it."

"Well, we can't all be warm and sunshiny like you now, can we?"

"It's all the love," he says dramatically, but I raise a single brow. "I guess under the circumstances, I understand. But come on, love is great." He pauses. "Love should be great."

"I agree, it should be." I shrug. "But it isn't always."

"You make it seem like love is a death sentence."

"Maybe it is."

I look up at him, and somehow, someway, his lips are still quirked up into a soft smile. He spins me around, and my dress fans out around my legs until I come back into him. My back is pressed against his chest as his arms cage me in, and his warm breath hits my neck, effectively sending chills down my spine.

"You know, Nina, even the darkest storms have to let a little light in eventually."

His lips are so close to my ear, I'm convinced they're touching me. But it's a phantom feeling, like the memory of our drunken kiss. I'm hot all over. From the tips of my ears, deep in my belly, and all the way to my toes. Jackson sets me on fire. He squeezes my hands gently before he spins me back around and recaptures one hand in his own. This time our chests are lightly touching, and those deep blue eyes are focused solely on me.

My cheek is just barely resting on him as his words settle over me, and I breathe in the hints of amber and vanilla wafting off him. I lean in. The physical touch, his touch, is comforting to me.

As I open my mouth to attempt a response, there is a tap on his shoulder from Lewis, mentioning something about some wedding duty or thing that needs to be done. Lewis gives me a smile as he waits for Jackson, and we step away. An instant chill hits me when his hands leave my waist.

He turns to follow Lewis as I begin making my way over to Harper and Sloan, but he turns around, eyes on me.

"Nina, you're not leaving until I get your number tonight. So, don't even think about it," he says, walking away backwards, sending me a wink as he catches up with Lewis. My lip twitches, but I just shake my head as I continue to my seat.

I collapse next to Sloan and Harper, very aware of the guy on the other side of Harper. Sloan slides me a piece of cake she must've grabbed me and hands me a fork. There is also a handful of the SweeTarts she brought on the plate, and I pop one in my mouth. They're staring at me, but I just pop more candy in my mouth and sip my champagne.

"So, I like him." Sloan grins, and I roll my eyes, taking a bite of the chocolate cake.

"You don't know him."

She taps her temple with the end of her own fork. "I can sense it. Just like when I told you you'd see him again."

I can't argue, so I stick my tongue out and turn towards Harper. "So, who is this?'

Harper wiggles her eyebrows. "This is Roman. Roman, my friend Nina." He reaches out a hand and gives me a smile as I connect them.

"Nice to meet you."

He's cute, and I see why Harper has been talking to him. He's got this soft but stable energy around him, the exact opposite of her. Dark brown skin and a short, clean haircut that compliments her fair skin and fiery hair beautifully. But if I know Harper, she'll hook up a few times and probably move on. Either way, he's a solid choice. And if he's still sticking around after being around these two, who I know have been talking about my drama, I like him already.

"Well, we're gonna dance now that it's picked up the pace a bit," she says with a smile, but she leans down to whisper in my ear, "I like him too." She finishes her cake and grabs Roman's hand, drawing him up to the dance floor.

My eyes trail after them as they fall into step together. I take another bite of cake and rest my head in my hand. "Today has been a lot."

Sloan gives me a soft smile and pats my hand, taking a candy for herself. "You're doing great, babe."

We sit there, eating our large slices of cake and drinking whatever each of us bring back from the bar for the next thirty minutes. Harper stays with Roman the whole time on the dance floor, and I'd be genuinely surprised if she doesn't go home with him or vice versa. My eyes flicker between them and the rest of the reception. Jackson is mostly with the other groomsmen or dancing. Lucky for me, whenever I look at him, he can't see me in the dim room under the hazy lights.

They flick to Myles and Emma every so often, and I hope they last. I hope they make it. I genuinely hope he's grown up and treats her better. Because she seems great. She's kind and inviting in the way she interacts with everyone, and he lights up around her. She lights up around him.

I'm brought out of my thoughts as Harper makes her way to our table, the tiniest beads of sweat on her nose. Roman follows behind her. She leans down and presses a kiss to each of our cheeks.

"Ladies, I'm heading out. I'll text you," she whispers, and she stands straight up as she grabs her clutch.

Sloan and I smile at each other and then at him. "Bye, Roman."

Roman gives an easy shrug in response, twisting his nose in amusement.

Only Harper would leave this wedding with a hook-up—it's impressive. As they leave, I lean back, exhausted from it all. Considering it's almost twelve in the morning, I'm ready to head out, too.

I look at Sloan, who nods, and we both stand. My feet are screaming at me, and I really want to go home, cuddle under my blanket with Jenko, and watch TV until I feel better. My eyes flicker around at the tiring crowd, people taking their seats or taking off their shoes. Of course, some people are still going hard, this is New York after all, and I probably would be if I wasn't drained. Physically and emotionally.

Jackson is nowhere to be seen in the dark room, so we both call our rides as we head toward the door.

As I exit the reception room, my name is called, and I turn around to see Jackson lazily jogging up to me. I glance at Sloan, who purses her lips to hide her smile as she steps off to wait near the elevator.

His cheeks are slightly flushed, the lightest pink haze on his tan skin.

"Wow, a guy can't even get a goodbye?"

I roll my lips into my mouth before answering and raise a brow. "Goodbye, Jackson."

Jackson shakes his head with a smirk and grabs my hand as I turn away. "If you thought I was letting you go that easily, you have a lot to learn."

"Jackson." My eyes flicker to Myles, who is standing with his arm around Emma talking to someone. "I can't."

"It's just a phone number, Nina." He pulls out his phone and holds it out, looking at me warmly. "Please."

I hesitate for a moment before taking it out of his hand and typing in my contact information. His eyes flicker between the new contact and my face before he slips it back into his pocket.

"I'll be contacting you about a real date soon."

I watch him for a moment, and I realize I could stare at him all night. The dimples, the sharp cut of his jawline, his eyes, darker now, which are watching me, flickering between my lips and my eyes and everything else. I step closer and rock up on my tiptoes and adjust his crooked bowtie, my fingers just brushing his skin. I keep them there a beat longer than needed to feel the beat of his heart under my fingertips before I drop my hands back down.

"Oh, *galán*, you're gonna have to work harder than that."

Jackson smiles, a full smile, which sends my heart into overdrive as I turn to leave, memorizing the image of him smiling so I never forget it.

Nine | Nina

This article must be perfect.

From top to bottom, it has to be perfection.

It's an in-depth, analytical piece on which fashion designers are making the move to faux fur versus the ones that aren't, finishing with why faux fur should become the new normal for the entire fashion industry, not just a select few.

I tug the end of my waves again, like I have been all day. Even though it's been almost two weeks since I begged Sloan to drunkenly chop it off, I'm still not used to it. My eyes are starting to blur. The sentences are looking a lot more like jumbles of letters than actual words at this point. But the head of my department, Miss Bisset, wants to see my draft before I leave tonight so she can possibly pass it on to Vanna Young. The end all be all.

Like I said, this article has to be perfect.

Because if it is, it'll be featured in the September issue of *Poze* in three months instead of just hidden away on the website. Along with that, if the article is approved and chosen for the physical magazine, I'll be given the opportunity over the course of the next few months to interview select designers.

So, along with my draft, I have to hand over the list of designers to interview that it would best benefit my argument while also showing the reasoning behind the other side.

I press my palm against my forehead as I take a sip of my now lukewarm coffee and pop a Fudge Stripe cookie from my stash into my mouth as I edit and re-edit the paragraphs. My phone beeps with a message, and I happily fall into the distraction.

There's one from Harper and Sloan in our group message, that Harper aptly named *Brooklyn Babies* after her favorite song, asking if we're still on for our Tuesday dinner as usual and double checking our orders. I respond with my usual.

But it's the other message, the message from Jackson, that warms my skin. Because despite my argument, he has barely stopped texting me since the wedding. I tap my recently re-manicured nail to open it.

Jackson: How's it going, sunshine?

I roll my eyes, but I can't help the giddiness that spreads through my veins as I type my response. On weekdays, he texts me at four p.m. on the dot. I especially cannot get over the term *sunshine*, which he insists on calling me even though I'm anything but.

If anyone is sunshine personified, it's him.

Me: Still alive, barely breathing though.

Jackson: That's a little dark for a Tuesday, isn't it?

Me: That's part of my charm

Jackson: If you're trying to seduce me, it's working.

Me: I promise you that's not what I'm doing.

I shake my head as I put my phone down, determined to get some work done before I leave for therapy. Before I can re-edit anything, Harper appears at my desk, her blue-light glasses hanging low on her nose.

"How's the article?" she says, collapsing in the tiny spinning chair I keep under my desk.

I take another fudge cookie and groan into my hands. "Not great, and I've gotta finish the draft before I leave in an hour."

She pats my hand. "You will." Her eyes flick up to my screen and back to me. "It looks pretty done to me."

"It has to be perfect." I shake my head and lean on my elbow. "Enough about my article. How are the shoots coming for September?

Harper smiles, her face lighting up. "So good. And I've got the lead on the fur campaign. So, when your article does get approved, it'll be your words and my photos. How sick is that?"

"That's awesome, Harps. Now it really has to be perfect. Leave so I can finish."

She plucks a cookie for herself and stands up, pushing her glasses back on her head. And after forty more minutes of deleting, rewriting, and editing, I print the article out. Miss Bisset is a stickler for printed first drafts. In my two years of working here, plus interning, I've only ever given her two other printed copies. But none of them for the September issue.

I throw my tote bag over my shoulder with the copy in hand, along with my interview choices written at the bottom, and make my way to her office. She's pacing, which means she's talking to someone on the Bluetooth in her ear. Aside from Vanna Young, whom I've only met one time, Miss Bisset is the most intimidating person I've ever met. But she's a damn good boss. Challenging, supportive, and brutally honest.

Miss Bisset stops talking when she sees me approach the office and leans against her desk. Her light brown hair is drawn into an immaculate bun against her fair skin, her sleeveless, lightweight sweater dress is ironed to perfection and paired with the signature Hermès belt around her waist.

"Come in," she says with her very light French accent, picked up from summers at her grandparents' house as a child.

I step into the office, which is always six degrees warmer than the rest of the floor, with a soft but nervous smile on my face. She holds out a perfectly manicured hand, and I place the most important piece of paper of my life, at the moment, in her hand.

Her eyes fan over it briefly before flickering back up to my face. "I'm excited for this piece. Miss Young is looking forward to reading it as well. We've both been keeping our eye on your work."

She says it with a stoic face, her lips forming their signature pout as she doesn't dare crease her perfect makeup. But I notice a certain softness in her eye as she looks over me, even if she never says it.

"I couldn't be more thankful for the opportunity."

I feel like I'm under a microscope between the warm office and the power her gaze holds, but I stand tall and straight. My tan paper bag pants are pressed neatly, with a sleek black bodysuit and black booties, and I feel all the more confident in my work.

"Thank you, Valentina. We should have the decision by the end of the week or by Monday," she says, placing the paper on her desk and moving around to the other side.

"Have a good night, Miss Bisset," I respond before pulling her office door shut behind me and letting out the deep breath I had been holding. I've never wanted an article approved more in my life. I make my way out of the office building and step into the sun that always seems to beat down in this spot at five p.m. My therapist's office is only five blocks away, and I start the walk, basking in the feel of summer in the city.

It's a whole different atmosphere than any other season. Winters are a different vibe with the decorations and Rockefeller, but also the insane number of tourists. Summertime, even with the hot temperatures and heavy humidity, the appeal of it is unlike any other. Trips to the Hamptons or Long Island, the liveliness of Central Park and rooftop bars.

I hop over a puddle left over from a rainstorm a few days ago as I cross another street. Even aside from all of that, it's the sun beating through the tall buildings and the breeze that comes with it. It's the sheer energy emitting off people. Even with our East Coast attitudes, we're just a tad bit warmer than usual.

Marissa's office is the same as usual, except she's got the curtains open, and the sun streams in onto the carpet as I collapse in the leather couch. It molds around me like it always does, and I breathe in the underlying scent of almond from her incense.

"So, tell me about the wedding? Better yet, how are you feeling?" Marissa asks me with a soft smile.

"It was a lot. Surprisingly, different from what I was expecting though."

She crosses and uncrosses her leg. "How so?"

For once, I'm not biting my lip or my cheek as I dive back into the wedding. The same sense of resolution I got sitting there listening to Myles read his vows, and Emma hers, washes over me.

"Well, I got some unexpected closure," I start, and she nods for me to continue. "In Emma's, his wife, in her vows she mentions that they met in college and started dating a few months after he broke up with me."

Her eyes widen just slightly, and I know she's recalling all our early conversations about my insecurities and anxieties about that time of my life. How he would call me or facetime me like everything was normal, but when he came home, we'd never be officially back together.

"So, that confirmed for me that I wasn't crazy. That I was right."

"While I'm sure hearing that wasn't wonderful, I'm happy that it wasn't this big emotional overload for you. That the overwhelming emotion you felt was closure."

"I was angry too, but it faded. I want to talk about relationships in general," I say, playing with the ring on my finger and turning it in circles.

"What about them?"

"Well, another thing I noticed was that Myles told her that I was an old friend. It's not the biggest lie in the world, but when you're inviting that person to your wedding? That's huge. And I think he's grown up but obviously not all the way," I ramble. "I know we've talked about my attachment style and that it's anxious, but I feel anxious about relationships in general."

"Are you concerned that everyone you view as a possibility will be like Myles? That any relationship will have all the same pitfalls as that one?"

Even though I've been coming to Marissa for almost two years, and she has always seemed to be able to hit the nail on the head or figure out what I want to say but won't, it surprises me every time.

"Yes. Pretty much. It's hard for me to have an open mind."

She takes a slow sip of water and leans back into her armchair, mulling over her words.

"I think a first step is being aware of things that actually make you anxious. Maybe look back at the things Myles did that you vividly remember making you feel nervous or jittery or untrusting. At the same time, you need to not compare everyone to Myles."

I nod along as she says the words, and it doesn't seem as hard as I make it out to be on my own. Because I know the red flags I paid attention to all those years.

"You can't walk into something new with the assumption that they will just be another him. Because our hope is, that they

77

aren't, that you've gained the skill to avoid those that are. But you have to give them a chance to prove that."

"I think that's the hard part for me. Removing the idea, that age-old tale, that every guy is the same."

Marissa nods with a small smile. "I won't say it's easy, but it is possible. The good thing about Myles's actions is that you know immediately what not to look for. What to put in the negative category versus the positive category."

"Like a pros and cons list." I smile.

"Like a pros and con list. Of course, as crappy as dating can be, it can be fun. You get to find new things you might like or dislike. The more you do it, the more you know. And it's about respecting your own boundaries. What you can push past and what you can't. What about love in general are you concerned about?"

I take a deep breath. I don't want to sound negative or ridiculous, but these thoughts have been heavy in my mind these past few months.

"A part of me is scared that even if I do find the right person, what if it's a lie? What if I love them more than they love me? But also, what if it's me? What if the reason Myles moved on or broke up with me is because I'm not enough, and what if everyone realizes that? I love the idea of love, but I'm terrified of it."

Jackson flashes in my mind, his easy smile and his apparent infatuation with me, which excites and terrifies me at the same time. Part of the reason I haven't said yes to a date is because I'm terrified of him getting to know me and deciding it's not good enough. Like Myles did.

"Love is scary, I know that. Especially when you haven't experienced the best of it. But you can't avoid it simply because of fear. You just need to be open to the idea, open to the possibility. And it's true, you won't be right for everyone, just like everyone isn't right for you. But there is nothing wrong with you." She sighs, looking at her watch. "We have to end here, but I want to touch on this when you come back, okay?"

I nod and give her a soft smile as I still my hands. "Yes of course. Same as usual for scheduling?"

She nods, and I stand, grabbing my bag and my earphones as I exit. "And Nina," she starts, and I turn in her doorway. "Just have fun with it, okay? Day by day."

My cheeks flush slightly as I give her a parting smile, popping my earphones in as I exit through the upkept building and back onto the familiar and welcoming dirty city streets. My music comes through the speaker as I make my way down to the subway station, knowing that food and my friends await me.

I pull my phone out to check my messages as Marissa's words flash in my mind, *day by day*. I click on Jackson's text bubble from earlier.

Jackson: Well, I think you should try.

Me: Try what?

Jackson: To seduce me.

Me: I don't think it'd be very hard.

Jackson: You're right, it wouldn't be.

I can't help but smile.

Ten | Nina

"Have you said yes to a date yet?"

I roll my eyes as I enter the kitchen, Sloan's voice echoing from the couch. Jenko is watching her with slightly annoyed eyes because she's sitting in his favorite spot where the sun streams in through the window and warms the cushion, but he flicks his left ear as I enter the main space.

The smell of coffee fills my senses as Harper pours one for her and one for me. She slides the almond milk creamer over after using it herself. Our reservations for brunch aren't until eleven a.m., so we're going through our usual Sunday morning routine, except Sloan is here. Usually, she meets us at brunch, but since her love language is quality time, I think she was missing us.

I take a slow sip of the hot liquid. "No, Sloan, I haven't. It's only been a few weeks since the wedding," I say as I collapse next to her, and Jenko jumps onto my lap into a small ball.

"Why not? He's cute, and he's into you."

Harper takes her seat in her armchair as the breeze comes through the open window. Sunday mornings in June are in my top ten favorite days to exist. The warm air, before it's too humid or too hot, the sounds of birds in the morning that Jenko watches out of the window, and the endless possibilities.

"I'm not saying I'll never say yes," I sigh, adjusting the light blue sundress I put on for brunch. "I just don't want to rush anything. I barely know him."

"You woke up in his bed." Harper deadpans, and I flip her off.

"I just want to get to know him better. And also, he's friends—best friends—with Myles. It just feels weird."

"Why?" Sloan asks. "To be frank, Myles treated you like shit the last two years you were dating. If you can even call it that. If he can move on and get *married*, why can't you? Who cares? Myles has no claim on you."

My chest constricts at her words, and I sink into my seat.

Harper nods, tucking her hair behind her ear. "Exactly. I get what you're saying, Nina, but from what I've heard, I like him. And I don't think Myles should get in the way of what you want or your life."

For Harper to already like him, the most protective one of us all, says something. She's always telling us what she thinks about someone we went on a date with or flirted with. And every day, when we're sitting on the couch or eating dinner, she asks to read some of our texts to see if he's passed the test. I guess that so far, he has.

"I don't want to let him get in the way. I'm just," I start, spinning my mug, "I don't know, I'm just taking my time."

I don't tell them that I don't want to get hurt again. Despite my last therapy session, and while I am taking it day by day, I am still terrified. I know that there's no reward without risk, no sunshine without rain, but it's much easier said than done.

Harper nods. "Well, we'll be here every step of the way whenever you're ready."

The sun just touches the tops of my shoulders from where we're seated outside of The Tavern. It's a rustic, industrial-style spot. Hard metal bars hold up the awning, blocking most of the sun's rays, and the same black bars line the window frames. Inside and out, cherry wood tables line the restaurant. All around us, green vines crawl up the bars, and plants decorate the space.

We sip on the waters we were given when we sat as we wait to order. Sloan takes a sip and glances at Harper. "Are you still talking to Roman? The one from the wedding?"

Harper raises a brow, flipping the menu even though I'd bet money she gets what she always does. "We're not talking. We're just sleeping together."

Sloan rolls her eyes, and I hold in a laugh, because while what Harper said is true, she also talks to him more than any of her usual hook-ups. She texts him all the time, even calls him some days when they don't see each other. But I'm not going to push her. If she doesn't want to admit she likes him yet, I am in no room to expect more.

"Whatever. When you admit it though, I am going to say I told you so to both of you," Sloan mumbles with a bop of her head.

I'm about to interrupt when two tall frames cast a shadow over the table from over the barrier between us and the street. We all look up, and my eyebrows shoot up when I see Roman and Jackson standing there.

"Well, hi." Roman grins.

Sloan's cheek twitches. "How ironic. We were just talking about you." I watch, amused, as Harper slaps her on the shoulder, though Sloan's wide smile never fades. Briefly, I make eye contact with Jackson, whose eyes light up under the sun.

Harper finally collects herself. "Do you guys wanna join? We can pull up chairs." She directs her gaze to me, a smirk on her lips, and if I was next to her, I would be the one hitting someone on the shoulder.

Roman and Jackson share a quick glance and then nod. "We'd love to." They walk around to the entrance as Harper finds two extra chairs and lets our server know.

Both men appear at the table moments later. Even though Harper and Sloan know who he is, saw him briefly in the bar, they've never officially met him, and Jackson takes the time to fully introduce himself as I take in his appearance.

In some weird coincidence, we're matching again. He's wearing a light blue, button-down shirt, the first few buttons undone, his tan skin peeking through, and simple pressed slacks. His blond curls are even lighter than last time, the glow of the sun brightening them, and they're pushed back by the Ray Bans atop his head, but a few stray strands pop out.

Finally, his eyes focus on me as he slides into the seat next to me. They trail slowly down my body and back up to my eyes, sparkling with amusement in their usual fashion. My body reacts almost instantly as I look back into his deep blue eyes and fight to keep the smile from my face. Little sparks of electricity bounce between us, and I swear I feel them land on my skin like fireflies.

Jackson spreads his arm across the back of my chair, and I raise an eyebrow at him.

"Fancy running into you again."

I feel the heat wanting to flush my cheeks as I raise a brow. "If I didn't know better, I'd say you were stalking me."

He leans towards me ever so slightly. "If I didn't know better, I'd say you were trying to avoid me." He holds his lips into a forced frown, almost like a pout.

"Well, if I was, it really isn't working now, is it?"

His lips pull into a full smile. "Sorry, Nina, it's gonna take more than that."

"I guess I'll have to step it up then," I say. "We match again." I point it out this time to make sure he understands I'm not actually annoyed with his appearance at our brunch.

Those blue eyes flick between my dress and his shirt before landing back to me, and the tension between us pulls just a little bit tighter as his gaze lingers. "We do."

I don't miss the way the shirt tugs at the lean muscles on his arms or the flash of skin where it's unbuttoned, and it sends a wave of heat over me that isn't from the temperature. Before he can say anything else, the waiter appears to take our drink orders.

Harper and Roman both order Bloody Marys which, as usual, Sloan and I turn our noses up at. "We're gonna do a pitcher of bottomless for us two," I say.

"Make that three," Jackson chimes in and flashes me a smile before turning back to the waiter, who smiles and nods before disappearing.

"Our third mimosa buddy. I love this," Sloan says and flashes Jackson her signature grin. I can't help the roll of my eyes.

"I'm honored to be included," he says, placing his left hand over his chest, because his other arm stays draped over the back of my chair. When he looks away to say something to Roman, Sloan lowers her glasses and raises her eyebrows at me before pushing them back up as the drinks are placed on the table.

We order our food. Harper gets her usual stack of French toast and a side of turkey bacon, while Sloan sticks to her omelet platter, and I get my usual waffle piled with strawberries and whipped cream.

We fall into easy conversation about basic stuff, like Roman's job in social work and with foster kids, how Jackson works at a high-end PR firm on Wall Street, and how they've been best friends since their freshman year of college and moved to New York together when they graduated.

I reach for my second mimosa and revel in the mostly champagne drink. As we wait for our food, I notice myself sometimes leaning towards Jackson. My eyes flicker to him during conversation to see the flash of the dimples or the easy way that he interacts. Drawn to him whether I want to be or not.

Sometimes, he's already looking at me, sometimes he's not.

But he's hard not to look at.

I like when he's not watching me because I watch him interact with my friends. It lets me gauge how they feel or how they interact with him. Sloan loves most people, especially people who are bright and earnest. But it's Harper I'm surprised by. She interacts with him, asks him questions, and laughs at all his cheesy jokes. She makes sure to send me a wink when he isn't looking too.

Thankfully, our food comes and is placed in front of each of us. We all dig in, falling into a comfortable silence. Jackson ordered a waffle like I did, except with chocolate chips and strawberries on the side. I practically cover mine in whipped cream, one quarter at a time, and add strawberries along the top as we eat. The only sounds are the car engines and our silverware until we fall back into conversation.

"You're telling me you like *22 Jump Street* better than the first?" Roman looks at me, shock written all over his face as he takes a bite of his breakfast sandwich.

"I love the first one. I can quote the entire thing front to back."

"She has a cat named Jenko. No one ever knows it's from those movies," Sloan chimes in, and that causes Jackson to let out a big throaty laugh.

I shake my head lightly as I see another table look over at us, just two girls that are seated behind us with their own pitcher of bottomless mimosas, but they just send me quick, easy smiles, and I turn back to focus.

"Okay, but the second one is just so good. The comedy is perfect, I'm sorry. Jenko's reaction to Schmidt dating the captain's daughter alone? Amazing."

"I'm with her on this one, Rome. I like the second better too." Jackson takes a sip of his mimosa since most of his plate is already cleared.

"You are a suck up." He points to Jackson who's laughing and turns to me. "And you, I'm questioning a lot of things right now. I'm so disappointed."

I stick my tongue out at Roman and take a bite topped with whipped cream and a strawberry.

"I wanna meet this cat," Jackson says. His eyes flick to mine, filled with amusement. "You got a little something—"

He reaches over with his thumb and swipes softly over the skin right above my mouth, and the dollop of whipped cream that he wiped off my lip is now on his thumb. My heart starts beating erratically in my chest at the simple touch, the light feel of his thumb on my skin. He sends me a sly grin before popping it in his mouth and then extending his arm behind my chair again.

Sloan kicks me under the table, and I know she's probably grinning from ear to ear.

Meanwhile, I'm just trying to catch my breath.

"No, you don't. That cat only likes her. He only puts up with us cause we're around all the time," Sloan says, and I shrug. I like that my cat really only likes me.

"We'll see. I'm a very determined person," Jackson responds, and I don't think he's just talking about Jenko anymore, but I don't bring any attention to it.

Mostly because I can barely focus on anything besides the last bite of waffle and the fact that his fingertips are lightly brushing the open skin on my back. Right where the tattoo that goes down my spine is, his fingers are strumming over the skin like guitar strings. Except softer, lighter.

Like he doesn't want to push too far, but he still wants to touch me.

"Are we still going to the Hampton house for your birthday?" Roman asks, this time directed at Jackson. *Hampton house?*

Oh, dios mío.

Jackson adjusts his sunglasses on top of his loose curls. "Hell, yeah. Are you still down?" Roman nods. "You guys should come." Jackson taps his fingers on my spine as he says it, as if to say *I'm talking to you.*

He looks at us girls, and Harper's got a huge grin on her face. We haven't made it down there this summer yet. We've had to resort to laying out on the rooftop of our building or the gym pool.

"I'm so down. When is it?"

"We're doing the weekend before my birthday. Probably leave Thursday, July fifteenth, in the evening and stay until that Sunday."

"I'd love to," Sloan says with a grin, bumping shoulders with Harper.

My lips fall into a frown as my eyes flick between the grins on everyone else's face. Isn't a weekend at the Hamptons too much? Even if it is over a month away. Spending that much time with Jackson at his Hampton house, even with a group, is a lot. And on top of that, I assume that Myles and Emma will be there.

"What's that face for? Valentina Andreá Arrieta Scott. We're going." Harper points her finger at me, and I roll my eyes, but I'm suddenly nervous and anxious all over. The sensation settling over my skin like a scratchy blanket I can't get off.

"What about work? Can we get off?"

"It's one day. Yes."

I glare at her, not sure how to express to her that it's too much, too soon, and especially for me to make a decision right away.

Jackson leans down, pressing his hand on my back. "Hey, it's no pressure. You don't have to answer right now, and you don't have to come if you don't want."

My chest constricts with conflicting emotions. Glancing over to him, I mumble, "Can I think about it?"

His fingers begin tracing over the lines on my spine again, sending goosebumps over my skin. A soft smile pulls at his lips, like he's got me right where he wants me. "You can take all the time you need, Valentina. I'm in no rush."

"Okay, thank you." I give him the tiniest smile. Just a hint.

He raises a brow. "For what?"

I shrug.

"You don't need to thank me. Yes, I want you to come, but you don't ever have to do anything you don't want to. Not with me."

The tension between us is like a tightrope tied to one another on both ends, and every time we're near each other it pulls tighter and tighter. I'm just waiting to see which side breaks first. I lean back into his hand, which is my first sign of defeat, and let the warmth of him spread over my skin.

I swallow, my brain going a little hazy, and take a sip of my drink and nod, leaning into his feather light touch on my back despite myself. Deep down, I know I'll probably end up going. Harper and Sloan want to go and will do everything they can to convince me, but despite what they want, it's also about me. And I want to make sure I'm okay with it.

Jackson not pushing, not insisting I come, makes me far more comfortable than I expected it to. And even though I try to deny it, I feel more and more drawn to him with every passing day.

I have a feeling that I am in far deeper water than I thought.

Eleven | Nina

When I was growing up, after dinner I would make my mom and dad sit down and watch *Project Runway* and *America's Next Top Model* with me religiously. Dad would be drawing designs for a client on a new building, Mom would be reaching out to families for her social work, and my eyes would be glued to the television screen, watching these brilliant designers and upcoming models.

Fortunately, I did take after my dad with his drawing talents. I would sketch designs. But I never quite acquired the fingers for sewing. Instead, I fell in love with journalism— fashion journalism. It's been my lifelong dream to work at *Poze*. Once I got the internship during my time at FIT and later a full-time job, my dream became to be published in the September issue.

It's Wednesday, and Miss Bisset has finally started calling different journalists in to announce whether their articles were approved or not. I'm impatiently waiting to hear about my own. Not even Fudge Stripe cookies can calm my nerves because my stash has sat untouched all day long.

Nervous doesn't begin to describe it.

On top of that, the possible Hamptons trip is growing closer. Every night, I lay in my bed with Jenko on my chest, thinking of every possible scenario that could occur should I go.

Most of my scenarios either involve Jackson and his undeniable charm or Myles, should he attend. I can't stop thinking about the wedding and what he was going to say before Emma interrupted us. I'm sure it was nothing positive, and I'm long past the point of waiting for—or wanting—an apology from him. But what would he think if I showed up? That I'm dating his best friend, even if I'm not *really* dating him? Drama would follow, and I'm just not sure I can deal with that.

I admit that I am extremely attracted to Jackson and his warm, inviting presence. Between the never-ending charm or the deep blue eyes, I'd be delusional to deny that I'm attracted to him, that I *am* into him.

I'm just scared of rushing in too quickly and getting drowned with no life vest in sight. Just like the past.

The sound of Miss Bisset's office door closing, a noise I've memorized in the last few hours, brings me out of my spiral, and I look up to see her wave a hand in my direction. I stand up and will myself to stop biting on the inside of my lip, which is already raw. My hands smooth over my light plaid patterned pants and simple coordinating cream shirt before I take two deep breaths.

Either way, it's not the end of the world. It's not like I'm getting fired and I'll never have the opportunity to be published again. I can always keep pushing at the September ones if this doesn't go my way. Because at some point it will.

Miss Bisset is dressed to perfection as always. Her navy dress pants and immaculate white top are impeccably ironed even as she sits in her desk chair. I swear her lips almost pull up into the ghost of a smile as I enter. Even if she does mask it quickly, it still sends my heart into overdrive.

"Miss Scott, please sit," she says, and I do just that. Not sure whether I should cross my legs or ankles to hide the fact that my left leg won't stop shaking with adrenaline. Because no matter what I tell myself, this is still a huge opportunity and would be a giant step in my career.

"So, I've got good and bad news."

Mierda.

"Good news, I adored your piece. Your maturity and the ability to open up the conversation on a huge topic in the fashion world, while making it seem accessible, was brilliant," she says, obviously starting with the good. Her eyes are twinkling with warmth, which makes me relax the tiniest bit.

"Miss Young loved it as well. Your piece has been approved and will be featured in the September issue. Obviously, you'll have time to edit it and interview the designers you were interested in. So, congratulations."

It takes everything in me to not jump up and start dancing in the warm office in front of my boss. The words *approved* and *September* just keep floating in big bold letters in my mind. A small smile forms on my lips as my leg stops shaking.

And then I remember there is bad news. Honestly, regardless of what it is, I don't think it'll bring down my mood much.

"The bad news is, Miss Young and I have decided we want you to exclusively write for the published magazine from now on. The online articles are a little less time consuming, so this will mean a heavier workload—"

"The published magazine?" I swear I don't mean to interrupt, but I don't think I could've stopped myself if I tried. This time she does smile.

"Yes, Miss Scott. You will no longer be writing pieces for the website. You will be featured and sent out on interviews for our published issues. The only work I'd like you to continue with on the online side of things is your editing. Your digital editing skills are extremely valuable, and I'd like you to continue that. If that is a feasible workload for you, that is."

Miss Bisset raises an eyebrow at that. A softness remains amongst her strong features and precise bun.

"Yes, absolutely. I'd be delighted."

She clasps her hands softly on top of her desk as her eyes focus on me. "I look forward to it. Good work."

I can't keep the smile off my face as I stand to exit the office. "Thank you, Miss Bisset." It takes everything in me not to squeal as I collapse in my desk chair. The first thing I do is text Harper and Sloan, who respond almost immediately with happy face emojis and gifs.

Then I send a text to Jackson because he's been asking about the article ever since I mentioned it casually at brunch. He answers almost immediately.

Jackson: Congratulations, hot shot. Might have to buy my first ever fashion magazine this September.

Me: You don't have to.

Jackson: I know that. I want to. I'm going to be new and improved. The next André Leon Talley.

I can't help the laugh that sputters out. I'd put a hundred dollars on the fact that he had no idea who that was without a Google search.

Me: Did you look up male fashion icons for me?

Jackson: I'll never tell.

My heart flutters as I reread his first response, and I throw my bag together as the workday ends. I can't wait to step out into the late afternoon sun and get home. Before I can, my phone rings, Jackson's name flashing at the top.

"Hello?"

"Hi, congratulations."

I roll my eyes, grinning because he can't see it. "You already said that."

"I know, I wanted to say it again." He pauses, and I wait, tapping my nails on my desk. "Are you busy?"

"No, I just got off work and was going to head home, why?"

"I have a proposition. It's not a date, I promise, but do you want to eat with me?" I chew on my lip, turning the idea over in my head. "Figured this might be a good way to convince you to come to the Hamptons. I'm still downtown. Well actually, I'm waiting outside your office."

I shake my head in disbelief. "You're downstairs?"

"I am."

Swinging my bag over my shoulder I start to head out. "What if I said no?"

"Well, I was hoping you wouldn't." He chuckles, and even through the phone it resonates deeply.

I take a deep breath and swing my bag over my shoulder, knowing I never would've said no. "I'll be down shortly."

"Is that a yes?"

"Yes."

"See you soon, sunshine." The smile is clear in his voice, and my stomach does flips at the nickname.

My heart is already beating heavily in my chest at the idea of seeing him again. Of being near him, the man who is as bright as the sun and for some reason, choosing to shine those rays over me.

Jackson

I tuck my phone back into my pocket as I wait downstairs for Nina to arrive. Luckily, my plan worked. Whether she agreed because she was in a good mood or because she genuinely wanted to come, I don't give a shit. Because she said yes.

I haven't been able to get this girl out of my head no matter how hard I try.

Like a moth to a flame, my eyes latch onto her figure as soon as she steps out of the building. I begin walking that way, taking a long, slow look at her. I take in every curve, every dip, every inch, attempting to memorize all of her. Finally, her brown eyes meet mine, and I grin instantly.

She seems less guarded today, and I hope it's because I've been slowly wiggling myself into her everyday life. Trying to make her more comfortable and take everything at her pace. Fuck, I'd do anything she needed already. As soon as I'm close enough, I reach up and grab her bag from her shoulder.

"Jackson." She deadpans, crossing her arms. But I notice her eyes roam over me, and the way she says my name instantly makes my blood burn.

"What?"

"Give me my bag."

I start walking away, towards my favorite hole in the wall pizza shop. Glancing back, she follows begrudgingly.

"No, I'm going to hold onto it. Come on, I'm hungry."

She catches up to me, walking by my side through the stream of people all getting off work. "Where are we going?"

"My favorite pizza shop." When we reach the side street, shaded from the sun by the tall skyscrapers, I gently place my hand on her back, leading her in the right direction. The heat from her body, even through her shirt, burns my palm in the best way.

When we get there, she glances up at me, her lips twitching slightly like she wants to smile. I wish she would. "Wait, I love this place," she says. The sign is simple, a faded red neon that just says *PizzaOne*.

I raise my brow, enjoying all the things that have tied us together since before we ever met. "They have the best pizza and you, have great taste." She eyes me, amused and I just grin, pulling the door open.

We enter, and the secret is that past the ordering table and around the corner, they have about four tiny booths in the back.

I nod to the chef, who knows my order by heart, and lead Nina to the back. She doesn't seem surprised, which means she probably comes here as often as I do.

"Pick a seat, and I'll go order."

She frowns. "You're not paying. You said it wasn't a date."

"It's not a date. I'm still going to pay though." She attempts to stride past me, and I step in front of her. "I'll just tell them not to accept your money. Just sit down and let me treat you. As a congratulations." I lean down, closer to her face, and to my surprise, her breath hitches just a fraction. "Please."

Her cheeks flood with color, and after a second she nods. "Fine. Thank you."

I smile. "My pleasure."

I wait until she sits down before returning her bag and walking back to the front to place the order. When I'm sure she won't follow me, I ask Tom, the chef, currently tossing pizza dough, who seems to know her, what she likes. He gives me a grin and spills her secret, which just happens to be extra cheese and mushroom, so I get her two slices of that and two slices of extra cheese for myself. And before I know it, I'm seated across from her with very large, hot slices of pizza before us. The light through the windows glints off the silver jewelry hanging on her ear as she tucks a hair back.

Nina sits back, pulling one leg up on the old booth and leaning on it as her eyes find my own. "Thank you, again," she says, softer this time.

"Stop thanking me. I wanted to." I study the sporadic little freckles on her face. They aren't clumped together, but instead there are larger freckles spread all over. Two on one side of her nose, a few on the right side of her forehead and her cheeks. The desire to trace them rushes in.

After a few bites each, she grabs a napkin. "So, when is the trip again?"

I try to hide a smile but fail. "The fifteenth. How are you feeling about it?" I unbutton the end of my sleeves and begin rolling them up as I wait for her to respond. Her eyes are latched onto my fingers and their movements, causing her to hesitate.

Nina clears her throat, meeting my eyes again. "I do want to come." She sighs, and my smile grows. "But I'm nervous."

"About?"

"Two things, I guess. It just seems like a lot very soon. We're not even—we're not . . ." She stumbles and taps her leg with mine under the table until she takes a deep breath.

"First off, I expect absolutely nothing from you on that trip. I just want your company, and I think you'd have fun. There is no pressure from me, Nina. I promise."

She seems to exhale a bit and settles back into the seat. "Then the other thing is Myles."

I knew that was coming, knew it had to be brought up at some point. And I'd be lying if I said I didn't think about it myself. As of now, I haven't said a thing to him. He didn't say anything about me dancing with her, so I'm hoping it hasn't crossed his mind. At some point I'll have to tell him, but I'm not there yet.

I want this to actually begin before it's threatened.

"Well actually, he never said he was coming. I don't think he or Emma will be there. If they tell me, I can let you know. I know it's more than just him coming to the trip; it's just him in general and the fact that I'm friends with him."

She glances down, taking another bite to avoid the statement because it's true. I understand the reservations. I don't know fully what happened between the two, but I know she's guarded. And I get that she's looking for any excuse not to try.

"I understand. I know that if this continues or turns into something else, he'll need to know. But he doesn't yet, and you shouldn't stress about it. If anyone needs to talk to him, it's me, not you," I finish.

97

Truthfully, I'm probably being a shitty friend, and I know I should be more upfront with him. But I don't ask for much. I do a lot for my friends because they're my family. They mean as much to me as my siblings and my parents. But I'm not sure I want to hear him say that I can't or shouldn't pursue her. It might be different if this was a few years ago when they first broke up. But they haven't been together for years. And he's *married.*

I want this chance for myself. Life is great, I won't deny that. I have a great job, great friends, but Nina makes me excited, makes me want to push for more. The idea of dating has never felt as exciting as it does right now, with her. I don't think that's a bad thing.

I lean forward, pushing my empty plate away, and rest my forearms on the table, closer to her. "And aside from him, I want you to come." My leg is now pressed against hers under the table, my foot hooked behind her own. "I want you to get to know me so that when I do ask you out on a real date, you say yes."

She meets my eyes, studying me. "I can ask you anything. Bug you all I want?"

"You can do whatever you want, Nina, if it means you'll come." My heart beats heavily as I await her answer.

She bites her lip, and my eyes are hyper focused on the movement until she takes a deep breath, and amusement appears in her eyes, past the hesitation. "All right." Finally, she lets herself smile, just a little, but it's enough for me. Enough to know I won't stop until I get a full smile on those lips. "I'd love to."

I grin again, leaning back in my seat and staring unabashedly at the girl across from me. I keep my leg hooked around hers under the table, and she doesn't pull away. I have no idea how I'm already so entranced by her, but I don't care.

There is something about her, something deeply special about her that Myles must have missed that I intend to fully uncover.

Twelve | Nina

"We all set?" Sloan asks, and with a nod from both Harper and I, she pulls the door shut behind her, locking it.

It's already July, and we're getting ready to go to the Hamptons. Time had flown by the past month. Jackson made me feel infinitely better when we had that dinner together after the news about my article. Since then, we've had a few more lunch slash early dinner outings, none of them dates. Just for me to get more comfortable. I have. He consistently texts me too, random updates about his day and always asking about mine.

He's attentive, and caring, and genuinely interested in anything I have to say, and sometimes I didn't know what to do with it all.

As far as he knows, Myles isn't coming to this trip, and what he said was right. Myles doesn't have a say on my dating life. Not anymore. So, I'm walking into this trip with an open mind and excitement at getting to spend time with my best friends, Roman, and Jackson.

As we head downstairs to meet Jackson, I don't question Harper about Roman like I want to. So far, what Sloan and I have been told is they are just friends who hook up. While it isn't new for Harper, because she isn't really a dater, I still suspect more. But I'll leave her to come to that on her own. We step out onto the street to wait for Jackson and Roman to pull up in Jackson's car.

I really, *really*, need to know who his company represents. Because it's all adding up. A high-rise apartment, a car in the city, even though he barely drives it, and a Hamptons house. Soon enough, a white jeep pulls into the loading area with its hazards on.

Jackson hops out and heads straight towards me. Before I can stop him, he scoops up my duffle bag. He grabs Sloan's as well, placing them in the back compartment of the jeep as Roman does the same with Harper's.

When he is back in front of me, he smiles and drapes his arm over my shoulder. His fingers drum lightly on my skin, setting off a feeling equivalent to a bunch of little sparklers going off.

"You guys all set?" Everyone nods. "All right, it's gonna be a tight squeeze in the back, so I apologize about that. But this one," he glances at me, "is up front with me." I try and fail to fight the heat crawling up my skin.

Harper waves her hand, smiling widely. "I think we'll survive." Sloan and Roman have matching grins, and I avoid eye contact at all costs as we move towards the car.

Jackson opens my door, puts the seat back and holds his hand out. "Up and at it."

He watches me with bright eyes. They're lighter as the late sun hits them, more like the light blue of shallow ocean water instead of the deep sea.

I place my hand in his and climb up into the seat. My entire body warms at the brief contact, and I try to steer my mind away from thinking about all the other places I want his hands. Cupping my cheeks, or on my waist, or his fingers lazily running over my spine again.

I am in *big* trouble.

He climbs in and lets his sunglasses fall over his eyes. He takes a second to adjust his seat for the three in the back and lets his phone connect to the Bluetooth. The cool air pumping from the vents contrasts with the heat of the mid-July sun that flows in through the roof and open windows. He pulls off into the traffic, which isn't too bad for a late Thursday evening. Hopefully we got off earlier than the other beachgoers and won't hit too much traffic.

I sneak a look back at Sloan, who is contently leaning in the open window, and Harper, who is leaned towards Roman's lanky body and showing him something on her phone, both locked into their own little world. As the first strums of a guitar come out of the speakers, I sneak a look a Jackson, who is already looking at me as he turns up the dial a little. The ring on his middle finger shimmers in the sun creeping through the window.

"Country?"

His dimples appear. "I made this playlist just for you. Hopefully you won't hate these."

My heart careens. We've talked about music so much, and he knows I'm not the biggest fan of country, that most times I hate it. He promised he'd make me a special playlist of ones he thought I might like, but I didn't believe him.

In the past, I'd been made promises by Myles, and none of them were ever followed through.

"On a scale of one to ten, how country is it?" I ask him, adjusting so I'm sitting on my left leg and leaning on the center console as the wind breezes through.

Jackson laughs loudly, and the sound hits me deep in my stomach. "I'd say it's a solid six, but it might be a seven sometimes," he says, shifting into the next gear as we start to venture out of the crowded city.

"I guess I can work with that." I run a hand through my hair, which is blowing wildly in the breeze, and since my sunglasses are packed away, I'm forced to squint against the wind as well.

"There's a hat under your seat, I think, if you want it."

I reach under, and sure enough, my fingers come in contact with a ball cap, a black Brooklyn basketball one, and I swiftly adjust it to my head so it won't fly off.

"This is one of my favorites. I think you'll like it." Jackson reaches for the volume before resting his hand back on the gear shift. I lean back into the seat, letting the contrasting temperatures wash over me as I listen to the song.

It's soft, which I didn't expect. In my head, country is tangy and loud, but the guitar and the voice are smooth. I even find myself tapping along on my thigh as I hear the low noise of Jackson humming along.

My phone beeps with a text, and Sloan's name pops up next to the name of our group message.

Sloan: You guys owe me.

Harper: For what?

Me: ???

Sloan: You know what. I can't believe I agreed to fifth wheel this.

Harper: Shut up. You love us.

Sloan: I never said I didn't.

Me: You guys are literally right next to each other. Tell Roman I say hi.

I roll my eyes and turn to look at the backseat. Roman is attempting to read the messages on Harper's phone as she holds it away, and Sloan, despite her text messages, has a smug smile on her face. I know she's not actually bothered by it or she wouldn't have come. One of the best things about Sloan is that she does what's best for her and doesn't ignore her own needs to please others.

My arm brushes Jackson's as they both rest on the center console as another song starts.

"All right, what's your favorite on this list," I ask, reaching in my small bag at my feet for my bag of candy.

"Wow, coming at me with the big questions." He hands me his phone. "Here. The passcode is zero-eight-two-eight. I'd say 'Homesick.'"

Even though it shouldn't, a warmth spreads over me. It's stupid, and we're literally not even dating, but how open and genuine Jackson is, it's already absolutely one of the most attractive things about him.

So, after I catch my breath, I type in the code and add the song up next, interested to see what makes it his favorite. As soon as it starts playing and his fingers start drumming along, I understand the appeal. Easy strums and melodic snaps wash over me as I watch Jackson listen to the song. I could watch him do almost anything, I think. His shoulders sway in time with the beat, and he mouths along to the lyrics.

Which alone make me swoon.

He sings along quietly in the driver's seat, and I can't keep my eyes off him.

"Is this where you get your charm from? Listening to cheesy country music?" I ask, handing him a candy.

He glances over, popping the candy in his mouth. "So, you admit I'm charming?"

I can't fight the soft laugh that escapes me as he continues to slowly break his way in. "Maybe a little bit."

Since the sun has lowered a bit, he's taken his sunglasses off, and they hang off the front of his top. His tanned arms are speckled with random freckles and a few white scars over his forearms. The loose blond curls look soft and fluffy atop his head, and my eyes trail slowly over the sharpness of his jaw and smooth skin.

He looks over at me briefly—I'm tapping along to the song now too because it's almost impossible not to—and his blue eyes meet mine. My breath catches in my throat as he does. Because even though it's a quick glance, and his eyes are back on the road in no time, it's like he sees all of me when he looks at me, no matter how fleeting.

"All right, play the third one next. I think you'll really like it," he says, and I break my eyes away from him and play the song up next. It's got a piano and light drumming in the background, and I lean into the seat.

I let the lyrics and the melody wash over me. Maybe it's the fact that he took the time to make this playlist, and call it *Nina's Playlist*, or a secret love for country I didn't know I had, but I love it. I love all the songs that have played so far.

"Okay fine, you win," I say, giving in. "I guess country isn't so bad."

He smiles wide, and the dimples pop. "Well, I am glad to hear that. We'll be listening to it a lot."

I smile, and I figure from our surroundings we've only got a few minutes left of the drive. The sky is painted in bright colors, red-hot orange and starburst pinks, with shades of blue, violet, and lilac peeking between. The salt permeates the air now, and I can see the water if I squint as what's left of the sun glares off of it.

It's colder now too since there isn't much light left, and Jackson rolls up the windows to create a bubble as I snuggle into my crewneck. I pop a few candies in my mouth and offer some to Jackson and the three in the back seat. We've all fallen into a comfortable silence as we start seeing some houses, although

I haven't moved my arm off the center console, and neither has Jackson, so they've stayed touching this whole time.

"You're joking. This is your house?" Harper says exactly what I'm thinking as he pulls into a stone driveway. Roman and Jackson both laugh at our shock as he parks the car.

It's stunning.

It's three floors. There's the ground floor with the garage but then there's a white staircase that leads up to the front door and a wraparound porch. There are rocking chairs at the front and tall, white wooden beams to support the roof. It's classic with modern touches. The entire house is painted a light seafoam green with lots of windows. From the front it's easy to tell that the house backs up to the beach because I can hear the ocean waves.

"What exactly do you do again?" Harper and I say in unison, giving each other a wink as we lock arms and the boys start pulling out the bags. Sloan just stares at the house. We are way out of our league here.

"I'm on the board at a PR firm, but I also represent a few people of my own." He taps the hat I'm wearing. One of the cities basketball teams.

"The team?"

"Not the whole team, just a player. A few fresh faces in other sports too."

I'm shell-shocked in place. Harper has to physically push me to start moving again. And I can't even come up with a snarky remark as I force myself to catch up to him. Jackson swings his keys around his finger with a very cheeky grin as we walk up the steps until he's turning the key in the lock.

"¿Quién? No puedes ser tan rico. Eso es . . . esto es una locura. No es possible." *Who? You can't be that rich. This is crazy. It's not possible.*

He stops in front of the open door, and I can hear Harper laughing behind me.

"Listen, I love this, you know I do. I want you to speak Spanish to me at all times, whenever you want, and I'll do my best to learn to keep up." I blush instantly as he looks at me with blue eyes worthy of drowning in. "But I need you to breathe."

Well, if he wanted me breathing, that wasn't the way to do it.

He chuckles softly and presses a hand on my lower back, ushering me into the house, Harper, Sloan, and Roman following behind us. The bags are dropped at the staircase, and I've finally taken in enough deep breaths to focus again.

Jackson's hand is still on my back, and I'm so hyper aware of the touch it's almost all I can think about.

The kitchen looks over the back of the house and wrap-around porch, which means we have a perfect view onto the sand. It's got clean white cabinets and dark granite countertops with stainless steel appliances. The island is big enough for at least six people to eat at, and the entire wall behind the countertops is filled with windows. To the left it opens into a formal dining room, but to the right it opens into a cute breakfast nook with French doors onto the porch.

"Are Myles and Em coming?" Roman asks.

Jackson shakes his head as he uncorks a bottle of white wine. "No, they never confirmed, so it's just us for now. A few more guys we know from work are coming tomorrow for the day," he responds, directing that towards us.

I'm fine with more people coming. I don't really care who comes as long as it's not Myles.

"All righty, well then how about pizza for us?" We all nod. "Toppings?"

"Pepperoni," Harper says, while I say "Mushroom," and Sloan says "Anything."

"Do a Sicilian, half and half," Jackson says and hands Roman the menu for a place nearby. He pours us all a glass and slides them over before looking at Harper, Sloan, and me.

"All right, room tour. Let's go, ladies," he says and pushes us towards the stairs, leaving Roman in the kitchen. "You got that Roman?"

"Yeah, I think I know how to order pizza," he calls, drawing a laugh out of us.

Jackson hands me his wine glass as he somehow picks up all of the bags. I watch his arms flex under the weight, but if it affects him, he doesn't show it, so I enjoy the view.

He stops at the room at the top of the stairs first and drops Roman's and Harper's bags, "Harper, if you want your own room, I can make that happen, but—"

She laughs but shakes her head, matching his grin. "I think we can hold down the fort in here together."

"That's what I like to hear," he says, and she carries their bags inside the room. He leads Sloan and me down to the left. "You two are in here," He pushes open the door and places our bags down right inside. The entire room is a pale, warm yellow.

He looks at me, bumping my shoulder. "You're welcome in mine, but I figured I'd play it safe."

I push him lightly on the chest. "A fool. You are a fool."

"Only for you though."

"You don't quit, do you?"

"Nina, please. I never quit," he says, sending chills down my spine at the way he says my name.

Just as I'm about to respond, Sloan interrupts, "All right, well, I'm going to get settled and let you two continue *that* somewhere else." She smiles, entering the room and shuts me out.

I blink, stepping closer to Jackson, who just laughs. He pushes open the door to the master, I assume, as he drops his own bags and takes the wine back. His fingertips brush mine as he grabs the glass, and he stays by my side.

It's beautiful. A pale blue with white accents and French doors that lead onto a small balcony. There is an adjoining bathroom and a decent-sized flat screen mounted on the wall across from the bed that's off to my right.

He sets his wine down on the dresser and shuffles through his bags until he pulls out a hoodie with *Georgia* written on the front and pulls it over his head, ruffling his curls a bit. It's rude that he looks that attractive in such a simple outfit, but it's not surprising that he's beautiful in everything.

I walk towards the French doors, and he follows, opening them for us, and leads us out onto the balcony. We stand side by side in the settling darkness. There aren't nearly as many lights out here, and I can see the stars for once. They light up the sky in little twinkles, some flickering out of view and back in. I can hear the waves crashing onto the sand and the low call of seagulls. Goosebumps break out over my leg when a cool breeze rushes by.

I am acutely aware of how close we are to each other. His familiar smell wafts around me again, and this time I catch the underlying hints of vanilla that I like so much. After another sip I look away from the darkness that is the night sky and the ocean I can't quite see anymore and turn towards him. A bright spot even in the dark.

And it hasn't even been a day, a full day, but I'm so incredibly happy I decided to come. To spend this time with him. To let myself enjoy whatever this is.

Thirteen | Jackson

turn to look at Nina, who is standing on the balcony next to me, tucked into a crewneck, her hair tucked behind her ears. Looking as beautiful as ever under the stars.

"I'm happy you decided to come."

She glances up at me, brown eyes warming. "I don't think I stood a chance at resisting your methods of convincing."

Chuckling, I shake my head. She was right. I had showed up at her work a few more times after the pizza, convincing her to come eat with me or even just walk with me. To be fair, I hadn't really left the girl alone. But I was ever so slowly starting to chip at the walls. That was easy to see because I'd been on the receiving end of a few soft smiles. She even stood closer to me now. So, it was working. At its own pace, at her pace. It was working.

"So, you think I'm irresistible?" I ask, taking a sip of the wine.

Her eyes widen, and her eyebrows furrow. "That is not what I said."

I grin, liking her flustered. "It's what I heard."

"*Necesitas checar tus oídos,*" she mumbles in Spanish, trying to hide her pink cheeks by taking a sip. I raise a brow.

I don't understand much Spanish since the last time I took a language course was my freshman year of college. And

I know that Google Translate isn't the best, but I keep it up on my browser for when I really need it, at least until I buy myself a dictionary or full on course and start really learning. For now, I glean enough from her tone to know it was something sarcastic.

"I'm going to take that as you agreeing with me."

She glares at me, but it's an empty glare because her cheek twitches. With one hand, she grips the railing, swaying slightly, and I watch.

"You are impossible," she mumbles, but finally, she *smiles*, and my entire body burns at the sight. Her entire face lights up, her molten brown eyes brighten, and it's one of the most beautiful things I've ever seen in my life. I'd do just about anything to keep that smile on her face. "When is your actual birthday?"

"July twenty-fourth."

"A true Leo baby," she says as a breeze passes by, and she stretches, pulling down the sleeves her crewneck, goosebumps appearing on the skin.

I cock my head. "Come on." Instead of waiting for her response, I softly grip her hand and pull her inside and take a deep breath, motioning to my room. Reveling in the fact that she hasn't pulled her hand from mine yet. "I figured since I picked all the music, if you wanted to, we could come up here and watch a movie or TV one night. Your choice."

Nina doesn't instantly deny it but raises a brow.

"Complete with a pillow wall, of course. I just got you here. I'd rather not chase you away."

Again she smiles, looking at the floor before back at me. "It's your weekend. I guess I can make that work."

I rub my thumb over the inside of her wrist, brushing over her pulse before squeezing her hand gently and letting it go. Being around her is like breathing in the air right before it rains. It's fresh and comforting. That's the only way I know how to describe it.

And I am so selfishly excited that she came this weekend, that I can spend all weekend continuing to figure her out, what she likes, what she hates. I don't know much, but I know a little from what I've picked up on.

She likes red. She wears it all the time, even right now with her crewneck.

She always wears a ring on her right pointer finger, and she spins it when she's nervous.

And despite having that hard exterior, she blushes easier than anyone I've ever met.

I know those things, little things that are starting to add up and form the girl in front of me, but it's already not enough. I want to know everything there is to know about her. All the little things, the big things, *everything.*

"What are you thinking about?" Nina nudges me, drawing me back into the present, with her empty wineglass in her hand.

My eyes roam over her face. The smooth skin, the freckles, the shape of her nose. "You."

"Jackson," she says it skeptically, and I frown.

"You asked, and I answered. I'm not making it up. I'm not bullshitting you. Promise."

Nina lets out a sigh, but her shoulders lose some of the tension that appeared. And I know that I'll never lie to her, never give her a reason to not believe me when I say something.

I tap her temple gently. "Hey, get out of there. You're here to have fun, okay? That's it." I don't give her time to fight it. "Now come on, let's go eat."

I step forward and hold my hand out, hoping she'll take it and knowing I'll keep trying if she doesn't. But Nina reaches out and grips my hand in hers gently, and my heart soars.

Nina

The hot July sun beats down on my bare skin.

I'm spread out on the towel, buried in my book, letting the rays darken my already brown skin. Along with the ocean waves crashing into the shore behind me, where my toes are buried in the sand, there's a low hum of music coming from the speaker Jackson brought and the occasional shout or squeal from everyone on the shore running in and out of the water.

I jumped in as soon as we touched the sand after breakfast, but since then, I haven't really left this spot. Harper and Sloan are asleep on the towel next to me, and every once in a while, Roman will run up, scroll on his phone and show me a funny joke, or Jackson will plop on our shared towel and doze beside me. Last time I checked, he and Roman were throwing a ball with the guys from their jobs.

They showed up at breakfast, introducing themselves with names I've sadly already forgotten, and pulling out their own alcohol stashes, which instantly earned thumbs up from us. They've been chill all day, talking to us like they've known us forever and just having a good time. So far, the weekend is going better than expected.

The feel of shockingly cold water droplets landing on my back draws me back to reality, and I turn my head just in time to see Jackson shaking his curls out before collapsing on his back next to me. I roll my eyes as he grins at me, stretching one arm over the top of my book.

"Hey!" I frown, but then think better of myself. "Actually, stay right there. I can use you as a book stand." Pulling my book from under his arm, I rest the spine on top of it.

"I can't believe you're just using me for my body," he says, his blue eyes twinkling in the sunlight.

"Oh, please." I tuck a lose strand of hair behind my ear. "You'd probably love that."

He watches me for a second. "Yeah, you're right. I'd let you use me anytime." I shake my head, fighting a grin and trying to focus on the page at hand. "Come on, come swim with me. Please."

My eyes coast slowly down his outstretched body, from his eyes to his lips quirked up into a smile to the freckle right under his left pec and the spattering of them on his right ribcage to the sand dusting his legs. I have no shame in the fact that I took my time checking him out, wondering all the places I could discover, not even when he raises a brow as I reconnect my eyes with his. I place my bookmark.

"Fine, but first you have to answer some questions."

He raises a brow, amusement lighting up his face. "Is this an interview?"

"Maybe."

He chuckles, his body shaking with it, and he adjusts, moving slightly closer to me, and our legs touch. "What do you wanna know?"

I rest my head in my palm, leaning on my elbow. "Anything. Your life, your job, what you like, what you hate, I don't care. But you have to be honest."

"All right, well first, I love my job. I love PR, love getting to help people show themselves to the world for whatever it may be. I got into it because it was a way for me to connect with people and often. Even in a professional setting, I love people, and I want them to be the best versions of themselves." He never takes his eyes off me as he continues. "I hate burnt toast and when people eat greasy food on planes. Third, I'll never lie to you. You don't have to ask me to be honest, Nina. I will always be honest with you."

He meets my eyes, and I inhale as he repeats the similar sentiment from last night. I want to believe him, and I know he doesn't mean little white lies, since we all have those, but he seems so sincere, so open about it that it's hard not to trust him. Because as of now, he's never given me a reason to not believe him.

I sit up, leaning on the heels of my feet, and his eyes follow me as I stand and hold out my hand. "Let's go swimming."

Jackson's eyes trail slowly down my body, taking in every inch of exposed skin and the red bikini. My skin burns from his gaze as he looks at me. They pause on the scattered ink on my skin, at least the ones he can see, before flicking back up to my eyes.

My breath catches in the hollow of my throat. The intense gaze sends a rush of heat that settles deep into my stomach and pulses with every breath. A playful smile graces his lips as he grips my hand and lifts himself. I step back, and he follows, not letting go of my hand, and my eyes narrow as his grip tightens.

"Jackson, don't."

The smile widens, both dimples appearing. "Don't what?" He steps forward and holds so tightly that I can't move and pulls me in and upwards, tossing me with ease over his shoulder, causing me to squeal.

He gives my butt a light pat, and my cheeks burn, and I just know he's grinning from ear to ear as he rests his hand fully on my butt.

Dios mío, gracias.

I lean up, placing my hands on his lower back, his skin warm and soft and grainy from the sand, and I attempt to shout for my friends. "Harper!" She lifts her head, startled, and grins as soon as she sees me.

"Have fun!" she shouts back, making no move to help me. Luckily for me, Roman joins in and drags her up and off the towel, surprise spreading over her features. I love karma. A few of the guys watch with amusement, two of them collapsing next to Sloan, who is also watching with a smile.

"Jackson, please," I whine loudly as the first splashes of water hit me from his footsteps. He adjusts, now cradling me as he wades in deeper, and the brisk saltwater splashes onto me. When it hits my butt, I look up at him, pleading. "Let me walk. I promise I'll swim."

"Baby, there's no fun in that," Jackson says, and my brain short-circuits at his word choice, and I barely even register his arms disappearing until the water starts hitting me.

Luckily, I recover quickly enough to grab his hand as he lets go and pull him in with me. Shock flashes quickly over his face as we get pulled under by a baby wave. My hair sticks to my cheeks as I emerge from the salt-water.

Jackson comes up next to me, grabbing my hand and pulling me towards him. I splash him, trying to get him away but failing as he captures my other hand.

"Are you having fun so far?" he asks, the water rising and falling around us.

I nod, completely honest. I think back to this morning, waking up in the pale yellow room with Sloan and walking downstairs to Jackson asking how I liked my coffee. And I think about the breakfast Roman made and how Jackson wouldn't stop playing footsie under the table with me. And how he has done and thought of everything to make me comfortable.

"Yes, it's great. It's perfect."

You're great, I think to myself and mean it. Because he is.

He smiles, shading me from the sun behind him and despite the cool temperature, I'm warmed just by him being near me. Like my own personal sun.

I think I might like it. Think I might really like him. No matter how much it scares me.

As he goes to respond, Roman shouts in the distance, and we turn our heads, looking toward the sand, and my stomach drops.

"Oh shit." Jackson sighs. He cracks his neck before pulling us through the water toward the shore.

My hand turns clammy, and I pull it out of his as soon as my feet touch the sand. He turns and looks at me, and I hope he isn't mad, but when I see Myles and Emma placing beach towels and chairs down, I can't help but feel the need to retreat.

Jackson gives me a small nod and smiles at me, and the understanding gleam in his eyes tells me he isn't mad.

But I'm frustrated that I feel like this. That I feel the need to pull away. That Myles showed up at all.

Everything was going great, and now I have no idea what to do or how to act. And I'm so sick of letting Myles have some stupid hold over my life, whether he knows it or not.

With a deep breath, I plaster a smile on my face and try to do everything in my power to not let this ruin my trip. Or ruin what I'm starting to feel for Jackson.

Fourteen | Nina

The orange flames from the small fire pit dance in the darkness and music plays from the speaker on a folded-out chair no one is using. All the evidence of dinner has been tossed into neat bags to take inside and throw away, and we all have red solo cups in our hands.

I pull the large *Georgia* hoodie that Jackson wore the night before tighter against my skin as a breeze comes in off the water, and his arm that's tossed over my shoulder pulls me in tighter to his chest.

Myles stands directly across from me; I can see his dark skin through the flames that flicker upwards, and I know his eyes are focused on Jackson's hold on me. Whether Jackson cares or notices I can't tell, but I look away and stupidly, drunkenly, I lift my cup towards Myles before taking a sip.

He just stares. And I sigh. Stupid, this was so stupid.

Ever since we stepped onto the beach, for me, there'd been an air of awkwardness everywhere I go. Myles's confusion was clear on his face when we approached him even though he tried to mask it quickly, but I could practically see the questions forming in his head. We played it civil, greeting each other with awkward hugs. Harper barely spoke to him at all, trying to keep calm, and so Sloan had to be the middleman. But as soon as the sun had started to set, I felt the need to drink to fight off the uncomfortable feelings.

Not that it's really working, but I don't care.

"I can't believe we lost today," Roman exclaims, alluding to the beach volleyball game we had played earlier. It had been all of us girls against six boys, and we had come out victorious, and Roman was still bitter. The other men had left except for two, Leo and Nick, both of whom were seated next to Sloan.

The four of us, including Emma, had made a pretty good team. She was kinder than I thought, and genuine, and really funny. And it kind of made it impossible to hate her, even if I wanted to. Which I didn't.

"Is someone still upset?" Harper coos sarcastically, and Roman raises an eyebrow as he quickly leans forward to pinch both of her sides, causing her to fall off her chair into the sand. "Dude, come on."

"Dude." He mocks playfully as she flips him off, and I can't help but laugh with Sloan, who's seated next to me. Roman reaches out a hand to help Harper up, and she takes it with a smile.

I take another sip as my right hand finds warmth by touching Jackson's back. My hand is slipped under his long sleeve and splayed across his hot skin. The alcohol has created a slight buzz, and I don't mind it. Because it makes me lower my guard a bit more. Despite Myles being here.

And I think Jackson likes it that I'm touching him, even innocently, because whenever I circle my thumb or move my hand even slightly, he sends me a deep gaze that sends sparks over my entire body.

But my hand falls when Jackson reaches for his phone, turning up the volume. "I love this song," he says and grabs my drink and places it in the sand upright. "Come on, we're dancing."

My heart stops for a second as my eyes flicker over the group. Roman is currently attempting to get Harper to dance, obnoxiously swaying their hands back and forth until she laughs. My eyes flicker to Sloan, who just leans back with her new friends and nods encouragingly. Even Emma smiles softly, pulling Myles up and into their own dance, unaware of the fleeting, cold look he throws my way.

I turn away from him and give in to Jackson, wrapping both my arms around Jackson's torso and slipping my hands under his shirt again. He lifts his cheek from the top of my head as I do, giving me a soft smile, and we're not really dancing as much as just swaying, but I don't mind.

I brush my thumb over his smooth skin, right above the band of his shorts, and I feel the vibrations of his soft laugh. "Why are you laughing at me?" I mumble into his chest, where my head rests.

"I'm not, really. It's just, you're a touchy drunk. I like it, a lot," he mumbles, his mouth closer to me so I can hear him. His lips brush the shell of my ear, and I can't help but shiver.

"I'm not drunk."

He snorts. "You've barely touched me at all, and now suddenly I'm a hot commodity? I'm not complaining, believe me, but you're drunk. At least a little."

I lift my head up, but the action makes his blue eyes spin, so I close them and rest my head back on his chest. "Maybe I am and maybe I am not." I hiccup. "But touching and all that, it just makes me uncomfortable sometimes."

"Nina, I've barely stopped touching you since we met. Why didn't you tell me to stop?" He asks, and he sounds serious, but his words are being jumbled by the alcohol.

With no inhibitions, I answer him honestly as my hands spread out on his back.

"I like it when you touch me, Jackson."

For a second, briefly, I feel his heartbeat speed up through his shirt right where my head is, and I like that I did that. I affected him. Because he affects me in ways I haven't felt in years, but also in new ways, ways I've never felt. I don't voice these to him, mostly because I'm scared, but I think I'm getting better. Or I'm trying at least.

Because I do want him to know I like when he touches me; it wakes me up, burns me in the best way. Or when he looks at me with those dark blue eyes that can be as light as crashing waves or as dark as the midnight sky, I can't think about anything else.

I look up when he still hasn't answered, and I'm shocked when I see a tinge of pink on his tan cheeks.

"Are you blushing?" I say, and I can't stop smiling. "I got you to blush. This is like a power trip, I love this feeling. So, so much."

He pinches my side gently, causing me to squirm. "We don't speak of this."

"But I like it." Hiccup. I mumble my next words into his chest, *"Es lindo, eres lindo." It's cute, you're cute.* And I feel his warm gaze on me. If he understood, he gives no indication, so my secret is still safe with me. "But I'm hungry, can we go get a snack?"

Jackson leans back to look at me, a warm smile on his face. "Yes, any requests?"

"A grilled cheese? Is that possible? I really want a grilled cheese."

The vibrations of his chuckle thrum against my body. "If it's a grilled cheese you want, it's a grilled cheese you shall get."

I push back a bit, dancing back and forth on my feet. "Really? You'd make that for me?"

Both dimples appear. "Yes, for you." I nod excitely and grab my drink from the sand as he grabs his phone. "We'll be back. You guys good out here?" he asks, and everyone nods, and I'm just thankful I *don't* feel Myles heavy gaze on me.

"Piggyback ride?" I ask, hiccupping as I grip my drink and phone in hand, and instead of answering, Jackson just takes my drink and sets it down, before holding out his arms. I climb up, and he hands me my drink. I take a long sip and hold it to him. "Want some?"

He squeezes my leg where he holds it after he takes a sip. "How much tequila have you had?"

I lean down, resting my head on his shoulder as he starts walking again. "Probably too much."

Jackson carries me up the small dune in the darkness until the light on the porch appears and casts a soft glow over the sand. He climbs the stairs easily and pushes open the French double doors, turning on only the light above the stove, leaving us in a warm glow. Easily, he sets me down on the island countertop, where I happily swing my feet, hiccups still racking my chest. Every time they do, Jackson sends me an amused glance.

I watch as Jackson moves easily around the kitchen, pulling out the bread and the various cheeses, butter, and water. He pours a large glass of it before doing anything else and hands it to me.

"Drink up." He crosses his arms, leaving no room for debate, and I oblige, downing the entire thing. To my chagrin, he just refills it but places it next to me this time.

The smell of butter melting fills the kitchen, and I sip the water slowly. "I have an idea."

He turns and leans against the opposite counter.

"After my wonderful sandwich, do you want to watch a movie?" I ask, making an effort this time.

He grins instantly, adding the prepared sandwich to the pan, and I hear the sizzle immediately. "I like that plan. Anything in mind?"

I take a slow sip and watch as his eyes stray to my bare legs and take them in, in a long sweeping glance. "I'll browse my options when we get upstairs."

He nods and flips the bread, and I finish my second glass. "The tattoo on your spine, it's in Spanish. Can I ask what it says?"

I smile. "It's the song 'God Only Knows.' It's for my parents. My dad and I used to play it every Sunday morning when we'd wake my mom up with breakfast. It just became our thing."

Jackson moves closer, until he's right in front of me. "That's pretty. Not as pretty as you, but pretty."

His voice is low, and it sends chills down my spine. I swallow, my heart beating wildly in my chest when he looks at me deeply. Jackson reaches up a hand, tucking a loose strand of my hair behind my ear. His breath fans lightly over my face as his other hand rests lazily on my thigh. My eyes flick between his darkening eyes, which are flared with heat, and his slightly parted lips.

The tapping of his fingertips on my legs sends small shockwaves over my skin and into my nervous system. Each one is more electric than the last, sending a swell of heat into my lower stomach that floods out to the very ends of my fingertips, and my cheeks flush thoroughly. My hand tightens around the glass in my hand until my fingers turn white as he effectively cages me in. Jackson's more intoxicating than any sip of alcohol I've ever had.

"I hate to do this, but the grilled cheese. It's gonna burn." I reach up and pat his cheek softly, hiding a cheeky smile as the smell of toasting bread fills the air.

His eyes lighten up as they flicker with amusement, and he laughs before reaching behind me, pulling the hood up over my head, and tugging the strings tightly until most of my face is covered. I feel the loss of his energy immediately when he pulls his hand off my leg, but I can still feel the soft touch on my skin like a ghost.

I watch through my obstructed view as he cuts the sandwich diagonally on a plate and hands it over to me. I greedily accept it and take the first bite, letting the different cheeses melt on my tongue, and then offer a bite to him.

"I don't ever want to eat anyone else's grilled cheese. This is the best one I've ever had. Seriously, you're a master. Have you considered going on *Chopped*?"

The deep laugh that escapes him echoes around the kitchen. "Mom's secret recipe," he says as I pull the hood off my head.

"She must be great."

"She is."

I smile and continue eating the best grilled cheese known to man. I offer him a few bites here and there, and then alternate by sipping my third water since coming inside. Jackson stretches his arms above his head, and my eyes go straight to the sliver of skin that appears above the band of his shorts. Thoughts and images start flooding my head all at the mere glance of his skin.

"I'm gonna clean up, take a quick shower, and then you can pick the movie, is that good?" he asks, sipping his own water. I jump down from the counter, landing with a slight stumble on my feet.

"No, I'll clean up. You go, and I'll meet you upstairs. You've done plenty, and I'm fine," I say and attempt to push him into the hallway. If he wasn't making it easy on me, I'm not sure I would've moved him at all.

I lean up and place a brief kiss on his cheek, my heart beating wildly, and when I pull back, I see a light dusting of pink on his cheeks again. Jackson shakes his head and holds up his hands in defeat. "Aye, aye captain. I'll see you upstairs."

I turn back and walk towards the sink, and through the window I can just make out the flames coming from the bonfire. Everything else is too far away to make out, so I grab the pan and the plate to soap them up as I put away the bread and the butter. Jackson already put away the cheese, as if to hide the recipe.

After everything is properly washed and drying on a dish rack, I soap and rinse the sink before shutting off the water. I know my stash of candies are packed away in my bag upstairs, and that should be enough for us during the movie.

As I shove my phone in my pocket and start to move towards the hallway, the French door opens, letting a gust of air in, and I turn. Myles stands in the kitchen across the counter from me with his arms crossed, and those dark brown eyes are trained on me. When we were growing up as kids to when we started dating, I could always tell when something was wrong or if he was upset. And even after all these years, the tell-tale signs haven't changed.

His eyebrows are ever-so-lightly furrowed, and his jaw is so tense I see the muscles twitch. His brown eyes go from warm and welcoming to cold and calculating.

My heart skips a beat or two or three as we stand there in an extremely palpable silence, and my teeth dig into the inside of my lip. My palms are sweaty where they rest inside the hoodie's pocket, and I pull a shaky hand out and run it through my hair.

"Nina, can we talk?"

Fifteen | Nina

Painful silence envelops the kitchen.

I want to turn on my heel and run tail-tucked out of this kitchen. The tension between us is like a stretched-out rubber band waiting to snap.

"Yeah, of course," I murmur, resting my palms flat on the counter, trying to ground myself with the feel of the cold surface and slow my heartbeat.

Myles swallows hard, and his eyes connect with mine, deep pools of brown that I used to love. Right now, they're cold as stone. "I was going to apologize."

I furrow my brows, trying to keep myself from nervously tapping my fingernails.

"At the wedding when we were dancing. That's what I was beginning to say. That I was sorry, for everything. For how I ended things, for how I treated you during school and when I came home. For not being honest, for leading you on."

I roll my bottom lip into my mouth. "You *were* going to apologize?" I say, noting his choice of words.

He sighs, running a hand backwards over his waves as goosebumps erupt on my skin, even buried in the warm hoodie. Myles trails his eyes over the sweatshirt I've been wearing for the past few hours, and judgement emits off of him in waves, but I hold my gaze.

"I'm still sorry. I am, but this? You being here, with Jackson? I don't understand. I thought I was crazy when I saw you two dance at the wedding. Thought it was nothing. But I was wrong."

For the love of god, he must be joking.

"Even if that apology was genuine, I don't want that from you." Anger starts to flood my veins, but I keep my voice even. "I spent far too long waiting for one, and I couldn't care less whether you're sorry or not. The best apology is changed behavior, and based on who Emma thinks I am, I'm not seeing much of that."

"I'm not talking about Emma and me," he counters, and I can hear how hard it is for him to keep his own voice level.

"Well, I don't want to talk about Jackson. That's my business, not yours."

"He's my best friend. I think I have a right to know."

I roll my eyes and take a deep breath. "You don't actually. You don't have a right to anything."

"Did you meet him at the wedding?"

"No, Myles. When I met him, I had no idea who he was," I say. I don't know why I even tell him, but if I can avoid this going any further that's my goal.

"But that didn't stop you."

"Stop me from what?"

"From sleeping with him."

The tell-tale signs of my anger start to appear.

My throat is starting to close, and my eyes prick, which only adds to my frustration. I press my tongue to the roof of my mouth and look to the ceiling until the pressure at my tear-ducts subsides. My anger is a combination of his accusing tone and the fact that I know he *knows* I haven't slept with him. Because he used to know me better than anyone. I know for a fact he's only saying this shit because he knows it'll hurt me, and the frustration and hurt is practically boiling my blood.

"Screw you. I don't owe you shit. Whether I am or am not sleeping with him is my business and mine alone. You're happy, Myles, or you should be. You're fucking married. Why don't you worry about that instead of me? Grow up."

Whatever alcohol is left in my system is only adding to my emotions, and I can't keep the bite out of my words. Because I've been nothing but supportive to him. Nothing but kind. For years, I've done nothing but cater to him. Today, I tried endlessly to ease the tension, and this is what I get.

His eyes are hyper focused on me. "I am happy."

"Well then act like it. Why does it matter what I do?"

"Because it's you. It's Jackson and it's you, Nina. It's like I don't know you anymore."

I curl my hands into fist on top of the counter and dig my nails into my palm. This is ridiculous.

"You don't know me anymore, Myles."

"But you're Nina. You—"

"I am nothing to you."

We stare off for a moment, but there are more words on my tongue, and I've been holding all of these emotions in tightly. Locked away in my own version of Pandora's box. Over time, I've turned most of my anger into understanding. My sadness into acceptance. But this?

Myles just took a hammer to the lock and let the box spring open.

"I am *your* nothing. You made that clear all those years ago. You're so full of shit. Me and you are nothing more than old friends, remember? I am not your girlfriend. I am not your old friend. We are barely even acquaintances."

His eyes narrow. "Why'd you come to the wedding then?"

At this point, I'm searching for the purpose of this stupid conversation.

"Why'd you fucking invite me?" I counter, and I'm no longer concerned with the level of my voice. "I went because I wanted to see you happy and moved on. I felt that I owed that to us, to myself, to see you happy. So, imagine how I feel right now. I was mature enough to go to your fucking wedding, and you're here bitter and angry about my life? It's bullshit."

"I just don't get it. This isn't you."

"Did I not make myself clear? You don't know me."

Myles clenches and unclenches his jaw as we stand there. It's painful standing in this kitchen repeating myself when I shouldn't even have to. I see something flash in the window under the porch light, but my eyes flicker back to him.

"It's all coming out wrong, I'm sorry. It's just—I'm hurt."

"Hurt? Fuck you, Myles." I huff and shake my head; my breathing is shallow, and my legs are shaking with adrenaline. "Nothing I'm doing is hurting you. You said you wanted to talk, but all you've done is berate me and attempt to make me feel guilty over something trivial."

I don't let him get a word in before I continue.

"What I am or am not doing with whomever I choose is none of your goddamn business. I'm done with whatever this is. This is nothing, we are nothing, and we haven't been for years. Get that through your head and treat your wife like she deserves to be treated."

My eyes prick again, and I'm not sure how much longer I'll be able to hold the tears back. I hate that I cry when I'm angry. I hate it. All of my emotions are like a crack in a glass, just getting deeper and deeper until it starts to shatter.

He opens his mouth to speak, but I shake my head. "Save it. I'm done with this conversation," I say, finally, and turn on my heel down the hall and head up the stairs.

My chest is heavy, and my head is pounding with the effort of holding in these tears as I grip my sides tightly with my own arms. I refuse to let Jackson see me like this, so I head into my room first, shutting the door behind me and collapsing on the floor, leaning my back against the bed.

I bring my knees up to my chest and lean my head back. The tears start their descent down my cheeks and onto my neck in a slow trail. I don't even know what emotion pushed me over the edge.

Anger, sadness, guilt. I'm so frustrated it's painful.

My chest shakes with the effort I'm exerting to hold in the sobs. Tears are one thing, but I refuse to sob over that assault-like conversation. Who does he think he is? Asking me questions about my life and my decisions?

I hold my hands gently on my temples as I force myself to take deep breaths, blinking every so often to speed along the tears. My teeth are digging into my lip as I try to focus on the feeling of that instead of the speed of my heartbeat, making sure to actively blow my deep breaths out instead of letting them sit on my chest.

I don't want him to ruin this for me. But I can feel it weighing me down already.

Despite it, I grab the candy, determined to try to salvage the night, and shove it into my pocket. I head into the bathroom next to my room before Jackson's. I run my hands under cold water and splash it lightly on my flushed cheeks, trying to cool them down and swipe the water directly under my eyes to fight the puffiness. After a moment, it looks more like I got winded running up the stairs than had a full-on crying fest in my room. My eyes are a little red like they always are after I cry, and my skin is hot, but neither of those are dead giveaways to a miniature breakdown.

When I enter, the only light illuminating the light blue space is ESPN playing on the TV, and there is already a pillow wall on the bed—a small one—because it's literally two pillows. Jackson is standing by his dresser, but he turns as I enter. He's got on low hanging sweatpants and nothing else.

But not even the sight of a shirtless Jackson completely erases the previous events.

He smiles at me warmly, his eyes flickering with confusion as he takes in my slightly disheveled appearance, because cold sink water can only do so much. Thankfully, he doesn't say anything about that.

"Ready?"

I pull out the candy. "All set."

"You know the way to my heart." He motions to the bed. "After you."

I place the candy on the pillow wall, place my phone on the nightstand, and climb in with my refilled water bottle under my arm. The feel of the soft sheets comforts me immediately as I snuggle in, leaning on the single pillow between us.

He climbs in on the other side and hands me the remote. I make eye contact with his deep blue eyes in the low light. They're still searching my face, and concern is clear in them, but I appreciate his not asking more than anything.

I scroll till I come across *Ghost*, and I pause. "Is this okay?"

"Anything you choose is fine, Nina." He glances at me and I click play.

Sitting there next to him, I want to chase the warmth I felt less than an hour ago. When I couldn't stop touching him and wanted to be anywhere close to him. But now, even though Myles is very much alive, it's like his ghost, the ghost of our relationship, is chasing me.

And I don't know how to fight it.

've known something was wrong since Nina climbed into my bed last night.

Her face was red, and her eyes were slightly puffy, but it was clear she didn't want to talk about it. Which was fine. She didn't say much when she woke up, curled into a ball as close to the edge of the bed as she could've gotten, and things hadn't improved at breakfast. It was awkward, and she was quieter than usual, only pulling Sloan and Harper away for a moment before the food was ready.

On top of that, every time I try to engage with Myles or talk to him, I'm met with a short, concise answer. It's obvious he's angry. He's never hidden that well, but the tension has pulled tighter every second since this morning and even now as we're on the beach. Roman and I are sitting back with Emma while everyone else had gone swimming. The girls were tossing the football back and forth last time I looked, but when I look up now, I see Harper following Myles out of the water, her hands moving wildly as Myles angrily holds a football in his hand.

"Uh-oh," Roman mumbles looking at the scene.

Even though I know it must be something to do with Myles and Nina, no one has told me a damn thing. And I have a feeling that everyone knows something but me, maybe excluding Emma, but she's been quiet all day too.

"What's going on?"

No one answers my question as we're interrupted by the arrival of everyone. Myles turns to look at Nina and strides closer to her, turning her towards him. His voice is low, but I hear the words loud and clear. "Can you control your friend?"

Nina furrows her brows, looking at him angrily as I stand up. "Don't touch me, Myles."

"She hit me in the gut, Nina. What's her fucking deal?"

She shrugs her shoulders. "I don't know, why don't you ask her?"

Myles shakes his head and steps closer, Nina's eyes flicking between Harper and Emma. "This is wrong, and you know it."

I clench my jaw and step up next to them. Myles glares at me, holding onto Nina tightly. "How 'bout you lay off?" I motion to his hold on her and step closer, causing him to step back.

Myles sneers, letting out a laugh that is void of all humor. "God, this is bullshit."

Emma speaks up from behind me, softly. "Myles, stop it."

He glances at her but fixes me with the cold, angry look once more. "You're so full of it."

Anger floods my veins as I start to put some pieces together. "Spit it out, Myles." And I know I'm not one hundred percent innocent, know that he saw Nina and I together last night and how I haven't really left her side.

I know he's putting together his own puzzle, but I also know he has a tendency to overreact, overexaggerate things, so I have no idea what he thinks is going on between us. Because as of now, it's not much. Yes, I should've told him right away, but I didn't.

And now we all have to deal with the consequences.

He glances between Nina and I, eyes latching onto where my hand is lightly touching her side. I didn't even realize I did it. I meet her gaze and nod gently to the towels, hoping she'll go sit down and remove herself from the situation. Thankfully, she does.

"I can't believe you," he says, watching the exchange.

I raise a brow. "Whatever I did or didn't do, I'm sure it doesn't warrant you acting like this much of an asshole."

He chuckles. "You know what you're doing. Why the fuck is Nina here?"

I cross my arms, my jaw clenching tighter. "What does it matter?"

"Just give me a straight answer, fuck. I'm not stupid. I saw you two at the wedding, and then I show up here, and she's here. You can't do that."

This time I chuckle lowly. I could easily tell him nothing has happened, because it hasn't, but it's none of his goddamn business, not when he's acting like this. "I can't what?" I want him to be an adult and spit it out.

"Date her. Pursue her. Whatever the fuck it is, it can't happen."

I nod slowly, as I glance around. I notice Nina and Emma next to each other. Guilt sits heavy on Nina's shoulders, but Emma looks anything but mad at her as they hold hands in the sand. Harper looks like she wants to tackle him.

"You mean I can't date your ex?" I narrow my eyes, and he stares angrily back as I step closer. My own anger growing. "The girl that you broke up with and are no longer with? That one?" He doesn't say anything. "Let me clear some things up for you. One, we're not dating." Which is true. For now. "Two, if I want to pursue her, considering I met her way before I knew she was your ex, I will." Also true. "Three, I was going to fucking tell you if it got more serious. I was going to tell you as soon as I got home from this trip that you didn't even tell me you were coming on."

"That shouldn't matter. You still hid it," he bites out.

And yes, he's got a point. I know what I did was wrong, and I'll own up to it.

"I know that. I should've told you from the beginning, you're right. But let's get one thing straight, this isn't about you being mad that she's here." I lower my voice so no one else can hear it, not afraid to be brutally honest. "You're mad she's moving on. Even though your fucking *married*, you're upset about it. Or at least don't know how to deal with it. And I'll tell you what, this is not how you deal with it."

"Fuck you."

Despite my anger, I'm also hurt. That he's not willing to even hear what I'm saying, to not even try to understand. We've been friends for years, best friends, and he's ready to throw everything away for a stupid fight. We're both in the wrong, I get that, but this is bullshit.

"Myles."

He purses his lips and holds up his hands. "I'm done with this. All of this."

I run a hand through my hair as I watch him stride off up the dune, past his wife and my friend, who watches with sad eyes, and my chest constricts at the sight. At everything. At the fact that my friend can't even listen to me, at the fact that he just strode past the love of his life without a second thought.

I look at Nina, who watches the whole thing with a careful gaze, and I feel like shit. This is exactly what she wanted to avoid when I convinced her to come here. She didn't want the pressure of anyone, of Myles knowing anything prematurely, and now that's royally fucked up too.

Even after a few deep breaths, I'm still so deeply angry. I don't want to make anyone's day worse or mope around when we've all been walking on eggshells all day, so I turn and stalk towards the ocean, wanting to be alone. Wanting to shove everything down and forget about it. I sit where the ocean meets the sand, letting the water run up and over my legs where I rest my elbows on my knees.

I'm not alone for long. I can sense her presence, attuned to it now, but I keep my eyes forward. She stands for a moment, hesitant, before taking a seat in the sand next to me. After a beat that feels endless, her shoulder brushes mine, and I exhale.

Turning to look at her, I see worry swims in her eyes. "Is that what was wrong last night? He said something to you." It's a statement not a question.

She sighs. "Yeah, in the kitchen."

I shake my head, chuckling dryly. "God, he's a dick sometimes."

Nina rests her hand on my arm, gently. "I'm sorry, for that fight, for all of this. I should've told you."

Without hesitation I meet her gaze again. "Nina, you didn't do anything wrong. You have nothing to apologize for. Not one thing." She opens her mouth, but I cut her off. "I should've been honest with him. That I wanted to pursue you. This is on me, not you."

"I don't want you to ruin your friendship. I don't want to be the reason."

"The only people that can ruin our friendship are Myles or me. Not you." We share a look, and I don't turn away until she exhales, hopefully agreeing with me or understanding what I'm trying to say. "I'm going to talk to him after this weekend, and we'll see what happens. But none of it is your fault."

The sun hits her warm, brown skin, highlighting all the sunspots, the random new freckles that appeared, and her dark brown eyes shine despite everything. Even now, I can't help but just enjoy her being next to me, just sitting here. How much calmer she makes me feel without even trying.

But I know she must be feeling a boatload of emotions that I'll never begin to understand. I've been in relationships before, none of them serious. But I've never been jaded or burned by anyone. Everything always ended easily. And I know that she's been hurt, burned by Myles more than I'll ever know.

I wish I could take it away.

Even though I can't, I remind her that everything is on her terms. I turn, facing her a bit more. "Listen, I know you must be feeling all sorts of things, and you don't ever have to tell me anything you don't want. But just try not to let him get in here any further." I reach up and tap gently on her forehead. "He doesn't deserve any more of your thoughts. It's your life, and you can do whatever you want, whether that's with me or someone else. He gets no say."

"Jackson," she says softly, looking down, and the way she says my name hits me in chest.

I smile. "Let's just try to enjoy the rest of the weekend. No pressure, no expectations, okay?"

Inside, I'm hoping that I still have a chance. That she wants to give me a chance. Because already, I don't want this to end.

Seventeen | Nina

I feel like I'm on a merry-go-round that keeps changing directions.

One moment, I feel fine, like the altercation with Myles never happened. That he never showed up, never confronted me or Jackson. They left shortly after everything. Luckily, I was able to pull aside Emma before they did and apologize. Instead of being upset or angry at me, she pulled me in for a hug and just held me there, and I held her back. She let me know she wasn't mad at me, that I wasn't at fault, and still I apologized again, to which she laughed. We made a promise to meet up soon, just the two of us. When I feel fine, I feel like I can continue getting to know Jackson and getting closer to him, because that's what I want.

The next second I feel like all this is going to lead to me getting burned again. That I'm dancing too close to the flames, and everything is going to end as quickly as it started. I feel bad because Jackson deserves someone who is open and ready and excited for this, not terrified of it.

Even so, if he is bothered by it, it never shows. He never makes me feel like there is anything wrong with me.

"I need to finish packing, you wanna come?" Jackson asks from where he sits across from me.

Harper and Roman are on a walk on the beach, despite the clouds and the occasional drizzle of rain. And Sloan is currently in the kitchen, checking her laptop for new appointments. I glance to her, and she gives me an encouraging nod, knowing all my fears and anxiety and trying to quell them.

I nod. "Yeah."

Jackson smiles softly, and we stand, heading upstairs to his room. I take a seat on the bed, pulling my legs up. He's been nothing but understanding since yesterday, making sure I'm okay, but I've noticed he's quieter today, upset about his friend and attempting to be the same sunshine boy we all know. Part of me worries he's just putting on a show, but it's not my place to say that right now or to force the answer out. I'm just doing the best I can for both of us.

"Hey," I say. He glances over at me. "You know it's okay to be upset, right? If you are." I meet his eyes, his hands holding a shirt closely. "Not saying we have to talk about it, but you've been nothing but kind to me, and I want you to know if you want to talk about it, you can. If you don't, that's fine too. But I'm here for you."

And I mean that, deeply. I may be unsure of what to do next, but we're friends now, at least in my mind. I want to be there for him.

He smiles, one of his dimples even appearing. "Thank you, Nina."

I nod, and we fall into a comfortable silence. My eyes flicker around the room, landing on a picture that I haven't seen before on his nightstand.

I reach up and pick it up, confusion flooding my brain.

It's a young Jackson, maybe ten or eleven, and two other kids who look nothing like him. One is clearly Hispanic, brown skin and deep hair, maybe a little younger than Jackson, and the other looks like the parents. She's got slightly lighter brown skin and kinky curly hair on top of her head. Jackson is holding her in his arms with a big smile as she tugs on his blond curls. The woman, who I assume is his mom, is smiling big, her arm wrapped around her husband, her white smile a contrast to her smooth dark brown skin. Even through the picture, I can see where he gets his energy from. She's warm and inviting and looks like she loves giving big hugs. His dad, who has light brown hair and fair skin, is watching her in the picture with a big smile on his face.

Even though I'm pretty sure it's obvious, I look up at him. "Is this your family?"

Jackson turns and smiles when he sees the picture I'm looking at. He pauses from packing, which is him neatly folding everything and then undoing all the work and tossing it haphazardly in the bag, and grabs the picture, taking a seat in front of me on the bed.

"Fun fact, I'm adopted," he says and purses his lips in a pose. I smile as I lean into his seated frame. "This is my mom Lula and my dad Michael. The best things to ever happen to me."

My heartbeat picks up as I see the joy spread over his face. Because I know it's genuine.

"After fostering me for a year, they finally accepted I was the greatest five-year-old ever and adopted me. And this one, Mateo," he points to the little boy, "came along when I was nine, I think. They fostered him for a year and then did the same thing."

I take a sip of the coffee I brought up with me and wait for him to go on.

"This is my parents' only biological child, Veah. She was a surprise to say the least. They weren't supposed to be able to have kids, hence the fostering, but one day my mom was pregnant."

He smiles, running a hand through his hair. "Don't tell Veah this, but I'm still my mom's favorite.

I roll my eyes. "How old are they now?"

"Mateo is three almost four years younger than me, so he's your age, I think, twenty-three? Veah is twenty, about to be twenty-one." He pauses, blue eyes flicking from me to the photo. "Jesus I'm old."

I can't help the loud laugh that escapes me because he looks mortified about his age, which is about to increase. "You're not old. You're only gonna be twenty-seven," I say and pat his cheek.

Jackson lays flat on his back on the cushy bed, covering his eyes with his arm. "You don't have to lie to me."

"Drama king," I say playfully, and he just pushes his thigh against mine in response. Underneath his arm, his lips curl into a smile.

Sometimes I swear he should be an actor; I take the picture from his hand and place my coffee on the table. "My mom would go crazy for your parents. She's a social worker and gets super attached to families when they end up adopting. Especially the ones that keep in touch."

"She sounds amazing." Jackson smiles before sighing gently. "I miss my parents."

A tiny wave of sadness washes over me as I watch him lie there. His hands are behind his head, and his eyes are focused on the ceiling.

"I talk to Mateo and Veah all the time, but my parents are always busy, so we miss each other's calls a lot. It's stupid but I always miss them this time of year. Labor Day was always a big day because I got adopted right before. So, it was always my holiday, and both mom and dad made it feel like that. Mom made me my own sweet tea and dad always took me to a movie that night." He glances over at me, those blue eyes shining. "I'd be lost without them, for sure."

"Is it hard to visit during Labor Day? Are they all still in Georgia?"

"Yup, same town, Peachtree Hills, Georgia. Same neighborhood, same house. Mateo and Veah both live in the city, only a quick drive away. Yeah, the beginning of September never fails to be busy work wise. If I have time, I usually come here. I visit other times, holidays and usually their birthdays, but it's just different."

I pause. I don't want him to think I'm pitying him. He doesn't seem like the type to enjoy being pitied, especially because he's built such a life for himself, but I also don't want to push pass the reality of it.

"They sound great. They all do. I'd be sad too if I couldn't visit as often," I say, tucking my hair behind my ear.

"I think I'm gonna try to fly them up in the fall. But we'll see."

I nod. "Well, there's no sweet tea that I'm aware of, but my parents go all out for Labor Day. You should come." I poke his laid-out frame. "I'd like it if you came."

My body warms as my heart pumps a little quicker. It's a simple invitation, but nerves dance over my skin, nonetheless. He turns onto his side and leans up on his arm, a few stray hairs curling over the top of his forehead. Despite my reservations still churning in my stomach, the invitation feels right. Just like that, any sign of sadness is gone, at least on the surface.

"Is someone warming up to me?"

I force my lips into a straight line and stare at him. "You annoy me."

His smile grows. "You don't mean that."

Those eyes stare into mine, and I can't fight the smile long, mostly because I can feel my cheeks getting warm as the heat crawls over my skin. "Yeah, yeah."

We talk a bit more about our families, just little things, and I feel his warmth as I sit so close to him. I want so badly to let him in, to let myself like him like I already know I'm starting to. To not pull away just because I'm scared of getting burned again. The more I'm around him and his brightness, I don't feel like I'm going to get burned or be blinded.

Instead, I feel like I'm opening my eyes and am about to touch the sun and live to tell about it.

. . .

"Nina." The sound of low music fills my ears, but I scrunch my eyes and curl into my crewneck. A low chuckle sounds in harmony with the song. "Come on, you're home."

I open my eyes slowly, confused by my surroundings for a moment. Instead of looking at the big Hamptons beach house, I'm back on my familiar dirty city street with streetlamps and horns blaring. We hit traffic immediately leaving the beach, and at some point, I must've passed out.

After blinking the sleep from my eyes, I'm face to face with an amused Jackson. He's slightly leaning over my frame that is curled into the seat and the center console with the dark cloudy sky behind him. His eyes twinkle.

My tired eyes flick between his eyes and his lips quickly. "I'm up, I'm up," I yawn.

I turn to see both Roman, Harper, and Sloan passed out in the back seat of the Jeep, and the soft rain continues to drip onto the soft top of the car. I sit up and stretch my arms out before turning around and pinching Harper's leg.

Her head shoots up from Roman's shoulder, and immediately her eyes narrow on my face. "You bitch, I hate when you do that," she groans and sits up, tapping Roman until he also wakes up.

Sloan blinks her eyes open, glancing to Harper. "How are you always so aggressive when you wake up?"

Harper blinks. "She pinched *me,* and I'm aggressive?"

I raise my brows, utterly amused by my two best friends. Sloan and I share a look. "Yes," we both chime.

"Well, hello, my beautiful people." Roman grins, and Jackson rolls his eyes as he turns off the car. I grab my small bag and jump out onto the sidewalk, pulling up my seat so the two in the back can get out. Jackson unloads all our bags, but instead of handing me mine, he just shrugs it over his shoulder, along with Sloan's, as Roman does the same thing.

The three of us lead the way up to the apartment. The familiar space greets us with open windows and the echo of rain. There's a note on the counter from my parents since they came and fed Jenko, which I'll read later. Jenko isn't in the living room, so I assume he's in my room, and I lead Jackson down the hall since he refuses to give me my bag.

"Where's the little guy at? I want to meet him," he says as he follows me. I open my door, flicking on the twinkle lights, and low and behold, Jenko is curled on my pillows. His ears perk up as his eyes take us in.

"You can just drop them on the floor. Thank you, you didn't have to carry them," I ramble with a soft yawn, still blinking sleep out of my eyes. Jackson doesn't say anything as he gently sets them down before making a beeline for the cat.

He reaches out a finger, and I wait for Jenko to shy away or act indifferent, but instead he reaches out his little nose. Jackson turns to look at me with a huge smile as I watch in genuine surprise as Jenko lets Jackson pet his head. Even more, Jackson reaches and picks him up, and Jenko goes without a fight.

I feel a bit betrayed here.

"Jackson and Jenko. We're kind of a dynamic duo."

I raise an eyebrow as I watch. "Two peas in a pod apparently." I shake my head, amused, and lean against my desk watching. Jackson meets my eyes from where he stands with my cat tucked into his arms. "Is there anything you want for your actual birthday? And don't say nothing."

Jackson trails his eyes over me, and I try to ignore my body's immediate response. The quickening of my heart and the warmth that starts to spread as he does. Even with a relaxed gaze, there's something deeply enticing about how slowly he looks at me, taking in every inch.

"An actual date."

I should've known. I roll my lips into my mouth before shrugging, my thoughts running to Myles and the drama from this weekend. I'm scared, I don't want it to be true, but I am. Still, even now, I am scared of what might happen.

Somehow, he must sense that. He stands, letting Jenko down gently, and steps closer to me. "Nina, I know this weekend didn't go as planned. I know that him coming was a wrench in everything, and if you want time, that's okay. But I really, really, want to take you out. Before he came, you smiled, you laughed, you had fun, and I just want to give you more of that."

My heart swells, and my head goes light, because I don't know what he sees in me. He's given me miles of space, showing me he's interested and genuine, and I've barely given him in an inch. Even after his fight, he made it about me, let me know I could do whatever I needed and still, even now, he does the same.

I don't think I'll ever deserve this sunshiny, selfless boy, but selfishly, I want him all to myself.

"Then a date you will get."

Jackson's face lights up, eyes sparkling with excitement, and the dimples pop immediately. The sight makes my stomach dip excitedly.

"Dreams do come true," he murmurs as he moves closer to me, close enough to touch, and I'm unable to help the small laugh that escapes me. I stand, pushing myself off the desk.

"Happy to be of service." Hesitantly, I step forward and wrap my arms around his waist. He tenses a bit, in surprise I think, before he returns the hug, and it's like being enveloped by the sun. "Thank you for this weekend, Jackson."

"Anytime, Scott," he says softly as his warmth curls around me. He squeezes me tighter before his arms loosen. "I better get Rome home before he falls asleep again. Punk."

I hit his chest lightly. "Be nice."

"I am always nice."

I roll my eyes and step back from him, but before I escape completely, he grips my wrist just a little tighter and leans forward. My breath hitches in my throat at the proximity, but he simply leans down and places a soft kiss on my cheek, pulling back with a smug smile.

"See you next Sunday. I'll text you with the details." He steps back, and I nod, my cheeks thoroughly warm. "Goodnight, Nina, and Jenko, of course."

Jenko gives a quiet meow in return, and I shake my head, following him out. I make sure to lock the door behind him and Roman, who gives me a quick hug before he leaves. I turn to see Sloan curled up on the couch under a blanket, asleep again. I go over to her and shake her.

"Hey, do you wanna come sleep in my room tonight?"

Her curls move when she turns over. "Did you say yes to a date yet?" She yawns, and I laugh, unsure of how this is her first thought.

"Yes."

She shoots up, wide awake. "You did?" I nod. She pulls me down into a hug, knocking the air out of me as we both land on the couch. "Nina, I'm so happy for you."

Harper appears with a frown. "Hey, where's my invite to the party?" She beelines for us and collapses next to us until we're squished.

"It's just a date," I mumble, but inside as much as I'm nervous, I'm also excited. So excited.

"Yeah, but you deserve it. So much." Harper pulls me into a hug this time, tightly.

Curled up with my best friends for life and the warmth of Jackson still lingering on my skin, I've never felt more welcome in my life. The drama sucked, but it also feels like a clean slate in a way. I'm walking away from Myles and whatever shitty things he wants to spit my way and into a different place with someone new.

Despite fear, I know I can't let it stop me forever. It seems like if I stumble or fall, Jackson will be there to try and set me back on my feet.

"Hi, *Mamá*."

I have to bite my lip to stop my groan from coming out as I step onto the subway and a flurry of Spanish comes out through my phone speakers.

"*¿Porque no me hablaste de este chico? ¿Cómo dijo Harper que se llamaba? Jackson?*" *Why didn't you tell me about this boy? What did Harper say his name was? Jackson?*

I am going to slap Harper when I get home. It seems she may or may not have let some information slip about my new dating life.

This is the downside of Harper practically being their second daughter. My parents talk to her just as often as—if not more than—they talk to me. Most of the time it doesn't bother me because Harper spent most of her life at my house and away from her deadbeat dad. Constant sleepovers, her own dresser, her own counter space in my bathroom. It's usually only when she spills my personal information that I feel any semblance of annoyance. But she is practically my sister, so I guess it comes with the territory.

I take a deep breath. "Because I'm still figuring things out, *Mamá*. I barely even know what's going on, but we have a date tomorrow."

"*¿Una cita?*" She practically shouts through the phone, and I have to hold it away from my hear, praying that the other people around me can't hear it. "*¿Es guapo? ¿Estas emocionada?*" *A date? He's handsome? Are you excited?*

"Yes and yes. Just don't tell dad, please. I'll tell him." I sigh, running a hand through my hair. "But I did invite him to the Labor Day party."

As I expected, she ignores my request to not tell Dad immediately. "*Mi vida!* Guess what?" she yells away from the phone, and I can just picture her dancing around the house until she finds my dad. "This is so exciting, *mi amor.* Although, you better bring him by before Labor Day. I want to meet him."

"*Mamá*, I need you to breathe. Can I get through the date first?"

"Sure, sure. But if I have to hear from my sweet Harper, who actually loves me, again, I'll never forget it."

"Yes, *Mamá.* I've gotta go, I'm about to be home. *Te amo,*" I sigh into the phone and wait for her response before hanging up.

This week has been ridiculous. Work was insane; everyone is editing and writing and preparing for the September issue. The cover feature keeps being postponed, which is causing an unnecessary amount of stress on every single person in the office. And now, my wonderful mom—and dad—know that Jackson exists.

Anyone I tried to date or talked to before never reached my parents' ears. Not even close. No one since Myles. So, for Harper to spill this, a name, and for me to admit there is a date—for my parents that automatically means its got potential. Add that to the fact that I have a date tomorrow, and you can change my name to Horrendously Stressed.

The walk up to my apartment door seems ten times longer and feels ten times more exhausting with my gym bag hung over my shoulder. I kick off my shoes at the door and pick them up to put in my room. The smell of food hits my nose immediately along with the low hum of Sloan and Harper talking in the kitchen.

As soon as I see Harper's frame bent over the counter, I glare at her. She smiles sheepishly at me as she nervously tucks her hair. "I take it you talked to your mom today?"

Sloan looks bored as she watches us, used to our never-ending antics, but I see her pour me a glass of wine out of the corner of my eye. I move everything to one hand so I'm able to pick up the glass, and I down half of it before looking back to Harper.

"*Tienes demasiada suerte que estoy muy cansada como para gritarte.*" *You're lucky I'm too tired to yell at you.*

I shake my head before heading to my room to change as Harper shouts, "I love you!" after my retreating frame. Her and Sloan are as fluent in Spanish as I am since they spent so much time at my house when I was younger and my mom made sure to spend time teaching them.

Jenko is curled up on my vanity instead of my bed, and he simply flicks an ear to acknowledge my presence. The sun has almost completely set, but what's left sends a warm light over my collages on the wall and has warmed the hard floor under my feet. A contrast to the cold air pumping through the air conditioning system. I don't hesitate to change into my sleep shorts and pull Jackson's *Georgia* hoodie that I stole over my head. The smell of amber and suede engulfs me, and straightaway, it washes away some of the exhaustion and stress resting on my skin.

I pad back to the kitchen, where the food has been allotted to plates, and I down the rest of my wine and pour another glass.

"So, how are you feeling about the Myles situation? Have you heard from him?" Sloan asks, glancing between us.

I shake my head, and Harper rolls her eyes, but sadness flashes in the gray of her eyes. He treated her like she wasn't a part of his life too, and I know she's sad, despite always putting up a front.

Maybe it's the exhaustion or the stress or my annoyance, but I can't keep my mouth shut. "Harper, you don't have to act all hard all the time. I know it upset you."

She turns her eyes on me. "No, it didn't."

"Harper," Sloan and I chime at the same time.

She blinks and looks away, training her eyes on her food. "Fine. Yes, it upset me, him saying 'your friend' like we weren't friends for years. Like I don't exist. I'd rather him yell. It's— whatever."

I sigh. "That's what you called Mom about, wasn't it?" It's silent except for the music playing in the background. She avoids both our gazes for a few seconds, slowly taking a few bites as Sloan and I wait.

"Yeah, it is," Harper mumbles softly. "I just told her how it made me feel. How he acted, how he treated us. I just needed to get it out. But of course, she didn't miss that we were in the Hamptons, and I let Jackson's name slip."

I nod, most of my annoyance dissipating at her honesty, and I send her a smile. "I'm sorry about Myles. He's just got to grow up. And he can't do it around us."

Harper breaths deeply. "It's not even that. I just, I've never seen him act like that. So malicious."

"I think he was—is—angry for a lot of reasons. I think he knew that if he tried to express how he was actually feeling, he would've realized he's not just angry."

I take a small sip. "I think he's hurt by the fact that Jackson and I, I suppose, didn't say anything. Even if that was out of a place of honesty. He wanted me to feel bad, to feel the hurt he is feeling but can't express. You and Jackson, though, are the easiest to take it out on when all he chooses to feel is anger."

Harper nods. "But why me?"

"Because you get angry back. You egg him on, which—while enjoyable—only makes him angrier. I usually just shut down, which he's always known."

"Yeah," Sloan agrees. "That makes sense."

"I mean, maybe I'm giving him too much credit, and I'm not excusing it, I just think that's what's going on. And I think he simply needs to grow up."

Both she and Sloan nod. "But let's talk about something else." I look at Harper. "Love you."

Her lips quirk. "Love you," she sighs. "As exciting as the weekend was, I don't know how I feel."

Sloan and I share a glance, but understanding floods my veins. "Roman?"

Harper shoves food in her mouth to buy herself some time. "Yeah. It's a lot. Like I think he likes me more than just fucking around. And that's too much."

Sloan clears her throat. "What's too much? Him? Or are you just worried you actually like him back?" I have to hold my laugh in. I cough softly to cover it as Harper flips us off.

"Obviously, I like him. As a friend. And the sex is great. And he's funny. And sweet."

Sloan pushes her mostly clear plate forward and rests her elbows on the counter, holding her head in her hands. "So, let's get this straight. Good—no, *great* sex. Good friend as far as we know. Great personality. I'm just not seeing what's wrong."

I sip my wine amusedly as Harper looks at Sloan with pursed lips. "What is this, an intervention?" she mumbles in response, pouring herself a large glass.

"Harper," I chide, raising my brows. "Stop avoiding it."

Harper squints at me. "I see the resident therapist has entered the chat." Sloan and I chuckle, but she continues, "Also, what is this? Attack Harper night? Can I breathe?"

"Just answer this, do you like him more than a friend?"

"I don't know." She sips, and I wait. "Fine. Yes. I think. I just don't want to get in too deep. Then there's expectations and rules and—"

"We're not saying jump into it and get married, Harps," I say with a shake of my head, knowing I'm being a bit of hypocrite, but I can't take my own advice. "You push everyone away. You always jump ship before the ship can sail. But I think a small part of you really, really likes him. Even if you can't see that."

Sloan smiles softly. "We're just saying, see what happens with him."

Harper sighs deeply, and I see her shoulders untense. Like she was wound up and she's finally uncoiling, even if it takes a damn intervention. "I will do my very fucking best."

Sloan turns in her chair, and this time her eyes are boring into the side of my head, and I know it's my turn. "Okay, wait, before I get attacked, I need dessert. Please," I say and clear the countertop, putting leftovers in the fridge and throwing out the takeout containers.

Harper wipes down the counter and splits the rest of the wine between our three glasses as I reach into the pantry and pull out all of our favorites. Fudge Stripe, Twix, frozen bite-size Kit Kats and peanut M&M's. Our pantry stays stocked with the goods.

I sit back down, popping a cookie in my mouth. "Proceed."

"You have a date."

"With Jackson,"

"Tomorrow."

I look between them, trying to make sense of any of the obvious statements they just tossed around. "And?"

"Are you excited? Are you miserable? Are you nervous? What is going on?" Sloan rushes out.

I blink. "Yes, I'm excited. Yes, I'm nervous." Even at the thought of the date, my blood warms and my cheeks heat up.

"I still can't believe you didn't kiss this weekend," Sloan says, popping a candy in her mouth.

"Right? Like how?" Harper agrees.

"I said I wanted to take it slow. Sue me."

"When you said slow, I didn't think you meant like a slug."

I gnaw on my lip, further irritating it after picking at it all day. "Well, excuse me if I don't want to believe something is too good to be true. It's just, it's too good. Something has to be wrong."

Sloan smiles softly as she shakes her head, her tight curls bouncing in harmony. "That's not true, Nina."

I raise an eyebrow because I don't believe that. This whole thing, Jackson, is just too perfect. Part of me wants to believe it, believe that he is truly just *that* interested in me. That he's just personified sunshine and he's choosing to shine his sunlight on me.

But the larger part of me is just waiting around for the other shoe to drop.

Like it always does.

Harper's sharp eyes are on me, no longer flicking with sadness or frustration, but instead a hawk-like focus. "I may avoid big time, but you live in a constant state of fear."

Sloan nods in agreement. "You assume that wherever you step the ground is going to crumble underneath you. So half the time, you don't even walk."

Yeah, that's pretty much what Marissa says. Although in slightly different terms.

I hide my smile because we know each other too damn well. "Okay, well you can hop off my ass because I like him. I'm doing my best."

Harper screams. Not a bloody murder scream, but an *I'm being chased but make it fun* scream. If that makes sense. My lips curl into a grin as I pull the hoodie up around my chin at their excited faces at my admittance.

"I feel like such a proud mom, of both of you." Sloan grins widely.

We all break out into laughter over our sugar high, and eventually, as the night gets darker and the honking of horns turns into every ten minutes instead of every three, Sloan makes her exit. She kisses us both on the cheek, her deeply conditioned curls brushing my cheek.

"Tell me everything, okay? I want to hear it all. Just have fun, babe."

"Yeah, yeah, I will," I say, and Harper and I both say "I love you" before locking the door. Harper and I clean up the living room, both preparing to retreat to our rooms. As we walk down the hall after leaving our living room dark and empty, I turn.

"Are you sure you're okay?" I ask, searching her face for any sign of distress.

She rolls her eyes in true Harper fashion. "It's a lot to process, but yeah, I'm okay. Now go, rest up, plan your outfit. I expect love and kisses and—"

"Good night, Harper," I call over my shoulder before shutting the bathroom door, effectively cutting off the sound of her laughter. After washing my face and brushing my teeth, I head into my room, where Jenko meows from his stretched-out position on my bed at my entrance.

I curl in beside him, clicking play on the movie that I didn't finish last night on my laptop. But I can barely focus on anything as I lay there, tucked into my dark room, petting Jenko's soft, calico fur.

My mind is only on tomorrow. The little gift I got Jackson is resting on my vanity, my outfit is hanging up already. I can't wait to see the cheeky smile grow on his face or the blond curls catch in the sunlight that always surrounds him.

And I can't stop running through the endless possibilities. The idea of kissing him, the possibility of feeling his fingertips on my arm or my cheek or wherever he decides to touch me, sends a wave of heat that leaves no part of my body untouched.

Because I do like him. I really like him.

I wish I could say that I was fine.

That I wasn't pacing around my room with my fourth cup of coffee in my hands or that I hadn't been watching the clock tick down every single minute until it reached two. Or that I hadn't questioned my outfit a million times.

However, that would all be a lie.

Porque estoy jodidamente volviéndome loca. Because I'm going fucking crazy.

I wait slowly, painfully, for three to roll around, the time that Jackson said he'd meet me at my apartment. Turning to the mirror, I glance over myself one last time. A deep red dress that billows to mid-thigh, with a lace top, and double straps over my shoulders. It's perfect. I hope. I reapply some mascara in the mirror and run a hand through my loose curls that have grown quickly, hitting right above the straps of the dress, and slip my feet into white Vans. After a few deep breaths and adjusting my bag, my phone dings.

Jackson: Your favorite fool has arrived downstairs.

I take one last deep breath in the mirror before heading downstairs. It's the perfect July day from what my weather app says. Low 80s and partly cloudy skies is practically perfect for the city. And hopefully, for whatever is planned.

The sun hits me instantly as I bound through my apartment and step outside. The rays reach out and fan over the tops of my shoulders, leaving me warm.

The sight of Jackson hits me even harder.

He turns just as I exit, with his hands tucked into his shorts and the top of his white shirt unbuttoned. The short, blond curls sway in the warm breeze that weaves its way through the massive buildings. Instantly, I'm greeted by his radiant smile that sends a flush of heat to my cheeks and a flare deep in my stomach, leaving me breathless when both his dimples pop.

As I move closer, his deep blue eyes grow bright and clear, excitement flashing in them, moving over every part of my body slowly, like the waves of the ocean, the ones that draw you in and pull you under in the most addicting way.

"Hi, sunshine." His voice is husky, and the sound practically sinks into my skin.

My lips quirk up. "Happy birthday."

"Well, thank you," he says. His eyes latch onto the dress I have on. A few seconds pass, his eyes lingering on every inch of skin before they flick back up to mine. The simple look takes my breath away. "Shall we get this date started?"

"We shall. Lead the way."

Jackson holds out his elbow, and I loop my arm through his, saving his gift for later as he leads me down to the subway. We step into a train, and before I can say anything, he cuts me off. "Don't even ask. Just wait patiently."

I sigh as we stand side by side on the crowded subway train. His smile relaxes from a bright grin to a soft, warm one, and even with the Sunday crowd around us, those blue eyes never stray far from my own. Somehow, on a crowded subway, I am blind to everyone else but him.

With each passing stop that we don't get off, any guesses I have are pointless. The subway ride ends after twenty minutes when Jackson pulls me off in Lennox Hill. I furrow my brows as he just pulls me along with a smile on his face.

Jackson leads us outside, back into the warm sun, and now, my only guess is something to do with Central Park. Because that's the direction we start walking in. After a few blocks, the greenery starts to peek through. The buildings are shorter, the crowds are bigger—especially on a beautiful day—and the tops of the trees are visible.

Once we're on a path, leading us—or me, since I'm the clueless one here—god knows where, Jackson turns, continuing his strut backwards. I raise an eyebrow as we fall under the cover of the trees, the sunlight peeking through every few steps.

"Where are you taking me?" I ask. He peeks over his shoulder every few seconds to make sure he's not walking into anyone, and every time he turns back around, his curls flow in the soft breeze.

He's only a few steps ahead of me when he stops completely, excitement sparkling in his eyes as he watches me for a second. "I can't decide if I want to tell you or surprise you."

I step off to the side and pull him with me, out of the way of others. I only hold his hand for a second, but it's soft and calloused all at once, and I want to memorize every line, every scar, on his palm when I have the time.

"Please tell me, pretty, pretty please?" I say adjusting my bag on my shoulder as I smile up at him, as convincing as I can.

He narrows his eyes playfully, considering me. "No. I'm gonna surprise you."

"Jackson," I whine, but he just laughs at my distress.

He steps closer. My breathe hitches in my throat for a second, my eyes trained on him until I'm sent into darkness when his hands cover my eyes. I swallow hard, trying not to think about the way the top of his chest touches my bare shoulders as he slowly walks us forward.

It feels like forever as I count each step painfully. Music fills my ears as we get closer to the mystery activity and the muted conversations of others as we pass. We stop after about a hundred counted steps, and he removes his hands from my eyes.

"Swan boats." Jackson is grinning as we stand in front of the large Central Park pond.

The large paddle boats float a few feet away on the dock. A lot of them are out on the pond, different couples and groups paddling away on the pond water. My eyes flicker back to Jackson.

"Paddle boats?"

He nods excitedly. "Yes, but swan-shaped ones. I've never done them before." And I laugh at the image of a tall Jackson cramming himself into one of these boats next to me.

I'm skeptical of the pond water and the boats in general, but it's what he wants, and it means I get to look at the goofy smile as much as I want. It's only fifteen for an hour I read as the couple in front of us pays.

Jackson begins to reach into his pocket, but I put my hand over his. "Don't even think about it, *galán*."

"Nina, it's a date. I'm paying." He eyes me.

"It's your birthday, so no, you're not," I say, raising an eyebrow.

I bump his shoulder gently and slide the booth attendant fifteen dollars in cash as Jackson gives up the fight for his wallet. We walk down the dock, past the geese floating on the surface and the few fallen leaves, the perfectly blue sky reflecting in the murky pond water, until we stop at one of the swans.

Jackson steps in first, tucking his own bag under the seat, and I wait until he's settled to step in. He holds out a hand from his seated position, and I grasp onto it, the warmth from his hands seeping into mine as I step in carefully. When I look back at Jackson, his eyes have darkened slightly as he trails them slowly from my exposed legs back up to my face as I sit down.

"See something you like?"

"Yes. I do." His voice comes out low and deep, and I can tell he means every single word.

And if my heart *was* beating, it isn't anymore. My skin tingles with the aftermath of his gaze, and my cheeks are blazing as heat floods every single pore. I'm probably as red as my dress. I clear my throat that has gone bone dry as I will myself to look back at him.

He's smirking when I do. "Oh, just start paddling," I instruct with an eye roll, and he does. We start pumping our legs in sync until we and the swan are moving away from the dock and towards the middle of the pond.

Jackson smiles at everyone we pass, which isn't something I'm used to or I'm sure half of New York is used to, but every single person smiles back because it's infectious and almost impossible not to smile back at him. We paddle through the water, with the late afternoon sun peeking through the trees that line the pond, and somehow, even the murky water looks beautiful from above. Geese and ducks rest peacefully, idly watching everyone in the boats.

"All right," Jackson says, looking at his phone where he has timer set for the hour and stops paddling, putting us at rest in the pond. "We're taking a picture with the swans."

"You are obsessed with them," I laugh.

He doesn't bother denying it and instead leans forward as he holds out the camera. That gives me a bit of anxiety at the possibility of him dropping it, but I lean forward with him. Our faces are so close our cheeks almost touch as we smile into the camera.

The swan head takes up so much of the screen, but I see the pure joy radiating on Jackson's faces as his dimples appear. I'm fully aware of his free hand resting softly right above my knee, the skin heating under his gentle touch. Little tiny shockwaves spread from his palm all over me.

"One, two, three," he counts, and I can't help but let my eyes flicker to him as the camera clicks. He takes another one, and I make sure to look forward for it, but all I want to do is look at him.

"I got this for you," I say, remembering my gift for him tucked into my bag. "Ignore the wrapping, I can't do it to save my life. But here."

Jackson takes it from me, his fingertips brushing mine. "You didn't have to."

I shrug, smiling softly. "I wanted to. It's nothing big anyway. Just open it."

He unwraps the gift easily since the tape is barely holding a corner together as it is, and confusion flits over his face at first until he fully sees the cover of the book. A huge grin follows.

"A Spanish-English dictionary? For me?" His eyes are trained on me, bright with excitement.

"All for you."

"This is great." Jackson turns it over in his hands a few times. "Now I don't have to use Google Translate anymore."

I raise a brow, my heart fluttering in the fact that he did that at all. Even though the app is questionable at best.

"You know what this means?"

"What?"

"This means you want me around, doesn't it?"

I do. My cheeks warm but I shrug, playing it cool. "Maybe."

He laughs softly, flipping through the pages for a moment with a cheeky grin before setting it down.

"Oh, and these." I pull out the Ziploc bag of sugar cookies I made for him. He takes it happily and I smile, unable to keep the emotion off my face.

We start paddling again as Jackson wants to play a first date version of twenty questions with the remainder of our time on the pond, and we mostly cover the basics. Every so often we paddle close to the edge, falling under the cover of trees until appearing back in the sunlight.

I find out his favorite color is green. Not lime green or a dark, army green, but the summer forest green. The green that reminds him of his hometown, when the trees are tall and full, and the grass is bright. The green that is full of life and promise.

He learns that my favorite flowers are marigolds because my dad used to buy them for my mom all the time. They were always in our house. On the kitchen table, on the coffee table, they would even end up in my room. So, it just overflowed to me, and when I got older, my dad started buying them for me too. Like when I got into FIT and the internship and eventually job for *Poze*.

I learn that Jackson's favorite snack are the chocolate Teddy Gram's and when he was younger, he constantly tried to sneak them into bed, which makes me laugh so brightly I can hear a little hitch of his breath, and it pulls the smallest amount of blush onto his cheeks.

I learn that nothing beats the sight of a pink-cheeked, blushing Jackson.

When I catch my breath from the sight, we toss more information back and forth. Like our favorite movies or music or songs, or childhood rituals, and what we were scared of, and eventually we start turning towards the dock as our time on the water comes to an end.

"I wanted to get food if you want. I brought a blanket we could sit on, or we could head towards the fountain."

I nod, then glance around. "Can we get Dippin Dots?"

He smiles, nodding as we step off the swan boat, now tied up by the attendant. I make sure my dress stays in place as Jackson reaches out a hand to help me step out of the slightly rocking boat. Once we're both squarely on our feet, we start walking in sync off in search of a food cart. Our arms swing close together, and the skin brushes together every few steps, causing lightning quick flutters in my stomach every time.

After walking down multiple paths, we finally come across a food cart not far from the huge fountain offering Dippin Dots, pretzels, and other various candies. There's a small line, and we take our place behind two families and two other couples. I try to keep my eyes trained on the menu and not the man next to me, but it's hard. His energy draws me in and makes me feel warm and welcome at all times. It's almost impossible not to look at him.

As we step up, I see him reach for his pocket again. I put my hand over his. "No."

"Nina."

"Jackson." I mock.

"Please let me pay."

I step forward, closer to the attendant since we're next in line. "No, you can pay next time."

All his fight dies. "Next time?"

I roll my eyes, but my smile gives me away.

"I like the sound of that."

"I thought you might."

We step up, and he pulls his hand away from his pocket. It's our turn in line, and the bright grin never falls from his face. I order pretzels, a cookies and cream Dippin Dots for me, and a cake batter one for Jackson. The attendant smiles at us. Jackson holds the ice cream cups and I hold the pretzels as I slide the man cash before bidding him a nice day.

Jackson leads us towards the fountain. People are sitting all around it, on the edge or on the grass nearby, spread out on their own blankets with their own food. Instead of taking us that way, I follow him to the lip around the fountain, and we sit on the concrete there instead. I lift one leg up, resting my knee, and keep the other foot squarely on the ground as he straddles the edge, facing me.

I take the first bite, letting the tiny circles of ice cream melt on my tongue.

"I don't mean to be dramatic, but whoever created Dippin Dots deserves a Nobel Peace Prize," I mutter over my next spoonful.

Jackson's laughter spreads over me. "Let me try yours. I've never had that flavor."

I glance up at him. "Never had cookies and cream Dippin Dots? You really are a fool." With a shake of my head, I hold out my cup dramatically, watching him spoon it, knowing he's about to taste the best flavor ever.

He nods. "Okay, that's pretty great. Give me another bite." He reaches out his spoon, but I pull it away with furrowed brows.

"Back off, cake batter boy." I take a slow bite, teasing him. "You picked your flavor, now suffer." He scoots closer as I inch away with a laugh.

"Come on, please." He sticks out his bottom lip in a pout in between bites of his own ice cream. I watch him with wary eyes. A curl falls over his forehead as I sit up further. His eyes dip down to my chest briefly, which sends a thrill straight through me, before they flick back up to my eyes.

I hold out my cup, letting him take a spoonful or two before pulling it back. "Greedy, greedy," I mock.

He reaches over and pinches my side gently with his hand. "Always such a smartass." I stick my tongue out at him before taking a big bite of my ice cream.

The sun sits above us, moving between some of the fluffy clouds that dot the sky. There's music coming from the other side of the fountain, mixing in with the occasional shout or loud conversation from other groups or kids running around.

I place my empty cup near my foot and rest my hand on my leg that's folded on the concrete, making sure my dress stays in place. He places his empty cup in mine as we start picking apart the pretzels, and he pulls out the dictionary I got him.

I furrow my brows as I lick a stray piece of salt away. "What are you looking for? I haven't said anything."

He sends me a glance. "Not recently, but earlier today you did. *Galán* or something."

I blink, cursing myself inwardly because I can't take the ego inflation he'll have if he knows I've called him that. "No, I didn't." But I say it too quickly.

His lip twitches. "Yes, you did. And now you're nervous and don't want me to know."

This time I move closer to him; my folded knee touches his legs. If I moved any closer, I'd be sitting between them on the concrete ledge. I rest my hand on his leg, and his eyes latch onto it. His skin is cooler than mine, a nice contrast, but still, he warms me.

"Are you trying to distract me?"

Innocently, "No." I pause and meet his eyes.

Eye contact used to make me nervous. In bars or on dates that never worked out, I always looked away. Or right past them at the wall to feign eye contact. But with Jackson, it's as easy as breathing.

"Well, is it working?" I ask, my eyes roaming over him. The blond curls, the freckles, the shape of him.

His eyes flicker to my lips and back up to me. "Yes," he responds shamelessly. He hasn't looked back at the book once and I could care less about the word now. I just want him to keep looking at me.

I can't help but smile, and I lean up, making myself taller as we sit close together. He watches my every move, not missing a thing. His lips are quirked up slightly, but I see his heartbeat in the crook of his neck, faster than usual as he waits for me to make a decision. I lean closer, forgetting everything else, all the people and the crowds around me, except for him.

"See something you like?" he repeats my earlier words to me, lowly. The tension between us is pulled tight and humming with energy.

My heart beats loudly in my chest, and every part of my skin feels like the soft fluttering of a butterfly landing on your finger.

"Yes."

My eyes flicker from his lips to his eyes to the way his skin glows in the warm sunlight. I'm nervous because there is no turning back from this, but I also haven't felt like this in years, and I refuse to run from this feeling. It's everything I've ever wanted to feel.

I push closer, and it feels like he wants this as much as I do. It sends a thrill through me, and I place my hands on the concrete and push myself upwards, effectively connecting our lips.

It's soft, warm, and everything I've imagined it would be. But better, so much better. He presses closer, leaning down, and his movements are slow, hesitant, as if he's scared that if he moves too fast, I'll run away.

But I kissed him, and I don't really want to stop.

At some point, he must set the book down because his hands come up to cup my cheeks. The movement surprises me, the touch gentler than I expected, and I pull back for a half second, meeting his gaze. He must like what he sees in my eyes because he pulls me back in just as quickly.

All hesitation disappears this time. The coolness of his hands, the chill of the metal band around his middle finger, and the contrasting warmth of his aura surrounds me. I still feel the smile on his lips, and I can taste the cake batter from his ice cream as his tongue swipes my lips softly, sending a wave of red-hot heat to pass over my skin and settle in the pit of my stomach.

The kiss is slow and purposeful, and everything I'm feeling overwhelms me in the best way. As he holds my cheeks gently, he surrounds me. His warmth, and the addicting smell of him, is everywhere all at once. One thumb brushes over my cheek, a wave of goosebumps following as my lips part for him without hesitation. If I could get closer to him, I would.

Our lips move in sync. It's not awkward. There is no finding a rhythm because we already have one. Perfectly. He washes over me like a wave, and I'm diving in headfirst. I'm breathless and burning, and I love it. I want to drown in it.

We pull back at the same time. His hands stay on my face for a moment longer. I lean forward, wrapping my hand around his wrist, his thumb brushing back as I give a final soft and simple kiss. Our hands fall away, but the feelings linger. I don't think anyone or anything could pull the big, dimple-bearing smile off his face.

My cheeks heat instantly as I attempt to catch my breath, my surroundings coming back to me. The fact that I willingly took part in a public display of affection without any hesitation. But with him looking at me like that, there was no way I could've stopped myself.

"So," he begins, and I think I'm redder than before as I push myself back, creating a bit of distance between us.

"Stop it," I mutter, trying to come back to myself, avoiding his gaze now.

He sits up straight, looking happier than ever as he watches me. I shake my head, ignoring the low hum of embarrassment I feel, even though it's nothing in comparison to the warmth he left behind on my skin. I try to scoot a bit further, but he doesn't let me, his hand landing on my leg, squeezing the spot right above my knee.

"You're hot when you're embarrassed."

My heart beats quickly in my chest as he watches me. "Stop."

Jackson moves closer again, my knee between his. "What, now I can't look at you?" he asks playfully, and I'm so distracted by him I forget to breathe for a second.

The effects of the kiss are still everywhere. I want to kiss him until I have every kind memorized, every move, the shape of his lips, all of it. I inhale.

"Well, yes, but stop looking at me like *that*," I say. I don't mean it. He can look at me however he wants.

He does. His eyes roam over my face, look at me like he sees all of me, slowly, carefully, like he's taking it all in and doesn't want to forget a thing. I glance away, taking in the crowd and catching my breath before looking back at him. He's still looking at me.

A soft look in his eyes and a softer smile on his lips. "No, I don't think I will."

haven't stopped thinking about Jackson.

Not once since our first date ten days ago.

So, when he called me after work and told me it had been a bad day and I could practically hear him trying to force a smile onto his face through the phone, I didn't hesitate to invite him over. He softly said, *really?* into the phone, as if he didn't believe me, and I insisted that he come see his buddy Jenko and that we could make whatever he wanted.

My music comes through the speaker on my counter, echoing through the empty apartment. I'm picking up random items strewn about to various beats of my playlist as I wait for Jackson. Homemade chicken noodle soup is simmering on the stove, my dad's recipe, and I set out butter on the counter for cookies or brownies later, whichever.

I don't know how Jackson copes.

I barely even know what an upset Jackson looks like, aside from that fight with Myles, which he'd shoved down almost immediately. So, I've done my usual bad day routine, and I'm hoping it works for him too. The oversized old black Nike crewneck of my dad's hits mid-thigh, and my leopard print shorts peek out at the bottom. Jenko's ears are perked from his spot on the windowsill, where the last rays of the setting sun hit his skin.

I can't contain the flutters of happiness that trickle over my skin as I sing along loudly to the lyrics at the fact that he's coming over. We haven't seen each other since last Sunday because of work, and maybe I can't stop thinking about it because it's new and exciting or because I've stopped fighting my obvious attraction to him or because, simply, it's Jackson, but I can't get him out of my head.

It doesn't help that my friends and my parents—well, my mom—are all enablers.

Our group chat goes crazy often. Whether it's Sloan and I berating Harper about how she's handling having possible feelings for someone or the two of them ganging up on me about Jackson, the questions only stop for the occasional meme or video.

My mom has called me at least seven times asking me to tell her about him. But aside from the date, Jackson and I have only texted and called on the phone a few nights, so there's nothing new to tell her. That's when she asks me to just repeat the date, detail by detail, again or asks me about him coming to Labor Day.

My dad is the only semi-logical one. Although, he's much more skeptical than logical, I think. Warning me to take it slow, that there's no rush, that boys are stupid. But that's usually when my mom, who still hasn't met Jackson, shouts in the background of our call that Jackson isn't a *boy* but a *man*. Then he throws in the occasional threat of *if he hurts you, I'll beat him up* like I'm sixteen again. I usually just shake my head and assure my dad that I won't be rushing into anything. I know he's just looking out for me. Mom is too, but she's just more excited about the whole thing.

She thinks its monumental that I went out on a successful date at all.

Dad would just rather I never date again.

A loud knock on the door that transcends the music brings me out of my thoughts. My heart beats quickly in my chest twice as I lower the volume and slide toward the door in my socks.

I unlock the door and am pleased to see a small smile on Jackson's face.

Jackson

Nina's warm brown eyes meet me at the door, and the sight alone alleviates some of the stress I've been feeling for the past few days. My eyes take in her legs peeking out of her shorts and the light flush on her cheeks.

"Hi." She moves out of the doorway. "Come in."

I kick my shoes off on the matt near the door as the smell of something cooking fills my nose. "It smells amazing in here." I look down to her as we walk down the hallway. "Hi."

She purses her lips, fighting a smile like always until a small one breaks free. "Hi," she says again, laughing warmly. She steps forward, hesitantly, and then wraps her arms around me.

Her hands splay out on my back, and the muscles loosen up as she does. The comfort of her touch grounds me, takes away everything on my mind. I don't know if she can tell, but she seems to hold on tighter for a few more seconds before letting go.

Jenko meows loudly from where I see him on the couch, and I stride toward him. "Oh, bud, don't worry. I'd never forget about you."

His ears perk as I approach him and reach out my hand. He lets me scoop him up, and I hold him gently as I make my way to the kitchen, taking a seat at the counter. There's a large pot on the stove. Soup, it smells like. Nina watches me hold her cat with a raised eyebrow as I scratch him between the ears.

"Want something to drink or should I leave you boys to it? I don't want to intrude on your romantic evening."

I bend down to whisper to Jenko but keep my eyes on the girl in front of me. "I think someone is feeling a little jealous." Jenko meows, and Nina narrows her eyes as I try to hold in a laugh and meet her gaze. "Oh, I didn't see you there. Do you have whiskey?"

She rolls her eyes, something that shouldn't turn me on, but it does. Every time. Shortly, I have whiskey in my hand as she holds a glass of wine in hers. I stand up, setting Jenko down and moving closer to her. Her cheeks turn pink instantly.

I tuck a loose wave of her hair behind her ear. "So, you made soup just for me?"

She takes a sip, and my eyes latch onto her lips. "Yes, I hope that's okay. I hope you like it. I also set out *Love & Basketball* to watch later. If you want, I mean. I know it's your favorite."

My chest constricts because it means the world and more that she went out of her way to do this, to do anything for me. I haven't told her anything yet. Haven't told her that Myles ignoring every single one of my phone calls or texts is affecting me more than I'd like. That I'm losing someone I considered a brother, a rock, and a constant in my life. All because I failed to be honest and he failed to listen.

And on top of that, my dad called me this week, on his way to the hospital for tests.

When I was younger, my dad had a heart attack and has had to be careful ever since. He said his chest had been tight and he had trouble breathing for a bit, so he's just going in for a checkup like usual. Said everything would be fine. But he let it slip that this isn't his first checkup, and that hasn't left my mind. It feels like I should know what to do, now that I'm older. But I don't. I just have to trust him when he says it's okay.

Even if it doesn't feel that way.

"It's perfect, Nina," I say, and she nods, moving to get bowls out and spoons. "Go sit down."

She glances at me. "Stop it, just let me."

I step forward again, grabbing the ladle out of her hand, holding onto her skin longer than needed. "Stop arguing with me and go sit down. Please." We stare off for a second longer before I win out. She steps past me, gently brushing her hand on my back as she does before taking a seat.

That slight touch lingers over my shirt like a burn, and I love it.

I spoon out two bowls worth and slide her a bowl before taking a seat next to her. Her eyes roam over my face, a hint of worry playing out over her features. We eat the first few bites in silence, and it's delicious. It tastes better knowing she did it for me.

"Is everything okay?" Her voice is soft as she draws up her knee to lean on.

After a slow bite, I answer. "I'm not sure."

I'm hesitant to tell her about Myles. Simply because I don't want her to look for a way out or find a reason not to continue this. We've only just begun dating, and she's finally letting her guard down. After all, she made the first move. Leaned in to kiss me first.

I've wanted to kiss her since the night from the bar. Repeatedly until it was branded on me. But I needed her to want it as badly as I did. I don't want this, my own issue, to be something that pushes her away.

She studies me. "You can tell me anything, Jackson. Even if it has to do with Myles." I realize that as much as I'm starting to learn everything about her, she is also doing the same. She has an uncanny ability to read me.

"It's not just him. If anything, he's the smaller problem. He just keeps ignoring me. I'm sent straight to voicemail and no text is ever answered. It's stupid and exhausting." I let it all out, unable to keep it in around her, not when she's so willing to listen. She takes a bite, waiting for me to continue. "But really, it's not him. It's my dad."

"What's going on?"

"He's in the hospital for some tests." I take a few bites, letting the information sit between us.

"For?"

"His heart. He had a heart attack when I was younger. Had to be careful about his diet and everything. Gets test done pretty often. But he said that this was the second round of testing in four weeks, and that," I shake my head, "that isn't normal for him."

I realize how easy it is to talk to her. To tell her everything that's weighing down on me. She pushes her empty bowl away, leaning her elbow on the counter as she sits next to me.

"And when I ask if everything's okay, to him, to my mom, to my siblings, they say it's fine. That it's just routine, but it isn't. And it pisses me off." I sigh, not wanting to be mad but not knowing what else to feel. "They don't want to tell me the truth, maybe because I'm so far away or maybe because I'm the oldest, but they keep downplaying it and keeping me out of the loop."

Nina is fully facing me now as I frustratedly run a hand over my head. "Have you told them that, that you feel pushed out?"

I laugh dryly. "No. I've always been the optimistic one; nothing ever gets to me. And I don't want to burden them with more shit on top of whatever is going on. I don't want to be a burden. If I'm the one they can come to, to feel better, then that's what I'll be."

Suddenly, her hand is on my arm. Steady. Her fingers wrap around my forearm as those brown eyes stare at me, warmly, filled with something fierce but soft. "Jackson. You aren't a burden. How you feel is not a burden."

I don't say anything. Just let her words sink into my skin.

She scoots closer on the stool, her grip firmer now. "You don't have to be the shoulder to cry on all the time. At least not with me."

Her words strike me like a shot to the heart.

I know that touch isn't her thing, so the fact that she hasn't let go, hasn't pushed away but instead moved closer, strikes me deep.

I've never had a terrible relationship. Short ones, yes, insignificant ones, yes. But no relationship I've ever been in was serious enough for talks like this. For shit that might scare people away. I don't understand how it's so easy for me to tell her everything, to just let it out.

"I'll work on it." I wrap my hand around hers on my arm.

Tracing over her knuckles and the back of her hand with my finger, feeling her skin on mine and the calm, comforting aura of hers that wraps me into it. I give her a soft smile and watch her brown eyes soften at the sight.

And I feel a little less heavy than I did moments ago.

● ● ●

I've learned a few things about Nina Scott tonight.

One, despite the semi-cold exterior she puts up, the well-guarded front, is that she likes taking care of people. Likes knowing that people important to her are taken care of.

Two, I learn I'm one of those people. Even if it's early, I've made the cut. I am slowly digging myself into her life. I hope that she continues to let me.

Three, she loves to bake. Which is how we ended up coated in flour.

"If you take one step closer to me, I will punch you," she threatens as I step towards her, and she steps back.

I've got a wide grin on my face as I hold a cup of flour in my hands. She knows damn well she deserves it. There are a few splotches of flour over my bare chest, and a handprint from her on my cheek, and I'm pretty sure there's some on my back. I watch her eyes trail slowly over my bare chest, my shirt hanging over the stool once the flour started being thrown, and take in every inch she can.

Pink starts crawling up her neck and onto her cheeks when she catches me watching her, all the blood in my body going south at her perusal of me. Her eyes quickly dart away and look anywhere but me now.

"It's okay to look, you know. I don't mind." I step forward, and she glares at me, but it's empty. "I know you like it."

"Shut up." She looks away again, but the flush deepens.

"Don't think I will," I laugh. "Come on, I just wanna give you a hug." The cup of flour shakes loosely in my hand.

"Don't sweet talk me, Ross," she says, dipping her finger into the cookie dough and taking a bite. None of it has made it into the oven.

"You and I both know sweet talking you is my specialty." Jenko meows at my words, and I'm really starting to love that cat as Nina turns to look at him, annoyed.

She mutters something to him, but I don't hear it as I take advantage of her distraction. Because now I'm directly behind her, and when she turns around, shock fills her gaze, and I waste no time in dumping the entire cup of flour over her. Her jaw parts as it dusts her shoulders, her stomach, and her face. She blinks, trying to clear it from her eyes, but I can't stop laughing at the sight.

A deep, full-bodied laugh, and god, it feels good to laugh. Nina is the only person who I thought of in the midst of everything that I had been feeling, and she didn't push my feelings down, didn't ignore them, instead acknowledged them and then insisted on making my day brighter. And she did.

I'm still chuckling when I stand back up, my stomach tight from excursion, and she watches me. Feigning anger, and I might've believed it, if her lips weren't twitching. And I want to kiss the dusting of flour off her lips more than I want anything else.

As I step into her space, she tilts her head back to look at me. "You look beautiful," I chuckle again, wiping the flour away from under her eyes.

My eyes latch onto the crook of her neck where her pulse quickens. I lean down, dusting my lips over her cheek and her nose until landing right above her lips, just enough to touch, and when they do, she steps back and rubs her hands, which have handfuls of flour, down both sides of my face.

"Sucker," she murmurs lowly, stepping back with a big smile on her face as she takes me in, equally as covered in flour as she is.

Immediately, I start to chase her. Dead set on getting that kiss. She moves to the other side of the counter right before I catch up to her, snaking my arm around her waist and pulling her into my chest. Her laughter fills the room and fills any space left in my brain that's not already occupied by her.

I lift her up, setting her on the counter next to the bowl of cookie dough, reveling in the huge smile on her face. Resting my arms on either side of her hips, I watch as she takes a long drink of wine and then leans forward and copies my earlier motions, wiping the flour from around my eyes.

She dips her finger into the dough when she's done, but before it reaches her mouth, I grip her wrist and bring her finger to my own lips. Wrapping them around her finger and the glob of cookie dough, sucking just enough to feel her pulse quicken under my fingertips. Pure heat runs through my veins as I look at her, pulling her hand away from my mouth but keeping it in my own.

"I wanted that." Her words come out breathlessly as she pouts.

"I wanted it more."

Her brown eyes flare with heat, and I can't look away. Not sure I ever want to because I don't want to miss a thing. I cup her cheek, brushing my thumb softly through the flour, the heat of her skin searing my own. I wonder if she's thought about kissing me as much as I have her since I dropped her off and left with a soft kiss goodbye.

With no more hesitation I lean in and press my lips to hers.

She lets out a deep sigh that I catch as our lips move together, and I can't help but smile against her lips as she melts into me. Her hand cups the back of my neck, burying her fingers into the base of my hair and pulling me closer. She tastes like chocolate and sweet wine, and I could get drunk on her alone. I step between her legs fully, pressing myself against the counter as close as I can get to her, and my free hand trails up the outside of her leg and to her waist, and I feel a shiver go through her.

I swipe her lips with my tongue, once, twice, teasingly until she parts them for me. Nina kisses like a slow catching fire. Gently at first, hesitant, until she lets herself burn in it. She kisses like she doesn't want to be forgotten, and I kiss her back to assure her that she never will be.

My thumb rubs right below her ear, and I feel the goosebumps form under my touch. I let out a soft groan at the fact that she, like me, is unable to fight this. Her nails scratch lightly at the back of my neck as she grips me, my skin white hot from her touch, sending all the blood in my body down south as my need for her grows.

I slow the kiss down, pulling back and teasing her, nibbling on her bottom lip and gripping her thigh. I'm not sure what does it, but she lets out the softest moan, and my smile follows immediately. I'd been fighting for that sound since our lips touched. She gave it away, and I'm never letting it go. Slowly, I'm learning her, and I'll continue to until it's committed to my memory.

She pinches my chest in response to my grin, and I chuckle, pulling away. Slowly, she uncurls her hand from my neck, dragging her fingers down my chest, through the flour, and I fight to catch my breath, my entire body hard and tight from the weightless feeling her kiss causes me.

"Quick question," I mumble, my lips brushing hers.

"Okay . . . go ahead."

"That word you call me . . ." Her eye widen, and I pull back to see it. "Do you really think I'm a prince?"

She groans loudly, pushing me back, and covers her face with her hands, and for the second time tonight, I laugh deeply. Again, she attempts to run away, jumping off the counter, but I grab her, pulling her closer.

"You don't get to run away that easily."

"You can pry the answer out of my cold dead body." Nina forces her lips in a tight line.

"Well, I already know the answer since I looked it up." I cock my head jokingly, and she hits my chest, glaring at me. "Come on, don't be mad. You can't be mad at me."

I lean in, determined to pull a smile from her face, knowing she's not actually upset. My hands go to her sides, tickling there until she starts squirming.

"Jackson," she breathes. "Stop it."

Instead, I grip both her hands in mine, interlocking our fingers, and pull her closer. Her skin is flushed and her eyes excited despite the frown she's trying to force. Gently, I kiss the corners of her mouth before pausing right above her lips. Finally, the corner of hers twitch up, and I kiss her again. Softer, slower, wanting to savor it, but it's just as addicting as the others we've shared. Except this one, it feels like she's taking all the tension, all the anger and frustration from when I first walked in the door, and making it go away, like magic.

If I ever thought she was just a girl in a bar, someone who wouldn't have been significant in my life, I'm being proven wrong every time I'm near her. Because every day I learn something that only makes me want her more.

I'm hoping that she wants me just as much.

Twenty-One | Nina

The September issue comes out in a week.

Seven whole days.

I *just* finished my last interview because Marc Jacobs is a very hard man to pin down. And even harder to schedule an interview with. From his previous, vague statements on fur, he was the perfect closing to the article. The one I must have on Miss Bisset's desk at exactly nine a.m. tomorrow morning. I shove the tape recorder into my bag and swing it over my shoulder.

The early August heat instantly surrounds me with humidity as I step out of the building onto the city street. Hot air lands heavily on my skin, and I immediately pull my hair back into a ponytail. My phone dings with a text from my mom asking me about dinner next Friday again. She is insisting I bring Jackson so she can meet him before Labor Day, see if he can hold himself to the standard she's created in her head.

Despite all my reservations and arguments insisting it was far too soon, my mom didn't care. She ignored every one of my attempts at avoiding it or making excuses, and honestly, I'm more scared of what she'll do to me at if I don't.

Of course, Jackson being Jackson had no qualms over this. So not only do I have to stay up finalizing this article and stress about it for the next week, at the end of that week, I'm taking a man to meet my parents. Way earlier than I would've liked, and there is absolutely no getting out of it.

Unless I was dead. Even then, my mom would probably pull me out of the grave by my ear lobe. Just as I'm about to text my mom back, Emma's name pops up in a phone call, and I don't hesitate to slide my finger across the screen and answer it.

"Emma, hi," I say, already chewing on the inside of my cheek. We've been meaning to get together for lunch or breakfast or something since the Hamptons, but between both our work schedules and my new dating life, it's been difficult.

"Hey, how are you?"

I nod and then remember she can't see me. "I'm good. Work is crazy but good. How are you?" *How is your marriage* is the question I don't ask.

She hesitates for a second. "Good, interesting." She lets out a quiet, dry laugh as I cross the street. "I was wondering, are you free next Saturday, the 20th? For brunch maybe, and we can finally talk?"

Mentally I go over my calendar, and when nothing comes to mind, I smile even though she can't see me. "Yeah, that's perfect. I know this little spot in Lower East, Aroma Café. They've got great food—unless you had somewhere in mind?"

"No, no, that sounds perfect. How 'bout twelve?"

"Sounds great, I'll see you then?" I ask, picking up speed to descend the stairs to catch the subway train home.

"See you then. Thanks, Nina." She says it softly, and we both say goodbye as I find a spot to stand on the crowded train.

The subway ride passes in its usual twenty-minute fashion. Maybe because I'm thinking about how Emma and Myles could be doing or because I'm so used to it, but either way, before I know it, I'm walking up the stairs of my apartment. As I turn the key and kick off my shoes to the smell of whatever Harper is cooking, I can't get either of them out of my head.

I really hope Myles is doing something—anything—to apologize or make it up to her. Even if he is, I hope he knows he should continue to for a long time. After treating her like that in front of us, after treating all of us like that. I really, *really*, hope he reaches out to Jackson or at least grows up enough to hear him out. Myles could always hold a grudge; the silent treatment was his go-to, and it doesn't seem like that's changed at all.

I know for a fact, even though Jackson keeps up his smiles and bright energy, that his relationship—if you can still call it that—with Myles is taking a toll on him. I couldn't care less if Myles ever talks to me again, whether it's with an apology or to judge me for my choices again, but I do care about his relationship with Emma and Jackson.

Part of me wonders if I was no longer in the picture what would happen. Would us not dating anymore repair the relationship with his best friend that's breaking at the cracks? Would the tension between Myles and Emma disappear?

Inwardly, I know it's not really my fault, but I feel guilty for causing any trouble with him and Jackson. With him and Emma. None of this would be happening if I hadn't been there that weekend.

And maybe this is all happening too soon.

A memory comes rushing back at the worst possible moment, attacking my brain when it's vulnerable, playing on all my old anxieties.

"Myles, please. Can you just tell me I'm not crazy?" I plead, my eyes on his overturned phone. He's been on it all night. When we got frozen yogurt sitting in the car, he was texting away in his left hand, holding it at an angle so I couldn't see it.

When we were in line for the movies, he barely spoke to me. Didn't hold my hand.

And he even answered a text message or two in the movie itself. Which he's never done.

I know we were on a semi-break this last semester, whatever that means, but even now that he's back for winter break, he's not here. Physically he is. But mentally, he's not with me. He's with someone else.

"I'm not talking to anyone important, Nina. Jesus, don't you trust me?" *His tone is sharp and unforgiving.*

I feel stupid for even bringing it up. I lean against his bedroom wall, staring to where he sits at the edge of the bed. Because I don't trust him, not anymore.

"Are we even together anymore?"

He furrows his brow. "Come on . . ."

"Did you talk to other people? This fall," *I inhale,* "I know we were technically not together, but did you?"

His hesitation is all I need. Apprehension is painted on his face, and my heart breaks again. All he's done since he left for college is break my heart. Different pieces at different times. Sometimes he rebuilds them, picks them up and tapes them together, but now, I don't think the pieces will ever be big enough to be put back together.

"Do you even love me anymore? Do you even want to be with me?" *My voice shakes, and I hate it.*

I hate how anxious I am for his answer, hate how despite my shattered heart, if he tells me he loves me I'll sweep the pieces into his palms all over again and watch him break me more until I'm nothing but dust.

He meets my eyes; brown eyes I used to love now only make me want to cry. All he ever does is make me cry. I've never hated him so much and wanted him to love me so much at once. And I wait for the words, even if it's a lie, that he loves me. Is still in love with me.

"I love you. I do." *The words are empty.* "But I don't know what I want anymore."

My breath hitches, and it feels like I can't breathe. I remember when he told me I was the only one, repeatedly. I was always the only one that he wanted for life.

But people change with the seasons, quicker than the summer temperatures hit the sky and the ground turns cold in the winter, covered in ice. I never expected Myles to change with them and to leave me here behind.

"You don't know what you want?" My voice is dry. Lifeless.

He moves until he's sitting in front of me, running his hands up my folded knees. "I don't want to lose you, Nina. You're still my best friend,"

I can't take any more, can't hear any more of this when he doesn't mean it. When it's all just to keep me close enough that he doesn't have to be alone. I'm sick of being gaslighted by him, but I don't know how to get away from the heat, the fire that's burning me over and over again.

"But I just—maybe we should take more time. I don't know. I don't know what to tell you. I don't know what to say to you."

I want to make him stop touching me, hating that because I'm comfortable with him I allow it. Allow myself to be strung along over again for love. When really, he doesn't love me, not enough, not like I love him. If he loved me, he wouldn't be hurting me.

If he really loved me, he'd let me go. And if I was secure enough, strong enough, confident that someone else might love me in the future, I'd walk away. But I know that I won't. That I'll continue to get burned until my skin is scarred forever.

"Hello, Nina?" Harper snaps in front of my face, and I come back to the present. "You okay?"

My chest hurts at the memory that bombarded me, reminding me of how terrible I felt during Myles's junior year and into his senior year. How I let myself be treated. I can feel the sting all over my skin.

I almost tell her the truth, until I see Roman sitting on the couch, surprising me. I force a smile. "Yeah, I'm fine. Just tired. Hey, Rome," I say, sitting down at the counter.

He flashes me a bright smile. "What's good, Nina?"

"Nothing new here, you?" I pull my notes from my bag to go over, the smell of food invading the space.

"Just waiting on this one to finish dinner." He sits next to me and points to Harper, who's watching me with sharp eyes. I look away.

"Patience is not your virtue," Harper grumbles with her back to us, bent over the oven, and when she stands, she's got pork chops in one pan and mashed potatoes in another. "Is this okay?"

Rome purses his lips, faking disdain, and I take a small sip, trying to shake off the residual memory of Myles's ghost. "I don't know, what about veggies?"

Harper death glares me. "There's fresh green beans."

"I'm allergic," Roman declares, his lips forced into a straight line, but humor dances in his eyes that Harper can't see as she lets out a huge gasp with wide eyes.

"Are you fucking serious right now? How allergic?"

"Deadly."

I cover my mouth and focus on my paper to try and hold in my laughter, happy for the distraction. Rome hits my leg with his, and I bite my tongue.

"Well, that's just fantastic. What am I going to do? These are things you should tell the person making you dinner, you know. As a courtesy. Like—"

Rome starts laughing deeply, and he tries to draw in a breath. "Harps, I'm fucking with you."

Harper turns around from pulling the green beans off the stove with a vengeance. Her gray eyes are laser focused on Roman's amused face, and I keep silent to avoid making matters worse.

"You're a punk," she says and throws a green bean directly at his face. He catches it smoothly and pops it in his mouth. "A fucking punk."

"Oh, come on, that was funny. It's not my fault you're gullible," he says, putting his big brown eyes to use as he stares her down softly. Harper rolls her eyes, her annoyed face finally morphing into a soft smile.

Soft Harper. Who would've ever thought?

She places each dish on the big countertop, and I stand up to grab plates and utensils and refill everyone's water. Harper takes her seat next to Roman, and I take over plating all the food before taking my own seat. The soft sounds of the TV fill the room as we fall into a comfortable silence eating.

"It's delicious, Harper, thank you," I mutter after swallowing a mouthful.

She sends me a wink. "Anything for you." I roll my eyes and continuing to eat.

"So, I heard about dinner next week. With your parents."

Both my head and Harper's swing to stare at Roman. He's got a stupid smile on his face.

"Excuse me?"

He nods, taking a bite and chewing so slowly that I'm sure it's on purpose. "Yeah, Jackson is super excited. He literally won't shut up about it. He's like a kid in a candy store."

"For gods sakes. My mom's gonna like him more than she likes me." I shove another bite of food into my mouth anxiously. Anxious about dinner. Anxious about all of it.

Anxious about letting someone get close to me again. The past few times I saw him I felt okay, making cookies in the kitchen, kissing him, feeling secure. But right now, I just feel dread, terrified of being hurt again.

"Trust me, he's also nervous," Rome says. "He wants to impress you. All the time."

My heart flutters in my chest deeply, despite my inner thoughts, and I feel warmth on my neck as I cast my eyes down towards my plate. God damn Jackson. Even when he's not around, he's around, trying to make me feel better.

"Well, you can tell him that he does a good job of it," I say softly. Hoping it sticks in my brain. Because he does. He does his best. Jackson has pursued me relentlessly, without abandon and without question of what he wants.

"Will do, captain," Roman says before returning to his food.

We fall into an easy conversation as we eat the delicious meal Harper made. Talking about the work that Roman is doing, the charity event that he's planning in a few months and how Harper is going to help promote it with her photographs. Darkness settles through the windows. Jenko does his usual nighttime routine of moving from the windowsill to his food bowl before finally disappearing into my room for the night, making sure to flick his ear at Harper.

After helping clear the counter and clean some of the dishes I turn to say goodnight to the two of them, who have settled on the couch together. They send me a smile before I disappear into my room with my laptop and a fresh cup of decaf. I hate decaf, but I won't sleep otherwise. Jenko is curled comfortably on my pillows. I pull out my notes from the interview and set them next to my computer, pulling my leg underneath me as I adjust. Luckily, before the interview, I marked my article where to add and adjust for new information, so I just have to plug it in and make sure the article sounds appealing while also getting the point across.

After a few minutes, my phone starts ringing with a facetime from Jackson, and I hesitate, wondering if he'll be able to tell something is wrong. If he'll be able to tell I'm second guessing everything. I swipe to answer it anyway.

"Well, hello there," he says with a big grin. His free arm is resting behind his head as he leans on his pillows.

"Hi." I take a sip of the hot coffee, making sure to lick the whip cream that lands on my lip before I lean my phone against my water bottle to stand it up.

"What're you doing?"

Sighing, I let my head fall into my left hand. "Finishing up my article. I've gotta have it on my boss's desk as soon as I get to work, and it has to be perfect."

"Well, I don't want to interrupt you. I just wanted to talk."

My eyes flick back to the camera screen. "No, no," I sigh, annoyed at the internal battle I'm having. I want to talk to him, and I also want to run. "Don't hang up."

Jackson sits up on the screen. "Is everything okay?" I type away for a moment before running a hand through my hair, feeling pathetic. "Nina," he says gently.

Fuck, I want to cry. He's too nice to me. He's too good, and I won't make it if this ends badly. "I'm just having an off day. I know I shouldn't unload on you with your family and everything—"

"Nina, that's not how this works. Please tell me what's on your mind," he interrupts gently, and I sigh.

"I'm just I can't stop second guessing everything. If we weren't doing whatever this is," I avoid the word dating because it feels too real, "Myles wouldn't be ignoring you, and your friendship would be fine. Emma wouldn't be upset. And I am terrified for you to meet my parents. It scares the living hell out of me because Myles was the last person to, and I know you're excited. I'm just scared. I'm scared of getting hurt again." My throat tightens, and I stop talking before I cry on the phone, shocked by my own honesty.

This is surely not what he called me for.

He meets my eyes through the phone, unwavering. "None of this is your fault. Myles reacting the way he did is not on you. How he treated you, or any of us, is not your fault. You're not dating him, you're not just his ex, you're a person, and you can do whatever you want. Please hear me when I say our friendship and his marriage are not your responsibility."

My chest tightens. The difference between how he's treating me when I'm upset, irrationally so, versus how Myles did, which is fresh from my memory, is astounding.

"And about your parents," Jackson starts, and I look up again, staring at him through the phone. "If it's too soon for you, that's okay. I will take this at whatever pace you need, and I need you to understand that. If you want to think about it and let me know, that's okay too."

"Okay," I say softly. Trying to soak in the words.

"Know that I have no intentions of hurting you. No intentions of taking you for granted or making you feel less than you deserve. I'm not going anywhere."

The fact that he's so willing to do whatever makes me comfortable makes my chest constrict. He is fully invested in this, in me, and I don't doubt him when he says he's not going anywhere, I just wish I could stop doubting myself.

Because Jackson Ross is too good for this world and too good for me. If I keep pushing him away, I'll never forgive myself.

"No, I want you to come. I'm scared, but I want you to come. Please."

He smiles, and I feel it through the phone. "I'd love to."

I shake my head at myself. "God, I don't know why you talk to me. I'm no fun."

Jackson raises a brow. "You're a ton of fun. Especially when you're drunk and you can't keep your hands off me." I glare at him through the phone. He just chuckles. "Sometimes you're a little snarky, like the glare you're giving me, but I like that too."

I feel the blush on my cheeks. "Stop flirting with me." Inside, my heart swells at how we go from a serious topic to his bright, charming self. I love it.

"If it wasn't clear, I like everything about you, Valentina Scott."

Everything from earlier feels lighter. Talking to him is easy. I don't doubt myself. He never makes me feel stupid, and he flirts shamelessly with me after. It's everything I didn't know I wanted. Everything I didn't know I needed.

"If you ever need time, or want to think about something, I'll never stand in your way. I promise." I nod, feeling appreciated, wanted. More importantly, believing him when he says that. He leans back into his pillows. "Now do you want me to go so you can get work done?"

I bite my lip. "No, will you stay on the phone? Please. If you want to talk to me that is."

His blue eyes light me up. "I always want to talk to you."

I want Jackson. And it's time to stop standing in my own way.

I don't want the brightest light I've ever known to walk away because I was too scared to let him in.

The man brought marigolds.

Jackson Ross bought a bouquet of marigolds to bring to my parents, or more specifically, my mom.

I'm terrified. After the article was finished, I took the weekend and reminded myself what Marissa and I have talked about. About giving life and love a chance. About trusting people when they seem genuine, and Jackson is the most genuine person I've ever met.

Earlier this week, he called again and asked what my parents liked to drink. Talked me through my nerves again like it was nothing.

Deep down, I know I will never ever meet someone as good and as bright as Jackson.

My heart hasn't stopped beating the whole car ride, and I swear Jackson can hear it because he keeps sending me warm looks as he drives. He leans on the center console, just close enough that the familiar scent of him fills my senses. His presence alone calms me, allowing me to push my anxieties down and live in the moment.

"Also, my mom may go in and out of Spanish, so if you need anything translated, please let me know, and my dad might try to come off intimidating and scary, but he's really not, and you really, really didn't have to get flowers or alcohol and—"

"Nina. Breathe." He meets my eyes in the mirror. "It's going to be fine. Promise." He reaches out and squeezes my thigh gently, three times in a row until I exhale.

We've just turned on to my familiar street in Brooklyn, and my fingers play with the hem of my jean shorts as he parks. Jackson smiles, not an ounce of nerves surrounding him as he takes the marigolds from my hands and hops out of the car. Almost immediately, he's at my door, holding it open.

"Come on, pretty lady, let's go," he says casually, the ghost of a dimple appearing. My cheeks heat immediately, and I step out, landing smoothly next to him.

His blue eyes make a quick coast down my body before flicking back up to my eyes, sending soft flickers of heat over the surface of my skin.

We walk side by side up to my childhood home, and before I can even reach for the door, it swings open. My mom stands there with a bright grin. She looks stunning, as always. Her black hair is immaculate as it falls down her shoulders over her flowy top and light blue jeans, and she looks flawless despite the simple outfit.

Her eyes widen when Jackson holds out the marigolds with a smile. My mom takes them, her hazel eyes flicking to mine, and I hold her look, silently begging her not to say anything, at least not yet.

"Hi, I'm Jackson. It's a joy to finally meet you, Mrs. Scott." Jackson holds out his hand, but that gesture is useless because my mom pulls him in for a big hug.

"Oh I know who you are. Please call me Elena. Come in, come in." She pulls away and steps back so we can enter.

"Hi, *Mamá*, nice to see you, too," I mutter with a raised eyebrow.

"*¡Cállete, mija!*" She whacks me gently on my butt as I walk inside behind them.

Instantly the aroma of food fills my senses, and I just know my mom's made her signature tamales, and I smell my dad's barbeque ribs as well. They pulled out the big guns for this I see, and it makes me smile.

Jackson leans down, eyes flickering quickly over my lips. "You never smile that easily for me," he whispers, and I side eye him, appreciating the fact that he's trying to make me feel better.

"Shut up." I bump his shoulder playfully.

My dad stands in the entryway to the kitchen, leaning against the wall with his arms crossed, his brown skin softly illuminated by the lights. Doing his best to emit *I'm a tough dad* vibe, but honestly, it's not working. The man looks intimidating, just like the college football player he was, but he's a big teddy bear on the inside.

Jackson walks toward him right away, confidently, and sticks his hand out. "Mr. Scott, what a pleasure. Jackson Ross."

My mom interlocks her elbow with mine as we watch. Dad's eyes flicker from Jackson's outstretched hand up to his face briefly before he shakes his hand and finally lets out a grin.

"Nice to meet you. We're happy to have you." My dad's voice is slightly mumbled and quiet as he says it, but the grin on Jackson's face when he turns around to look at me says it all. Blush fills my cheeks, and I cast my eyes downward, biting my lip to hide a big smile.

Mom leans into my ear, *"Mi amor el es lindo. Ustedes hacen una linda pareja."* My love he is cute. You two make a nice couple.

"Mamá, para, no somos una pareja." Mom, stop, we're not a couple.

"Todavía no." Not yet.

I ignore her as we walk forward, all convening in the kitchen. Mom works quickly in getting the flowers into a vase.

Dad notices them, and his eyes flick right up to mine; the deep brown color holds mine as he sends me a knowing look.

"Okay," I clap my hands together, trying to rid the nerves coursing through my body. "Who wants a drink? I'm drinking." I walk straight towards the liquor cabinet.

"Oh, wait," Jackson mutters quickly. "I forgot something in the car. I'll be right back. Please excuse me." My parents wave him off, and he swiftly makes his way out the front door.

Jackson reappears before I can find anything good with two bags in hand and hands one to each of my parents. My mom pulls out a bottle of Pueblo Viejo, and my dad pulls out a bottle of Knobs Creek whiskey.

Dad eyes the bottle with a raise of his brow. "Sucking up to us, Ross?"

A grin grows on Jackson's face, his hands tucked into his pockets. "Yes sir, I am."

Mom hits my dad on the chest as his body racks with a chuckle and places their bottles on the counter, pulling out four shot glasses. "Well, since we have fresh tequila, may as well, right?"

"Only one for me. I'm driving," Jackson says standing next to the dinning chair I took a seat in a few seconds ago.

"*¿Donde lo conseguiste, mija? En marte?" Where did you find him? Mars?* Mom asks, her eyes twinkling, and I shake my head.

Jackson rests his hand on the back of my chair, curling his fingertips into the ends of my hair and tickling my back, reminding me he's still here.

"*No se todvaía estoy tratando de averiguarlo." I don't know yet, I'm trying to figure it out.* I shrug, meaning that, causing her to laugh as the boys look on.

My dad is pretty much fluent in Spanish, but Mom and I use it more. Just more our thing since he really only learned for her. I'm grateful that he doesn't spill to Jackson what we said. Not that he ever would, but I'm still thankful.

I lean back into the chair, into Jackson's fingertips, as my mom pours the shots, the smell of tequila briefly overpowers the other smells wafting through the kitchen. I stand as we all form a small circle to cheers our glasses. Jackson's hands never leave my back, and I purposely ignore both my parents' eyes as we tip our glasses.

"So, I'll take one more," I say instantly.

Dad sends me a look, and I roll my eyes. "How's work?" he asks, setting up the small table in the kitchen. I help him by placing the silverware as Jackson and my mom start mumbling to each other as she dishes out servings.

"It's good. I got published in the September issue. It's out, on newsstands everywhere. Assuming they put it in. I actually haven't looked because I'm terrified."

He raises his eyebrows, pride flashing in his eyes. "My baby in the September issue? Glad to hear all those *Top Model* and *Project Runway* binges paid off." He comes to stand right next to me, bumping my shoulder gently, eyes flicking to Jackson and back to me. "And this boy over here? You like him?"

"Dad," I say quietly as he raises an eyebrow, "Obviously I like him. You think I'd bring him here if not?"

He looks over to the blond standing in my kitchen, laughing with my mom. "No, I guess you wouldn't."

He kisses me on my cheek without saying anything else, but he pats Jackson on the back when he passes him to place the steaming plates on the table. I take my seat and motion for Jackson to plop down next to me. Both of his dimples are on full display at the plate of food in front of him, steaming vegetables, tamales, ribs, and rice.

I don't know what about that moment hits me.

Jackson sitting in my childhood home, in the kitchen, meeting my parents. Maybe it's the way the muscles under his tan skin flex lightly in the short sleeve button up, or the bright smile he's had on his face all day, constantly flashing his dimples at me, or maybe it's the way he's constantly touching me with a light graze, the pad of his thumb or his palm. Or the way his deep blue eyes flash with warmth every time they land on my face. Like they like whatever they see or that looking at me causes the same exact reaction in him that I get whenever he's around.

This all-encompassing feeling of the sun warming your skin from the inside out.

Whatever it is, I like it. I don't want it to stop.

I know this wouldn't have happened if I hadn't taken this step forward. Pride surges through me. Maybe it's stupid, but it doesn't feel like it. It feels like I've cleared a huge personal hurdle.

I pull my eyes away from his face as we start to dig in, but not quickly enough.

"¿Ves algo que te gusta?" See something you like? My mom has a smug smile. "So, Jackson, what do you do?" she continues, giving me no time to respond.

He's mid-bite into my dad's ribs, which makes me chuckle at the tiny splattering of barbeque sauce next to his lip. After a moment he responds, "I work in public relations, down in Tribeca."

"That's impressive. Good business to be in, especially here," my dad says.

Jackson smiles, "It is. Couldn't imagine a better place. It's certainly a special industry. What do you do for work, Mr. Scott? Mrs. Scott," she gives him a look, "Elena, Nina's told me all about your social work. My mom would adore you."

She grins, always ready to talk about her work, but let's my dad speak first for once. "I'm in architecture. We're actually working on a huge project for Brooklyn next year if all goes well."

"That's awesome. I really enjoy when new construction starts, watching the building from the beginning and seeing what it turns into. A strange fascination of mine." Jackson takes another bite, this time of my mom's tamales, and I can tell he loves it. "But I think both of you should quit and become professional chefs. This is unreal."

I laugh softly, digging into the various foods on my plate as both my parents beam. Mom's joy is written all over her face with a big, blinding smile. While my dad's is softer, it shimmers in his eyes as he looks from me to Jackson.

"*Oh, es bueno,*" Mom says, sending me a wink.

"*Sí mamá, lo sé.*"

It goes quiet for a moment as we all dig in. Jackson and my mom go back and forth on her social work and his own personal experiences with it. It's all going so much better than I had expected. It wasn't that I thought it was going to be a huge drama fest. I was just paranoid, anxious something would go incredibly wrong. But it hasn't.

I also thought Dad would be a much harder person to please. But in fact, I think he's as susceptible to Jackson's charms as the rest of us.

Jackson listens as much as he talks, and he lets my dad go on about the project, and I see my dad's appreciative glances when his eyes flicker to mine. My mom goes back and forth in Spanish, mostly out of habit, about cooking or her social work, and even then he listens, with me quietly whispering translations to him as I eat.

Our plates are practically cleared now. Jackson leans forward onto the table, but the hand closest to me snakes over to my leg, where he just gently rests his palm. His thumb moves in small, rhythmic circles on the inside of my knee as I finish my own food.

It takes purely physical effort to not stare at him and to retain some dignity in front of my parents. Especially with the addicting way the pad of his thumb feels on my leg.

I take a sip of my drink, forcing myself to look up at my parents, like I haven't been staring at the blond next to me for what feels like forever.

My dad's warm eyes flicker between us. "So, did Nina invite you to our Labor Day party? We'd love to have you."

Jackson taps my knee with his thumb and smiles at me. "She did, and I'd love to come. I hear you guys go all out."

My mom grins. "We do. We're happy you'll be able to make it." Dad nods in agreement. "How about dessert? I made cake?"

Jackson's blue eyes flicker from her to me. "So, that's where you learned to bake."

My parents both get up, Jackson and I standing with them to help clear the table before my dad points. "Sit. Both of you. We can handle this."

I shake my head, leaning forward and resting it in my palm as I connect my eyes with Jackson's.

"You okay?" he asks me. I nod because I am.

"Not too crazy, right?" I ask him.

"Not at all. Honestly, you're crazier than both. I should've known."

My jaw falls open, and I narrow my eyes. "Wow. And to think what this could've been," I mutter, feigning disappointment with a small shake of my head. It doesn't matter because I know he sees right through me.

My dad turns his head as he holds out plates for my mom to scoop slices of cake on. "Where are you originally from, Jackson?"

"Georgia, born and raised until after college."

Mom leans closer to me. "¿Un muchacho sureño? Me gusta." A southern boy? I like it.

I roll my eyes as my dad and Jackson share a look. "Eventually you'll pick it up. If you intend to be around it long enough."

I glare at my dad because we're not even dating and he's already throwing double meanings into his statements, but he ignores me, humor lighting up his eyes.

"Oh, I intend too. She bought me a Spanish English dictionary for my birthday, and I've been learning on my own." Jackson smiles. "Do you speak it?"

Dad laughs, but I also see approval written all over his face. "I do. Until they pick up the pace, and then I don't even try."

My mom places slices of cake on the table in front of all of us, and they both seat themselves again.

"Hopefully she hasn't said anything bad." Jackson raises a brow, his blue eyes twinkling, and my heart beats harder in my chest, butterflies erupting in my stomach at the quick look.

"Oh, hon, she's not saying anything bad at all." Mom winks at him and sends me a sheepish smile, like she feels bad for outing me. Which she doesn't.

My cheeks flood with heat immediately, and I avoid eye contact with everyone except my slice of cake, which is my only comfort. Jackson leans back now, arm behind my chair like it was at brunch, and slyly twirls the end of my hair.

"That's good to know."

Dad smiles. "But you already knew that didn't you?"

Jackson grins. "I had a feeling, sir. I just had to check."

I groan, shoving a huge piece of cake in my mouth just to avoid having to speak. Because it's obvious that tonight I will be outnumbered. I think my parents like him better than they like me.

Not that I can even blame them.

The man is literally irresistible.

As if he can sense me thinking about him as I eat my mom's delicious cake, he taps lightly on my spine like he always does.

I flick my eyes up to my parents. "You guys are traitors."

"Not even they can hide the truth, Nina. Just embrace it." The confidence drips off Jackson's words, and I ignore the flare of heat in my stomach as I roll my eyes at him.

We finish the cake, and even though he's right next to me, I can't stop thinking about him. It's stupid, but him meeting my parents, albeit earlier than I would've liked, and my parents liking him feels like a really important thing.

It's given me a feeling of security that envelops me. Like I'm not crazy for feeling this way about him.

Jackson helps my mom clean up the kitchen before we get ready to leave as my dad leans next to me in the hallway. "He seems great, sweetie," he says softly, and I lean against him. "He better make sure it stays that way."

Ah, there's Mr. Tough Guy.

I hit him on the chest with the back of my hand. "Dad."

He holds up his hands before wrapping them around me in a hug. "I'm just kidding. You seem happy. He seems great. I'm happy for you."

"I'm scared," I admit. He squeezes me, and I exhale.

"That's part of life. Just don't let it keep you from living it. Okay?"

My heart flutters as I squeeze him back. "I love you."

"I love you too."

I watch my mom give Jackson a quick hug and a kiss on the cheek before they walk over. He shakes my dad's hand again before Dad pulls him into a hug.

"Ready to go?"

I nod in response.

"Again, thank you guys so much. It was really wonderful to meet you." His blue eyes shine as he twirls his keys on his fingers.

"Anytime. We'll see you at the holiday," Dad says as they walk us out, and Mom kisses me on the cheek. "Bye, sweetie," she calls before gently shutting the door behind us.

It's dark out, no sign of stars in the sky. Only the streetlights illuminate our walk to the car. I'm almost positive my parents are watching us, and I can envision the stupid grin on my mom's face as Jackson opens the door for me like always.

He holds out his hand to help me step up. I put my hand in his, and he gives it a squeeze before shutting my door and climbing in on the driver's side. The drive back into the city is surprisingly easy, and we fall into a comfortable silence as I watch the buildings pass us by. The playlist he made for the Hamptons trip is on in the background, and I'm not ashamed to say I know every single word to every single song.

I realize I don't really want the night to end.

He leans into his seat and looks over at me at a stop light, his left dimple—which is always first to show—peeks through just slightly. "Why are you looking at me like that?" he says quietly, blue eyes searching.

My own flick over the smooth planes of his face, from the curls to the freckles to his lips and back to his eyes. "Because I can," I say reaching out and tugging softly on a curl. "Do you want to hang out?"

His dimple pops a bit more. "Hang out?"

"Watch a movie or something, I don't know. I just want to spend time with you."

Jackson's cheeks flush ever so lightly. "So you do like me?"

I roll my eyes, fighting my own smile. "You know I do," I admit softly, even though it's not a secret. In fact, I think it's quite obvious.

"I do now." He intertwines his free hand with mine, resting it on my thigh. The stoplight changes, and he drives on. "You have lunch with Emma downtown, right? You can come to my place if you want and go from there?"

I bite my lip. "Is that okay with you?"

His eyes connect with mine instantly, and that ghost of a smile turns into a full-fledged grin. "It's more than okay with me, sunshine."

Valentina Scott is in my bed.

Not a pillow wall in sight, and she looks fucking beautiful. Her hair is pulled back loosely, framing the warm brown skin of her bright cheeks. My T-shirt is draped over her body and every addicting inch of her is branded to my memory.

Meeting her parents went terrific for me, and I take it as a step forward that she decided to let me come. Ever since we've left, it seems like a weight has been lifted off her. I'm hoping that she's ready to let me in. To let me show her that she deserves everything good in the world a million times over. I would do just about anything to ensure she knows that. To make her believe it. But for now, I'll take the barely-there, warm smile she gives me as I approach.

I settle in next to her, placing the two waters on the nightstand with only the TV light on. Blurry city lights stream through the windows. "Your parents are great."

She turns towards me. "Yeah they are something. They adored you."

"I'm happy to have made a good impression," I say genuinely, stretching out my legs.

"I don't think you've ever made a bad impression in your life, Jackson," she mutters softly, her brown eyes meeting mine.

205

"Well, I certainly made a good one on you." I raise a brow playfully, and she reaches out and flicks my nose with a smile, one of my favorite sights. Before she can pull her hand back, I grab it and intertwine our fingers, the simple touch igniting my entire body. "How do you feel?"

Confusion fills her gaze. "About?"

"Everything. This, I suppose."

She nods, leaning further into the pillows, but doesn't pull her hand away. "I feel better. I just, I get anxious sometimes and get into my own head. I'm scared of wanting this, of getting hurt, but—"

My heart beats deeply in my chest, in a way only Nina can make it. "But what?"

"I want you more."

There's no self-control left in my body when those words leave her lips. With her hand in mine, I tug, pulling her closer until she's draped over my chest, and I let her sink onto me, surprise and heat flashing in her eyes. I reach up, still slightly reclined against the headboard, and bring her lips to mine. Her skin is soft against my palms, and her lips feel like they were made for me. My other hand goes to her bare legs, feeling the smooth skin underneath my fingertips.

I don't take the kiss any further. Just nip and tug at her lips, gently, roaming my hand up to tickle her side with my fingers until she's breathless and laughing as I show her how much I want her. How much I want everything she's willing to give.

I pull back and trail my fingers up and down her spine and twirl the ends of her hair, but her eyes keep flickering to my lips, and I harden against her. I adjust us, not wanting her to think I invited her over for that or expect it of her. She moves onto her back, and I lean up on my elbow, one hand tracing her stomach over the material of my shirt.

She turns slightly, half on her side, and hits me with a look I don't think I'll ever erase from my memory. "Can you keep kissing me please?" She says it shyly, and my head goes a bit hazy.

My hand stops, surprise filling my veins until I grin. "I thought you'd never ask." She laughs softly at my words, and I lean down, connecting us again.

Electricity flows through us, my skin to hers, my lips to hers. Every kiss before this means absolutely nothing to me as she erases every kiss I've ever had. She rolls over, into me, and her hand comes up around the back of my neck, her fingers fanning out on my skin. I groan at the sensation of her hands on me, heat flooding my lower body.

Her skin is hot, burning hot, under my palms everywhere I go. The curve of her hip, the backside of her thigh, warm and supple under my palm, and her legs, soft and inviting.

I pull back for a second. "You know we don't have to do anything, right? I'm in no rush," I mumble against her lips. And I mean it. I'd wait forever to touch her if I had to.

She smiles against me. "I'm not opposed to a make out." She leans in, then stops. "Unless you don't want to?"

The chuckle reverberates through my body. Instead of answering, I just pull her closer. I kiss her slower, deeper, learning every movement of her lips. As much as I want to sleep with her, tonight or any, to erase everyone before me, I know I'm not going to. When I do, I want her to know fully that she's sure, that she's ready. That the risk of opening herself up is worth it.

But I'll do whatever she wants until that moment.

My hand trails lower, brushing the end of her T-shirt and the skin of her lower stomach. She shivers, and I grin, loving how affected she is. Loving that she's letting me in, little by little. I'm painfully hard, stretching against my sweatpants, but tonight I don't care about anything but her.

I brush against her stomach, her soft skin, moving my hand lower and lower, roaming over her hip and her butt, squeezing it as she presses closer to me. Neither of us wants to come up for air. She pushes her leg between mine, and my skin burns everywhere she touches.

Lightly, my fingers brush over the band of her underwear, and she sighs and pulls back. "What?" I ask, amused. I want to hear her say it, even as she pushes closer.

I want her to claim what she wants. Openly and proudly.

"Jackson."

"That is my name, feel free to wear it out." I smile, brushing my fingers over her cheek, tracing the dotted freckles.

Nina pauses, pulling at her bottom lip. Both her hands are on my bare chest, and it's impossible to focus on anything that isn't her.

"I wouldn't be opposed to you touching me either." Her cheeks pink up, but she keeps her eyes on mine. A groan clogs my throat at the look she gives me with those brown eyes, and I swallow. Her voice is quiet but firm. "Touch me."

Her fingers brush my skin, and the grin spreads without my permission, and I nod, leaning closer. "Anything for you."

The pink of her cheeks deepens at that, and at the same time, my lips touch hers and I slip my hand down, touching her, just barely, where she wants. She exhales deeply, all the tension escaping her body as I press my fingers against her. I document every reaction. She's warm, and she lingers on my skin, even through her underwear, and I can't take it anymore. I have to feel her skin on my fingertips.

My eyes were closed when we were kissing, but now, as my hand slides under and she's warm on my fingertips, I blink them open. I want to see her. I want to see everything.

She moans as our skin comes in contact, the center of her pulsing against my fingers as I circle, teasing her, pushing her higher and higher. Nina circles her hips, her leg squarely between mine as she attempts to fuse us together. Her kisses pause when I finally find her clit and move slowly until I find a rhythm she likes, one she responds to, and I know I have when she stops kissing me altogether, but her hands grip tighter. One is curled under me, spread along my back and pulling me in while the other grips my sweatpants, her knuckles curled tight. Her little puffs of air hit my lips as I continue. I trail my lips down away from hers, over her cheeks and onto her neck. Her grip tightens, and I nip and bite and kiss my way around her neck until the smallest moan passes her lips. The sound goes straight to my groin, and I groan softly against her neck, kissing my way back up.

I go slowly, determined to tease her, and I move back up, watching every reaction that passes on her face. The flicker of her eyes when I press my fingers against her, the flush that grows from her cheeks to her neck to her chest when I press a finger fully into her.

I lean in, brushing our lips again, fully capable of multitasking. "Look at me." Her eyes stay closed until I push a second finger in gently, feeling the deepest part of her tighten around my fingers.

Her brown eyes hit mine, heat flaring as she finds me looking at her. She blinks a few times, her hand moving from my sweats to my arm, curling around it tightly, holding me to her. I keep my fingers moving in a rhythm and my thumb pressing on her as her breath quickens. She's quiet, letting out a few sighs and soft moans, and I categorize every single one. Her eyes start to flutter closed, but I want to see them when she comes.

"Eyes on me, baby," I say against her lips, and she listens.

And she looks beautiful. Flushed and warm against me, skin burning itself to mine. I never have and never will see a girl that's prettier than her. She tightens around my fingers, and I groan, painfully turned on by her body's reactions as I chase her higher, her eyes locked on me the entire time.

Her nails dig into my arm, and I revel in the pain, revel in her physical reaction to my touch. Again, her eyes start to flutter closed, the brown hazy as the low light of the TV casts shadows against her skin. I lean forward, closer to her. My lips brush over her cheeks, over the bridge of her nose, and land right above her own lips, which are parted letting out little puffs of air. Her legs are squirming, trying to get closer as I keep a steady rhythm and keep circling my thumb. Her hand tightens around my wrist. And she finally lets it all go, pulsing around my fingertips and my thumb tightly. She physically loosens in my hold, her head coming forward to rest on my chest as she catches her breath. Her hand stays splayed on my back.

Slowly, I pull my fingers away and push her chin up, away from my chest, and pull her into me. Every inch of her is perfect.

Helplessly, I pull her closer, intertwining our legs more if possible, needing to taste her lips and feel her against me. My arms are wrapped tightly around her, hands trailing up and down her spine until my hand curls around the back of her thigh. Her chest heaves up and down against mine as she comes back to me.

"Hi." I smile, taking every second in.

Her bright cheeks and warm, sleepy brown eyes are a sight I hope no one on this earth ever sees again but me. "Hi."

"You're beautiful."

And when her lips curl into a smile right before touching mine, the simple act enough for pleasure to flood my veins, I see a future I never have before.

he sun is streaming through the windows.

But the sun isn't what woke me up. It's the slow, soothing circles of Jackson's fingers on my hip that did it. The small puffs of air that land on my neck where his head is buried in my hair. Each one sends a trail of goosebumps down my spine.

As much as I want to stay there, I want to see him, early morning with hazy eyes and tousled hair, so I twist around, and his arm tightens around my waist as I face him now.

His eyes are half open, still lazy with sleep but focused on me just the same.

Always on me.

"Did I mention," his lips quirk up as his words come out lowly, "that I love sleepovers?"

I reach up, running a hand through the haphazard loose curls on his head until softly patting his cheek. "Really? I wasn't sure."

He kissed me until I fell asleep last night. Barely let me touch him, said he was only focused on me, fully on me, and selfishly I basked in it.

Amusement flashes in his eyes, an eyebrow raising in the hazy morning light. "How is it that you're a smartass this early in the morning?" He punctuates his words with a squeeze on my side, causing me to squirm as he holds me tighter.

"It's in my blood." I lean forward. "And you can't deny," I brush my fingers over each cheek, "that you like it," I finish, my lips hovering above his.

He pauses for a second before reaching up and gripping my chin softly, pulling my lips to his. It's slow and soft and warm, like the morning sun, and the opposite of everything I've ever known. Jackson tugs lightly on my bottom lip with his teeth before pulling away, only to lean back in and kiss me again, this time with a smile on his lips.

This morning feels like a fresh start. I haven't thought of anything but Jackson and giving it my all. Starting to figure that this risk—despite the fear that runs deep—might be worth the treacherous drive just to see the view with someone like Jackson.

"What time is brunch?" he mumbles, like he doesn't want to break this little morning bubble we're in.

I roll over, grabbing my phone from the nightstand, and check the time. "I need to leave in an hour and a half."

He grins with his eyes closed and pulls me closer. I smile softly as he pats my hip twice before resting his hand. "Want me to make coffee?" he asks, lips brushing against my cheek.

I just nod, and before I know it, I'm following him out of his room. We make a pit stop in the bathroom where he hands me an extra toothbrush before we move out and into the bright kitchen. He puts on a record, letting music fill the space as he gets the coffee maker ready, and I look around. Since the last time I was here I was practically running out, I roam every inch this time. And then I see a stack of magazines on the edge of the countertop.

I walk over, seeing the familiar cover of *Poze* staring back at me. "Jackson." I hold one up, and he turns to look at me, crossing his arms over his bare chest with a grin. The stack is ridiculously high, and I can't even begin to guess how many copies he bought. "What in the world is this?"

He shrugs. "I bought them."

"Why so many?"

"I've been passing them around at work, the whole building, to my coworkers and my clients. Even took them to the pizza shop." The coffeemaker churns in the background as I just stare at him.

"You're just handing out random fashion magazines?"

He pulls out two mugs. "Well, I bookmarked your article in each one."

Speechless, I just stare at him before looking at the pile and sure enough, seeing a little tiny sticky note at the top of each and every magazine. "I don't—why would you do this?"

"Well," he moves towards me, "One, because I wanted to. Two, if I buy all of them no one else can read your work, and three, because you deserve it, and everyone so far has loved it. The article was brilliant."

"You actually read it?" My shock only grows. He raises a brow, and I think if Jackson says he's going to do something, he does it. I've never had that before. Besides my parents, no one ever cared about my work this much.

Stepping forward, I look at him, the golden energy around him, the daylight practically drawn to him, and I wrap my arms around his waist, falling into his warmth.

I think I might like this; I think I could stay like this forever.

• • •

"Valentina Scott, if you don't tell me everything, I will kill you." Sloan's voice is clear as day through my earphones as I walk down the crowded street.

I roll my eyes, adjusting my small shoulder bag. "It wasn't a big deal."

"He met your parents, and you spent the night." She fights back. "It was a big deal, and I want you to tell me."

Quickly, when the traffic pauses, I cross the street, leaving one block until Aroma Café, where I'm meeting Emma. "All right, all right. I have to go. I'll tell you later."

"Tonight?"

"Yes, pinky promise."

"Okay, great. I love you," she says, and I just know she's grinning.

"Yeah, yeah, I love you too," I say before hanging up the phone.

Ignoring the small crowd of people waiting for a table or a seat at the trendy bar top, I head to the hostess and give her the name of the reservation. She nods and grabs two menus. I arrived five minutes early just so I could be here first. There's really no reason for me to be so nervous or for my heart to be pounding in my chest, but it is.

I sit down, immediately taking a sip of one of the waters already placed on the table, close my eyes, and force myself to take a deep breath. When I open them, Emma is walking towards me. Her hair is half pulled back, with the rest of the long strands flowing behind her. Her eyes search around the restaurant, a smile forming when she sees me.

I greet her in a brief hug before pulling back. "Hi, how are you?" I adjust my seat, crossing and uncrossing my legs under the table.

Emma smiles, slipping her bag to hang on the edge of her chair. "I'm good, I'm good. Just life. You?"

I nod knowingly. "I feel you. Work has been insane this week." She moves to respond, but the waiter comes over to greet us before she can. After we both order drinks, coffee for both of us, a brief silence falls, and I build up the nerve.

"I'm so sorry, Emma." I shake my head, trying not to tap my nails on the table. "I'm so sorry. For everything."

She furrows her brows. "Nina, you didn't do anything wrong." I open my mouth to argue. "No, I'm serious. In no way is any of this your fault. Myles is the one who said you were old friends; Myles is the one who threw a fit and attacked you for moving on and blew up at his best friend. Not you."

My eyes focus on the water in my hand instead of Emma's completely understanding and far too forgiving smile. "I'm still sorry."

"Well don't be. Please."

I nod slowly. "How is everything, since then?"

She bites her lip, taking a slow sip of water. "It's been something. Obviously, it hasn't been that long, but we've had a few serious talks." I raise a brow; the Myles I knew and the one I've seen recently doesn't do serious or logical. "At first, I didn't know what to ask or how to even understand what he was feeling. But I asked if it was a shock thing or something more."

My eyebrows shoot up. "And?" My heart pounds.

"He said it was shock. I'm not excusing him, but he's been open and honest about everything. We've gotten in a few fights since, and he's apologized a million times. We've also started talking to a counselor. Together and separate. I always wanted to before we got married, we just never had time. But I told him it was something I needed."

"What did he say to that?"

She quirks her head, her eyes focusing on the table. "He agreed. We've gone twice already. I told him he needs to talk to you and Jackson and grow up. Make amends and all that."

Make amends. I guess we'll see about that. Before I can respond, our coffees are placed on the table, and we order our food. As I thank the waiter, I'm focused on the sad, nervous energy that's emitting off of Emma. I pat her hand until she looks up.

"I think that sounds good, Emma. If it's any consolation, the Myles I knew would've never even tried. I know it's a weird subject, with everything that's happened, but he loves you. I can tell."

She smiles, taking a sip of her drink. "You have so much faith in people. Even when they don't deserve it."

I shrug. "We're human." I take a sip of my drink, leaning back slightly and tucking my hair behind my ear.

"Maybe I'm putting too much faith in him though."

"Emma, if you wanted to leave him, I would go with you to a lawyer." She chuckles. "But you love him. He loves you. And you're a good person. You don't seem like the type to give up so easily. If all you're asking of him is to be open? To talk? That's nothing. The least he can do is prove that he's willing to change. Because you deserve that."

Emma watches me carefully, eyes wide, but I continue.

"He acted poorly, and you're doing everything you can to make this right. If it doesn't work, you tried." I smile. "And that's what matters. *You* tried."

Emma's eyes are watery, just pooling with tears, but she smiles anyway, shaking her light brown hair before wiping the tears away. "Oh my god, gross. Enough about this." She waves her hand. "Please, how are things with you? With Jackson?"

I blush instantly. "It's really great. Too great probably."

She laughs but shakes her head. "He's a good guy, Nina, and you're amazing. I couldn't imagine a better match."

My heart flutters in my chest. "I just don't get it; he can't be that perfect, right?" I laugh, running my finger around the ring of my glass. "I don't know, I never thought I'd ever feel anything like this. Ever."

"I'm happy for you, really, really happy. You deserve it." Emma smiles, brightly this time. "And he's not perfect, I can say that, but trust me when I say he's pretty close."

I lean back. "Yeah, he really is."

The waiter puts down our steaming plates of food. "God, isn't it fun gossiping about boys? When they just have no idea it's happening?"

I laugh softly before taking a bite of my waffle and whipped cream. "There really is nothing better. Harper and Sloan would love this conversation."

"This may be weird, but would the three of you want to do dinner one night or go get drinks? I really loved them—that is if you think we're friendly enough for that. I know this is a slightly strange thing, but—"

"Shut up, absolutely. I'd love that." I grin, taking a big sip of my drink.

Emma smiles, nodding, and the rest of brunch is easy. Talking and laughing until we're both pink-cheeked and our voices are hoarse. As we leave the restaurant, back under the partly cloudy skies where the sun just peeks through, I pull her into a tight hug.

"Keep me updated, if you're comfortable, okay? And we'll plan something with the four of us?" I say, squeezing her.

She squeezes back. "I will. And you as well. I want updates on everything. Thank you for this, Nina."

"Anytime, Emma. Really, I mean it." We hold one another for one more second before letting go and turning to make our way down whichever street we came from.

I never thought I would've ever had brunch or even be semi-friends with Myles's wife. The statement still doesn't make complete sense in my head, but after sitting there with her, I know that he won't find anyone better.

Myles and I never would've worked in the long run, even without everything that happened. He was too selfish, and I was too willing to give at the time, too willing to do or say whatever I needed to make him stay. Neither of us ever would've grown up if we had stayed together.

But Emma, she's demanding respect, she's trying to help him grow and not just appeasing him. If I'm being honest, she could walk away today and find someone amazing, who wouldn't make those immature mistakes. But Myles would be taking a loss if he let her go. A big one. So, I'm happy to hear that he's willing to do what she asks, to take the steps to fix the problem instead of running away like he used to.

As I walk down the street, back towards my apartment, and think about the Myles I used to know. The Myles I remember, the immature one, the one always ready to take and only ever give when it benefited him, the one that would've never been willing to change, I realize something.

I realize, that maybe, as much as he doesn't know who I am anymore, I don't know who he is either.

And that's a damn beautiful thing.

Twenty-Five | Jackson

The fact that Myles agreed to talk today surprises me more than anything.

Honestly, I expected him to tell me to fuck off and that'd be that. Although, I don't anticipate this meeting going any better. I uncuff my shirt sleeves, rolling them up on my forearms, and lean back into the high-top seat. The low lights of the bar and old rock music playing overhead fill the modern space.

My brain is running a million miles an hour, trying to make sense of losing someone I consider—or used to consider—my brother. I know I made mistakes and should've told him instantly; I just didn't think about it, and that's on me. But everything since is on him. I've tried, and up until this week, he's ignored every call I've made.

For once, work is the easy factor, the one I'm in control of. I take a sip of coffee as I type away on the laptop I have pulled out. The board of directors has been implementing a new policy at the firm that needs to be looked over before being put into place. My eyes scan the screen, reading until Myles appears at the table.

I look up, closing my computer and meeting his gaze. After a hesitation, he gives me a nod in greeting before sitting across from me. The tension is heavy. Something I never thought I would experience with him. When we were both in college, the one year we got to play together, we were in sync, inseparable on and off the field. It's how we stayed close for so many years. Always vying off each other's energy.

There is none of that here.

He leans back, his eyes cold. "You wanted to talk?"

I sigh, seeing how this is going to go. "I did." The bartender drops a water off, and I wait until he's walked away to speak. "I want to apologize. For not telling you what was going on."

He takes a sip of the water. "You mean that you were dating Nina?"

The use of *were* pisses me off, and I clench my jaw. "I am still dating Nina."

Even though we haven't really discussed titles or what exactly we're doing, in my head we're dating. And it's the only way Myles will hear what I'm saying.

I sit up further. "I didn't intend for this to happen, Myles. When I met her, I had no idea who she was."

"It didn't stop you when you found out."

I roll my eyes, running a hand down my face. "Does it matter? If I stopped dating her, what about your life would change?" He says nothing, and I raise a brow, annoyance buzzing over my skin. "What would you do, divorce your wife?"

"Of course not," he bites back, flexing and unflexing his hands. "I don't want Nina back. I want Emma. We're talking to someone; we're working on things."

"So, then why does it matter if I keep dating her or not? Are you going to forgive me if I apologize or are you still going to act like you've been wronged?"

Honestly, it's exhausting. This isn't the Myles that I met in college, the one that became like a brother to me. This isn't even the Myles that Emma fell in love with and married.

I wonder if this was the Myles that Nina knew.

If it is, everything makes so much sense. Why she's hard-pressed to push things away, to always put others first, to always offer people what they might want to hear. It makes my fucking skin crawl.

He leans forward, his hand gripping the glass tightly. "You were my best man at my fucking wedding. You were the first friend I ever made in college. And you start dating my ex and you don't even tell me? It just upset me."

I crack my neck, forcing myself to take a deep breath. "I get it. I know I was wrong, and I'm trying to make up for it." I should stop there, be the bigger person. But I don't. "But you're so determined to hold this grudge, this claim over Nina when you don't have any. I'm not your childhood best friend betraying you, Myles. You're a grown man, as am I. And I was going to tell you. But I have a feeling even if I did, you would've reacted the same way."

He rolls his eyes. "That's not true. I would've had time to process."

I furrow my brows. "Process what?" I laugh dryly. "It's not like you just broke up. You're married. What did you need to process? That the girl you let go of years ago was finally no longer yours?"

He sighs and lets his head drop for a moment, but my sympathy meter is running low. Most of my sympathy is for Nina, if this is what she had to put up with, and for Emma, for this side of her husband appearing when it should be the happiest months of her life.

"I don't know."

With a shake of my head, I square my shoulders. "No. I think you do. I think you moved on, you met Emma, got married, but as soon as Nina showed signs of moving on, you couldn't deal with it." I hesitate, but I ask the question anyway. "Are you happy with Emma?"

"Yes," he says, sure of himself, meeting my eyes, and I believe him.

"Then what is the deal, Myles? Nina came to the wedding so she could see that you were happy and moved on and this is how you react to her?"

"Oh, and you're so sure of that?"

My brows almost hit my forehead. "Yes, I am. Pretty sure she told you that herself in the Hamptons too." Guilt and surprise flash through his eyes. Maybe he's surprised that Nina and I actually talk about this shit. But I don't care. "She came to see you happy, and the fact that you even think there was another motive means you don't know her at all. You don't know her anymore, Myles, and you simply don't have a right to."

"And you do?" Myles sits up, glaring at me.

"Someone does, whether it's me or someone else." I sigh. "I didn't come here to fight over Nina. Even if I did, you're not in the running anymore."

He runs his hands over his face, his wedding ring glinting in the light. "I know that, I do, and I don't want to be—"

I interrupt. "You do know it. So you need to act like. And if you really love Emma, if you're really happy, you'll realize it sooner than later."

My phone vibrates on the table, and I don't have to look to know it's Nina. It's Thursday, and the past few, we've been getting pizza after work. Looking at the Rolex on my wrist, it's close to when she gets off, and I need to leave soon so I can meet her outside.

"I know it's not what you expected, but if you were really my brother, my friend, you'd find it in there somewhere to be happy for me. I made a mistake, Myles. You've made your fair share of them. We all do. But this isn't how you treat someone you care about."

I stand, tucking my laptop away into its case.

"Wait." Myles stands too. "I am happy with Emma. I love her. We're trying, and I've been honest with her. I wish I had an answer or an excuse for how I acted, how I've been acting."

I nod. "You two are great together, Myles, everyone knows it. And you don't need an excuse. If you were hurt by my actions, fine. But you just can't keep treating people like they've mistreated you when all they've done is live their lives."

I wish I had more to say, but I don't. I hope that he means it when he says he's trying with Emma. Talking to someone, talking things out, and working through whatever he needs to work through. Maybe it's guilt at treating Nina how he did, maybe it's something else, but I'm not the one to dig it out and try to fix him. No one can fix Myles but Myles.

So, I just give him a parting nod and begin to turn away.

He stares at me, a mix of emotions swimming over his face. "So that's it? You have nothing else to say?"

"What else do you want me to say? I'm not going to stop dating Nina because you can't figure out your own shit when you have a great girl at home. I'm sorry I didn't tell you sooner. I am. You're still my friend, but this—this isn't you. Feel free to call me when you come back."

Myles tucks his hands into his pockets as I begin to walk away. The tension pulls tighter the further away I get until it snaps. I won't be the one to mend this friendship. I can extend as many hands and chances as I want, and it still has to be Myles's decision. He'll have to decide whether a girl that hasn't been a part of his life for years is worth losing more than just a friend over.

But fuck this, I'm not going to let this taint or ruin everything between Nina and me. This weekend is Labor Day, and I get to spend it with her and her family, who has taken me in with open arms. I couldn't be more excited that she's fully started to let me in, to be a part of her life, of her routines, of her traditions.

Myles isn't a factor in my life that I can control. He has to figure out what he wants and how to handle it. I've done my part. Because Nina brings me a sense of peace I didn't know I was looking for. There's nothing he could say or do that's going to make me give her up so easily.

I pull my phone out of my pocket and dial Nina.

"Hi," she breathes over the phone, and the knot in my chest loosens at her voice. "I'm on my way down now. I'm just packing up."

I turn left down the street and back towards her office. The bar was only a block or two away, and knowing her, I'll still be there before she's downstairs. "Take your time."

"How was it?"

I sigh, cracking my neck again and rubbing the back of it with my free hand. "As well as expected. I miss my friend, but that's not him. At least not the friend that I knew."

"Yeah," Nina says softly. "I don't know who Myles was or is or—I don't know. He's hard to read. You never really get what you expect." She pauses, but I can tell by the pause she's got something else to say. "Jackson, I'm the reason this is happening, that you're losing him. I don't want to be."

"No." I don't hesitate. "You are the reason for a lot of things, good things. But you are not responsible for him. Or for what's happening. Don't ever think that way."

I would give her a whole goddamn list of the good things she's responsible for if she wanted it. Even after that conversation, I'm more focused on seeing her face, knowing just the sight of her will ease the tension tightening my body.

"Okay, if you're sure," she says, and I hear the sounds of the elevator through the phone just as I reach her building. I lean on the concrete half wall nearby, where I always wait.

I chuckle at her words. Because I have never been so sure of anything in my entire life.

"Valentina, if there is one thing I'm sure of right now, it's you."

It's silent for a second, and I bet she's rolling her eyes. And then she appears at the doorway of her building, pushing it open and stepping outside. Every time I see her, it's like the first time, and she looks goddamn beautiful in the evening sun.

The phone is still pressed to her ear, and as she approaches, I see her teeth pulling at her bottom lip. "Speechless?" I ask through the phone, grinning now.

"*Te odio*," she says, and the smooth sound of Spanish on her lips never fails to send chills down my spine.

"No, you don't." I hang up the phone just as she approaches, the sound of her heels clicking on the pavement.

With an eyeroll, she tucks her phone away into her bag, which I grab before she can swing it back onto her shoulder. She still tries to fight me when I do, and it's not that she's not capable, I just like doing it.

"I see you've been practicing your Spanish." Nina tucks a curl behind her ear.

I lean down, brushing my lips over her cheek, hoping to see the pink flush that always appears, and when I pull away, I'm pleased to see it spread. "This girl I know got me a dictionary. Figured it was time to use it." Her lips twitch. "Ready?"

She doesn't say anything, just puts her arm through mine.

Her brown eyes look up at me, dark and beautiful in the sunlight. And finally, her lips tug into a small smile, erasing any tension that she didn't already get rid of. Nina steps closer, into my space, and I welcome her into it. I would welcome her anywhere. If I had it my way, there'd never be any space between us.

She's fallen into my life easily, and I hope despite everything going on, she stays.

"**C**ome on, Harper, let's go already," I shout from the kitchen, tapping away at my phone, letting my parents know we'll be there soon.

It's already Labor Day. The past two weeks have flown by in an instant. Ever since Jackson met my parents and I talked to Emma, I've felt better. More willing to put my guard down and finally let Jackson in. Let him treat me the way he has been since the beginning but letting myself enjoy it. For once in my life.

He hasn't talked to Myles since their lunch, and he hasn't brought up his dad recently, but I need to ask him about it. Make sure he isn't keeping it in for my sake. I don't want him to think that he's just a shoulder to lean on, at least not for me. It'll take work, but I want him to know that I'm here for him, to listen and hear him, for whatever he needs, like he has been with me.

"Is that the sweet tea you made him?" Sloan smirks, standing next to me. I blatantly ignore her, sending another message, this time to Veah, thanking her for telling me Jackson's mom's recipe. I'm sure it's not perfect or anything like his mom's, but I hope it's close.

His sister and I have talked a lot over the past two weeks, ever since she ended up facetiming one Thursday when we were getting pizza. It started as a normal, brother-sister call until she caught glimpse of me and the brightest, smile came over her face. They may not be blood related, but she has the same easy-going energy he does, even over the phone. It turned into her and I talking for an hour till Jackson decided he needed attention and dragged me away. He had no shame in hanging up the phone on her.

On top of that, Jackson and I have just spent a lot of time together. Lazy touches, his fingertips on my spine or the outside of my leg, trailing up and up, or mine roaming over his chest and smooth back when we listen to music some days. We haven't done anything further, despite the longing growing in my chest every time I'm near him. But most days I just enjoy the simplicity of being touched the way he does. Gentle and searching, like he's learning every inch.

"All right, let's go." Harper enters, with her bag over her shoulder. "Don't forget your precious sweet tea for your boyfriend," she sings, and when she walks past me, I tap the back of her knee with my foot playfully.

"He's not my boyfriend," I mumble as we lock the door behind us.

"Not yet." Sloan swings an arm over my shoulder, pressing a kiss on my cheek with a smile. I try to fight it, but I can't help but smile in my best friend's hold. The sun hits us as we walk to the subway, the city buzzing with life on the holiday weekend.

We arrive at my house quickly, walking the sidewalks of our old street, where the three of us use to run around, in and out of the bodega on the corner or the donut shop two blocks over or just getting into trouble. The side street is already packed since this party has never had an official start time. I see the neighbors I grew up around, their friends and families. Anyone that's close enough comes to this event.

Jackson is about to meet everyone who had a hand in raising me, who watched me grow up, and that is way more terrifying than him just meeting my parents, but I'm not scared. Just excited.

We walk up to the stoop in front of my house, and it's crowded too. Some of the younger guests are throwing footballs in the front street, kicking balls down the sidewalk, or sitting on the stoops and holding the plastic cups my mom gives out for her parties. Music is blasting from a speaker somewhere, filling the air. When they see us, they wave and shout hellos as we walk in.

The front door is wide open as usual, but my mom is there. "Girls, come in, come in." She grins, motioning us to the kitchen. She pulls Harper and Sloan in first for a hug, which isn't even surprising anymore. But dad pulls me in, and I smile as he kisses the top of my head.

"Where is the blond?"

I raise a brow. "He's coming later."

"What's this?" He taps the pitcher.

"It's sweet tea. For the blond." I mock.

He leans back, holding my shoulders and looking over me with a watchful gaze. "You made him sweet tea? Are you sure you're my daughter?"

My cheeks heat. "He said it's his favorite, and he hasn't been home to have his mom's, and Labor Day was practically when he got adopted, and I—"

Dad chuckles, his dark skin crinkling. "I think it's very sweet. I've just never really seen this. You weren't like this with what's his name." I know damn well he remembers his name. "Maybe it's because you were younger or—I don't know. It reminds me of your mom."

My lips pull into a smile because my mom and I are the same. She acts like she's not sappy and in love but would literally do anything for my dad, and apparently, I am doing the same. I wish I could say I was surprised, but I'm not.

He pats my back and takes the pitcher and puts it in the fridge, falling into an easy conversation with one of our longtime neighbors. My mom finally stops chatting with my two friends long enough to really notice me.

"*Mija*, where is he?" She motions as if I wasn't allowed to come without him.

I kiss her on the cheek. "He's coming, *Mamá*, a bit later."

She purses her lips and nods, patting me on the cheek. "*Bien, bien.* I have people who want to meet him."

"People?" I raise my brows. "*Mamá*, what do you mean?"

I don't get a chance to finish my statement because she quickly hushes me and pushes me in the direction of the backyard to go around and see if people need anything. My head is slightly blurred because I'm spinning over what she's told everyone about my personal life. I quickly shake it off and make the rounds, leaving Sloan and Harper to fend for themselves.

In the end, I'm happy for the distraction because time passes much quicker as I walk around and say hi to people I haven't seen in a while, and it means I'm not thinking about Jackson the entire time. Even though, in the back of mind, I still am.

I want him here.

Not even caring if him being next to me means unending questions or knowing looks. I know that he'd hold my hand, his thumb tracing small circles over my palm, or twirl the ends of my hair, and I would answer anything they asked with him there. Maybe I should be worried at how quickly all these feelings have come to fruition and how overwhelmingly beautiful they feel, but I'm not.

Finally, I finish my rounds and grab a drink before searching for my friends. The sun lands on my face as I walk through the open front door of the house to find them sitting on the stoop, watching people throw footballs back and forth.

I collapse next to Sloan and poke Harper on the cheek where she sits one step below, leaning on Sloan's legs. My phone dings as I take a sip, and my lips tug into a smile.

Jackson: Walking up now. I didn't realize I was dating a celebrity, sunshine. :)

The little smiley face pulls a quiet laugh from my mouth as I look up to the street. He's nowhere to my right, but when I look to my left, I can just make out a blond head of hair. Soon, he's close enough I can make out the small smile on his face.

But something is off. The dimples aren't fighting to appear, and he's talking on the phone, animatedly, while trying to keep the smile on his face. Even his shoulders are slightly hunched, when usually he stands like he doesn't have a care in the world.

I won't push right away, but it's one of two things, and I hope he tells me. As he walks closer, he hangs up the phone, and his eyes land on me as I bring the cup to my lips, trying not to worry too much.

He sends me a wink, and even from a distance, the familiar warmth spreads up my neck and onto my cheeks. Certain people have figured it out as I see a few neighbors and friends glance between us, but I couldn't care less. Jackson's shoulders straighten as he picks up the pace just slightly as he nears me.

"Ah, here comes lover boy," Harper snarks quietly, and Sloan tugs her hair.

"You're one to talk," I reply, insinuating the relationship between her and Roman. That she insists on calling a *situation*. And she shuts right up. Sloan laughs, and we share a warm glance.

"You guys are so mean to me," Harper mumbles, but she smiles, not meaning it.

I stand and lean against the stone railing of the steps as I wait for Jackson.

One of my old family friends shouts, pulling my attention for a second. "Valentina Scott, is that who I think it is?" The grin pulls on Miss Lisa's face, her deep-set eyes warming as she smiles, and my face immediately heats up when the entirety of the street turns their head.

Because if Miss Lisa, who I love, is anything, it's loud.

I sigh. "Yes Miss Lisa, I don't know what *Mamá* said, but yes."

She smiles. "You got a pretty one, honey, make sure you keep him around." She winks, and I just shake my head at her antics.

"I'll do my best."

Harper lets out a *whoop* in the background, and at this point, with every eye on me, I'm pretty sure I'm the actual color of a tomato. I glance back to Jackson, who is grinning now, both dimples on display.

"Miss Lisa?" he says, stopping in front of me, twirling his keys around his finger. She turns, raising her eyebrows with a smile and nods. "I believe it'll be me who will be lucky enough to keep her around."

I swear to god, at least five jaws pop open, including mine and Miss Lisa's, as he says it. So casual, so unashamed, and I think I might be on fire. "Nina, if you drop him. One of us will snatch him right up," Miss Lisa shouts, chuckles following her words before she turns back to her previous conversation.

"Hi, baby," Jackson says, this time so only I can hear it as he leans down and presses a soft kiss on my cheek. His hand softly pats my butt through my jean shorts, effectively setting the rest of my body ablaze.

I gaze up at him over my cup. "Hi. Fair warning, my mom apparently told the entirety of Brooklyn her daughter was dating, and they all know who you are, so I'm apologizing now."

"Are you sure you don't have a star on the Hollywood walk of fame I don't know about?" He squints playfully, and I swat his chest.

"Seriously, I'm sorry."

"Seriously, Nina, if I could tell the entire world, I would." He leans down, lips brushing my temple. My chest feels like it's going to explode.

Before I can respond, Harper chimes in because she can't go three seconds without eavesdropping. "Do you guys need to get a room already?"

I roll my eyes as Jackson says hello to her and Sloan, kissing them both on the cheek. Something about Jackson treating my friends as well as he treats me makes my heart pump.

But I meet Harper's gray eyes. "Just for that, I'm telling mom about Roman and that you're dating."

"You wouldn't."

I raise my cup. "Watch me." I grab Jackson's hand. "Well, let's go inside so you can say hi to my parents and get that over with. I also have something for you."

"Is it a room, like Harper suggested? Because I'd be interested."

My hair flies over my shoulder when I look back at him. "Shameless." I drag him inside.

He tugs me back slightly, his chest coming into contact with my back, as my heart careens in my chest, and I feel his breath on my cheek. "You like it."

My mouth is dry, and it takes me a second to recover, to figure out how to put one foot in front of the other. "Behave," I mutter, and he grins like he never said anything at all, and I resume pulling him forward.

As soon as I can see the kitchen, my mom's eyes land on Jackson and she brightens immediately, pulling him forward out of my hand and into a hug. Dad watches amusedly from his spot next to the fridge, mostly because that's where the beer and whiskey are stocked, and he likes to be prepared.

"It's good to see you. I'm so glad you came," my mom exclaims and lets him out of her death grip.

He smiles, reaching out to shake my dad's hand. "I wouldn't miss it for the world. Thank you again for having me. I told Nina I didn't realize I was dating a celebrity."

My dad scoffs, a smile playing at his lips as I lean against the table. "Welcome to the club. Took me a few years to realize I was too."

My mom glares playfully at him. *"¡Callete, mi amor!* Please, make yourself at home. Make sure Nina gets you anything you need—"

"*Mamá*," I exclaim, and she just winks at me, bringing a chuckle out of everyone watching us in the kitchen.

"Well, I'll leave you two to get settled. But I'll be back to introduce you to everyone." She ushers everyone out of the kitchen, leaving my cheeks aflame yet again as my dad just smiles and grabs another beer.

I think my mom could run the world if she wanted to, and no one would dare argue with her.

"Good to see you, Jackson. Glad you could come," Dad says, patting him on the back before heading out back.

"Have I mentioned I love your parents?"

I roll my eyes, setting my cup down on the counter. "Yeah, once or twice."

I open the fridge, suddenly terrified he'll hate that I attempted to make this sweet tea, and I hesitate before telling myself to man up, because it's *sweet tea* for god sakes. I wrap my hand around the handle and bring it out, setting it on the counter. When I turn around, his eyes are on me as he leans on the counter with his arms crossed, his tan skin a nice contrast to the simple black T-shirt he wears, and the easy confidence of his flows off him.

"I made, or attempted to make, sweet tea." I tug on the inside of my lip. "I've been texting Veah, and she tried to tell me how your mom did it, and I'm sure it's not your mom's, but I wanted you—"

He breaks out into a full-on show-stopping grin.

Dimples on full display as he pulls my hand and tugs me closer to him. Both of his hands cup my face, and my entire body is fluttering as his thumb moves over my beet red cheeks. Those blue eyes flash with appreciation as they flicker over my face. He looks at me like I'm everything and then some.

I swallow dryly as my eyes flicker around, making sure that no one is in the kitchen. Because when he leans down and presses his lips to mine, I practically fall into him, wrapping my arms around his waist. Everything he does sets me on fire, from the tips of my toes to the top of my head. It's like he strikes a match and I walk right into the flames every time. Low heat unfurls everywhere, from the pit of my stomach to where my fingers press into his lower back.

A low sound escapes his lips, and my heart stops. Before it turns into something it shouldn't, he pulls back but presses his lips to mine three times in quick succession, which takes my breath away all the same.

"Thank you." His thumbs tap my cheeks lightly. He starts to say something else but clears his throat, and I'm worried. I go to ask, but he gives me a soft shake of his head. "Later. Promise."

I go to argue, but voices from the party grow louder as they enter the house. I hand him his cup and move to stand next to him, attempting to create some appropriate space.

Instead, he wraps his free arm around me and pulls me in front of him. And then he tucks his hand into the front pocket of my jean shorts.

It takes everything in me to not take that hand and pull him far, far away from the people at this house to somewhere else, where it's just us.

The voices get louder and deeper, and I already know who it is before they even come into view. My dad and his three best friends from childhood. They, unlike my dad, are actually intimidating. They look like my dad, same stature, various shades of brown skin and bright smiles, when they do smile. They, like my dad, never really liked Myles. And have never seen me bring anyone else home.

"Ah, here he is. The man of the hour," Uncle Mike—who's not really my uncle but may as well be—says, a single eyebrow raised as he takes us in with his arms crossed.

Jackson tenses slightly behind me, but doesn't remove his hand, and I glance back. By the look of it, he's very unaffected. Aaron and Will give me big smiles, equally eyeing the boy behind me until my dad rolls his eyes and hits Mike on the back of his head.

"Chill out, Mike, for the love of god, she's not even your daughter." My dad shakes his head, taking a seat at the table.

Uncle Mike makes a motion with his hands. "I just want an official introduction," he says.

I smile as I take a sip of my own drink. "Well maybe if you asked nicely, I'd give you one. Kindness is key, Uncle Mike, haven't you learned that yet?"

Aaron and Will laugh. "God, I've missed you, Nina," Will says and opens his arms. I pat Jackson's hand and step forward and embrace him and then Aaron and then Mike, who rocks me back and forth.

"It's good to see you guys. It's been too long."

Jackson never takes his eyes off me as he stands there sipping his tea, which one, warms my heart that he's drinking it at all, and two, his gaze still sends chills down my spine.

I motion to him, and he steps forward, and I grab his hand briefly. "Jackson, this is Mike, Aaron, and Will. My dad's groupies and the uncles I never asked for. And this is Jackson." I smile.

Jackson sets his cup down and shakes each of their hands with a smile. "It's nice to meet you guys, even if you may want to interrogate or kill me."

They all laugh, and my dad snorts. "See, I told you he was funny."

I roll my eyes as we stand there chatting for a bit. Uncle Mike, who's really the only intimidating one, loses the façade way quicker than I expect. He and Jackson actually hit it off. I update them all on the article because if Mom or Dad weren't around and they were, they were also subject to the *Project Runway* and *Top Model* marathons.

Eventually, we end up all sitting at the dining room table and Mike is Jackson's new biggest fan. Aaron and Will right behind him. They laugh about basketball and sports. He even talks art with Aaron, who's been collecting since he was in college. My dad chimes in every once in a while, but I feel my father's gaze on me, and I know he's watching me watch Jackson.

Watch Jackson seamlessly fit into my life like there was always a space for him.

I turn to look at him. The sun is lower in the sky now, peeking through the kitchen window and setting a warm glow over the room, and my dad gives me a knowing smile.

Normally, I'd want to run and hide, but I'm in far too deep to care anymore. He leans over and pats my leg. "Proud of you."

I furrow my brows. "For what?"

"For just being you. Not settling for less than you deserve and chasing your dreams. I'm just—I'm proud of you."

A smile breaks across my face, and I lean over and kiss him on the cheek. "I love you, Dad."

"Love you more, kiddo." He winks, but then stands and claps. "Come on, boys, I'm in the mood to school y'all in some street ball."

All their heads turn towards my dad, and the energy shifts immediately. For kind of being old, their competitive and childish spirits haven't left the building. They used to cause trouble when they were younger, and I have no doubt they'll continue to. Jackson chuckles as they exit the kitchen, and I stand up, reaching my hand out.

He grips my hand in his and I smile up at him, his eyes warming when I do, and I can't wait to show him the house. The place I existed and grew up in without him and hopefully get to make new memories in with him. I drag him through the house, ready to spend some time alone with him until real life comes knocking again, like it always does.

Jackson

Nina's childhood bedroom is somehow both exactly what I imagined and totally different.

There are collages all over the walls, outfits, clothes, old-fashioned magazine covers and quotes all taped and glued together. I take another sip of the sweet tea she made me. It's not Mom's, no one will ever touch my mom's, but this is Nina's.

It's good. Really. And the fact that she went out of her way to make it for me makes it even better. I set it down as she climbs up onto the window seat and crosses her legs.

"What are we doing up here?" I ask her, the sounds of her family's Labor Day party reaching us all the way up here. It's loud and inviting and a welcome distraction from what's happening in my life.

She shrugs, meeting my eyes. She never used to do that. Always finding something else to look at or focus on. But not anymore. "I just wanted a minute alone with you."

I nod and take a seat next to her. Instantly, because I need the comfort, I grab her hand and pull her closer until she's situated with her back against the wall next to the open window and her legs draped over my lap with my hand on her thigh. Hesitation shines in Nina's eyes.

But she doesn't shy away. "Jackson, what's wrong?"

"My dad's in the hospital. Again. Has been for a week, and they didn't tell me until this morning." Her hand that was tracing circles on my arm stops, and I laugh dryly. "They didn't tell me because they didn't want me to worry."

Nina moves closer and threads her fingers through mine. "I'm sorry they did that. That wasn't right." Her fingers find mine, spinning the ring on my finger repeatedly.

I lean my head against the wall, eyes on the street below before landing on her face. "I understand why they did it," I say, but it's a lie. I don't get why they didn't tell me. And I'm so fucking angry, but I don't want to be angry at them.

Nina sees right through me, her lips quirking in a sad smile. "It's okay to be angry, Jackson. It was wrong for them to wait. He's your dad too." She presses her fingers into my palm. "Did they say how long he'd be admitted?"

"They don't know anything. And I don't know how to be here while he's in the hospital, and I don't know if he's going to go home. I'm sure he'll be fine, but I want to see him." My eyes roam over her face, the scar on the bridge of her nose, white against her brown skin. The full lips, a freckle on the bottom one, and her warm eyes.

"Then go see him. Can you take some time off work and go home?"

I sigh. "I'm nervous if I go then it means something is really wrong. Part of me just wants to be here with you. And I don't want to leave when things are going so well."

She adjusts until she's kneeling between my drawn-up knees, looking straight at me. Her skin is warm, and her touch puts me at ease. "You don't have to have it together all the time, Jackson. You don't need to be the one to lean on out of any obligation. Things aren't always perfect, and life can't always be sunny. But I'm not going anywhere."

There's a gentle look in her eyes, and I know there will never be another girl like her. She may walk with a rain cloud some days, always prepared for the worst, but then she turns around and dances in it. Tries to make the best out of it and take others with her.

I know I'm leaving. I have to go see my dad. Just in case, just to make sure he's okay and to spend time with him. Considering I don't know what type of life I would've had if it wasn't for him and my mom.

"I know I've been difficult," she starts.

I shake my head. "No, you haven't. But continue."

She rolls her eyes, and the sight loosens the tightness in my chest. "I'm with you, whatever you need to do, whether it's here in New York or in Georgia with your family, I'm still with you. I promise."

Twenty-Seven | Nina

"**S**o, he's leaving? For how long?"

I rub my hands over my face and roll my shoulders back. "I don't know, Harper." I sigh before throwing my clothes in my bag.

"And you're okay? I know he's going home for a good reason, but are you okay?" Her gray eyes flicker up to me. They stare into mine, and I bite the inside of my lip, pulling at the skin painfully until I drop it.

"It sucks. I'll miss him, but the whole situation sucks. And me being upset about him going for a bit isn't the same as his dad being in the hospital." I shrug, zipping the bag closed. It's packed for tonight. I'm heading to Jackson's since he leaves tomorrow and even though I didn't ask to come over, he invited me as soon as he booked the flight this week.

Harper shrugs. "Didn't say it was. I just wanted to check on you."

A sad smile forms, and I lean in, flicking her on the forehead in appreciation. I adjust the sweatshirt I have on, which is really Jackson's, before gently swinging my bag over my shoulder. After a quick glance in the mirror, Harper follows me out into the living room, where I grab my water and keys and throw them in my bag.

"Okay, well, just text me if you need anything."

I smile. "I'm not going to war, Harper."

"All right, fuck you, I was trying to be nice." She grins, and I roll my eyes, calling out a goodbye before shutting the door.

It's mid-September, so it's still warm, but the east coast humidity isn't bad for once, and the breeze that flows through the buildings sends light goosebumps over my legs as the sun starts to set, painting the sky a light pink. The subway isn't dead, but it isn't packed either: a few people scattered around, some with headphones hanging out of their ears or holding books in their hands.

My phone starts to vibrate in my hand, and Veah's name pops up on my screen. I slide my thumb over quickly. "Hey, Veah, what's up?"

"Hi, Nina," she says, and she sounds exhausted, just like Jackson did when he told me about his dad in my bedroom. "I just wanted to say thank you."

"For what?" My brows furrow as I stand up, getting ready to get off the subway.

"For convincing or encouraging Jackson to take off work and come home." She pauses, and I can hear her small inhale as I step back into the street. "He's mad at us because we didn't wanna say anything until we had to, and I don't like when he's mad at me, and I feel bad and—"

A sad smile tugs at my lips. "Veah, it's okay. You don't have to explain to me. And he's not mad at you, I can promise that."

And I can. Because he's not mad at Veah. He's not really mad at anyone anymore. He's just processing.

"Well, I just wanted to say thank you. He talks about you all the time, not just to me. To Dad, to Mom, to Mateo. We all wanna meet you soon. Hopefully, under better circumstances."

My chest swells with emotion as the breeze wraps around me again, and I pull my sweatshirt closer as I approach his building, my bag gently hitting my back with every step. "I'd love to, Veah. But seriously, just enjoy your time with him. You don't need to thank me."

"I do." I can hear her smile over the phone. "You're awesome, like really awesome."

A small laugh escapes my lips as I look both ways before ignoring the red hand and crossing the street. "No, that's all you. I'm practically obsessed, and I haven't even met you."

Her laugh comes across the speaker, causing my lips to pull into a grin. "Ditto. All right, well, I'm sure you're on the way to my brother's—"

I interrupt. "Are you stalking me?"

She laughs again. "Just my intuition, you know? Anyway, I'll let you go. Thank you again."

"Stop thanking me, but you're welcome. I'll talk to you later," I say as I open the door to his building. The doorman smiles at me as the call ends. He greets me before buzzing Jackson's room and letting me through to the elevators.

The ride is quick up to his floor. I walk down the familiar hallway, remembering the very first time I walked down this hallway, except in the opposite direction, towards the elevator. To think that I expected to never see him again.

It's weird to think that he's leaving. And I don't know when he'll be back.

My knuckles barely graze the door before it opens for me. I raise a brow. "Were you staring out the peephole or something?"

Jackson smiles. "Yeah, I'm actually expecting someone. Did anyone come in with you by chance?" He looks around playfully over my head before his eyes flicker back to mine.

"Oh, you are? No problem, I'll head out and send them up."

I begin to turn around until I feel his hand wrap around mine, and he pulls me back quickly. His blue eyes flash with amusement as he pulls me into the apartment and shuts the door, wrapping his arms around me tightly.

"I don't think whoever you're expecting would appreciate this," I mumble, looking up at him.

He rolls his eyes. "Oh, shut it."

I narrow my eyes. "Make me."

Jackson doesn't bother responding, he just leans down and presses his lips against mine. Instantly, I feel the tension in his shoulders lessen and warmth unfurls all over my skin and deep in my chest. It's beautiful and strange to think that I have that effect on him. Feeling the strain and the stress and the emotions almost evaporate at a simple touch, even for a second, is beautiful.

He pulls back, but not even an inch. I still feel the ghost of his lips against mine as they curl into a soft smile. "Hi," I mutter softly as his hold tightens briefly before lessening completely. He grabs the bag off my shoulder and slings it over his own as we walk into the open kitchen. And I don't think I'll ever get over how stunning his apartment is.

Full-sized windows line the walls of the open concept area. The living room and kitchen are flooded with pink and orange light from the setting sun. The black couch and black accents of the décor contrast with grays and whites of the counter tops and the walls that are decorated with sporadic artwork and pictures of his family. There are candles on the coffee table and on the island countertop. A few books have strayed from the bookshelves that are next to the TV mounted on the wall and are spread on the countertop and dining table.

The September issue of *Poze* sits front and center on the coffee table.

Simple black barstools contrast the white counters, and Jackson sets my bag down on one of them. There are marigolds in a vase on the counter, and the rest of the kitchen is simple:

all white counters with stainless steel appliances and warm overhead lighting. But the little accents like the kitchen magnets and a collection of shot glasses on the wall make it feel as warm as the rest of the apartment.

In here, the picture of the sun setting over the city skyline is just as beautiful as it is in his bedroom. I turn from admiring the room like I always do. The quiet sound of a Billy Joel record plays from a speaker, and I take a seat at the island.

"So, what're we doing tonight?" he asks, leaning across from me, his lightly tanned forearms resting on the cool surface.

"Anything you want. I just wanted to spend time with you before you left." I smile up at him, grabbing for the glass that I assume is his water and taking a sip. He raises an amused brow but doesn't say anything.

"Takeout and movies okay? Not up for much else." His words are quiet, and the tension slowly starts to rebuild in his shoulders as he stretches. I pad around the counter, kicking my shoes off and leaving them under the chair, until I'm next to him.

"Yeah, that's perfect. Want me to make cupcakes?" I rock my shoulders to the beat of the song in a playful manner, hoping to tug a smile from his lips at the mention of one of his favorite desserts. And I succeed.

"You could make me anything and I'd love it, but I do love those. With the extra chocolate chips?" He grins, and my heart flutters in my chest as I nod.

Jackson turns around, moving towards his fridge, and pulls out a bottle of the sweet Moscato that I like and two glasses. "I got your favorite. Two to be exact."

"Trying to get me drunk?"

He pours two very large glasses. "I might be. You're very touchy when you're drunk. You know I like that."

I raise a brow. "I touch you all the time."

Jackson comes over and places my glass in front of me. "I'm feeling needy."

Instead of answering, I wrap my arms around him, sliding my hands under his T-shirt until I feel the warmth of his skin on my palms. "Better?"

He looks down at me, wetness pooling in his eyes and I can see how badly he wants to go home. It's obvious he's afraid of what he might find when he does. Mostly because he tries to hide the clouds and the storms. Always tries to find the sun. But sometimes we can't push away the rain, no matter how hard we try. Not even Jackson.

But he just nods, resting his chin on the top of my head, and my heart beats deeply and slowly in my chest. Jackson surrounds me not only physically but emotionally as well. He's the brightest light I've ever known, and I wish I could take way the pain that's dimming that. Not just for me but for him.

But I can't do that. All I can do is hold him.

So, that's what I do.

● ● ●

"New York State of Mind" comes through the speakers as the track changes. The speaker system in his house allows us to hear the record player even from the bedroom, and he hits a remote, turning the volume up.

I'm sitting cross-legged next to him as he leans against the headboard, swaying his shoulders playfully to the song. "I love this song," he mutters, blinking his eyes open.

I take a sip of my wine. "Never would've guessed. Not like you're obsessed with Billy Joel or anything."

Jackson blinks, his blue eyes sparkling. "Smarty-pants tonight, my god."

My tongue swipes out, clearing the stray wine, and his eyes quickly flicker down, focusing on my lips and causing a burst of heat in my stomach and all the way to my toes, leaving a tingling sensation in its wake.

He reaches over and squeezes right above my knee, pulling a small squeal out of my lips. "Hey now, that hurt." I pout.

"No, it didn't. You're just ticklish and don't want to be tickled, so you say ouch. Like always."

I open my mouth to argue, but I can't because he's right.

"And for that, you should feed me a bite of my cupcake, please." Jackson grins, and my heart beats quicker for a moment, but I lift the plate in my lap, which previously held four full cupcakes and now only has one and a half left.

I pick up the fork, which I'm only using to avoid getting crumbs in his bed, and hold it out to him, and he makes a slow, dramatic show of taking it off the fork. I raise a brow, because if he was trying to be seductive, which is something he doesn't need to try at, he failed and only succeeded in getting frosting on his nose.

Jackson ignores it and just leans in for another bite, swaying his shoulders again to the song. He takes the piece of cupcake, singing the song lyrics in between his bites, and his last words are mumbled, "*New York state of mind.*" He licks his lips to get the stray crumbs of cupcake and a rush of heat takes over my body.

I roll my eyes as he does, ignoring my body's response.

He takes the plate out of my hand and places it on his nightstand, and before I have time to prepare, he's sitting up and pulling me onto his lap so that I'm straddling him. Blood rushes past my ears as my adrenaline spikes when his hands slide under my sweatshirt and rest on my waist as he holds us flush to one another.

"You have a little something on your nose," I mutter, but my voice is breathless, and he moves his thumb in slow circles, and I swear my heart skips a few beats.

The smirk pulling at his lips and the dimples fighting to show tell me he knows that.

He cocks his head slightly. "Do I? Interesting." I nod, and he quickly leans forward wiping the frosting on my cheek. I squeal, trying to pull away, but his hands keep me locked in place.

A smile grows on my lips, even though there's frosting on my cheek and still some on his nose. His hand squeezes my waist, and I squirm slightly.

"Hey, you got something on your cheek, did you know that?" He smirks.

"No, I never would've guessed. I wonder who did that?"

Jackson shrugs. "I don't know, but I'll clean it up for you."

He leans forward and kisses the bottom of my cheek and slowly flicks his tongue out to clear the beginning of the frosting trail off my face. I swallow hard, my breath catching in my throat as he moves up my cheek, and with each separate press of his lips, he slowly licks the rest of the frosting off my cheek. My entire body is humming, and an instant, hot heat unfurls in my stomach, scattering across the rest of my skin.

My heart is beating so loudly I'm sure he can hear it as he pulls back to smile at me, both dimples on display again.

"You're a little red. Everything okay?"

I attempt to push away from him, the heat still blooming in my cheeks, but his tight grip keeps me exactly where I am on his lap. And I can feel his entire body harden beneath me, lighting me up all at once.

"Stop teasing me."

His lips quirk up. "Tease you? I never do that."

I sigh dramatically, looking away as if looking for an escape until he pinches my skin lightly and my eyes flicker back to the

247

hazy amusement in his own eyes. Neither of us speaks for a few minutes. The silence fills the space, not in an uncomfortable way, but in a way in which we can both be. Both of us in the same space, not saying anything because we don't need to.

I watch him watch me. He does so lazily, slowly, as if he has all the time in the world to do so. I take the time to make sure I have little details memorized. Like that his freckles are heavier and closer together on his left cheek than on his right. The small white scars on his chest from playing—and falling—too much as a kid in the woods of Georgia. The shape of his lips and the feel of his fingertips.

I commit those two to the deepest part of my memory.

Jackson's voice is soft and low when it breaks the silence. "Thank you."

Those two little words made me feel content when Veah said them to me over the phone, but when Jackson says them, it feels like my heart is going to fall apart. His eyes are focused on his hand, which is currently playing with the bottom of my pajama shorts, brushing my skin every few seconds.

"You don't need to thank me. I haven't done anything." I rest my hands on his chest. Knowing I'd do anything he needed without hesitation.

"You've done everything. So, yes, I do. Just accept it." He taps my nose with his hand before letting it fall back to my skin, albeit a little bit higher. A small smile pulls at my lips.

His hand snakes around to my lower back, holding me where I am tightly while his other rests on my thigh, brushing back and forth.

The silence returns, and I press a soft kiss on the side of his lips. "I'll miss you," I say against his skin.

His eyes drop to my own; the grip on my leg gets tighter. As emotion builds in my chest, fervor for Jackson also starts to heat my blood. I want to be as close to him as I can tonight, emotionally, physically, in any way possible.

I look up at him, trying not to bite the inside of my lip, and try to further ignore the negative side of me that's been in my head since I found out about his dad. Try to ignore the small sinkhole that feels like it's getting bigger every second we get closer to tomorrow.

Jackson doesn't say anything. He just reaches up and cups my face, his thumb brushing over my cheekbone softly. I lean down and press my lips to his, losing myself in him, in the moment that's quiet and peaceful and safe inside his room. His arm wraps tighter around me, still underneath the sweatshirt, and my skin is on fire but not because of the heavy hoodie.

The dim light from the bedside table paints him golden in front of me. His hands grip the bottom of the sweatshirt, and his eyes flicker briefly to mine. I wiggle my brows playfully and nod, watching as amusement flashes in his eyes. Until he slowly pulls the sweatshirt off and the look in his eyes is replaced with something else.

"You're never gonna give that back, are you?" he murmurs before his tongue swipes my lips.

I pull back, breathless. "Wasn't planning on it. Do you want it back?"

His hands roam my back, cooler from the air hitting it, and my waist, and he pulls my bare chest against his. "No. Keep it. Keep everything."

My heart swells, and I have a feeling we aren't just talking about the sweatshirt, but I just kiss him, hard enough to make an impact, to make sure he remembers that I'll be right here waiting while he's gone. Knowing there isn't much else I can do while he deals with everything.

I ignore the sinking feeling, ignore the doubts. I ignore anything that isn't Jackson.

He's going home for a reason, a good fucking reason, and I'm hoping like hell everything is okay. That his dad is okay. That his family is okay. That he is okay.

But I realize deeply and suddenly that I am terrified to lose him.

So, I focus on having him while he's here. How he touches me like I'm something special or the way he kisses me with intent every single time. He pulls my hips down, pressing me onto him, and I feel it at the deepest part of me, and I want him everywhere.

My thoughts, my body, my heart, my life, I want him everywhere.

One hand comes up and cups my cheek, pulling me closer as our lips dance together. The swipe of his tongue on my lips sends a wave of heat to my core. His other hand brushes back and forth on the band of my lace underwear, teasing me, his fingers slipping under every few seconds before drawing back. I roll my hips over his, chasing the feeling, and I smile against his lips when he lets out a soft groan.

I lean back, my hands trailing down his chest, messing with the band of his sweatpants. When I look up, his blue eyes are dark with lust and a warmth that makes me feel whole.

"Do we need these?" I ask, and he shakes his head, one of his dimples appearing.

Slowly, I scoot back and drag his sweatpants off and toss them behind us, leaving us equally clothed, in only our underwear. His boxer briefs are tight, and just looking at the sight of him—long, lean muscled legs and a smooth stomach, up to the blond curls dancing over his forehead—lights me up.

"Come here." He motions, and I narrow my eyes, feeling playful where I sit back at the foot of the bed.

His eyes flicker down, over my bare chest to where black lace covers the rest of me and back up. The slow perusal sets me on fire, and I'm ready to walk on the sun. Jackson sits up and moves quickly. His hand wraps around my ankle, and he pulls me forward, sliding me across the bed gently yet roughly enough for me to lose any air left in my lungs.

"Trying to run away from me, Scott?" His hands are on either side of my head, my legs drawn up so that he can rest between them, and I revel in the weight of him.

I reach up and brush a curl out of his face. "Not anymore."

He kisses me, harder this time, rolling his hips over and over me, sending little shockwaves over me until I have to pull away to catch my breath. Again. I grip the back of his neck as he places kisses against my cheek, down to my throat, nipping and licking every step of the way. He traces my collarbone with his mouth, with light kisses, and his tongue dances over my skin, placing a kiss on the hollow of my throat in between.

"Jackson," I pant, trying to move my hips against his to alleviate the ache growing between my legs with every second. His thumb plays with the underside of my breast, teasing the skin.

He leans up, smiling against my lips. "I'm just getting started." Despite myself, I blush deeply.

He kisses his way downward, over my ribs, trailing his fingers after his tongue, over my hips until he reaches my underwear. My heart beats wildly in my chest when his fingers curl on the edge of the lace. I glance down, already consumed by him and am greeted with the sight of him already looking up at me. I nod and when those blue eyes light up, it might actually be the last thing I ever see.

Jackson looks at me like he's never seen light before.

Tightly, he holds my hips down as he kisses around right where I want him. He nips the sensitive skin all the way from the back of my knee up my thigh, alternating between that and soft, open-mouthed kisses, up to where my hip meets my pelvis and across.

"I love this tattoo," he murmurs against my skin as he traces the ink on the side of my left hip. "And this scar." He kisses the scar on the top of my thigh I got when I was younger. "And this spattering of freckles." He traces my lower stomach. "There is no part of you that I'm not obsessed with."

He reaches up and intertwines his fingers with mine and places them on my hips. Holding me down while holding my hand.

And I'm burning for him, pulsing everywhere. "Please," I pant, twisting closer to him.

I'm fully unprepared when I feel the slow drag of his tongue, and I bite my lip to keep the moan from escaping my mouth as I squirm, trying to get closer. My back arches slightly again as his tongue continues to swirl and he sucks on the sensitive spot, his left hand firmly intertwined with mine, holding my hips against the bed as I try to scoot closer, try to do anything to help the pressure pooling quickly in the pit of my stomach.

He pulls back briefly, and I look down as he glances up, lust flaring in his eyes before he leans back in. Jackson gives another slow lick and finally slides a finger into me. My teeth let go of my lip, and I can't help the moan that escapes past my lips as his finger slides out and two slide back in, curling upward as his tongue continues in slow, steady motions. I squeeze his hand tightly, trying to ground myself.

He slows down the movements of his tongue and speeds up the curling of his fingers, and I try to hold the loud breathy noises from escaping past my lips as I bury my free hand into his curls, trying to find anything to hold onto. He chuckles against me, the vibrations causing my stomach to tighten further as my heart beats thunderously in my chest. My entire body is tingling from my ears to the tightness in my stomach as he sucks lightly on the sensitive bud and curls his fingers all at once, sending me into a frenzy as every single sensation explodes throughout my body, leaving me dizzy as the orgasm flows through me.

Fuck.

As I come down, he slowly kisses his way back upwards and hovers over me, his eyes shining, and he licks his lips once before bending down and kissing me. Feeling every inch of him as he grinds his hips against mine and brings the hand that still holds my own up next to my head. I'm still a little breathless from moments before, so I pull away, leaning my head to the side to try to catch my breath as his lips latch onto my throat.

"You are absolutely fucking stunning, Nina," he whispers against my skin.

I toy with the band of his briefs, and he doesn't hesitate to shimmy them off. He tosses them off to the side and reaches in the nightstand. He comes back to me, a condom in hand, and I reach down and curl my hand softly around him and watch as his eyes flutter closed, his head falling forward into my shoulder.

Jackson presses soft kisses where my shoulder meets my neck as I slowly glide my hand up and down him until his hips start to move in time with my hand and I can hear his breathing hitch. I push gently on his shoulder until he's lying on his back and I'm straddling him. His eyes widen slightly before his lips curl into a smile when I lean down and kiss him again, slowly and deeply.

I gently tug the condom out of his hand and slide it onto him before deepening the kiss further as his hands grip my hips. I pull back just slightly as our noses touch, and bite his lip gently, causing him to chuckle, before guiding him into me.

I bite my own lip as I let him stretch me, trying and failing to keep the breathy noises inside, feeling his fingers dig into my hip as I gently cup his chin with my hands, unable to breathe deeply with all the sensations flowing through me for a second time. It takes a second for me to adjust, but when I do our eyes connect as he thrust his hips up gently, causing my breath to hitch.

With each rise and fall when our hips meet, I twirl mine slightly, slowly, relishing the sound of the breathless moans leaving his mouth and the firm grip he has on my hips. I lean forward, deepening the feel of him until I kiss right under his ear and his throat as the speed increases slightly, reveling in the groan that escapes his lips.

Committing the sound to memory.

The pressure builds again between my thighs and deep in my stomach, and I grip his shoulders tightly as one of his palms spreads flat on my back, pressing us together tightly. I can feel his chest rise and fall with every short breath, and his fingers dig into my back.

And before I know it, he's spinning us over until I'm on my back. Quickly, he has my hands intertwined with his, and he holds them above my head, stretching me and taking control.

"Jackson," I breathe out as he rolls his hips in a terribly addicting rhythm. "You're killing me." My fingers curls around his as my pulse quickens and my skin heats.

He leans down, lips brushing the sensitive skin of my neck. "You killed me first."

A laugh bubbles past my lips but it quickly turns into a breathless moan. He settles in between my drawn-up knees, pushing them out with his body. I fight to have my hands back, burning to touch him as he strokes slowly. And I need him to kiss me, to do anything but torture me slowly. Jackson trails kisses everywhere but my lips, over my hot chest, my heart pounding painfully, up my neck as he takes me higher with each stroke.

My body is burning, all for him, and I would've waited years more if it meant he was at the finish line.

"Come on, baby," he says huskily against my lips.

Every time he calls me that, I forget my name for a second. And in the haze of my pleasure, I almost beg him to never call me anything but that again.

"I want it all Nina," he whispers softly against my neck, nipping at the skin. "Every inch of you, every sound that leaves your mouth." He slows, drawing out the torture he's delivering so beautifully well. "I want you."

I dig my nails into his palms where they're held hostage and push up against him, feeling him everywhere as my body tenses. He lets go with one hand and drags it down my hot skin until he's pressing against me in rhythm with his body.

My grip tightens as he brushes his lips against mine. "Only if you give me the same," I murmur against him. After a moment, he slips his tongue between my lips in a silent but addicting answer.

I can feel a tremor pass over his body as the sensations burn through me. And the loud, throaty groan against my throat he lets out as he comes echoes in my head and all around me over and over again. The pressure peaks again and blossoms out, setting my nerves on fire in one single burst, spreading all over my skin until I'm slowly burning in the best way seconds after him.

This man might very well be the death of me.

His body slows, his breath still coming in short pants as I sink into the mattress and my entire body relaxes, my hands still in his hold. After a moment of us just simply catching our breath, he leans up and kisses me softly, warmly, relaxing me further. He lets go of my hands as we lay there, him on his side and me tucked as close to him as I can get. My leg between his and my chest against his own.

The silence is comfortable, it always has been with him. But I want to hear him talk to me.

"Tell me, have you always been this beautiful?" I ask. I brush my thumb over his nose and press it against his lips. He nips it in response, his cheeks flushed. From my words or our actions, I'm not sure. When he stays silent, I continue. "I mean it. Not just your looks Jackson, but everything about you. Your optimism, your quiet strength, the way you care about people." I shake my head, moving closer. "The way you care about me."

Jackson smiles softly when I blink, clearing the emotion from my eyes. "Don't even try it, Valentina. Have you seen yourself?" The heat of his body seeps into mine. "You're one of the most loving people I know. You would go to war for the people you love, and you'd make them cupcakes for the journey there. You're confident and you're funny and you light up entire rooms when you enter them." He traces over the dark spot on my bottom lip. "I can't get enough. Of you, of everything that makes you who you are. And your smile, I think I love that more than anything."

He leans in, tugging at my bottom lip with his teeth before ending it in a soft kiss. "And I hate that I'm leaving because I'm going to miss you too."

It feels like flowers are blooming on my heart at those words. Even though he's leaving, and I have no idea what will happen, if his dad will be okay, if he will, I enjoy the fact that I'm feeling something I never thought I'd feel again.

Except it doesn't feel like falling this time. It feels like flying.

And I hope neither of us has to crash.

T|he Georgia heat suffocates me as I step out of the sterile
hospital environment.

The front desk greets me as I exit, for almost the fifth week
in a row, and I recognize almost everyone on staff by now. I could
do this in my sleep. Every day, I head down the left hall towards
the cardio department, to the D elevator up to the fourth floor,
turn left, and walk past the first nurses' station, and head eight
rooms down to the left. And to leave, I just retrace my steps.

I hate how easy it's become.

The weight sits heavy on my shoulders.

The first two weeks I was here, it wasn't so bad. My dad
smiled at me, giving me a big hug and ignoring his instructions
to not get out of the hospital bed. He was still strong with the
lean strength he always carried with him from building all
sorts of things for Mom or for the house, the strength he had
from always moving, always finding something to do, and his
volunteer hours at the fire station. And he was so happy to see
me. My entire family let me spend most of the first week with
him alone, only stopping in to say hi or make sure he was doing
okay.

I got to talk to him about Nina.

His eyes had a knowing look when I first brought her up as

he settled in with the banana bread she had made—at the last second—for me to take. "What's she like?" he asked.

I kicked my feet up on the bed from my chair. "I'm not sure I have enough words, Dad. She's brilliant. She's funnier than she gives herself credit for, at least to me she is. She makes me laugh all the time without even trying. And she's got a tough exterior sometimes." I smiled. "But she's also somehow the sweetest person I've ever met. Puts everyone above her own needs even when she shouldn't. And she's gorgeous."

"Sounds like how I feel about your mom," he said, leaning back. "You were such a sap when you were younger, always making Valentine's cards for school and bringing everyone gifts. You were the most loving child I'd known, and you only wanted love in return. I remember you asking about girls in high school and then stopping in college 'cause it wasn't cool to talk to your dad, but I always told you, you'd know. Didn't know how to explain it, and you didn't get it. But you would, one day."

"I get it. I get it now," I said, and he smiled, saying more with the simple pat on the hand than he could with his words. Like he knew just as well as I did.

I've known for a while, but it settled in fully sitting there with him.

That whole first week, Nina and I facetimed whenever I wasn't at the hospital, which wasn't often and was usually late, but she answered every time. Usually at her desk working on an article or curled up into her bed. Finally, I caught her during the day so she could meet my dad. He took the phone out of my hand before I could blink, and they hit it off instantly. He told stories about me as a kid, like teaching me how to drive stick shift or ride ATV's or playing basketball together. Nina told him about the magazine and how I bought them for her, about the swan boats and how excited she was to meet him. My heart had swelled in my chest at the sight.

Since I had been away for Nina's twenty-fourth birthday at the beginning of October, I sent three separate packages. At work, she got delivered chocolate covered strawberries, a weakness I'd discovered from talking to her parents. A bouquet of marigolds and tulips at her apartment, since I found out she loved those from Harper and Sloan. And since she still had an old-school CD player in her room, I sent her the burnt CD of the country playlist. We'd talked from when she got off work until she fell asleep, and she'd listened to my horrible rendition of "Happy Birthday," despite her protests, and I was rewarded with a smile. The one she saves just for me.

It felt like even though I wasn't there, she was with me.

Those days my dad was smiling and walking, and doctors were hopeful.

But now, it's been almost five weeks.

And he's still in the hospital. We all smile less and sit in silence more. Every passing day, my shoulders get a little heavier and the distance between Nina and I gets a little bit larger.

We don't talk as much; I only call when I don't feel overwhelmed by everything since I'm working from home and practically living in the hospital with my dad. I haven't talked to her on the phone in over a week and have had to settle for sporadic text messages.

It's not that I don't want to. I want to talk to Nina all the time, every day. But it's harder and harder to put on a smile when my dad is getting worse.

His heart is declining, he's constantly getting tests done, EKG's, echo's, scans, the whole nine yards. Him and I talk about everything under the sun, sports, New York, what he is—was—building, and I tell him about Myles and how we haven't talked, because I'm ignoring him now, and I talk about everything except what life would become if my dad was no longer here. He tries to get me to talk about things, about what might happen,

259

and every time I ignore it. Settling deeply into denial. Wanting to spend as much time with him as possible without addressing the possibility of losing him.

And not that Nina needs me to fake a smile on the phone, but I'm also running out of things to say.

Watching my dad decline is sending me somewhere I've never been, and I don't want anyone to worry about me. So, instead of pretending, I just don't say anything.

But I have time now, and I don't hesitate to press her name, at the top of my favorites list in my phone. She answers after the second ring as I climb into the car I rented, sighing as I lean against the seat.

"Hello?" She sounds hesitant. The sound of her voice lifts my shoulders a fraction. But right now, it's not enough to make a difference.

I miss Nina so much, but I don't feel like the person she knew anymore.

I don't feel like anyone except someone who might lose their dad.

Nina

"Hey," Jackson sighs out, and instantly, I know this isn't going to be a night where I can distract him or send him any light. Sadness seeps through the phone.

This had been one of those weeks that just won't go my way. It feels like the entire world is working against me, and no matter how hard I try, no matter how positive I try to stay, the world laughs in my face and sends something else. I thought that when I left work today, because it was Friday maybe I'd catch a break. But no. Apparently spilling my coffee all over myself this morning wasn't enough—or accidentally deleting my article.

The final straw was someone spilling their entire smoothie on me on the subway home.

It took everything I had not to burst into tears.

There's nothing I can do to make Jackson feel better. And there's nothing I can do to stop the anxiousness I feel in my veins.

"How is everything?" I hate that I asked that. I want to cry, for the third time today. Because it doesn't seem like his dad is going to get any better. And I hate that he has to go through this, that his entire family has to go through this.

He laughs dryly. "Shitty. He's not getting better. They think there's a diseased vessel or something, so they're going to try surgery soon. But he's never going to get any better."

"Jackson, I'm so sorry."

"It's fine."

"It's not fine—"

He huffs. "I know it's not fine, Nina. Nothing is fine. Everything fucking sucks." He sighs again. "I'm sorry. I didn't mean to snap at you, I just—" His voice breaks, and the sound cracks my heart open like thunder does at the beginning of a storm. "I don't know what life will be like without my dad. I don't know what a world without him looks like."

My eyes flutter closed, and it feels like my chest is on fire from holding back tears, and I can't imagine how he's doing right now. Because I would be the same.

"But I called to tell you that and to tell you that I had to cancel my flight." I forgot he was supposed to come home, just briefly, early next week, mostly for work. "I can't leave. I'm taking time off work. And I'm sorry."

"It's okay. You don't have to apologize."

"I do. I miss you, but everything is just hurtling towards me right now. And I'm sorry I can't be there or be present. I just need to prepare for this."

I lean my head back, willing the tears to stay in my eyes. They don't listen. "I get that, Jackson. I miss you too. But I'm here however and whenever you need me, whatever that is."

It's silent for a moment. And not the comfortable kind. This silence is filled with unsaid words and deeper meanings neither of us wants to talk about. His dad dying. Him not coming back. Me unsure of what he needs. Him pulling away. Everything crumbling down under his once sure and steady feet.

"Okay, well, I'm gonna go. I've gotta get home to my mom. But I'll talk to you soon, okay?" he says quietly, the music in his car playing softly in the back.

"Okay," I whisper.

Neither of us say anything for a moment or two again until we both say a quiet goodbye and the beeps of an ended call echo in my ear and chill me to the bone. I grip my phone tighter for a moment before dropping it on the couch next to me. Before I decide to throw it at the wall and watch it shatter.

Mierda.

Why do parents have to die? I know that we can't fight loss, that it will happen eventually no matter how good or bad of a person we may be, but it still *fucking* sucks. Part of his entire world is going to fall from beneath him, and I don't know what to do. I don't know if he wants me there and is scared to ask. I don't know what he needs, what he wants, because *I'm* too scared to ask.

My entire body feels off as I stand up from the couch, wrapped in a blanket because I can't seem to get warm. Goosebumps that won't go down rest uncomfortably on my skin, and I know that I shouldn't, but I grab the wine out of my fridge and pour. Anything to get warm, anything to forget everything.

Today, this week, the past few weeks have been awful. My only highlights of them had been when Emma came over Tuesday night and joined our dinner. Told me that her and

Myles were doing better and that's he's talking to someone consistently. She fit seamlessly into the group dynamic, and it was great. The night allowed me to take my thoughts off Jackson and my anxiety for once.

The other bright side is I don't think this week could get much worse.

As I bring the glass to my lips, there's a knock at my door. My eyes shoot to the clock on the oven. It's too early for my parents to be here after dinner, and Harper and Sloan both have keys. I take a deep breath and quickly pat my cheeks with cold water to make myself feel like a person again. A glance through the peephole tells me that hopes of my day not getting any worse are fucking wrong.

I open the door and come face to face with Myles, who stands nervously, shifting his weight between his feet, with his hands in his pockets, and I have absolutely no idea what to expect at this point.

"Hey, can we talk?"

blink a few times to make sure I'm seeing this correctly. That Myles is at my door asking me to talk again. Sure enough, no longer how long I close my eyes, when I open them, he's still there.

"Sure," I sigh and step back, letting him inside. As he walks in, I run a hand over my face and realize I probably look ridiculous.

He stands around awkwardly for a moment before taking a seat at the countertop, and I stand across from him, my hands gripped around my water glass. "I'm sorry to pop up like this."

I nod. "It's fine. You can't stay long; my parents are stopping by soon." Which is true. They promised to stop at my favorite bakery after their dinner. Somehow knowing I needed them without me saying it.

"Of course. This won't take long, I promise."

A sigh escapes my lips as I play with the bottom of the hoodie, looking anywhere but at Myles. "What exactly is this, Myles? What are you doing here?"

He looks around, eyes flickering from the living room to the kitchen and back to me. "I'm sure Emma's told you we've been working on things." I wait. "And I'm here to apologize for what happened. I was an asshole, and I had no right."

I swallow, taking a sip of my water to soothe my dry throat.

He runs a hand over his hair and rubs his chin as he sighs. "I am sorry, Nina. You didn't deserve that. You or Jackson. There's no excuse for my actions." He shakes his head slowly, his eyes closed for a second. "You and Jackson are two of the best people I know. I just never expected to see you two together. I'm not here to make excuses, so again, I'm sorry. I'm not saying this fixes anything or we have be friends. I just wanted you to know."

I'm pretty sure I'm in shock. I've never, in my entire life, heard the words *I'm sorry* from Myles Henderson. To be hearing them now, after being treated like shit, is astounding and something I never expected. I was happy to hear about him and Emma working through things, but I never expected him to knock on my door and apologize.

He's right, we'll probably never be friends. But this makes him slightly easier to tolerate, especially as I become friends with Emma.

"That's not all, though. I'm sorry for everything. For everything I never apologized for all those years ago when we were kids. I was an asshole who didn't know what he wanted and thought he could have everything. I was wrong, and I was wrong for ever treating you or anyone, like that. So, I'm sorry."

I think if my heart stopped in shock right now that would be fitting. It's beating so quickly, I wouldn't be surprised if he could hear it. I never in a million years ever expected anything like this from him.

"Thank you, Myles." I blink, trying to form more words, but I don't know if I can. "That means more than you know." Myles gives me a sad smile.

"It took me too long, but I'm trying. To be better."

I nod, a small smiling forming on my lips.

Emma makes him want to be better, and that's all I can ask for.

"That's not the only thing, though," he adds, and my eyes shoot up to his, my heart beating deeply in my chest.

"What else is there?"

Myles hesitates and inhales, holding the breath before letting it out in a deep sigh. "It's about Jackson."

My eyebrows furrow. "What about him?"

"I've tried to talk to him, which hasn't worked out. But Emma has, briefly, and she told me about his dad. He won't answer my calls, and I don't blame him, since I did the same."

I nod, gnawing the inside of my cheek. "His dad isn't doing well. Neither is he." It feels weird to be talking about Jackson with Myles. Feels like I got sucked into some parallel universe and everything is tilted on its axis.

His brown eyes meet mine, and all it does is make me miss Jackson's blue ones.

We fall into silence for a moment, both of us just sitting in my kitchen not saying anything. The only sound is the TV I left on and the occasional honk of a car driving down a busy street.

I come back to my senses and circle around to his original statement. "Okay, but I know that, so why are you here? To talk to me about my—about Jackson." I hesitate.

The word boyfriend sits like a weight on my shoulders. Because I realize we never defined anything. Not that it mattered. We weren't in a rush; we both knew we were exclusive. I just don't know what to call him in front of Myles, and my heart hurts in my chest for a second.

I take a deep breath. "What about him? Is there something I don't know?" And even though he doesn't ask, I pour him a water, sliding it over the countertop, and he grips the glass gently.

"No, I just don't think you've seen this side of Jackson before, and I figured the least I could do is give you some advice."

I stand up a little straighter. "I don't really want your advice, Myles. I didn't ask for it." My words don't come out as harsh or as stern as I would like them to, but I have very little fight left in me after this week as it is.

"Believe me, I know. And I know that I'm overstepping in many ways, I just—I want to help. Just this once, please let me. You don't even have to listen if you don't want to. But I've seen Jackson going through tough shit with his family before. Mateo had a rough time in high school, and I know how Jackson reacts."

I take another, much bigger sip, my eyes flickering around my apartment, a space that Myles has never been a part of until now, and he's offering help. "Fine."

There's a sad smile on Myles's face as I reluctantly accept whatever help he's trying to offer. I wonder if he realizes how different we are now from how we were, how different our lives became from what we expected.

"He's going to shut down. If his dad doesn't get better." He sighs. "He's going to shut down. And make it seem like everything is fine or that he has it handled. Like he doesn't need anyone."

Immediately, I can feel the tears fighting to make another appearance, but I won't cry in front of Myles ever again.

"But he does. He's not going to ask you or admit it," Myles leans forward, resting his forearms on the counter, "but I'm telling you he does. He will. Maybe not yet, but if his dad dies, he is going to. I just wanted you to know."

Myles is the first one to say the word. Jackson and I both dance around it when we talk about his dad. We certainly don't talk about him dying. But I think we both know what's happening. It hurts to hear the word.

"I don't want to push him away or suffocate him. I don't—" I shake my head because I don't even know what I'm trying to say anymore.

"I know I broke your trust a long time ago and never got it back, and this isn't me saying I've earned it, because I know that

I haven't. But on this, trust me. You will not. I think that should it happen; you need to go down there."

My eyes widen, and it's not as if I hadn't thought about it. That if he needed, I would go, but I don't want to overstep.

"Not right now. I know you have to work. But if something happens, I'm telling you to go. Jackson's going to need you whether he says it or not."

I nod, but I barely feel the movement as I digest the words. "Okay."

His eyebrows shoot up. "Okay?"

For the first time today, I laugh. Not a big one, just a small hiccup of one, but still, it feels nice. Even if it is with Myles. "Did you expect me to put up a fight?"

He cocks his head to the side with a smile. "Honestly, kind of."

My lips pull into a sad grin, and my grip loosens on the glass. "Yeah, well, I don't have any fight left in me. I just want Jackson, and I want him to be okay."

And I know that a scared me, one scared of putting myself out there, of being there fully for someone, of admitting how much I want to be with them, would've never said that out loud. The real me, the grown up and more mature me, wants to be there for him. Even if that means simply standing by his side so he's not alone.

Even if some part of him won't want me there.

So, I will happily take the advice given to me about how to deal with this situation, what to do. Even though this all still absolutely sucks, and even though I've been told he's going to shut down and pull away. I understand why it's happening, and I understand it still hurts.

I will do everything in my power to make sure that he gets through this.

No matter how much it hurts in the process.

I stand up straight, and even though I still want to cry, can still feel the weight sitting deeply in my chest and pricking at my eyes, in this moment, I feel a little bit stronger. I never thought I'd have Myles to thank for that. But I do.

"Thank you, Myles. I mean it, all of this—thank you." My lips curl up slightly, and I wrap my arms around my torso.

He stands up, warmth fills his eyes, and he nods, plucking his keys out of his pocket. "You're welcome. It was long overdue." I walk him to the front door, our footsteps pattering softly over the floor. "Seriously, Nina. I'm sorry, and I hope everything works out okay. You deserve it. You deserve everything. I hope you know that."

"Thank you, Myles." I swallow hard, the words just adding to every other emotion building in my chest. And I don't know why I ask, but I do, "Are you happy?"

He meets my eyes, and my chest tightens. I don't want Myles. Haven't for a long time, and especially not now. But the little girl that used to run down the streets with him, walked through the halls and watched him grow up, still needs to hear it. I'm not a hateful person. I'm not going to wish him pain or hope that his marriage fails. Life is different than those two little kids ever thought it would be, but I think we each found something else, something that fits better. So, I just need to know that he's happy.

His lips turn up. "I am."

I nod. "Good, I'm glad." My voice doesn't falter, and he exits shortly after.

After locking the door, I head into the living room, collapsing onto the couch to wait for my parents. I sink into the cushions and take a few deep breaths, knowing that I can't predict what the next few weeks will bring.

As much as I wasn't expecting Myles to show up, his advice gave me a little bit of ground. Something to lean on should I need it when I have no idea what could happen.

With Jackson, with his dad, with us. But I know I'll do whatever needs to be done for him. He pushed his way into my life, and I'll do my best to make sure he gets through this, however I can.

Thirty | Jackson

Octtober came and went, and the lingering warmth it left into November came and took my dad with it. Leaving only an endless chill behind.

The last two weeks were hard, harder than I ever expected them to be. After his surgery, he came back okay at first before getting sick in the hospital with postoperative pneumonia. He was too weak to fight it off.

Now, my mom doesn't have a husband.

Veah, Mateo, and I don't have a dad. Not anymore.

It's been three days, and it still doesn't feel real because only two days before that, he was laughing, smiling—coughing, yes—but he was my dad. We were talking about bringing him home. Veah had snuck in takeout from his favorite spot, and all five of us sat around, eating and joking like we used to.

He kept telling us cheesy jokes and kissing my mom in front of us despite our protests. At the end, right before they kicked us out of extended visitors' hours, he told us he was proud of all of us, how much he loved us, and he let me know, when I bent down to give him a hug, how happy he was that I'd found someone like Nina.

Looking back, we should've known something was wrong. He wasn't usually sentimental, and I should've fucking known.

But I didn't. Now I'm sitting in my childhood bedroom with no dad to call, no dad to talk to, and no way to process anything.

I haven't talked to Nina since I told her, and that weighs me down too, sits on me like a weight, pushing and pushing. Adding to the guilt I feel at not coming home earlier, not spending more time with Dad despite practically living in the hospital room, not seeing something was wrong.

I still remember the way she held in her own tears on the phone. It was a Wednesday, and as soon as I was out of the hospital room, desperate for fresh air, I had called her.

She was breathless when she answered with a soft hello, and everything came crashing down. I'll never forget how I felt saying the words out loud to someone who wasn't my family.

"Hey." My voice had choked up almost instantly.

"Jackson?" she said, hesitant and pacing in the background. "You can tell me."

I wanted to disappear. "My dad is gone. He's not here anymore."

He's not here anymore. I think those were the hardest words I'd ever said in my life. The silence was deafening and had stretched between us as she searched for something to say. But we both knew there was nothing to be said.

"I wish there was something better to say, but I'm here for you, however I can be."

She'd talked me through a mini breakdown or a rant or whatever one can call it. I ranted about Veah, how she won't admit she's not okay, how she keeps asking us if we're okay when we all know she isn't and that none of us are. Mateo left almost instantly and has been in and out ever since, avoiding all of us. Mom didn't say anything at first, just cried.

Now, I haven't talked to Nina since. Three whole days I've spent living in a weird haze of a world. And I feel like an asshole, but I'm barely functioning as it is, trying to keep my family together, trying to check on them, and if I talk to Nina, she'll make it okay for me to break down fully, and I don't have time for that. I don't have time to not be okay.

Not with the funeral tomorrow.

There's a knock on my door, and it pushes open, my mom appearing. Her dark skin is duller than usual, tired, but she's still my mom, and she isn't crying, and it makes me feel just a fraction better.

She sits next to me. "You ready for tomorrow?" she asks, and I nod and then shake my head. My eyes flicker up to my suit that's hanging up on the door to my bathroom.

"No. Are you?"

She sighs deeply, leaning her head on my shoulder. "No. I'm not."

I wrap an arm around my mom, the women that adopted me, made me feel loved and needed, and hold her close.

"I miss him so much already."

My eyes prick, and I stare up at the ceiling, willing the tears away. My mom doesn't need to see me cry, she needs me to make sure she gets through tomorrow. "Me too, Mom. It doesn't seem the same. Everything seems off."

We sit together in silence for a bit. Somehow, even though he hasn't been here the entire time since I've been home, the house feels quieter. Emptier. My mom pats my leg, turning to look at me. "Did you tell Nina about the funeral?"

Guilt pricks again. "No. She has to work and has a life, and I'll just see her when I go back."

My mom sighs. "She'd want to be here for you, you know that, right?"

Deep down I do know that. But I cannot face everything yet, and Nina will bring it out of me as soon as I see her. "Yeah."

She pats my leg like she used to do right before she was gonna say something important. "I know what you're doing."

I look up. "You're being the big brother. My first son. You're trying to take care of us, and I love you for it, but you've gotta take care of you too. And asking for someone you care about to be with you when you need them is not weak. It's strong."

She goes on. "I love you so much, baby, and your dad did too. But it's okay to let it out and to lose it like the rest of us. This is hard, and it's going to be hard for a long time, but if you bottle it up, it's just going to get heavier." She pats my cheek. "And if you keep it in too long, I'll never get my sunshine boy back. While you're taking care of us, please make sure you're taking care of you too. It's what your dad would've wanted. It's all he ever wanted."

"Mom," I sigh as she stands.

"No. You don't have to listen to me now. It's okay." She smiles for the first time, a sad one but a smile. "I just worry about you sometimes, okay? I'm a mom, please let me worry."

She wipes her hands on her light blue jeans and leans down, cupping my cheeks like when I was a kid. We look nothing alike. Never have and never will, but she is my mom through and through, and my dad was my dad. I wouldn't have asked for anything else on this earth but the life they gave me.

Mom squeezes my face and kisses my forehead. "Let's just get through tomorrow together, okay?"

I stand up and hug her tightly. "I love you."

I just hope we get out on the other side.

• • •

The first thing that happens when we get to the funeral is a bunch of old firefighters greet me instantly. My dad used to volunteer when I was younger and was always around and hanging out with his old friends. The former chief, Collin, my dad's best friend, hugs me tightly, patting my back before grabbing my mom's hand.

"If you need anything at all, you let us know, okay?" he says gruffly, the emotion clear in his voice. Veah squeezes my left hand, where she's holding on tightly, and I squeeze it back.

"Same goes for you, okay?" My mom says to the chief, patting his cheek. He gives her a smile, and they let us head in first to prepare.

The front of the room where we'll stand for the viewing is set up beautifully. My dad's urn is on the table with a collage of photos of him with us and with his friends. I chose to put his favorite baseball cap up there, Veah and Mateo chose their own things, and my mom put the tie he wore on their wedding day on the table.

Veah clings to my hand as we walk through, and for once, she's quiet, her eyes wet with tears, and I just wish I could take it away. Mateo is silent on my right as Mom walks in front of us, head high and putting on a brave face. We set up, taking our places, and before I know it, people are filing in. Shaking hands with them, hearing them tell stories about my dad is breaking my heart little by little, but I manage to hold back the tears. Each story is like a weight added to my shoulders. It gets heavier and heavier as people tell me things I never knew about my dad. Stories from the firehouse, about how he actually had to save a cat from a tree one time or how he almost burnt down a classroom in high school science. Every detail is so perfectly my dad, but it breaks me little by little.

I never let go of my sister's hand, and at one point she has to step back, and I shield her from the crowd as best I can. Mateo keeps his head high, but I see the tense set of his jaw and how he shakes out his hands after greeting everyone.

As much as I love taking care of them, I would never stop, I realize I'm a fucking idiot because I wish Nina was here.

I wish I had her to lean on.

I look around the crowded room. The line is shorter now as people take their seats, and we'll start the ceremony soon. The next person says hi with a soft voice to Mateo, the first in line, and I look to my left to see a familiar face. Nina's brown eyes flicker to mine as she shakes my brother's hand. He gives her the tiniest smile as she squeezes his hands before moving closer to me.

Shock fills my chest, and Veah squeezes my hand, leaning up. "Thought you might need her here after all." My chest tightens, and Veah gives me a soft smile. "You've been taking care of us. It was my turn to take care of you."

I'm speechless as Nina steps in front of me with a sad smile on her face, but her warm brown eyes make me feel safe instantly. Straightaway, I pull her forward and wrap my arms around her tightly, breathing her in as I bury my head in her hair. Her hands spread out on my back, pulling me closer. I hold on for as long as I can before pulling back.

"Hi," she says, and I'm so stupid for thinking I could've done this without her. She intertwines her fingers with mine briefly.

"Will you sit with me? When I'm done?" I ask, right to the point. I'd keep her up here with me if I could.

She reaches up and fixes my suit collar, spreading her hands down the shoulders. "Of course."

Before moving on she leans up and kisses me on the cheek, the simple act piecing a small crack in my chest back together. Nina hugs Veah with the same fervor, and my mom holds her the longest of all of us, even though they've never met. They both have wet eyes when they pull away. I nod towards the first row, and she takes at seat at the edge. Her arrival makes it a bit easier to breathe, and I think I might actually make it through the funeral.

When the viewing ends, we take our seats, and as soon as I'm next to her, she grips my hand tightly in hers, intertwining our fingers. I place a kiss on her temple, the emotions fighting to break out of my chest. People speak, and my eyes burn with unshed tears every time someone new tells yet another story I've never heard. Veah goes up, but when she gets up there, she freezes, and I instantly go up with her. I hold back the few tears that threaten to fall when we tell a story of when she was first born and how Dad wouldn't put her down because he was scared she'd break. She smiles and cries and holds my hand. Mateo is silent the whole time, fidgeting and avoiding looking at anyone, but I know that is just how he copes and I'll let him.

Mom closes it out, telling us all what a great man he was. A great husband. A great father and an even better friend.

By the time it is over, everyone has wet eyes, but we've all laughed at least once, determined to celebrate my dad's life. Nina is by my side the entire time. Either holding my hand or drawing little shapes on my thigh to distract me when I need it.

When we step outside into the gloomy day, I can't help but hug her again. We rock back and forth slowly, my thumb rubbing under her ear, on her back, everywhere I can get.

"Thank you," I mumble into her hair. "I'm sorry I didn't tell you."

"It's okay," she says into my chest, her warmth seeping into my cold body. "I understand."

My family waits off to the side. We're having the wake at our house with only Dad's closest friends, keeping it small.

I pull back. "Where are you staying?"

"I'm at a hotel down the street."

"Okay, well, let's go get your stuff. You can stay with us from here on out."

She shakes her head. "Jackson, I'm only here until Sunday, and I don't want to overstep."

"That's two more nights. And Mom will never let you stay at a hotel. So, let's go and get back." She still looks hesitant. "Please, Nina. I just need you with me."

Nina's eyes soften under the gloomy Georgia sky, turning them molten. "You're sure I won't overstep?" I rub her palm with my thumb before pressing in, a silent reassurance. "Okay, okay. Anything you need."

My lips turn up, and I lean down, pressing a kiss against her forehead and lingering there. She exhales, never letting go of my hand. I let my family know I'll be driving with her in her rental before making it to the house. My mom nods, giving Nina a warm smile as Veah pulls her in for a hug. Even Mateo hugs her, squeezing her tight.

Nina comes back to me, taking my hand and leading me to her car. Our shoulders brush as we walk in silence. But I don't need her to say anything. She came even though I didn't tell her and my sister did. She came.

Before we climb into the car I pull her back into my chest. Confusion flickers in her eyes. "What? Did you forget something? Do you need something?"

"I just need a moment." I lean back against the car, pulling her between my legs. Instantly, her arms wrap around me. "Can I have that with you, just for a minute? Before we go?"

Nina rests her head on my chest. Holding her tightly, I rest my head on top of hers.

"You don't have to ask Jackson. You can always have that." Her words are soft but they mean more to me than I could ever explain.

Bending down to her height, I press my lips against her neck in soft kiss. She sighs and I move my lips to her ear, "You are the best thing that's ever happened to me."

Despite everything, I love it here.

I love Jackson's childhood home, his mom, his siblings. All of it.

Everyone that had come over for the wake left a few hours ago. Earlier, Veah and I put all the food away.

"How are you," I asked.

Veah gave me a smile, but I saw the sadness on her face, in her eyes. "I'm okay. I'm worried about all of them, and that keeps me distracted. Mateo doesn't talk, and that freaks me out. And Jackson just takes care of all of us, and that worries me in a different way. Basically, I'm just sad and worried."

I didn't hesitate to pull her into a hug, between wrapping up baked mac and cheese and roasted chicken, and she wrapped her arms around me. I felt her shoulders shake, but I didn't say anything. I don't think she wanted to cry, and I didn't want to make her feel worse, so I just held her there.

A bit later, I helped Mateo move the furniture back to where it was earlier. He didn't say much, just kept clenching and unclenching his fist until he accidentally knocked over a plate, shattering it on the hardwood floor. He cursed and kneeled next to it. I got a dustpan and swept it up, and he met my eyes with a silent thank you.

I've never lost a parent; I don't know how any of this feels, so I'm just trying my best. Taking their moods as they come and doing whatever I can to help them however that might be.

When everything was said and done, we all just sat in the living room watching movies. For a bit, I felt like I was intruding, that the family needed some time together. Veah and Mateo sat on the floor, pushing their snacks back and forth, while Mrs. Ross sat in the recliner that she told me her husband used too, and I stayed next to Jackson on the couch. But I just felt like they needed to be with each other, so I offered to make hot chocolate for everyone.

I stand, waiting for the milk to heat, as I watch through the hall. Jackson leans over the couch to steal snacks from his siblings, and his mom laughs, a small one, but it's still a laugh. I search the kitchen for the mugs and pull down five of them. When I turn around, Mrs. Ross is standing in the kitchen a few feet away.

She's a beautiful woman, and I see the resemblance between her and Veah instantly, the only difference her darker skin. "Thank you for coming today. It meant a lot to him."

I shrug. "I wanted to be here for all of you. I was worried I overstepped at first."

She shakes her head, giving me a soft smile. "No, you didn't." She looks back to the living room. "You're the only girl he's ever brought home." Shock fills my chest, and my eyebrows rise as I make eye contact with her. "I hate the circumstances, and I wish my husband were here to really meet you, but I'm also intensely happy for my son."

Tears prick at my eyes at all of it. Stupidly, at being the only girl he's ever brought here, and sadly at the fact that while I met his dad over the phone, I'll never really get to know the man who had a part in raising Jackson.

I smile despite myself and shake my head. "I'm just a girl who happens to like your son."

Mrs. Ross pats my hand, "You are far more than that, sweetie. But aside from that, thank you for being here for all of us. You helped in ways I can't describe today when we got back here. They've all told me so much about you. And I know we've talked on facetime, but it's nice to have you here." She steps forward, her warm eyes reminding me of my mom as she pulls me in for a hug. "Thank you for being there for him, even when he thought he didn't need it."

This time I can't help the tears that slide down my face. I try to wipe them away quickly. "You guys are amazing, and I'm just doing what I can."

Her warmth and motherly aura wrap around me as we stand together. A shadow appears in the corner before either one of us speaks, and I turn, seeing Jackson leaning against the doorframe with his arms crossed. He gazes at me, slowly but fully before meeting my eyes.

He steps forward, towering over his mom's shorter frame and kisses the side of her head. "Stop making my girl cry, Ma," he says softly, but I hear it all the same. I feel warm all over. She holds him for a second before pushing him in my direction, and I'm thrilled to see the ghost of a smile appear on his face.

"I'm gonna go get changed and grab your bag from the car. I'll be right back. Do you need anything?"

I look at him, still dressed in a button down and his tie. "No, no, I'm good here. Go get changed, and your hot chocolate will be ready soon."

Jackson just nods and kisses me on the cheek before leaving me slightly flushed in the kitchen.

Mrs. Ross's eyes light up at the sight, but she doesn't say anything, and we fall into a quick, simple routine. She tops the drinks with whipped cream after I finish mixing it all together.

After the drinks are handed out, I settle back into my seat, waiting patiently for Jackson to return.

I'm worried about him, and I can't focus on the movie in front of me. He hasn't cried, not really. A few tears at the ceremony, sure, but I don't know if it's really sunk in yet, and I'm walking on eggshells waiting for it to. I don't want to push too hard and not enough at the same time. I just want to be there for him.

So, when he doesn't return after almost twenty minutes, my worry deepens considerably. I make eye contact with his mom. Mateo is passed out, his head on Veah's shoulder, who I'm pretty sure is also asleep.

"You should go check on him," Mrs. Ross says quietly.

My throat tightens. "You don't want to?"

She shakes her head, her eyes warm. "He's too worried about me to let me be his mom. He needs you, whether he'll say it or not. I think he needs you right now more than anyone."

My heart breaks and swells all at the same time. I nod and stand, padding silently through the hall, past the kitchen and up the stairs. There are pictures all over the wall, and I pause to look. His dad is everywhere, with a bright smile. There's a picture of him and Jackson from when he was younger, ruffling his son's hair, then one of him and Jackson in suits at his graduation, and more. The pictures repeat with all his kids and then endless amounts of them as a family and him with his wife.

It's a beautiful wall, but it also reeks of sadness now, tainted by the recent events. The entire house feels somber, weighed down by the loss of someone so monumentally important the foundation can't help but sag under it all.

I find Jackson's room on the last door on the left. The door is slightly ajar, so I knock before pushing it open. His room is clean and drastically different from his apartment now, and I love it, like a blast to the past. His bed is against the wall, a TV across from it. Two bookshelves and a dresser and old posters and pictures. But he's nowhere to be found. His closet is closed, but the bathroom door is ajar with a light peeking out.

I set both hot chocolates down on his nightstand and tap on the door. "Jackson?"

When I don't receive a response, I push the door open. He's sitting on the closed toilet with his elbows on his knees, still dressed in what he wore earlier, and there's a beer bottle on the counter. He looks up as I step in, eyes rimmed in red, and his jaw is tight.

My heart tugs. "Did something happen?"

He shrugs, and I step closer to look at him as he tugs his tie. "I can't get my stupid tie off. It's too tight." Jackson pulls at it again and again until I step in, bending slightly. I cup his cheeks and force his head up so I can press my lips to his forehead. He exhales deeply at my touch.

"Hey." He meets my gaze, and the sight of unshed tears in his blue eyes hurts me to the core. "Let me." I uncurl his fingers from the tie, and he lets me. His hand finds purchase on my hip, playing with the fabric of my dress before sliding downwards and cupping my thigh as I work on loosening the knot. Despite the grief, his touch still makes me come alive.

"I walked up here, and it all just felt different. He's been gone, but the house felt emptier today." He squeezes my leg as I untie the knot fully, leaving both sides of the tie hanging over his chest. "I miss him. I miss him so much."

I run my hands over his shoulders repeatedly. "I'm sorry. I'm so sorry," I whisper, cupping his face and tilting it back to look at me. Sadness and frustration gaze back at me, but there's something softer there too, warmer than moments ago.

"And I'm sorry for not calling as much. I missed you so much. I just didn't know what to do or how to do any of this. I'm sorry I disappeared."

"I missed you, but don't apologize to me. You didn't do anything wrong."

"I did," he says. "I didn't tell my dad I loved him enough, didn't spend enough time with him, and then I just disappeared when I needed you. I don't know how to do any of this. He'd be so disappointed in me."

My heart cracks, but I keep my face stern. "Look at me. Have I ever lied to you?"

Confusion flickers in his eyes. "No."

I rub my thumb over his cheek. "Believe me when I say your dad knew you loved him so much. You spent every day with him when you were here. He knew how much you cared about him and looked up to him and loved him. He knew that, Jackson." A tear falls from his eye, and I press it with my thumb. "He would not be disappointed in you for anything. You lived a life he was proud of, you made a life for yourself, and that's all he would've wanted."

He looks at me, blue eyes glistening with more tears, and I wish I could tell him everything will be okay and have him believe me. That this feeling will lessen one day. But all I can do is reassure him until he's tired of hearing it that he isn't disappointing anyone. He's just a human being who lost his dad.

"I promise, Jackson. You didn't shut me out. I'm right here. And your dad loved you so much. I could see it through the phone. I will tell you that every day forever if you need me to."

Suddenly, he stands and has his arms wound tightly around my waist. I hold him just as tightly, my fingers digging into his back. "I'm not going anywhere." I squeeze him even tighter when I feel him start to shake, small, barely-there movements, but I feel it under my hands, and I rest my head on his chest as his arms pull me closer to him. Keeping me there.

And in the low glow of the bathroom light, after the loss of his dad, after wondering if I was doing the right thing by coming here after Veah called me, after weeks apart, I know that I would do anything for Jackson.

Because I love him.

I am so in love with him. With everything about him. The layers that make him who he is. The person who might need help but won't ask for it. The sunshine for everyone else on a cloudy day. The man who never wants to see a gray sky and does everything he can to ensure others don't have to. The man who doesn't know what to do when the clouds come in but tries to fight them anyway.

There is nothing I wouldn't do for him.

I think about what me and Marissa talked about a week ago. How the girl I was with Myles was always willing to change for him, be what I thought he wanted me to be. But with Jackson, I've blossomed. I was scared to overstep, to come here, but I was also scared to fail Jackson, to let my anxieties win like I believed I had failed Myles for so long. But I haven't. I haven't failed Jackson. Marissa reminded me that I can only fail if I don't try. And that we're just taking a hard situation day by day.

I'll continue trying for this man as long as he lets me.

I thought I'd been in love before. But sitting here, wrapped up in Jackson as he lets out tears he's held onto for so long, I don't think that's true.

What I feel for Jackson, the warmth that floods my veins or spreads in my chest whenever he simply looks at me, the tiny sparks that erupt over my skin whenever he touches me or smiles at me or enters the same room. I know I've never felt anything like this before.

So I squeeze him just a little bit tighter as I hold him, and I'll do anything for him. To keep him here and warm and safe from any more harm.

Because I have never loved anyone the way I love Jackson Ross.

The man who makes me feel as though I'm lucky enough to have walked on the sun itself.

"Here,"

I blink and roll over, taking the cover with me as the smell of coffee fills the room. Light spills in between the curtains, and I sit up. Jackson's watching me, warmth dancing in his eyes as he holds two mugs in his hands.

"We can go downstairs. I don't want to be rude," I mumble, still half asleep.

He sets both our mugs down on his nightstand and carefully climbs in next to me. "No one else is up, so we can stay in here."

He clicks a remote for his stereo that sits on the dresser, and low, soft music comes through the speakers. He sits back against the headboard as I cross my legs next to him, running a hand through my hair, which I'm sure is a mess. Meanwhile, he looks perfect.

"I need to go fix this," I mumble, motioning to myself and attempt to crawl over him. He stops me, his arm easily wrapping around my waist.

"No," he mumbles into my hair, squeezes me, and my lips curl up into a smile. I lean into him for a moment before moving back to sitting at his side. Happy to see he's in a slightly better place this morning, after Friday night and yesterday, even if it's only for a bit.

Grief takes time. But moments that bring a smile to your face and make you remember why life is the way it is, those happy moments still exist. Moments like this one.

Friday was an emotional rollercoaster all day until I finally convinced him to crawl into bed after getting him undressed in the bathroom. He had just wanted to lay down, lay next to me, and I would've given him anything he asked for.

Saturday, yesterday, was better. It was just us and his family all day. Eating leftovers, mac and cheese and chicken and everything in between. Mateo finally ate, at least for the first time since I'd been around him, and Veah laughed, deeply, when Jackson threw a roll at his head. The sound of them all laughing, the fact that they were still able to feel joy despite everything, made me feel at ease. We sat around playing board games all day. Sometimes they would talk about their dad, remembering his favorites or telling funny stories.

When that happened, Jackson, whose side I never left, would touch my knee or my thigh or hold my hand, and I was happy to ground him there. To remind him I was and would always be here for him. His mom would sometimes give me a knowing look, making me blush. And Veah and Mateo treated me like I'd always been around. Teasing me like they did everyone else, like I was just another family member.

Jackson, well, he just made me feel like I was home.

That night, when we went to his room and watched a movie on his laptop, I pressed my lips against his to say all the things I couldn't say out loud yet. Kissing him enough that I hoped he knew.

"I think you should stay. *Poze* can go without you this week." Jackson's voice brings me back to the present.

"I think my job needs me, unfortunately." I roll over so I'm on my stomach, looking up at him.

"Well, can you tell them you have a needy boyfriend?"

My cheeks warm. "Boyfriend, huh?"

He grins sheepishly, his leg brushing mine under the covers. "Yeah, I never asked you. That was rude of me, wasn't it, to assume?"

No, I want to say. *Please assume I'm yours because I am. All yours, Jackson Ross, and have been for longer than I even knew.*

"I thought it was hot, but I guess I wouldn't mind some groveling either." I shrug, feigning boredom, and both dimples appear in his cheeks.

Jackson turns on his side, his eyes never straying from mine. "You've been my girlfriend in my head for a while, so I figured it was time."

I swirl a circle on his arm with my finger, acting as if my heart isn't about to beat out of my chest at his words. "Aw, you think about me?"

He rolls his eyes, and I'm thrilled to see the lightest dusting of pink on his cheeks. "Oh, shut up. You're a brat." In response, I gently flick his chest, and he grabs my hand and squeezes it.

"Yeah, well, you still think about me, so." I stick out my tongue playfully. He pulls me closer with the hand he holds, turning back onto his back until I'm resting lazily on his chest.

"Like I said," he starts quietly, his nose inches from mine, "brat." And punctuates the word with a kiss on my nose. After a moment I lean forward and peck him on the lips before resting my chin on my hands. Taking him all in. Happy to see that sadness isn't the first thing I see in his blue eyes.

"When are you gonna come back. Do you know yet?"

He shrugs, and I feel the movement underneath me. "I'm not sure yet. Maybe a week or two."

My heart beats painfully, and even though I understand it, I still miss him in New York. Miss having him around all the time. I try not to let it show on my face, but he sees right through me, in the most Jackson way possible. "Don't worry, I won't be leaving you alone when I get back."

A smile takes over my face whether I want it to or not. "Yeah, yeah, yeah." I gently tap his chest before I sit up, reaching for my coffee again. Before I can take a sip, he grabs it out of my hand and sits up. "Hey! I need that," I pout.

He raises a brow and taps my lips with his finger, taking my breath away, before holding out his free hand. "Come on, I'm making you breakfast before your flight." I smile and crawl out after him, quickly slipping on a sweatshirt and following him downstairs. The house is quiet, and I don't want to leave in a few hours.

I catch up to him and grab my mug from his hands, a smug smile on his face as we enter the kitchen. He starts pulling things out of cabinets left and right, and I watch from the sidelines at first, sipping on the still hot coffee. After a moment, I find his phone on the counter and turn on some music, low enough not to wake everyone else but loud enough that we can both hear it.

"French toast and bacon okay? It was my dad's favorite. Figured I'd make enough for everyone," he says softly, handing me a bowl and eggs.

I lean up on my tiptoes and kiss him on the cheek. "Sounds perfect."

Stepping to the side, I find a clear spot on the counter and crack the eggs into the bowl before tossing the shells. He quickly starts the bacon on the griddle, and the smell, along with the coffee, immediately fills the kitchen. We work quietly for the most part, aside from the occasional humming along to the song or the slight clang of a pan, but soon enough the French toast is frying in the pan and the pile of bacon is growing.

Veah appears with curls piled on top of her head in a bun, and in seconds Mateo is behind her, and he pulls her in and messes up her hair. She frowns. "God, you suck."

"You love me," Mateo says, and she rolls her eyes, ignoring him.

"Morning," Veah mumbles and kisses Jackson on the cheek and pats my arm as she passes. She starts pulling out plates and silverware and puts them on the table in the other room. "Mateo, make yourself useful and get the creamer out and whatever else—syrup too."

"Bossy." He shakes his head but gives me a smile as he does what she asked.

"Is Mom up?" Jackson asks, flipping the bacon and then leaning against the counter as I take another sip and check my flight for the fifth time.

"Yeah, she'll be down in a second," Mateo answers, and Jackson nods, taking the second round of French toast off the pan, sprinkling it with powdered sugar, and covering it so it stays warm with the rest.

I carry the plates that are ready into the dining room, the first stack of bacon, some fruit, and waters.

"Are you sure you need to leave? You're much more pleasant than Jackson. I think you should stay," Veah asks as she takes a seat, and I laugh, a smile spreading on my face.

"I already tried that," Jackson chimes in, and I roll my eyes.

"I'd love to stay, but I have to go back to work." I place plates down in front of each seat and lean forward over the chair with a smile.

"Well, just know we'll welcome you back anytime," Mrs. Ross says as she enters the room, and she kisses everyone, including me, on the cheek before she takes her seat. Jackson walks in with the rest of the food—the smell of cinnamon and syrup filling the dining room—and sets the plate down on the table before sitting next to me.

"Yeah, seriously, please come back. Jackson's a pain on his own. You're great," Mateo chimes in over a large forkful of French toast, and Jackson tosses a piece of bacon at him in response.

Seeing them act like this makes the air easier to breathe.

I can't help the small laugh that spills out of me, and Jackson smiles at me, and I look around at the family around me and couldn't be more thankful for them. This extra family, who just lost one but have welcomed another without a second glance, without a second thought, with open arms.

They've gained another forever or as long as my time allows me. I'll be by their side.

· · ·

The car ride to the airport was quick, quicker than I really wanted. I don't want to leave; I want to be wherever Jackson is. The entire car ride he held my hand, always touching me, and I loved it, loved every second of it.

"So, you'll tell me when you know for sure when you're coming home?" I ask, looking up at Jackson as he pulls my bag out of the car. He nods, a small sigh escaping his lips. His eyes roam over me, and I furrow my brows. "What's that look for?"

"I want to come home, to the city. I just also want to be here. I'm going to miss you." He grabs me and pulls me into his chest. I wish I could take everything he's feeling away.

"Jackson, there's no rush. I only asked because I'll miss you. I always miss you."

He looks sad, much more so than he did all day. After breakfast, we went for a walk down the streets he grew up on, hand in hand. Then we came back and flipped through photographs, Jackson telling me about his adoption and showing me videos of his Labor Day parties and telling embarrassing stories about his siblings.

Then we sat out on the porch like he used to do with his dad, with me on his lap and his hand on my hip. I sat there and realized how lucky I was to have met him, to have met all of them.

"I just," he runs a hand through his hair, "I don't feel like myself. I just feel lost."

The sound of a plane taking off rumbles loudly overhead as we lock eyes. I think he's just scared, scared of life without his dad, which is normal. He just wasn't ready for it. I don't think anyone ever is.

My eyes prick with my own tears, but I hold them in. "You are the same person. Life is just a little different now. And it's going to take time to get through it. To get used to it."

He grips my hand in his, rubbing his thumb over my knuckles slowly. "I just don't know how to do both. To live life while I can, be the man you deserve, and deal with all of this shit. And the person I want to ask isn't here anymore." His voice cracks, and I can't help the tear that falls. "So, I guess I'll be home as soon as I can figure out how to do that. To be who you need and someone who knows how to deal with it."

"No one knows how to deal with this. That's why it sucks so much."

I sigh, the words on the tip of my tongue because I didn't want to say them when he was surrounded by all of this, but I want him to know how deeply I am in this with him. Internally, I think it's hilarious how much I've changed. In the beginning I was terrified of being burned again. Of not being wanted as much as I want him. Of never experiencing the love I always wanted.

Of thinking love would only break and end and never heal. When in fact, loving Jackson is the easiest thing I've ever done.

I reach up and cup his cheek, feeling his warm skin, tugging a curl at the nape of his neck, and watch those blue eyes watch me with so many words unsaid and so many things to work through. I'll be there every step of the way whenever he's ready.

"Jackson, I don't need you to be who you think I need. I just need you, the you that you are now and have always been. I love you so much." I smile softly as shock flickers over his face. "I love you, Jackson, and I'll still love you today and tomorrow and whenever you come back." I wipe away the stray tears on my cheeks.

His lips part, and I shake my head. "I don't need you to say anything. I just needed you to know. You may not feel like it right now, but you are still the brightest person I've ever met. And I'm so happy to have you in my life. So you take as long as you need."

Jackson's own tears fall, just a few, and the sight pulls a wet laugh out of me. A small one, but it does. I lean on my tiptoes and press my lips to his, hoping he heard every word I said and listened to it. Because I meant it.

It's a soft kiss, his hands eventually coming up to hold my cheeks, and my heart swells. He's still there, the sunshine in the dark for me. "You come back when you're ready, okay?"

Part of me hates how emotionally open I'm being, how vulnerable I feel. But if I didn't open myself up, to pain or to love, I wouldn't feel anything at all. What a waste that would be.

Jackson nods, wiping a tear on my own cheek. "I'm sorry I made you cry."

I roll my eyes despite myself. "Shut up, Jackson. I'm not sad, I'm just in love with you."

He pulls me into a tight hug, and I don't hesitate to wrap my arms around his waist. He rests his cheek on my head, and I lean into him, breathing him in. "You're gonna be late."

I nod because he's right, but we stand like that for a little bit longer until he finally pulls back and picks up my bag, draping it over my shoulder. "I'll be back soon," he says, tapping the center of my lips with his thumb before tucking his hands in his pockets.

I can't help it, I give him one last kiss before I turn and head into the airport. He watches me, and I wish I could stay and help him through this, but it'll be a process, and all I can do is love him through it.

"Take your time," is the last thing I say before heading inside. I feel his eyes on me every step of the way, can feel all the emotions from here.

I go through the usual airport procedures mindlessly, thinking about how easy it is to love him. After Myles, I was terrified of putting everything out there, of putting all my emotions into one place and into one person. Letting Jackson see those parts of me is still scary in a way, because it's new, but mostly I just feel an excitement that I've never felt before. Because Jackson makes me feel everything so much deeper than I ever have before.

Nothing about loving him is wrong or hard, it's as easy as breathing.

Compared to the past, it's like pitting the sun against a speck of sand.

Jackson may not be my first love, but he's my eye opener. I get it. Why everything is about love. The books, the songs, movies, and poetry, everything makes sense. Why people can't stop writing about it, dreaming about it, craving it.

I lean back into the airplane seat, looking out the window. Whenever he's ready, I'll be there. I'm not waiting for him in a way that I need him to go on with life. I'm pretty sure he loves me. But he's been through a lot, and I'll wait for him to realize he doesn't have to try to be anyone else but himself. The person he's always been.

And when that happens, I'll still be in love with him.

Thirty-Three | Jackson

My hand grips the steering wheel tightly as I turn right into my neighborhood, the music low in the background because I'm not listening to it anyway. For the first time, I'm not overwhelmed by grief or the loss my dad. All I can think about is Nina.

I love you.

I shake my head, feeling both heavy and light. I feel guilty for not saying it back, for dumping all this stuff on her over and over again. But then she goes and does that, tells me she loves me, something I didn't even realize I needed in that moment until I heard it.

I lean back into the smooth leather of the car seats, my dad's old truck instead of the rental, and it still smells faintly of him. I don't know how to describe it except that it's *Dad*. But it also smells a bit like Nina now, like fresh rain and flowers, and the scents combined comfort me.

So does the fact that she loves me.

Even though I had to let her walk away right after to get home, I know I'll chase her down for the rest of my life if she lets me.

I climb out of the truck, tucking my phone into my pocket as I walk back inside. No use in texting her now since she's on the plane. The smell of food immediately hits me, and I head straight to the kitchen to see Mom and Veah both sitting there, sipping water. I grab a beer for myself.

"Did she make it to her flight on time?" Veah asks, popping a tortilla chip in her mouth.

I take a pull of the beer and nod. "Yup, she's all set. Should be landing in a little less than two hours."

She smiles. "She's great. Honestly, better than I ever expected for you."

I flick my little sister on the forehead and grab a few chips for myself.

"Well, she certainly, made you all smile again. She was great, Jackson," Mom says this time, flipping over whatever is in the skillet. "When are you going home? I know you're not staying here long without her now." She raises a brow, and I lean next to where Veah sits on the counter.

"I want to go back soon," I say, but I hesitate.

"But—" My mom gives me a pointed look.

I give her a knowing look. I can't ask my dad, and I need to ask my mom. What to do. If she thinks I'll get through this. If she thinks Nina will be there when I do.

Veah narrows her eyes at me and whines, "No, come on. Don't kick me out. I'm not the annoying little sister anymore. I can help."

"Veah, hon, give us a second, okay?" Mom says for me, and I spare her a thankful glance, taking a seat at the counter while my sister grabs her tortilla chips and heads to the living room. "What's going on?"

I rest my head in my hands before looking up. "She told me she loved me." Her eyes light up, but I go on. "I feel like I don't deserve it. Not after everything. I feel lost, like the world's off kilter and I'm not the same man she met all those months ago."

"Oh, sweetie." My mom sits next to me. "The world is off for us, and probably will be forever in some ways. But you're not a different person, you're just going through something. That doesn't mean you don't deserve love and happiness. You've always been my sunshine boy, but that girl, Nina, lifted you up when you needed it. And you let her."

"I didn't say it back. I was in shock and feeling overwhelmed."

"That's okay."

I shake my head, feeling like the little kid that always came to his parents for everything. Except now I'm grown up. It's funny how we never stop needing them.

"When are you going back?" Mom asks, meeting my unsure look.

"I'm not sure. I thought about going back Sunday or the weekend after, but I don't know." I want to be here because I want to be in the house I grew up in with my dad, and to be here with my family. I also really want to follow Nina home.

Mom smiles knowingly. "Jackson, baby, don't stay here and sit in the grief with us. Unfortunately, it'll follow you. Go back to New York and be with Nina. I know you want to."

I smile, shaking my head and standing up. Easily I pull my mom into a hug. We stay like that, and I know she's right. Sitting here, chasing my dad who isn't here, isn't going to make this any easier, not that much will, and I won't lean on my family. I won't let myself. But I will lean on Nina.

Suddenly, there are arms wrapping around me from the other side. "I heard. I'm sorry, I couldn't help it, and I love you, Jackson," Veah mumbles into my back.

I chuckle. "Love you too. You really should stop eavesdropping, you know."

She steps away and pinches my arm. "Jerk." But then she hugs me again.

We pull away, and Mom wipes under her eyes. "Go book a flight."

Veah chimes in, "I'll help!" I flick her on the forehead again.

"Shut up." I grin, happy I talked to my family about everything. "All right, well, I'm going to go up and figure it all out. I'll be back down when dinner's ready. Let me know if you need help." I take my beer and a few more chips and head up the stairs, stopping only at Mateo's old bedroom, where the door swings open. I don't expect to find him there, but he's packing up clothes, probably ready to head back to his apartment, and I lean against the door frame.

"Hey, you okay?" I ask quietly, my eyes flickering to the pictures of him and dad on his dresser.

He turns, rubbing his eye with his thumb. "Okay as I can be right now. You?"

"Yeah, doing my best. You know, if you ever need to get away, you can always let me know and fly up to the city. You and V are welcome anytime, you know that."

He sits on his bed and nods, but he starts to smile, bright against his brown skin. "Yeah, I know. Nina was great. Heard you're in love."

I roll my eyes. "You and Veah, always so damn nosy."

Mateo shrugs. "Can't help it, we learned from you. Seriously, she's great. I'm happy for you, Jackson. Dad would be too."

I start to head out, patting the doorframe. "Yeah, well, I'll buy you guys a ticket, and we can all do something soon, okay? I miss you guys."

"I know it was for a shitty, terrible reason, but having you here was great. I miss having you around."

A grin spreads. "Aw, you miss your big bro?"

He rolls his eyes and turns around. "Yeah, yeah, get out." I laugh and head down to my own room, thoughts swirling in my head.

Part of me does want to stick out the week, spend a bit more time with Mom and Veah and Mateo while I'm here. Spend a bit more time where Dad used to always be. And the other part of me wants to go home and get Nina and hide away in the city. I crack my neck and rub my hand across the back, kneading out the knot that's formed when my phone starts buzzing.

Myles's name blinks back at me. Like it has for the fourth or fifth time this week. Each one I've sent to voicemail. So I'm not sure why I answer this one, but I do, sliding my thumb across the screen carefully.

"Hello?" I sit down on my bed.

He hesitates. "Hey, I've been trying to catch you."

I sigh. "Yeah, I know."

I don't offer an apology because I don't have one. Even though I do miss my friend and am not blind to the way I went about pursuing Nina, though I never intended to keep it from him, the way he acted and treated all of us wasn't okay.

"I just wanted to let you know I'm sorry about your dad. And that I'm here for you, and so is Emma. I know I don't have a place to say that, but I'm gonna say it anyway." He pauses. "I'm sorry, Jackson."

After a deep inhale, I respond. "Thank you."

"Did Nina make it down?"

My brows furrow, confused as to why he's asking me about my girlfriend. "Yeah, she did. Why?"

"No reason. I saw her a few weeks ago to—well, it doesn't matter. I just knew she was nervous about coming down if need be."

Even though I hate to admit it, there was a time he knew me better than anyone. Knew how I'd react, knew exactly what I would do. I'd be lying if I said I didn't miss my friend, but I'm also hesitant about letting him back into my life, especially now.

"Yeah, she came down. It was good. And thank you for calling," I add, because that's as much as I can give to him right now.

"Good, well, not good, um, you know what I mean. Well, one day when you're back, if you're open to it, I'd like to talk. Maybe," he rambles, and I nod to myself.

"We'll see, Myles. Not sure about all that right now. But I'll let you know; tell Emma I say hi, okay?" I take another sip and shortly after he says he will, we say an awkward goodbye and hang up the phone.

I'd be open to talking to him. If Nina can, and he put her through the ringer for years, then I can man up and do it too. I just don't want to. At least not yet. I need to get back on my feet without my dad to fall back on before I open another wound.

I look around at my old childhood room that felt full of life when Nina was here, but now it just reminds me of my dad, and it makes me cold instead, the chill spreading over my skin.

Almost instantly, I open my laptop, pulling up the familiar airline, and look for flights.

I still see her dark, wavy hair blowing behind her as she walked into the airport after telling me she loved me. Drastically different from the guarded girl I first met. I'd wanted to say those words for weeks, before I found out about my dad, but she beat me to it. I didn't want to say them when I was losing him, didn't want my memory of that and of Nina weighed down with grief.

But she said it anyway, fearlessly. She's come out of her shell and let me in, and I'm not going to ruin that or miss out on it. There have been multiple times I knew this was deeper than I thought. I knew she was something far more special than I could've anticipated when she pulled that ballcap out from under my seat on the way to the Hamptons.

Knew I was in deep when I made her a grilled cheese in the kitchen and couldn't stop thinking about the smiles she gave me that were all mine. Or when she invited me over and made me soup, I knew she cared deeply and endlessly about those she let into her life, and I was honored to be making my way into it.

I knew I loved her when I saw her in her parents' kitchen when we went for dinner. When she had been talking with her dad, she'd looked over her shoulder and smiled at me. A soft one, a *Nina* one in the yellow lighting of her family kitchen. I knew she was it for me.

A picture of my dad and I stares back at me from my dresser. I remember a conversation we had once when I was young and learning about death. He told me he wanted to be celebrated. He wanted us to live for him, not stop living because of him. I don't know what life looks like without my dad; that will come with time, and I'm sure every day will bring new challenges, but if I can go through them with Nina . . . with her by my side, with her to lean on, I think I'll get through it. Think I'll make my dad proud.

I look around at my empty suitcases, and I shake my head, emotions flooding my body.

There's no damn way I'm waiting to go see her, to go tell her how I feel. Nina has this way of making everyone feel seen and heard, and I watched her do it with my family and felt her do it with me. She lights up my entire world, and after everything, I think she deserves to know that sooner than later.

Thirty-Four | Nina

'd hoped that my anxiety wouldn't kick in after getting home from Georgia.

About telling Jackson how I felt, about putting myself out there.

But I was wrong. Anxiety sucks, and I wish my brain would just shut up and let me breathe. Let me enjoy this.

But for the past three days, I've been reeling. Just thinking about how I have to wait to see Jackson, about how I stupidly hope he's going to say it back even though he's shown me time and time again how he feels.

I sigh and eat another Fudge Stripe cookie. But quickly, they're ripped out of my hands, and Harper is standing over me with a pointed look on her face. "Nina. Stop eating the cookies. They aren't gonna make him come home any sooner."

A scowl crosses my face. "Don't be rude to me. I'm sensitive right now."

She raises a brow from across the table. "Obviously."

And I hold her glare until we both break out in a laugh. I know I'm being dramatic, but I don't care. Jackson and I have talked since I left, but not about anything important. It's okay. It's only Wednesday, so I haven't called much, mostly because I do want him to enjoy his time at home and only return when he's ready. I'm also scared I'll start babbling and say something stupid, like asking him to marry me.

"Nina, what are you really stressing about?" Harper watches me, breaking off her own cookie.

I sigh. "I just—I've never done this. Never dealt with grief like this, never opened myself up like this. Certainly never told anyone I loved them first." I run my hands over my face. "It's stupid. I'm just anxious."

"You lost your grandparents in high school and college. You helped me through the grief of having shitty parents and claiming yours. You've dealt with all types of grief, losing close friends, losing Myles, losing your family members. There is no right or wrong or better way to help Jackson than to do what you can."

I raise a brow. "When did you get so sentimental?"

"I hang out with you too much." She deadpans before smiling. "And telling him you loved him? There is nothing fucking wrong with that. I don't mean to be sappy, and I won't be in five minutes, but you're doing your best.

"No, I know. I'm just being stupid."

"You're not stupid. You're just in love." Harper smiles, poking my cheek. "It's nice. And that man loves you. Whether he said it or not, you know it's true. I know it's true. The whole fucking world knows it's true." I snake my hand out and grab another cookie, and she continues. "And soon, he'll fly home and tell you that himself. So I can stop."

"You're so mean to me," I pout.

"Oh, shut up. I love you."

I roll my eyes. "I love you too. Now go or you're gonna be late. Leave me alone to wallow." I wave my hand at her as she throws her trench coat on over her sweater. Roman is taking her somewhere tonight, got tickets on sale to a concert, I think.

"No more cookies. I counted. I know how many are left."

I stand up and grab another just to spite her. "Do not judge me and my emotional eating. Now go." I practically shove her towards the door. She stumbles as I push her forward and stops to slip on her shoes.

"God, you are pushy when you're emotional," she says, grinning, and I roll my eyes again.

"You're annoying."

She winks and stands up, adjusting her purse over her shoulder as she wraps her hand around the door. "All right, well, if you spiral just send me a text or call Sloan. I expect all the tissue boxes to be full when I get back," she says, and I close my eyes and rest my head on the wall, waiting for her lecture to end. Her eyes soften, just briefly. "Love you. You'll be fine."

I head back to my laptop as the door opens and closes. The music in the background fills the space, a soft melody as I pull up an article I need to be working on. My phone buzzes next to me, Jackson's name flashing on the screen.

"Hello?"

Jackson's voice comes through the speakers. "Hey, are you busy?"

"No, not at all, why?"

"Can you do something for me really quick?"

I furrow my brows in confusion, eating yet another cookie. "Yeah, of course, anything. Is everything okay?"

He chuckles lightly. "Yeah, it's fine. I sent you something and it should be at your place by now. Can you check?"

I stand. "Yeah, Harper just left though, so she would've told me about a package, but I'm looking now." I free my hand from where it's tucked into my sweatshirt sleeve as I walk to the door.

I pull it open, and instead of a package, there's a Jackson in front of me. Shock floods my veins. Harper is walking backward behind him in the hallway, making a heart with her hands. I would laugh except I'm too surprised.

He has a soft smile on his face and two bags with him and his phone held against his ear. "Hi." At my appearance, he hangs up the phone.

I'm speechless for a second, my mind trying to catch up with what I'm seeing—that he's really here. "Hi. What are you doing here?" I ask. Standing nervously in the doorway.

His dimples fight to appear. "Landed about forty minutes ago. Came straight here."

"How was the flight? Come in, I'm sorry, please come in." I want to smack myself at my rambling, and I know he's amused because I can see the upturn of his lips as he enters, shutting the door behind him.

The music I had on plays in the background as I stop awkwardly in my kitchen, waiting for him to enter behind me. I hop up and sit on the counter simply to stop my fidgeting.

He walks closer to me, dropping his bags gently, until he's standing in front of me, and his hands lazily rest in his pockets.

"So, it's soon. Why are you back already?"

"Would you like me to go?" he asks, and I blush deeply, hearing the joke in his tone.

"No, no, stop. I just—I don't know." I sigh, realizing I'm rambling.

Jackson shrugs, but his eyes are light with humor, and he ignores my jumbled words. "You got something—" He reaches out with his thumb and swipes right beside my lips. He surrounds me fully now. "That kiss you gave me in the airport wasn't really a good enough goodbye."

My entire body heats and the blush pools in my cheeks as I cast my eyes down. His left hand rests on my thigh, drawing little patterns with his thumb as his other cups my chin and forces my eyes up to his. I don't have time for a breath before he's leaning down and kissing me, and it takes only milliseconds before I relax into it.

I'm not sure why I was scared at all.

"I got home, and it just felt empty. Dad isn't there, and you weren't there." He shrugs, tugging a loose hair of mine before dropping it. "You told me to come back when I was ready. I was ready."

My entire body goes weightless at his words.

Jackson leans in and kisses me again, cupping my cheeks softly. He pulls back, his lips resting over mine. "I love you, Valentina Scott."

Now my heart stops for a whole different reason.

His lips brush against my ear, my neck, everywhere. "I love you so much more than I can ever explain."

The words from his lips wrap around my body, my heart, and imprint on my skin. My eyes stay closed because I'm scared that if I open them, I'll realize this is a big dream and he won't really be there. But he kisses me again, softer this time, and I open them when he pulls back, his blue eyes trained on mine. Because I am so in love with Jackson Ross that it hurts, and hearing him say it practically makes my heart burst.

"This would be about the time you say it back," he whispers playfully and pinches my side, causing me to squeal as my entire body comes to life.

I purse my lips and shrug, playing along. Happy to see him in such a good mood.

He narrows his eyes playfully, hands still on my side. "Is it 'cause I made you cry?"

The question draws a laugh from me, and I shake my head. My hands tug him closer, gripping his shirt. "Hmm, maybe." I sneak my hand under his shirt, feeling his skin on mine.

"How can I make it up to you?"

"Still figuring that out," I breathe, semi-distracted by his hands and how they haven't stopped touching me. He steps closer, in between my legs, trailing his hand up the outside of my thighs and up my sides.

I haven't seen this playful side of him in so long I almost cry on the spot.

"Want me to keep touching you?"

I hum. "That could be a start."

"Kissing you?"

"Always."

His dimples appear, and I reach up and poke one, unable to help myself. Jackson leans forward, placing soft kisses on my cheek and my nose, surrounding me as his hands begin to tickle me again. I fight his touch, laughter bubbling out of me as he does it.

"Okay, okay, please. I love you," I breathe out, still laughing. "I love you."

He exhales. "Thank god, I was worried."

I laugh again, unable to stop smiling. "You're so cheesy." He leans back, grabbing a cookie from the container behind me, not bothering to defend himself.

"Thank you for everything, Nina. I don't want to talk about it, but thank you."

I hop down and hug him tightly to me, not bothering to say anything. "Are you staying over?"

He rests his cheek on my head, my heart swelling like it does every time he does that. "If you'll have me."

I nod and step back, grabbing one of his bags and dragging it to my room, willing him to follow me. And he does. He sets his other bag by my desk, and I watch from where I lean on the edge of my desk as he grabs a few clothes out. Jackson approaches me and places his hands on either side of my hips and bends down to meet my gaze.

I can't believe he loves me back. This beautiful, bright man, who is going through something I can't imagine, loves me. And I'll never forget it.

I sigh into him, gently holding his T-shirt in my hands, but he doesn't move. Just holds us in place. "I have a request," I say. He nods and I press my thumb against his lips. My heartbeat quickens when he kisses it softly.

"How can I fulfill it?"

"You don't want to know what it is first?"

Jackson smiles, hands roaming over my lower back and my butt. "Nope. If you ask, I'll do it. To the best of my ability."

My heart just about soars. Loving this man is the best decision I've ever made. "I just wanted you to kiss me again."

"That's easy baby," he murmurs, pressing his lips against mine. They move together like they were always meant to. I relax into him completely, not thinking twice about it. "I have a request of my own."

I nod, blinking my eyes open and meet his gaze. Jackson smiles cheekily. "I'm needy. And I expect I'll be asking you to remind me quite a bit. All the time, really, when you least expect it."

I smile. "Remind you of what exactly?"

He presses his lips against mine and holds them there. "That you love me."

Externally, I laugh lightly at his words.

Internally, my heart has officially left my chest and walked itself right into Jackson's hands.

I twist his shirt and whisper against his lips, "Always."

He smiles before kissing me back, fully this time. His request is too easy. I'd tell him whatever he wanted. Whenever and wherever. Because I have never belonged somewhere more perfectly than I have here. With Jackson, *in love* with Jackson.

There's nowhere else I'd rather be.

Thirty-Five | Jackson

Grief doesn't go away. I've learned that. But I've also learned that a hard moment doesn't have to be a hard day. That I can lean on someone, Nina, when I need it. She's held me up more times than I can count since I came home mid-November. She keeps me on my feet, keeps me smiling throughout it all.

Every day I wish my dad was here so I could talk to him. Tell him about Nina, about life, about anything. Just to do it if I could. But I can't, so I do everything I can to live how he would've wanted me to.

Every morning since I got back from Thanksgiving, when I flew back down to see my family, I've woken up with Nina next to me. Either at my apartment or hers, I wake up with her hot skin touching mine or her hair brushing over me. Today, like many others, I had trouble sleeping, tossing and turning as quietly as possible as to not wake her up like I had before.

When I felt the light touch of her fingertips on my hand that was spread, tapping nervously on her stomach, I exhaled a sigh of relief. I hadn't even realized I was doing it until she intertwined her fingers with mine. She pressed her back further into my chest, grounding me.

She leaned back so I could see her. Sometimes, those nights were my favorite. The tired, hazy look in her brown eyes, and the way her touch woke me up inside and out. I leaned over, softly pressing my lips to hers, and she sighed, and I caught the puff of air in my mouth. My skin burned, my spine tingling at her kisses, the way she pressed against me, and the soft skin. Quickly, in the middle of the night, in the darkness, we'd slipped off the little layers we did have on. And Nina had sighed my name like she always does, anchoring me to her more and more each time, and I couldn't hold back. She'd brushed her fingertips over the length of me, and seconds later I was sinking into her, completely enamored with her.

I wanted her to need every part of me as much as I needed her.

Those nights, when she knew I was struggling, she told me extra. With her touches, sighs of how much she loved me, and each night I felt a bit better than I had. Knowing I had her with me.

Right now, I can't wait to get off work and meet her before heading back to her place. We take turns, a few nights at my apartment before we spend a few nights at hers, with Jenko. And he loves it. Usually curls up in the bed with us, purring away. I don't care where we are. It makes no difference to me as long as we're together. The clock ticks by as I type away, looking over a contract, and thankfully, it hits five a lot quicker than I expected. Through the windows, the light of the December gray sky beams in.

I pull on my winter coat as I pull my phone from my pocket. There's a text from Nina telling me she'll meet me outside my office. That was five minutes ago. After shutting down my computer and grabbing my case, I head toward the elevators. They're full, everyone leaving for the day, and we all step off on the ground floor at once. Nodding a few goodbyes to familiar faces, I head straight to the doors and into the cold.

Instantly, I find Nina in the crowd. In a tan coat that isn't warm enough for the temperatures and a knit hat pulled over her hair, she rocks back and forth on each foot, probably trying to stay warm. She turns, and even from a distance I see her brown eyes light up, and I grin.

Her cheeks are flushed from the cold when I approach.

I take her gloved hand in my own. "Are you insane, Scott? It's freezing." I pull her in for a quick hug, trying to warm her up as best I can.

"Yeah, yeah, yeah," she mutters into my chest. "Now come on. Don't forget we're going out tonight." I nod, not dropping her hand from mine as we walk through the streets. Christmas lights gleam off the buildings in the gray sky as we head towards the subway.

"Let's grab a hot chocolate." I grin, pulling her to a stop at the food cart. "Two hot chocolates, extra whipped cream on one of them, please." Quickly, I glance at her, squeezing her palm before handing over some cash.

I hand her the one with extra whip first and walk to the side of the street, away from the afterwork crowd. "Hold this." I give her my own drink, and she again bounces on the balls of her feet, her breaths coming out in little clouds.

"Jackson," she whines, the sound hitting my skin like a drug, "come on, it's cold."

I raise a brow. "No shit, Sherlock. You need a better coat." With a roll of my eyes, I reach up and adjust her hat, which is leaving her ears exposed, and tug it down until it's right over her eyes. "Whoops."

She laughs softly as I flip it up, uncovering those beautiful eyes and smiling at her. Then I pull her coat tighter and use the skimpy tie it has to bind it around her waist. She hands me my drink back as we begin walking, her hand in mine, and head into the subway train. Somehow, despite her having the one with extra whip, like she always does, I end up with some on my nose.

She pulls off her glove and wipes it off with her finger, her simple touch erasing the cold.

"Thanks, baby." I lean down and press a kiss on the side of her head, inhaling her familiar perfume.

Despite our various displays of PDA, I know it's not her favorite. And while I would have no issues kissing her on the subway or anywhere, despite the amount of people around, I know a kiss on the head shows her enough how much I always want her. She leans against me, her head on my shoulder until we come to the stop near her apartment and make our way inside.

I hang up our coats on the rack near her front door after kicking our shoes off. "I'm going to need a nap if we're going out. I'm old you know," I mumble, and she rolls her eyes.

"You're not old."

"Despite that, I want to nap, and I want to nap with you." I grab her hand and practically drag her to her bedroom. She sets the hot chocolates on her desk and sets an alarm as I reach for the small drawer she gave me for clothes, just like the two drawers she has at my apartment, and tug off my work clothes.

Her eyes watch me, heating up as I slip on sweatpants and a long sleeve shirt. And the look in her eyes causes a spread of heat from the base of my spine all the way to my neck. I take a seat on the edge of the bed, staring at her. "Everything okay over there?" I say, feeling my smile spread.

Her cheeks flush as she slips on a large sweatshirt and out of her leggings, drawing my attention. "You're too pretty," she mumbles when she meets my eyes again. "It's not fair, it's distracting."

I grab her hand and pull her closer to me, my hand wrapping around the back of her thigh as she rests her hands on my shoulders. "That's how you make me feel all the time."

My thumb rubs back and forth in the hollow at the back of her knee, feeling the goosebumps rise under my touch. Easily, I pull one knee forward and it lands next to my hip. Shamelessly,

I scoot back and pull the other forward until she's straddling my hips.

"I thought you wanted a nap," she says, her hands on either side of my head.

"I do. Doesn't mean I don't want to kiss you first."

Her eyes light up, and she leans down, giving me a soft kiss before moving along my throat, placing a trail of soft ones there too. I squeeze her legs until she squeals and gives me what I want. Her lips find mine again, her tongue lightly teasing them until my hand comes up and grips the back of her neck, deepening the kiss until we're both breathless.

We settle into her bed after a moment. I throw my arm over her waist. "How are you today?" Nina asks gently.

It hits me in the chest.

Nina has a way of checking in on me without making me feel suffocated. She doesn't chase me around and attempt to make sure nothing is wrong, because that's not life, and she never expects me to talk about it if I don't want.

But every few days, she checks in. With a simple question like the one she just asked.

"I'm good today." And I mean it. I miss Dad all the time, but on easy days, it's a low hum, not an overbearing ache.

"You promise?"

I nod, kissing her nose. "Promise. You know I'd tell you."

She nods, her body loosening into my touch as we lay there. I flex my hand before roaming over her back until landing on her butt and giving it a pinch.

"What?" she asks, but there's a smirk growing on her lips.

"Say it."

She grins, her bright smile taking my breath away. "I love you."

Rolling into her, I bury my face in the crook of her neck, smiling against her skin. I place a few kisses there. "I love you too."

Thirty-Six | Nina

"Come on. Emma said she's inside and is holding a high-top for us," Harper says, pulling Roman along with her as we all walk towards Bar 13.

"Harper, dude, why are you sprinting?" Roman jokes, practically jogging to keep up with her fast walk. She glances back. Her orange-red hair flows softly against her face as she raises a brow at him.

"Because I'm fucking cold. Now come on."

Roman smiles with a shake of his head. "You are aggressive."

The rest of us laugh. Sloan, Jackson, and I walk behind them, not bothering to attempt to keep up. Harper hates the cold more than anything and can only stand to be outside in it for approximately five minutes. The bar is busy but not overflowing yet, and we enter, waving to the bouncers we recognize, and head back to where Emma told us she was sitting.

She smiles. Her brown hair flows down over her outfit as she leans up and waves when she sees us, and my eyes instantly land on the shots lined up on the table. I grin, knowing it's tequila.

We all stand around the table, and she wiggles her eyebrows. "Figured tequila would warm us up," she says with a laugh and goes around and gives us all a quick hug before landing next to me on a seat.

She leans in towards me. "So, we may have a slight issue." I turn more towards her, Jackson giving me a quizzical look that I ignore for the moment. "Myles may or may not show up."

I raise my brows in surprise. I don't really care one way or another if he does. We've put most of our issues to rest, and I accept that being friends with Emma means I'm going to have to see him occasionally in casual settings. I get that. But I'm not worried about me as I sneak a glance to Jackson. I'm worried about him and Jackson being in the same room.

Because Jackson has made it clear, after he told me about their phone call and Myles's multiple attempts to apologize, that he's just not ready. And I may not really know Myles anymore, but I know enough to know he's persistent and is probably at his wits end at being avoided. I know that Jackson has Roman and other friends, but it doesn't mean he can't be upset about losing Myles. He suffered two losses this year, different from one another, but losing a friend is still a loss.

I lean towards Emma, away from Jackson's listening ear. "I mean it could be good or it could be bad, but honestly it needs to happen one way or another, so they can move on. At least it's in a crowded bar." I shrug and grip the shot glass, and Emma smiles, agreeing silently.

Jackson's arm wraps around my waist gently, and he leans down. "Everything okay?" he mumbles against my ear, and I feel shivers down my spine.

"Yeah, I'll tell you in a minute," I respond, leaning up and placing a quick kiss on his cheek.

"All right, cheers!" Sloan shouts, holding up her glass with a smile, and we all touch our glasses to hers, hit them gently on the table, and tip back the liquid. The tequila burns in the best way, warming me instantly from the inside out as I stand around with all my friends.

I lean forward on the table as Jackson goes with Roman to grab drinks from the bar, and Sloan leans over. "You two are disgustingly in love, and I love it. Just thought you should know."

With a roll of my eyes, I tap her nose. "Shut up."

She pulls me closer and hugs me tightly. "I love you and love to see it, honestly. Took you long enough."

I pat her butt gently. "You suck," I laugh. "I love you too." I glance over at Jackson and Rome at the bar, the same bar where we met in the cold of the last February, and he turns his head, connecting his eyes with mine and winks at me from afar. I shake my head with a smile.

"Like I said, disgustingly in love."

I don't bother answering her this time. I just give her the finger, and she laughs infectiously as we fall into an easy conversation until the boys return. Jackson slides me and Sloan our drinks. Jackson has easily become fast friends with both Sloan and Harper, getting along better than I could ever have imagined. I take a sip, leaning my head on his shoulder as he drinks his old fashioned.

"What were you gonna tell me?" he says, and I lean up, already having forgotten to warn him about Myles. Just as I open my mouth, Emma pinches me, and I look over the crowd to the door and see Myles entering the bar, slowly taking off his coat.

I flicker my eyes to Emma and back up to Jackson, who is oblivious. "Myles is coming." He coughs lightly, furrowing his brows. "Or actually Myles is here." I nod towards the door where Myles has now found us and is slowly making his way over.

"Jesus Christ," he mumbles, and my heart beats slowly, and I grab his hand and tug his head down to mine.

"It'll be fine, Jackson, I promise. And I didn't know until about five minutes ago, and I'm sorry."

Those blue eyes flash with humor despite him being annoyed. "Nina, I'm not mad at you. I just don't want to talk to him."

He never fails to reassure me over the littlest things, and it's something I didn't even know I needed until he came around.

I smile. "It'll be fine, and it'll be quick. And if you want to leave after, we can go get pizza and go home, okay?"

"Extra cheese?"

"Extra cheese." I squeeze his hand just as Myles appears at the table.

Harper eyes him but thankfully, doesn't say anything, and Roman gives me a glance and pulls her away. I assume to go dance, and I smile, nodding at him as he removes her from the situation. As he moves past, he gives Myles a quick hello, and I see Harper huff beside him, and I try not to laugh.

Myles places a kiss on Emma's cheek, and Sloan and I watch to see what happens with careful eyes and held breaths. He looks up, greeting all of us, "Hey, guys." He hesitates, draping his coat on Emma's chair behind her. "Jackson, can I talk to you? I'll make it quick."

I see Jackson's jaw tense just slightly, but he nods and pats my butt before downing his drink and walking with Myles over to the bar. "This should be fun," Emma jokes, and we all laugh, the tension having evaporated at the table with the two men gone for the time being.

I watch them as casually as possible as I sip my drink and talk with Emma and Sloan. About work, about Christmas plans, and life in general. Emma tells us how therapy is going with her and Myles. Sloan is almost fully booked every day at the salon. I tell them details about upcoming articles, but none of it is that exciting in the winter. It's the easy season there, at least for me, and especially after September. So, I'm just enjoying Christmas time and getting to write articles for print and the website.

It feels like the boys have been talking forever. My eyes flicker back to them occasionally during our conversation, trying to read Jackson's facial expressions. His mouth is set straight, but from here it doesn't look like he's tensing his jaw or prepared to walk away. He just looks slightly indifferent as Myles talks with his hands, but he starts nodding along, taking sips of another drink, and finally starts talking too, and I smile softly, happy that he's at least trying or at least being open about how he feels, I hope.

"How do we think this is gonna go?" Emma asks, her eyes on the two of them as well.

I take a sip. "Hopefully they'll at least be able to be civil, that's all I want."

Sloan nods. "I think they will be. I think it was a bit rough, but it seems like they both want to move forward."

Finally, after what seems like hours, even though I've barely finished my drink, I'm surprised to see them hug. It starts off a bit awkward, even from here I can see the distance that they're maintaining, but after a moment something changes. Myles pats his back, and my heart hurts, because I just know it's about his dad. They pull back, and the slight awkwardness returns when they separate, but it was a step. Each one took a step.

Myles has shown he's trying to grow up, not just saying it. I'm not saying he's earned forgiveness yet or will, but I hope Jackson realizes it's okay to miss someone even if they made mistakes.

They walk back with easy smiles on their faces, talking as they do. Myles sits right next to Emma when he reaches the table, handing her another drink.

Sloan glances between the four of us and downs her drink. "I'm gonna go dance. I'll see everyone later or maybe not. Love you lots!" And before any of us can respond, she's gone, into the crowd.

"Be safe!" I shout after her, and she gives me a thumbs up before disappearing.

Jackson comes back to me, standing directly behind me and wrapping his arms around my shoulders until my chin is practically resting on his forearms. I sip my drink, leaning back as we start casually swaying to the heavy bass reverberating through the bar. When I realize Emma and Myles have fallen into their own conversation, I tug on Jackson's shirt.

He doesn't unwind his arms from around me but leans down. *"¿Estás bien?"* I lean my head on his arm and look at him. A smile starts to spread on his face, and my stomach erupts into flutters.

I know he wants to learn so I'm trying to be better about speaking it more around him.

"Not perfect, but I think we'll be okay. He apologized for his actions, his words, and so did I, for not telling him what was going on. He said he's trying, and I can see that," he says, mouth brushing against my ear. "And he said he was sorry about my dad. He always loved my dad. They got along really well. I told him we could just see what happens."

Softly, I squeeze the arms that are around me with my palms. "I think that's great, that's enough. You don't have to be best friends again, but I think that's good."

"Well, you're my best friend, so I think that's fine," he mumbles.

I snort softly, acting like his words didn't just leave another brand on my heart as he takes more and more pieces that I'd gladly give up to him.

I take another sip. "Do you wanna stay or go get pizza?" I ask, and for once in my life, I don't feel the need to stay all night. Not that I don't enjoy being wrapped up in a crowd, especially at my favorite bar. I love it, I love this place. But right now, I'm content either way. If he wants to go, I won't complain because instead of being surrounded by random strangers I'll be surrounded by Jackson.

"Let's go. The sooner we leave, the sooner we get pizza and the sooner I can take those clothes off."

I blush instantly. "Jackson Ross," I huff, a little breathless, and I feel his laugh vibrate through his chest. Of course, I'm not denying that's how I'd rather be spending my night too.

"God, I love it when you say my name," he whispers against my cheek, and his lips are warm, and it doesn't take much convincing. "Come on, I'll get you French fries."

I turn and look at him. "Let's go."

He laughs, louder this time, and nods, grabbing our coats from our chairs. "All right guys, we're heading out." He gives Myles a brief handshake and hugs Emma before I do. Myles nods at me, and I smile, tugging on my coat and taking Jackson's hand in mine.

I follow Jackson out of the bar, and as soon as were in the cool air, he grabs my hand and leads us to our favorite tiny pizza shop on this side of the city. It's barely big enough for five people, and we always end up eating at the window outside anyway. Once again, I'm not wearing a heavy enough coat, and he knows that immediately because he takes his off and puts it around my shoulders. He's smart and is wearing a crewneck, and I'm not going to complain about the extra warmth.

He walks backwards in front of me now with a big smile, swinging my hands back and forth.

"Jackson, you're gonna hit someone."

"No, I'm not. You're my eyes and ears, and you're gonna warn me." He just continues, pulling me closer and further away with every step.

"I'm your eyes and ears, huh? That's a pretty important job," I say as I pull us to avoid a drunken group of friends who just grin at the antics.

"It is, so don't fuck it up." He wiggles his eyebrows, and I laugh; the smell of pizza fills my senses as we get closer.

I tick my fingers. "Eyes, ears, don't fuck it up. Anything else?"

Jackson raises a brow and stops, pulling me in front of him. "Nope. Add pizza and then going home to the list, and I think you've got it covered."

I nod, biting my lip, and I glance around to see that the street's pretty empty and back to his waiting blue eyes, and I lean up and kiss him softly, gripping his sweatshirt in my hands.

Because little does he know, I'm already home.

Thirty-Seven | Jackson

Christmas has never been my favorite holiday. I like it, but I just always preferred other ones more. Thanksgiving for the food or Labor Day solely because it was about me.

But Nina's parents' house is filled with food and drinks and all our friends, and it's warm. Basketball is on the TV on mute while classic Christmas music fills the space.

Nina's parents were kind enough to welcome my entire family over when they said they would fly up for the holiday, and now we're all spending it together. Mateo and Roman and Harper are all joking around, sitting on the floor by the Christmas tree in the window, while Sloan and Veah are on the couch, gossiping about god knows what.

I'm sitting in the armchair next to them, but I'm not paying any attention to anyone but the girl sitting on the edge of my chair, her legs draped over mine and hanging over the other side while my hand rests on her ankle. Her dark hair falls in waves down her back, much longer than it used to be, and her eyes are bright and warm, and I don't even remember life without her in it.

"So, do you want your last present now or later?" she asks, excitement flashing in her eyes. I look around, confused because we did presents earlier in my apartment with my family before we came here, and she didn't bring anything else with her besides the gifts for her parents.

"You got me enough, Scott." I squeeze her leg softly, aware of her dad on the other side of the room.

Nina leans back. "It's not a physical thing,"

I furrow my brows because now I have no clue. She already got me a few vinyl records, Elton John and Billy Joel, along with a new watch and tickets to a concert in the spring.

"Remember that question you asked a week or two ago?" She leans closer, taking sip of her drink. "Well, our lease will be up in March, and if you still want me to, I'll move in with you. And Jenko, of course."

The stupidest grin spreads on my face as she watches me, and her cheeks flush instantly. I'll never get tired of the red flush she always gets. "Of course, I want you to. That place doesn't really feel the same without you anymore."

She's spent so much time at my apartment that I can't really imagine it without her in it anymore. When she's not there, I'm at her apartment anyway.

Nina leans forward and hugs me the best she can in our position, and her hair hides me from view, so I place a few kisses under her jaw before pulling back, letting her familiar smell, her warmth, her love wrap around me. The necklace I got her dangles near her collar, a white gold sun pendant with her birthstone in the middle and a small *J* charm, and I reach up to play with it before my hand drops back down.

Harper, who's on our left, leans towards us and whisper yells, "Get a room." Nina gives her the finger before turning back to me. I laugh at the exchange, loving how seamlessly everyone fits.

Living in the fact that soon enough, she'll be living with me full time and there will be no more back and forth. No more overnight bags or planned out weekends because she'll be with *me.*

"I don't wanna wait. Can it be March?" I ask, drawing circles on her ankle.

She rolls her eyes, and I smile again. "I think you'll survive."

I laugh and my eyes flicker over the group again until making eye contact with Nina's mom, and I nod my head ever so slightly. Soon enough, her mom and my mom are calling her over to help them in the kitchen since the food is almost ready.

"Be right back," she mumbles and kisses me on the cheek before walking over to our moms. Roman watches with a smirk on his face, and I take a sip of my drink and stay seated until she's out of sight. As soon as she is, I go over to her dad, who's talking to Mateo now, and ask if I can talk to him quickly. He tries to hide a smile and nods his head in the direction of the hallway.

"So, what did you need to talk to me about?" Mr. Scott asks, and I wasn't nervous before, but now I am as I glance back to the kitchen hallway. "Don't worry, they can't hear us in here." The smile fights to escape on his face, and I have a feeling he knows what's going on.

My hand tightens around the glass in my hand, my finger drawing through the condensation. "Well, I know that you guys aren't super traditional, and neither am I, but I'll be asking Nina to marry me, and I wanted to tell you. Make sure you at least approved. I know how much you mean to her and figured it may not be a requirement, but something that might be important to her."

He raises a brow, but amusement spreads. "So you're asking me or telling me, Jackson?"

This time I grin because I'd ask her no matter what he said. "I'm telling you I'm going to marry her. Regardless of the answer, I'm not letting your daughter walk out my life. But I admit, it'd be nice to know you approve. I already talked to her mom."

Finally, the smile breaks through, and I exhale a breath I didn't even know I was holding as he pats me on the back. "Come with me," he says quietly, looking over his shoulder before heading upstairs.

We pass Nina's bedroom and don't stop until we're at the end of the hall and the door opens into an office space. There are bookshelves against the wall filled with knick-knacks and different types of books, and a large desk sits right near a window.

Her dad leans over, and I hear the unlocking of a drawer, and when he turns back around, leaning against the desk, he's holding a box in his hand. "I bought this for her mom as a gift one year, an anniversary present. A better ring. When we got engaged, I didn't have much money saved up, so I always wanted to get her a ring I thought she deserved."

I smile, leaning against the chair. Watching and waiting.

"But when I got home and looked at it, it didn't feel like her. And so, I told her, ruined the surprise, and let her look at it. Elena didn't even want it. Didn't want any other ring than the one that was on her finger." He smiles warmly, and his brown skin crinkles as he does. "But we both decided we'd save it for Nina. Neither of us have family heirlooms or anything special to us that could've been passed down. And the band is vintage and reclaimed, so this is the closest we came to something like that."

I cough lightly, feeling the emotions build under my skin. Not just the ones I have for Nina, but the ones her parents have for each other and her. Being here with him makes me miss my dad more than I thought was possible. And also makes me thankful that this is a family I'm blessed to be around.

"I know you just lost your dad, and you'd probably be wanting to talk about the girl you're planning on marrying, and I know she's my daughter and I'm biased, but I approve, Jackson.

You never needed to worry about that with me. If you ever need anything at all, I hope you'll ask."

My teeth clamp down, and I tense my jaw as my grip tightens on my glass. "I miss him all the time. But having your daughter in my life, having you and Mrs. Scott in my life, helps remind me how great life still is. So, thank you for that Mr. Scott. I appreciate it."

He dips his head. "You're welcome. I'm happy you and Nina found one another. Although, it is very soon." He smirks, and I exhale again as the room lightens again and chuckle.

"Don't worry, I've asked Harper and Sloan. They've told me she wants to date for at least two years before anything else. She wants to enjoy every stage, so that's what we'll do. I just figured I know now so why not ask you." I grin, feeling the heavier emotions sink deeper, letting joy fill the space again. "But also, you don't have to give me that ring. If you and her mom want to give that to her that's amazing. I never expected you to give me anything. I don't want you to think you have to."

I swear I see pride flash in Mr. Scott's eyes, and he ignores my statement. "So you're gonna hold on to this ring for two years?" He holds out his hand, the box resting in his palm.

I grin and stand up. "Yes sir, I am. Or for however long I need to."

He nods proudly, and pulls me in for a hug, slipping the box into my hand in the meantime. "Welcome to the family, Jackson."

Nina

This is already the best Christmas I've ever had.

My parents' house is full of life and the smells of all our favorite foods and almost every person that means anything to me. Basketball is on in the background on the TV, and everyone is loud and talking and laughing, and I love it. The best part, or two best parts, are Jackson is here and it's snowing, on Christmas. Which almost never happens.

The house is decorated completely but tastefully with carefully string lights and the Christmas tree in front of the big window in the living room. I take a sip of the drink Dad made for today, I think a whiskey and cranberry recipe he found online, and surprisingly, it's pretty good. Everyone is still spread around the living room, I think, but I stand in the kitchen with my mom and Mrs. Ross as we get ready to put out the buffet spread of food.

Biscuits are covered by foil, the buttery smell filling the space along with the ham that my mom just took out of the oven and my dad's chili on the stove, with bacon bits on the side and shredded cheese. My mom also made rice and beans, and there's more, of course. It's a complete mixture of all our favorite things, and it's perfect.

I'm pulling out plates when Jackson and my dad enter the kitchen from the living room, laughing about something quietly before Dad comes over and helps me reach the dishes I can't. He places a kiss on my cheek as he does before doing the same to my mom as he tries to steal a bite of food and she swats him away.

I avoid eye contact with Jackson on purpose as I move throughout the kitchen. I can feel the familiar pricks against my skin of him watching, and my cheeks warm as they always do. I don't last long with my little game because all I want to do is look at him, and when I do, he grins widely, both dimples popping, knowing he won whatever this was. Smoothly, he nods his head slightly and wriggles his fingers by his leg, and I walk towards him in response.

"Are you having a good Christmas?" I ask as he leans against the door frame.

His eyes twinkle. "I am. Are you?"

I smile. "The best."

"Because I'm here, right? I thought so."

I laugh at his cheesiness, hating how much I genuinely love it. Before I can say anything, Harper and Mateo walk by. "You two make me want to vomit—in a cute way. Kind of," she mutters, and I roll my eyes as Mateo takes it a step further. He hits Jackson over the back of his head gently, and Jackson responds with a quick slap to his chest, and the laughter bubbles out of me.

I look back at him as they enter the kitchen. "You kinda deserved that."

He snorts softly, blowing out air. "You secretly loved it."

I reach out and take his glass out of his hand and take a sip, as mine is sitting empty on the counter near the biscuits. "I'll never tell."

"You don't have to. I know you." Jackson's blue eyes shine with lightness and humor, and I can't help but let the smile out. I take another sip of his drink. "But come on, the snow from this morning has been sticking, and it's beautiful."

I squeal excitedly and practically jump up and down as I set his drink on the kitchen table. "The snow is sticking, so we're going outside," I yell to anyone who even cares to listen, and Jackson laughs as I drag him down the hallway.

Of course, he makes me pull on my coat, the new one he bought me for Christmas, and it falls past the length of my long sleeve sweater dress. I slip on the old fuzzy boots I always leave here over my stockings as he zips up his own coat. Jackson pulls open the door, and I'm surprised to see just how much snow has fallen in a few hours. Not enough for a snow angel or anything crazy, but the snow is heavy and soft and perfect for snowballs.

I grin, pulling him down into the empty street as the snow falls around us. When I turn back around, his hands are in his pockets, and he's just grinning at the snowflakes landing on his blond hair, his slightly red cheeks, and his nose. They dust his skin softly, falling over his freckles, and he looks happy.

I can't help but stare because last year, Jackson Ross wasn't a part of my life. Now, I hope that he'll never not be a part of my life. Because everything is better with him. Life is brighter and warmer and exciting, and it feels endless with him.

Jackson Ross is my all-time, the only one I want to do life with, ever.

He looks down, turning his smile to me, and my heart beats quickly in my chest. "It never gets old."

I cock my head to the side.

"The snow. Even though I've been here for years, it never gets old. It's always exciting."

"Yeah, I feel that way about a few things." I grin because it's like he read my thoughts, even if he doesn't know it. I crouch down quickly and ball up snow in my gloved hands.

"Nina, don't you dare."

I wiggle my brows. "Oh, come on, don't be a party pooper, Jackson."

Before he can stop me, I fling the snowball at him and watch it hit him square in the chest. He shakes his head and laughs, and before I can prepare, he's running towards me through the snow, and I squeal, turning quickly, trying to get away. Easily, he catches me and is wrapping an arm around my waist pulling me back into his chest. His other hand comes up filled with snow, and he plops it on the top of my head.

"You suck," I whine, and push back into his chest as snow falls into my eyes, but the laugh bubbling in my chest escapes regardless.

But when I pushed back, he lost his footing a bit and starts to slip. I reach out, grabbing his head to try to steady him, but instead, we both end up in the snow, bright laughter spilling out of us as we sit up. He grabs my leg, right above where my boot ends and pulls me closer to him, dragging me through the fluff.

Jackson reaches up and brushes the flakes off my face. Off my cheeks and my nose and my lips. I watch him do it, enamored with even the simplest of actions that he does, and smile. Even with the gloves, I feel the familiar singe of his touch on my skin and into my veins.

"I can't believe this year is almost over," I mumble, scooting closer to him. "Are you doing okay today?"

I look up at him, snowflakes landing on his eyelashes, and he blinks a few times to clear them. I'm sure he misses his dad, and I know there's nothing I can do about that. He was a little upset when we woke up this morning. He didn't say anything, and I think having his family there helped. But he was up throughout the night. Every once in a while, he'd pull me closer, and I could feel the deep breaths he would take.

He looks at me. "Yeah. Better than I thought. I miss him, and I wish he was here. Wish he got to meet you and your family, but he wouldn't want me to waste my time being upset." He lets out a sad chuckle, and I nod, holding his hand in the snow.

"Well, it's okay to be sad if you want to be."

Jackson shakes his head, his eyes never leaving mine. "I don't want to be. Not right now. Losing my dad was the worst part of the year. But my favorite part of this year would be you, Nina." He cups my cheeks, and even in the cold, I can feel my eyes prickling with tears.

"Yeah, well, mine would be you too," I say softly, surrounded by the snow and by Jackson.

He smiles, the dimples showing in his cheeks as he leans forward and kisses me. It's quiet and soft, like he is, but it's also blistering and sends little sparks over my skin and into my bones like he always does.

"I love you," he says against my lips.

I smile. "I love you more."

Jackson made me believe in love again. That it was pure and warm and everything anyone has ever dreamed about. He's healed almost all my scars from the past, erasing the burns and doing everything he can to make sure a new one will never touch me.

I know that love isn't easy, that it's not always smooth sailing. That life isn't always bright, that sometimes it's hard to find the sun. Like when he lost his dad. Things were hard, but he was open with me when he could be, let me be there for him when he couldn't talk about it. I've learned that love isn't just the highs but being there through the lows.

I think we both learned that everyone has to let a little light in sometimes. I think that love is finding someone who makes that challenge just a little bit easier. Someone who makes life just a little bit brighter.

I just know that my favorite part of every year to come will always be Jackson Ross.

Epilogue

Two years later

"You ready?" Jackson asks, kissing me swiftly on the cheek as he grabs my bag from the bed, even though I am perfectly capable of grabbing my own bag.

I nod, sticking my phone in my back pocket and pulling my sweater on as I follow him out of the bedroom and into the bright living room of his—or our—tall apartment. The city is on full display as he makes sure everything is off and packed for the week, and I grab the leash hanging over the dining room barstool.

"Hi, bubs, you ready to go?" I grin, leaning down to Bane, whose six-month-old, lanky, already huge body immediately starts shaking with excitement. He shoots up and rubs his head into my chest, and a laugh bubbles out as I scratch his ears.

We're heading to the Hamptons for the week. It's the day after Christmas, and we figured what better place to spend New Year's. All our friends will be joining us in a few days. Jenko is at my parents' house. As he's getting older, the only two places he can truly stand are here and their home, so we don't drag him to the Hamptons anymore, but he's always with us in spirit. But Bane, the six-month-old Cane Corso that we got on my birthday in September, loves it there. Loves it anywhere we go.

I snap his leash on, and he pads by my side excitedly, Jackson watching us with a smile as he twirls the keys to the Jeep. I grab the two water bottles on the counter, my eyes flicking up to him. "Can we stop for snacks?"

He raises a brow, but when Bane lets out a small bark in conjunction with my idea, he just laughs. "I need gas, so yes, anything for you two. I'm outnumbered anyway." He chuckles, and my smile widens.

"You and Jenko outnumber me. It's only fair."

I walk past him, patting his butt on the way, and hold open the front door for him as he carries the bags. Bane trots happily next to us, his floppy ears moving with every step as we head down to the parking garage. Even now, a few months later, I'm not over the shock of Jackson's surprise. We'd both been talking about getting a dog for a bit, but I never expected him to surprise me with a trip to a shelter that had received puppies.

Jackson had walked me blindly into that shelter, and when I heard the yips and yells and he uncovered my eyes, I practically tackled him to the ground with excitement. This little three-month-old puppy came right over to us, placing his head in my hand, and that was the moment we left with Bane.

I lean my head on Jackson's shoulder as we descend in the elevator until we stop on the parking floor and head to the Jeep. He places the bags in the back as Bane bounds into the car without any help and I swing myself into the passenger seat.

I turn on the music as he pulls onto the street. It's only three on a Thursday, and since it's the day after Christmas, it's actually pretty dead as we drive to the nearest gas station. It's cloudy and gray, and the clouds look heavy. I think it might snow. At least, I hope it does.

"Any special requests?" Jackson says as he hops out of the car, and I shake my head, reaching my hand back to pet Bane. His soft fur immediately comforts me. "All right, be right back, baby."

My blood warms as he shuts the door behind him because even after two years, nothing's really changed. Of course, things are different. We live together and have for almost two years; we have a dog, and life is simply better. Not to say that everything is always easy. That would be unrealistic. We've fought, over stupid shit like which shelf to put groceries on in the fridge or how to arrange the pantry, but those fights always end in us laughing or joking and wrapped up on the couch.

We've fought about other things, but honestly, I can't remember the serious fights, because they aren't many. Because we never go to sleep angry or at least without talking about things. I never push him too far because he still likes to hold it in, but I let him know I'm there in the silence, through touching him or just being near him. Jackson's getting better about telling me when something is bothering him or when he needs space. And he makes sure to let me cool down or sit on the floor or manically clean everything before I'm ready to talk.

There are no secrets, nothing is ever swept under the rug and left for later. We address it, we move on, and we go back to how we are, we go back to normal. But it's not like it happens that often. Things are still amazing.

Our normal is amazing.

For the most part, being with Jackson, living with him, is everything I wanted it to be. I know how he takes his coffee, and he knows how I take mine; he knows what I like for dinner, and I know what mood he's in based on the album spinning on the record player. Living with Jackson Ross is simply the best. I get to go to sleep with him and wake up with him, I get to annoy him whenever I want. It's living with my best friend, and I couldn't ask for anything more.

I didn't think it could be better, but then we got Bane, and I'll walk in on them cuddling or vice versa. Even Jenko settled into loving the big puppy, and rainy days or our off days will often turn into the four of us on the bed or the couch, and it's moments like those it hits me how much I love him.

Not that I forget, but every day there's something that reminds me just how special he is.

I'm brought out of my thoughts when he appears at my door, bright blue eyes and a dimple peeking through. "Here, got you Twix and Sour Straws." He plops the candy into my hand, and I reach up and poke the dimple.

"Thanks," I respond, dumping the candy on my lap as he leans in, waiting for the gas to fill the tank. He nods, the soft smile never leaving his face as he reaches a hand back for Bane.

"'Sup, buddy? You excited for the Hamptons?" he says, his voice higher and warmer as he talks to the puppy, who just wags his tail excitedly. I grin, watching them. "Yeah, me too. Uninterrupted time with my favorite person."

Bane lets out a tiny bark in response, and I laugh, feeling the familiar flush of my cheeks as Jackson's eyes flicker back to mine. He grins and leans in through the window and presses a quick kiss to my lips. The feeling of his lips on mine still lingers even as he moves back into the driver's seat and sets us officially on the way to the Hamptons.

Most of the way is spent in a comfortable silence or singing along to the playlist I have on shuffle with horrible voices and loud laughs with each other. His hand almost never leaves my knee, tapping along to the beat or just resting quietly.

I adjust my legs again, and look at Jackson, who has one hand on the steering wheel and the other resting on my leg. "So, the realtor got back to me."

His blue eyes flicker to mine, a slow smile spreading. "And?"

Trying and failing to keep the smile off my face, warmth fills my chest. Because as much as we love his high-rise apartment, we've also decided we want more charm, more history, more New York. We're not buying, because who knows if we'll stay in Manhattan forever, but we got approved for a new long-term rental. A brownstone. Mostly with the help of Jackson and his flourishing career.

"Brownstone is ours if we want it." I grin, and he squeezes my knee as Bane sticks his head through the seats excitedly. Jackson looks over again, and I can see the pure excitement shine in his eyes and the way he leans back in the driver's seat.

"God, I want to kiss you right now."

I roll my eyes, patting the hand that rests on my leg. "You can kiss me when we get there."

He raises a brow, confidence pouring out of him. "Oh, I will." Bane barks, and I chuckle lightly, leaning back to pet him.

"Don't worry, baby, I love you, and I won't leave you out," I coo to the dog, who wags his entire body with endless energy.

"You love him more than me," Jackson pouts dramatically, and I look out at the scenery, the blue water peeking through the houses and the smell of salt and sand, and I know we're almost there.

I hit his arm. "Shut up, that's not true."

"Ow, and now you're abusing me? Jesus." Unblinking, I stare at him, and his lips start to upturn into a smile, and he glances over again. "Kidding, kidding. You'd never hurt me."

He's right. I'd never hurt him. Well, maybe a pinch here or there, but I'd never do anything seriously to hurt the man who has given me everything I never even asked for.

I don't say anything though. I just smile as we drive down, closer to the coast and the place that we both love going so much. The sun is just starting to lower in the sky behind those thick heavy clouds, but colors are starting to peek as he pulls into the driveway. The house is beautiful as always, and he turns down the music as he puts the car in park.

I start to open my door, but Jackson stops me. "Hold on, I just wanna go make sure the heat turned on in time and it's warm enough." He smiles and takes the house key from the glovebox, leaving the car on, but still, I kick open the door and let my legs hang out.

He grabs the bags first and takes them with him as I pet Bane behind the ears from the front seat until Jackson appears near the door again. "All good, let's go," he says softly, reaching around me and turning the car off, the keys jingling as he tucks them into his pocket.

Bane bounds forward and out of the car, landing easily, and sits patiently at my side when I hit the ground. Jackson stands with his hands in his pockets right behind me, cheeks flushed from the cold.

"Oh, wait, I hid a new toy for Bane under your seat. Can you grab it?" he asks, reaching a hand out for the pup. I nod and lean back into the car, reaching under the seat.

With searching fingers I don't feel anything reminiscent of a dog toy. "Jackson, nothing is under here," I breathe out as I reach further back. Then my fingers brush against something.

It's soft and smooth and velvety, and it's definitely not a fucking dog toy. I wrap my fingers around it and pull it out. Not quite seeing what's resting in my palm. I blink and blink again before looking at Jackson.

"What is this?"

Bane is sitting by his side with his ears perked, and Jackson has the smallest of smirks growing on his lips. "What does it look like?"

I stare at him. "It looks like a little black box. What the fuck is it, Jackson?"

He chuckles. The sound is low and deep and spreads fire through my veins—or would if my heart was beating—and he steps closer. "Open it, Nina."

My hand shakes as I flip open the box, and I don't even have time to breathe before my eyes fill up with tears. Blood rushes past my ears as Bane starts barking in excitement, and his body is wagging by my side as Jackson comes to stand right before me. I'm not even looking at what's in the box; I'm just looking at him.

"I wasn't really sure if this was the most romantic or the best way to do this," he starts, and my grip tightens so hard my knuckles turn white. "But I remember our first drive to the Hamptons, and you pulled that ball cap out from under the seat and put it on your head and smiled at me. It's a stupid memory, but it's one of my favorites. You smiling at me in that moment. I knew I was done for then. Knew it was you."

He reaches forward and grabs the box from my hand, and I just stand there, watching him. "I knew I wanted to do it here, just wasn't sure how, and then that just popped in my head and," Jackson shrugs, his left dimple popping, "this just felt right."

The dog barks again, and I laugh, but it's muffled by me trying not to burst into an absolute mess of sobs. Jackson reaches up and brushes my hair back, behind my ear, sending sparks that feel like tiny butterflies landing on my skin.

"You are the absolute love of my life, Nina. There is no one else I'd rather do life with, even though you love that dog and Jenko more than me." I hit him on the chest, and now tears are freely flowing down my face. "I remember life before you were in it, barely, but I do. It was fine, but you came in, and everything just fell into place."

His words are simple, but with every single one my heart stops in my chest over and over again, and I simply cannot fathom the love I feel for him. Because *better* is the only way to describe it. It's simple and concise, but it's true. Life is better together.

"You are the best person I've ever met, my favorite person in the world, and I wouldn't have made it these last two years without you. Life is hard, I know that, and not everything has to be perfect, but you, you make life easier. Better. Brighter. You make it easier to breathe."

I don't think I could control the messy sob that comes out of my throat even if I wanted to. My hands come up and cover my face to try to hide the tears as my body swells with emotion. From my tiptoes to the top of my head I'm alight with every single emotion I've ever felt and the overwhelming love I feel for Jackson.

He pulls my hands away from my face, his eyes gleaming, and his lips are pulled up into a smile as he tips my chin up, just as he lowers to one knee with Bane sitting right next to him.

"Will you marry me?"

I can barely form words, so in all of my emotional glory, I just hug him tightly, practically tackling him to the cold ground of the driveway. His arm wraps around my back, and he holds me tightly as I bury my hands in his hair.

"Yes." My voice is scratchy and barely audible. "Yes, Jackson, a million fucking times yes," I murmur.

His grip tightens as we just lay there, Bane jumping excitedly behind us until I sit up and let Jackson breathe. Bane comes over and shoves his head in my hands and I laugh. I'm still only looking at Jackson when he slips the ring on my finger and sits up, cupping both my cheeks, which I'm sure are flushed and patchy and bright red, but he doesn't care.

Both dimples shine through. "I love you so much."

"Good, 'cause you are stuck with me now," I mumble before leaning forward and kissing him, letting all of this sink in. I'm engaged to Jackson Ross.

When I pull back, I look at the ring, the silver band studded with simple diamonds and a stunning six prong solitaire, and it glimmers in the cloudy sky, and my eyes start prickling again. Because it's simple and perfect and beautiful even amidst the clouds, just like Jackson, just like the time we've spent together.

He pinches my butt, mumbling against my lips, "Say it back."

Bane barks from where he lays right next to us, his head on his paws and his tail wagging over the pavement as he watches us. I laugh and brush my thumb over his cheek, over the freckles I have memorized and the little scar on his cheek and the way his breath hitches just slightly and the way I get to spend the rest of my life with him.

"I love you forever, Jackson."

• • •

Dad snakes his arm through my own.

Looking up at him, my heart beats nervously in my chest as I squeeze his forearm. He smiles down, gray peppering his neatly trimmed scruff and his head, but he still looks young.

"You ready, kid?" he asks, clearing his throat as he pats my hand.

I look out the back window of the Hamptons house onto the beach, where everyone is seated in a neat semi-circle. Flowers are situated to form an aisle. Jackson waits at the end, with Roman, Mateo, and Myles standing next to him. The house doesn't even look like the house anymore—it's been transformed. A neat, modern bar is set up on the back porch that we extended a year ago and seating is arranged both on the deck and inside as well. The same flowers, down on the beach, line the deck stairs and are arranged beautifully around the décor.

I hear the music start, and the girls who are lined up on the porch turn around with smiles, Emma at the front, followed by Veah, and then Harper and Sloan. Harper sends me a wink as she and Sloan take the tail end of the walk since I made them both my maids of honor, and I grin back, watching them walk down the stairs and onto the sand in sage green.

I think back to the proposal, almost two years ago. My nerves are firing, but I've been ready since the day he asked me.

"Ready as I'll ever be." I squeeze his arm. "Is it normal to be nervous?"

He reaches out and carefully adjusts the shoulder strap of my deep V, lace-covered dress. "Yes, it's normal. I'd be more concerned if you weren't." He smiles and walks us forward to the door, and my heartbeat quickens. "But that boy out there loves you." He reaches for my left hand, twisting the engagement ring. "Held on to this ring for two years, you know."

My eyes widen, glancing down to the ring. "No, he didn't."

Dad grins. "He did. He would do anything for you, Nina. You are the best daughter, the best person I ever could've helped raise. Parental love and romantic love are different. Not really comparable. But if anyone could rival the love I have for you as my daughter and my friend, it's him. I have no doubt that he'll do everything he can to make you happy and you'll do the same for him. And that's all I care about."

I lean up on my tiptoes and kiss him on the cheek. "Thanks, Dad. I love you."

He opens both of the French doors, and warmth surrounds us immediately. The smell of the sea and the salt permeates the air as we walk across the porch. We pause on the steps, and I finally look up to see Jackson's eyes are locked on me. Suddenly, I feel like I can do anything. Bane sits next to him, all grown up and ears perked. Jackson keeps his eyes on me as I slowly step down the stairs with my dad next to me, holding me tightly, just in case I fall.

His mom is standing next to mine, both of them in tears, and I feel tears prick in my eyes when I see the empty seat we chose to leave for Jackson's dad. I tried to drag Jenko out here, but Mr. People Hater refused. But I saw him sitting on the windowsill of the bedroom right before I walked out, so I know he's watching too.

Mine Would Be You

My feet hit the sand. It covers my skin, and I know this is the final stretch. I can see him clearer now, blue eyes shining, and the ocean dulls in comparison. Both dimples are on full display just before he dips his head with a shake and squeezes his hands tightly in front of him. Roman pats him on the back, and Bane nudges his hand as he looks back up.

I try to fight my own smile, but I can't help it, because he's looking at me like he always has. Like I'm the only thing that exists. Like I'm the only sun in the sky.

Before I know it, I'm standing before him and my dad is kissing me on the cheek and patting him on the back. But Dad pulls me in for a tight hug. "I love you, kid. You deserve the best." He squeezes my arms before pulling away and going to his seat, leaving me with tears in my eyes.

I look up and see the wetness in Jackson's eyes as he takes my hands, and my heart flutters, warmth spreading over my skin like the mist of the ocean when you get closer to the waves.

The justice of the peace, Uncle Mike, starts talking, but I'm barely listening. "You crying over me, Ross?" I whisper because we're in our own little world. Squeezing his hand tightly in my own, thumbing over his ring finger that won't be so bare in a few moments.

He raises a brow, a dimple peeking through. "How can I not when you look like that?"

My cheeks heat, and I pinch his palm as we both turn to pay attention. It's a short introduction, and I feel myself getting nervous as we get closer to the vows. We didn't do traditional— traditional has always felt impersonal to me—so we decided to write our own. And I'm going first. I turn to face Jackson completely, the white lace dress blowing softly around my legs.

Dad is smiling at me, but I can see the emotions written plainly on his face. Mom is holding Mrs. Ross's hand tightly, and all our close friends and distant family sit in the small crowd with smiles. I look back at Jackson and his gorgeous blue eyes and the crisp suit he has on, and for a second, my nerves fall away.

I'm marrying the love of my life.

Uncle Mike smiles at me and nods, willing me to start. Jackson squeezes my hands, and I let out a soft laugh as Bane barks, bringing a laugh from the crowd.

"All right, all right, I'm going," I say, my lips pulling into a smile. "Jackson, you came into my life so brightly, filled with optimism and joy and everything I never knew I needed. Whatever clouds were over me became small and trivial in comparison to you. You are my favorite song. Melodic and comforting and endlessly beautiful. You are my color green. Vibrant and full of life. You are better than the candy you always buy me from the store, you are better than the grilled cheeses you always make me when I'm sad, you are better than country music—that you forced me to love on a Sunday drive in the summertime. You are better than everything I have ever known and will ever know."

He smiles at me, soft and warm, as I finish. "I promise to be there for you when you need me and even when you don't. To support you at the highs and the lows and to hold your hand through whatever challenges we may face, forever. You have pieces of me I never thought I'd give away, but I felt no fear when I gave them to you. You are the most exciting part of my future. You are the best part of my life. You always will be."

Jackson shakes his head, and I bite the inside of my lip as he grips my hands, and I can't help but grin. He's the cheesy one, the sweet one, the one with the words, but it's nice to know even after all these years I can get to him too.

"Well, jeez, I don't know how I'm gonna beat that," he jokes, and I laugh. The crowd lets out a small laugh as well as I push him gently with my hands. Uncle Mike nods to Jackson, and he smiles back as he twirls the engagement ring on my hand.

"You were the best surprise of my life, Nina. When I walked into that bar that night, I didn't have any expectations, and then you walked up and surprised me. And even now, every day, you surprise me. In the way you fearlessly love those around you, including me. In the way that you are always there to pick me up or push me through or bring a smile to my face. Every day you surprise me by reminding me that everything I feel for you is indescribable. Every day, there is something that reminds me how lucky I am that you are in my life and how lucky I am that I get to love you. You always say I remind you of the sun, but you remind me of the moment right before it rains. When the sun is still peeking through, but the air is fresh and clear. And there's that little bit of light still in the sky. You are my light."

My eyes prick, and I'm squeezing his hands so tightly I might be cutting off the circulation. If I breathe too deeply, I'm scared I'll break out into sobs, so I focus on his hands and Jackson in general to ground me. To remind me this is real.

"So, I promise to always make sure that light is there. Not just for me, but for everyone who is lucky to have you in their life. I promise to let you clean whenever you're upset and do whatever you tell me to do." He grins. "I promise to be by your side through everything life will throw at us—even though, I think together, life is easier. And I promise to make sure you always know just how much I love you, every day for the rest of our lives."

I'm happy I don't have to say anything because I don't think I could. My throat is closed, and my entire body is filled with a boatload of emotions I don't know how to process. I don't know how I got so damn lucky.

Uncle Mike clears his throat, and I'm surprised to see tears in his eyes as he looks at us. "Whew, okay. You two." He smiles and shakes his head. "The rings, please."

Jackson's mom steps up with the rings, and Uncle Mike takes them and hands them to us. I hold Jackson's in my hand.

We picked the bands out together, so they match, both white gold. His is smooth and mine made to match the engagement ring.

Slowly, we each slide the ring onto each other's finger, and I can't help but play with the ring on his finger. I love that it's there now, the finger no longer bare. A part of us on his hands.

Uncle Mike claps his hands together. "Well," He looks at Jackson, who he has grown to love so much it's actually ridiculous. "You may now—"

Jackson doesn't wait for him to finish before he's grabbing my cheeks in his hands, the cool band of the ring on my cheek, and pressing his lips to mine, lighting my blood on fire in the slowest burn. Each piece of me alight with life. I hear laughter in the background, Uncle Mike muttering something about the importance of patience, and all our friends chuckling around us, but all I feel and all I know is Jackson Ross and the feel of his lips on mine.

My husband.

• • •

"Presenting Mr. and Mrs. Ross!" Uncle Mike says through the microphone he felt he needed to buy as we walk down the stairs hand in hand onto the makeshift dance floor created over the sand.

Jackson holds my hand tightly in his as we descend. Everyone claps and Harper shouts in excitement from the side, I look over to see her and Roman holding hands with big smiles and Sloan and her boyfriend cheering loudly. Everyone is smiling and cheering, but no one is happier than I am as I look at Jackson.

His cheeks are flushed with excitement and his eyes flicker over to me. He squeezes my hand under the warm early summer sun as we make our way to the center of the dance floor for our first dance.

As Jackson pulls me to him, I'm taken back to the first time we danced at a very different wedding when I was in a very different place in life. A little nervous and a little hesitant on love, even though he seemed so sure of himself, even then. His arm wraps around my waist now, and I feel his fingertips spread out on my lower back as his other hand holds mine.

The soft music comes through the speakers, filling the outdoor space along with the sound of waves crashing in the background as Jackson pulls us into a dance.

He looks down at me. "So, are you happy? With the wedding, with everything?"

We spin, and I raise my brows. "It's perfect. We could've gotten married anywhere, with just us, and I would've been happy."

I'm thrilled with how we planned the wedding. It's small and personal and at my favorite place in the world, the Hamptons house, and it's Jackson. So, it's perfect. But I would've been happy to marry that man anywhere.

Jackson pulls us closer, his fingers tapping on my spine. "You look beautiful." He shakes his head with a soft smile barely pulling his lips up. But it's warm, and it makes butterflies erupt in my stomach, even after all this time.

I hug him tighter. "You look pretty great yourself, husband."

He spins us, the song filling my heart with the lyrics and the melody, and it's exactly how Jackson makes me feel. He does his signature spin, pulling my back into his chest as he leans down, his lips brushing my cheek ever so softly.

"Wife, wow." He presses his lips harder to my cheek and it sends a shiver down my spine. "I'm never gonna get tired of saying that," he whispers before spinning us back and pulling us back together.

I grin, the dress spinning around my legs as we fall back into step and I squeeze his hand. "You don't have to, because I'll never get tired of hearing it."

Both dimples poke through as the sun shines down on us and surrounds us. "You're my wife. This is the best day, can we do it again?" He leans down, and I laugh, the sound filling my chest and his proximity filling my heart with an overflow of emotions.

"We can do anything you want; we're married."

I don't think we're dancing as much as we are swaying at this point, but I don't care. It's about us and it's our day and our moment and I wouldn't have wanted it any other way.

"That we are, baby, that we are." Jackson's hand finds my rings again, and he spins them around and around like he's memorizing the way they rest on my hand. "I love you, Valentina Ross."

My nose crinkles when I smile wider if that's possible. "And I love you."

He pats my butt quickly, and I rest my head on his chest as the song starts to come to an end. This is just the beginning. My heart is full, and I feel at peace, wrapped up in Jackson as we sway back and forth to the song and enter this new chapter together. He's my rock and my best friend and my person. And the best person I've ever met and ever had the honor of loving.

Obviously, marriage doesn't change everything about life, it's not a restart or a re-do, but it is a new beginning in a way. Today feels like the first day of the rest of my life—the life that I get to spend with Jackson Ross.

Forever.

For the extended epilogue, head over to my website!

Acknowledgements

It feels very strange even beginning this section of the book. Somehow, after the writing, the endless editing, and everything in between, this is the hardest part. When I started this story right before the pandemic hit, I never envisioned finishing it that winter and picking it back up to turn it into this. This is at once, both fulfilling a lifelong dream of mine and also the scariest thing I have ever done. And I certainly wouldn't have done it without any of you. Thank you for loving the very rough first draft of Jackson and Nina's story, for loving them like I did, and for pushing me on this journey. There are no words that can express how grateful I am for all of you. Thank you a million times and more for taking this into your hands and helping me put it out into the world.

To my mom, who for once kept this a secret from the rest of my family and for helping me along the way. Even though I'm secretly hoping you never actually, ever read this. Thank you for always encouraging me and forever being the optimist. Dad, please never read this, I'll never look at you again. Thank you for never failing to push me when I needed it and being kind, when I needed that more. Life would be very different without the both of you in it.

To Kennedy, I am forever grateful to call you my friend (my bestie forever actually, you are stuck with me). I cannot say how thankful I am to have met you when I did, I don't always understand why certain things in life happen, but I'm eternally grateful this world brought you into mine. I cannot wait to be roommates and shout your brilliance from every rooftop in the city.

To Sabine, the SpongeBob to my Patrick. I have so much fun with you; parallel parking in Philly, bonding over our love of grilled cheeses, rom-coms and being certified horse girls. You are awesome and I am so thankful for you. You were the first person I told about *Mine Would Be You* and it wouldn't be here without your support.

To Jules, I love you more than you love this story (no matter what you think). You deserve everything good and kind in this world and more.

To Liya, you are an angel—not only to me but so many others—and I'm sorry to say you are stuck with me for life. Thank you for always being excited with anything I send you, I can't explain how much it means to me.

To Steph and Jenni, thank you a million times over for putting up with my questions. Helping with translations and giving feedback. For being my indecisive air signs with me and somehow helping me make decisions. And for being the Sad Girls Club, I love being sad together and I love you both.

To my twitter friends: Mia, Foo, Jay, Emaan, Jordyn, Emry, Shan, Zoe, Est, Kay, Ivanna, Pome, Kelsey, Hope, Ali, Amaal, Maria, Em, Hannah, and everyone else (I'm sorry, I'm panicking and overwriting, and I will message you all a million times) on twitter, on Instagram, anywhere and everywhere, thank you for being my friends. Thank you for supporting everything and being excited over things when they haven't even been written. I truly can't wait to share everything with you all.

Thank you to April, for helping me edit this manuscript, everything you did was beautiful and only helped me improve. To Ashley, for helping me along the way and helping me learn. To Murphy Rae, for creating a beautiful cover. To Elaine, for the beautiful formatting. Thank you to every single one of you.

And lastly, thank you to the readers, for picking this book up. For loving it as much as I do, I hope it meant something to you. I hope that every book you pick up, you find something for yourself. And to reading, I simply wouldn't be the person I am today if books didn't exist.

The best place to keep in touch and
stay up to date is my website:
www.kjamilaauthor.com

Instagram @kjamilaauthor
Twitter @kjamilaauthor
Tiktok @kjamilaauthor
Facebook @kjamilaauthor
Pinterest @kjamilaauthor
Goodreads @kjamila
Amazon @kjamila